OTHER BOOKS BY JON LAND

*Published by Forge Books

JON LAND

A WALK IN THE DARKNESS

A TOM DOHERTY ASSOCIATES BOOK
NEW YORK

This is a work of fiction. All the characters and events portrayed in this book are either products of the author's imagination or are used fictitiously.

A WALK IN THE DARKNESS

Copyright © 2000 by Jon Land

Seven Sins excerpt copyright © 2007 by King Midas World Entertainment, Inc.

A Forge Book
Published by Tom Doherty Associates, LLC
175 Fifth Avenue
New York, NY 10010

www.tor-forge.com

Forge® is a registered trademark of Tom Doherty Associates, LLC.

ISBN-13: 978-0-7653-6114-1
ISBN-10: 0-7653-6114-0

First Edition: March 2000
First Mass Market Edition: April 2001
Second Mass Market Edition: May 2008

Printed in the United States of America

0 9 8 7 6 5 4 3 2

For my readers, new and old:
Thanks for coming along for the ride.

ACKNOWLEDGMENTS

WE MEET AGAIN. Or, perhaps, for the first time. If that's the case, welcome. If you've been with me before, welcome back and I hope all has been well since last we met.

The idea for this one again grew out of a lunch at Bolo on New York's east side with Natalia Aponte, the greatest editor in the universe. I say that in all seriousness because Natalia's influence is on every page of *A Walk in the Darkness* and they are all better because of it.

If you've been with me before, you've probably noticed it can be a struggle to find new ways of thanking the people who appear on this page every book, especially Toni Mendez and Ann Maurer, who've been with me for all twenty-two titles. This time I'll simply say thank you; it's not enough, but no words could be.

Likewise for Tom Doherty, Linda Quinton, Jennifer Marcus, Chris Dao, and Irene Gallo at Forge Books. I feel bad for other authors who don't know what it's like to be published by people who care about their books as much as they do.

Along the way of this one there was also Wiley and Rita

Archer, Moshe Aroche, Irv and Josh Schechter, Richard Marsh of the *Dearborn Press and Guide*, Barbara Schlevin, John Thurston, Bill Letizia, Mark and Barbara Land, Reverend Stephan A. Silipigni, and especially Rabbi James Rosenberg. Jim's a fine writer in his own right, whose mastery of Judaism, Israel, and the Torah is equalled only by his suggestions for plot points.

A final and special thanks to Emery Pineo and Nancy Aroche, both of whom will be stepping away from the middle school blackboard after more than thirty years in the classroom. Enjoy your retirements, Emery and Nancy, but, remember, I still know where to find you.

For everyone else, there's a tale to tell. So turn the page and let's begin.

The people who walked in darkness
have seen a great light.

—ISAIAH 9:1

PROLOGUE

THE PLOT

THE OLD DOCTOR heard heavy feet sloshing through the mud before he saw the two shadowy figures lugging a third between them.

"I've been waiting since sundown, Captain," the doctor said, holding the door open. "Hurry up and get him inside."

The soldiers carried the man into the dim glow cast by the room's oil light. They smelled like the rank and spoiled street muck that coated their feet. Perspiration, strong and salty, glistened on their brows and dropped from their cheeks. The trail of blood that had speckled the mud in their wake followed them across the stone floor.

"Lay him on the table," the doctor ordered. He closed the door behind him and made sure all the shutters were latched. "He is still alive, I presume."

"We wouldn't have bothered, if he wasn't," the captain replied, straightening the unconscious man's legs upon a heavy wood table matted with straw that crackled under his weight.

"A fool's errand, nonetheless," the doctor said, approaching the table with lantern in hand.

"We all have our orders." The captain frowned. "To follow whether we approve of them or not."

"I'm not a member of your Roman guard."

"You are a citizen, all the same."

"But not a miracle worker." The doctor moved his lantern closer to the prisoner and ran it along the length of his body, stopping at his head, where plum-colored blood soaked the table in a widening swatch. "Do your superiors really expect to get away with this?"

"They have no choice."

The doctor looked up from the prisoner and swallowed hard. "And this has no chance."

"Just do your part. What happens afterward is not your concern."

"And if I refuse?"

"My orders are to kill you."

The doctor laid a goatskin bag containing his instruments on a stone pedestal within easy reach of the table. "Then I suppose I should get started."

He lifted a pot from the open flame where he had set it long before to boil and placed it too on the pedestal next to a rag. Next he removed the first instrument from his bag and inspected it in the dull glow of the oil light.

"All the same, Captain, even if this works it will change nothing."

"You'd better hope it does," the captain said grimly, "for all our sakes."

THE DIG

H OW DOES THE work go today, Sayin Daws?"
Winston Daws redoubled his handkerchief and dabbed the
sweat from his forehead. The four-post tent shielded him
from the sun, but not the heat and humidity. "Slowly," he
told Kamir, the Turkish work foreman who had just returned
to the site with fresh supplies.

Kamir shrugged and his forehead wrinkled with concern.

Daws went back to the microscope set on the table beneath
him, hoping to find some clue in the minor writings and
artifacts his team had found thus far. Around him the group
of young archaeologists were busy excavating twelve separate square trenches. Their painstaking work progressed very
slowly, and he had begun to fear that the lack of tangible
finds would begin to take its toll on their eagerness and en-
thusiasm. The group had been at it for nine weeks now, the
many abandoned spots that had yielded nothing noticeable
from the darker dirt used to plug holes. The sum total of
their descent through the ages barely filled five airtight storage canisters, one for each of the different uncovered layers

distinguishing the ancient settlements that had been built atop each other.

But Daws had reason for optimism. Recent finds of iron fragments indicated they were at last drawing closer to the target era of the first century A.D. This coming as the sun began to bake the air with the daytime temperatures unseasonably stretching well into the nineties.

Kamir hovered next to Daws under the tent that provided the site's only shade. "Perhaps, Sayin Daws, today is the day you will tell me what you are really looking for."

"This is strictly an educational expedition, Kamir. You know that."

"As I know what it cost you to secure the necessary permits." Kamir smiled slightly, showing a hint of his pearl-white teeth. "Two of the Turkish officials were my cousins."

Daws again moved his eye from the microscope. "You have waited all these weeks to mention that?"

"Because it occurs to me that your young disciples do not know the truth either." Kamir's eyes filled with trepidation. "And that they may be in danger."

"That is not your concern."

"Two of them are also my cousins, Sayin." The foreman shielded his eyes and gazed outward. Beyond the tent Daws's students were busy at work, their faces tinted a pale coral by the breeze-blown dust. "That makes it my concern."

"This is Ephesus, Kamir," Daws said, recalling his earliest study of the region as a London schoolboy. Located on the Aegean coast in southwestern Turkey, the rolling, fertile plains and hills of Ephesus had yielded such finds as the Basilica of St. John, the Library of Celsus, and purportedly the final resting place of the Virgin Mary. But this site was located in the middle of the area's arid bushy lowlands miles from any other reported find, an area known only for mundane and previously charted settlements that had never produced anything of profound significance.

"And in Ephesus there is *always* danger," Daws continued, "which explains why I have already taken the precautions I have."

Kamir and Daws both eyed the four Turkish soldiers positioned strategically about the perimeter. They were rotated in three shifts, on duty twenty-four hours a day. But that was only a small part of the expense being incurred by Daws through the course of this expedition. In addition to the field archaeologists, there was a surveyor to make the plans, a photographer to maintain a visual record of selected finds, a registrar and draftsmen to receive and record those finds, and technicians to treat and preserve the most delicate discoveries. The day-to-day feeding and housing of such a large staff was a massive undertaking in itself that had already begun to take its toll on Daws's resources.

But the import of what he was seeking required that he not abandon the search, especially now that at least limited evidence of the era in question had been found.

"Still, Sayin," Kamir persisted, "my fear is that—"

"Bir sey bulduk! Bir sey bulduk!"

The excited shout came from one of the excavated trenches, the deepest where one of Kamir's cousins had been at work all morning. *"Iste! Cabuk!"* the young man shouted. *"Sanlrlm, aradiglmlzl bulduk! Cabuk!"*

Kamir swung fast toward the now standing Daws. "He says that—"

"He found something," Daws completed, and reached for his camera before heading toward the trench.

"Cabuk! Cabuk!" Kamir's cousin continued to urge excitedly.

Daws eased the camera's strap over his head and dropped down into the trench, closely followed by Kamir. He could see the face of the foreman's cousin was encrusted with chalk-white dust and yellowed dirt. Sweat painted streaks down his cheeks and forehead. The young man thrust a yellowed finger toward a depression in the layer of earth he had uncovered, Daws recognizing the fortuitous discovery as a tomb, where the most meaningful finds were often made.

He knelt over the depression and shifted his camera aside so it wouldn't be in the way. Then he pulled a small whisk broom from his back pocket and used it to gently brush away dirt and pebbles from a rectangular object, realizing it was made of wood. A small chest that was easily large enough to contain precisely the find he was searching for.

Coughing the relentless dust from his lungs, Daws gently eased the chest from the depression in which it had lain for nearly two thousand years. The iron latch was still in place, preserved by the hard claylike texture of the dirt. Daws eased a pencil beneath the chest to check the integrity of its underside. Then, after being satisfied it was intact, he lifted the chest gingerly from the ground.

"Is this what you have been looking for, Sayin?" Kamir asked him.

Straightening slowly, Daws turned toward his foreman with the box in hand. "Let's open it and find out."

DAY ONE
THE PRESENT

CHAPTER 1

DANIELLE BARNEA FLIPPED the air-conditioning switch up higher as the hot sun of the Judean Desert baked her through the car's glass. The wave of nausea she had felt passed quickly, and she returned all of her attention to the road. She had gotten the call while sitting in the doctor's waiting room and had driven from the clinic straight to the West Bank.

The final stretch of the drive to the crime scene took Danielle east through the Judean Desert toward the Dead Sea along a flattened dirt route. Around her the land was arid and scorched, only thin patches of gray vegetation scattered across the rock-strewn landscape. She could feel the dryness even in the cool air flooding the Jeep's cabin. Besides occasional nomadic bedouin tribes, she knew there were no settlements anywhere for miles.

At length, Danielle approached a makeshift military checkpoint just up ahead. She flashed her ID and an Israeli soldier swiftly waved her through toward a campsite set in the lee of the hillside another mile up the road. Israeli Defense

Forces vehicles rimmed the encampment, along with enclosed jeeps bearing medical markings. White rectangular tents erected over worktables fluttered in the wind. Four miniature Quonset huts with canvas flap fronts rose haphazardly out of the desert like unwelcome brush, now watched over by armed soldiers. Danielle noticed wooden plates nailed to boards driven into the desert ground named three of the huts after American hotel chains in hastily scrawled printing: HOLIDAY INN, MOTEL 6, and HOWARD JOHNSON'S. A trio of old Land Rovers were parked to make use of what little shade there was, while not far away a pair of covered cargo trucks roasted in the sun. Up a steep rise, just beyond the camp, she could see a doorway-sized opening into the jagged stretch of hillside, also guarded.

As she drew her Jeep to a halt near the others, Danielle got her first glimpse of the bodies covered by white plastic that crackled in the heat and wind. She climbed out of the car and walked toward the scene slowly. She noticed an Israeli army captain conferring with an old bedouin man in flowing white robes that billowed outward and headed toward him. The bedouin's hands trembled badly, his eyes red, drawn, and gazing somewhere else. The Israeli captain saw her and slid away from the old man.

"Pakad Danielle Barnea, Captain," Danielle greeted, handing him her ID.

The man took it reluctantly. "Captain Dov Aroche. We weren't told anyone from National Police was coming," he said, returning her identification after a cursory inspection.

Danielle chose to ignore his words. "You were first on the scene?"

"Yes."

"Then someone from your office was simply following procedure."

Captain Aroche did not relax. "I was under the impression this was a military matter, military jurisdiction."

"If there are security issues, yes. But the murder of foreign nationals is a civilian matter, unless terrorism is involved. Do you have any reason to suspect that here?"

"We have fourteen bodies, all shot to death, apparently from very close range as they slept. Beyond that, I don't know what to suspect at this point, Pakad."

"How many were American?" Danielle asked Aroche.

"Twelve."

"Archaeologists, I was told."

The captain nodded. "I guess no one told them these hills were picked clean years ago."

Even though no stranger to carnage, Aroche sounded plainly unsettled. Danielle could smell tobacco smoke on him and a half-empty cigarette pack protruded from the lapel pocket of his shirt, the plastic hanging down over his name-tag.

She looked over his shoulder toward the old bedouin man. "He found the bodies, I take it."

The captain nodded. "There were four bedouins bringing supplies not long after dawn. The old man sent the others to go for help. They came upon one of our patrols three hours ago now."

"What else has he told you?"

"Nothing. We can't make sense of his language, even if he stopped ranting."

"Ranting?"

The captain nodded. "He seems to know one of the dead. We have just finished compiling a list of their names from IDs we were able to recover."

"Show me this list."

Aroche hedged. "I'm not sure if I have—"

"Now, Captain."

Aroche shrugged and reluctantly led Danielle to the hood of a truck that had become his temporary headquarters. Atop the hood lay an assortment of wallets, passports, and identification cards. Aroche snatched a pair of pages from beneath a rock that had kept them from blowing away in the breeze.

"It's preliminary," he explained, handing it to Danielle with some reluctance, "but we still believe it to be complete."

"Very good, Captain," Danielle said, grateful for the time Aroche had saved her.

She scanned the handwritten list cursorily, until the ninth name stunned her. She swallowed hard, took a deep breath, and felt the hot, dusty air burn her mouth.

CHAPTER 2

ISRAELI SOLDIERS HAD parked their jeeps diagonally across the road, blocking Ben Kamal's access to the Judean Desert. There were other ways to reach the reported crime scene, but only in the kind of utility vehicles capable of handling the terrain. This route running east from Bethlehem toward the Dead Sea, though unpaved, was naturally flat, manageable even for Ben's Peugeot.

Ben snailed his car to a halt even before the Israeli soldiers signaled him to stop. They took a long look at his white Palestinian license plates and then eased their hands to their automatic rifles.

The leader, a sergeant, walked to the passenger side of Ben's car. The private hung back, bringing a second hand to his rifle.

"You have entered a restricted area," the sergeant told Ben. "I must ask you to turn your vehicle around."

Ben produced his identification instead. "Inspector Bayan Kamal of the Palestinian police."

He had now spent five years as a detective in the West

Bank after returning to his homeland to help train the Palestinian police force. His family had immigrated to the United States in 1967 shortly before the Six-Day War, though Ben had never considered a return until tragedy left him with nothing but memories in Detroit. Such a homecoming became an opportunity to start fresh with no baggage, he thought.

Until he created some. While attempting to train the fledgling Palestinian police force in proper investigative techniques, Ben found himself mired in the case of a murdered cabdriver suspected of collaborating with the Israelis. Meeting the man's widow and children gave him all the motivation he needed to uncover police corruption and a trail that led to a trio of officers who had killed and mutilated an innocent man.

The resulting outcry when the police officers were found guilty by a Palestinian military court led, ironically, to Ben himself being labeled a traitor. He realized he had drastically misjudged the landscape and the politics, found himself shunned as an outsider who had run out of places to which he could flee. He thought he could outlast the atmosphere of mistrust, but after five years had found relative isolation to be the only way to accomplish that.

The Israeli army sergeant inspected the ID, matching the picture of Ben's face. He flapped the wallet closed and returned it, unimpressed.

"I am sorry, Inspector, but you are out of your jurisdiction."

"I am here at the request of Pakad Danielle Barnea of the National Police."

"I know of no such request."

"She is the chief investigating officer at the crime scene in question."

The thick bands of muscle lining the sergeant's neck tensed. "And my orders are to deny access to the area to all but those who have the proper authorization."

"My pass allows for free passage anywhere in the West Bank."

"This particular area is currently under Israeli control." The soldier shifted his weapon from his shoulder so it was within easier reach. "If you do not vacate the area, I will have to detain you."

Ben turned off his car's engine. "This land was ceded to the Palestinian Authority in the latest phase of your government's withdrawal. I have the official maps right here. Would you like to see them?"

The sergeant leveled his rifle. The barrel trembled slightly. "Please exit the car now! I am placing you under arrest."

Directly in front of the Peugeot's hood, the private snapped his weapon to his shoulder and aimed through the windshield.

"Do as I say!"

Ben caught the look in the sergeant's eyes and opened the door slowly. The sergeant backpedaled enough for Ben to climb out, then instantly resteadied his rifle.

"Turn around! Hands on the roof!"

Again Ben did as he was told, cocking his gaze backward to see the sergeant shoulder his weapon before he approached.

"Face forward!" the sergeant ordered, and Ben felt his neck jerked downward, reduced to the same height as the sergeant, who was at least four inches shorter than Ben's six feet.

The angle allowed Ben to see himself in the car's side mirror. The dust and a thin jagged crack distorted his face, gave it a grotesque, misshapen appearance like something from a sideshow attraction. Not that he liked the real version much more, even though his skin remained smooth and relatively unmarred for a man of forty. This while many Palestinians wore their scars proudly and enjoyed explaining in which war they had suffered each one. Ben's hair was lighter than most of his countrymen's as well, a medium shade of brown; thick, wavy, and full. A young man's hair, he often mused, layered above a much older man's eyes.

The sergeant's hands started frisking at his shoulders and

worked downward, quickly feeling the outline of the pistol beneath his jacket.

"Beretta nine-millimeter," the sergeant said as he yanked it out. "Good gun."

"Israeli military surplus."

"I think I'll hold on to it for now."

And Ben felt the sergeant's hands continue their probe, while the private kept his gun poised in front of the Peugeot's hood. The sergeant got to Ben's jacket pocket and jammed a hand inside, emerging with his portable mini-disc player trailed by the small attached headphones.

"What's this?"

Ben turned enough to look at the sergeant. "It plays music. The radio in my car doesn't work."

"Where'd you get it?"

"A friend gave it to me."

The sergeant gave the disc player a closer look. "The instructions are in Hebrew."

"An Israeli friend."

Before the sergeant could respond, a four-wheel drive vehicle with darkly tinted windows and yellow Israeli license plates came to an abrupt halt. The driver's door opened and the soldiers snapped to attention as a woman with a National Police badge dangling from her neck stepped out.

"What is going on here?" demanded Danielle Barnea, her eyes falling on Ben.

CHAPTER 3

"WHY ARE YOU searching this man?" Danielle continued.

The sergeant regarded her nervously as the private lowered his rifle in front of the car. "I, er, we . . ."

Danielle's boots clattered atop the pebble-strewn road. She stopped in front of the sergeant only long enough to flash her identification.

"Didn't Inspector Kamal tell you he was here on my orders? Are you the man I informed over the radio to expect his arrival?"

"I—"

"Never mind. Return his gun and possessions immediately."

The soldiers looked at each other, then back at Danielle. The sergeant approached and returned the Beretta to Ben.

"Forgetting something?" Ben asked, holstering the pistol.

The sergeant slid the portable mini-disc player from his pants pocket and handed it over.

"Thank you," Ben said.

"I will take things from here," Danielle informed the soldiers as Ben and the sergeant glared at each other, "if you don't mind."

"Of course, Pakad," the sergeant relented, though it was clear that he did mind.

Danielle, of course, should have been addressed by the feminine "*pakadet*." But being the youngest woman ever to attain the rank of Chief Inspector of the National Police had led to her identification card being mistakenly printed with the first name "Daniel." The correction had been made almost immediately. Her formal rank, though, had stuck and spread quickly, a matter of tradition now, as well as respect for her prowess as an investigator. In fact, all her subsequent identification cards continued to call her "*pakad*." This after a military career in which she became one of the first female soldiers selected for duty in the elite Sayaret, the Israeli Special Forces.

As of late, Danielle had found herself comparing the old picture on her identification to the face she saw in the mirror. Remarkably, she looked the same. Her wavy auburn hair still tumbled to her shoulders. Her brown eyes were as bright and vital as five years ago, her weight exactly the same thanks to an obsessive dedication to daily workouts. And yet she felt so different, another person entirely, especially over the past three weeks.

Danielle waited for the two Israeli soldiers to head back to their vehicle before approaching Ben.

"That could have been nasty," she said. "They would have kept your gun."

Ben leaned back against his car. "I was more concerned about the disc player you gave me. Now tell me about these American archaeologists murdered in the desert. . . ."

She watched him smoothing out the wires connecting the player to the small headphones. "It would be better if I show you."

"The courtesy of the call was much appreciated, Pakad, especially since I haven't heard from you since you missed our . . . appointment last Wednesday."

"I'm sorry."

"That makes two weeks in a row."

"I've been very busy," she said, not meeting his gaze.

"Are you going to be busy this Wednesday?"

"That's not important now."

Ben caught the uneasy tone in her voice. "Why did you call me here, Pakad, when it is clear your people have assumed jurisdiction?"

Danielle produced the wallet she had taken from the crime scene. "One of the victims, one of the Americans, is named 'Kamal.' "

Ben accepted the wallet almost reluctantly and opened it. Danielle watched the color drain from his face as he inspected the identification, started to reach out a hand to comfort him, then pulled it back.

"It's my nephew," Ben said so weakly the wind almost swallowed his words.

FOR SEVERAL LONG moments, he could only stand there staring at his nephew's college identification card, hoping there was some mistake. His gaze was so empty he seemed to be looking past the wallet's contents instead of at them. "My brother's son. You're saying he's . . ."

Danielle turned away. "Let's take my car."

"It's been so long, I barely even recognize him," Ben mumbled, falling into step alongside her.

"Then perhaps . . ."

Ben shook his head painfully. "No, Pakad. The student ID is from the University of Michigan, Dearborn campus. My brother is a professor there. I remember him telling me that is where Dawud enrolled."

"You haven't spoken to your brother very often, have you?"

Ben's gaze was fixed straight ahead. "Three times since I returned to Palestine. Maybe four."

Danielle left it there and got behind the wheel. It seemed to take Ben a very long time to come around to the passenger side, but when he finally climbed in, his face had hardened, reddening even as she watched.

"How was he killed, Pakad?"

"Shot. They were all shot."

"How many?"

"Twelve Americans. Two others."

"Witnesses?"

"One, maybe: a bedouin man on the scene."

"I'd like to talk to him," Ben said, staring out the window.

CHAPTER 4

AT THE CRIME scene, Ben lunged out of the car ahead of Danielle. She rushed to catch up with him.

"You are not here in any investigatory capacity. I want you to understand that. Let me do all the talking."

Ben didn't slow down. "Just take me to my nephew, Pakad."

Captain Aroche, the ranking Israeli soldier on the scene, stepped out in front of him before Ben could enter the hastily staked-out crime scene.

Danielle hurried to draw even. "Captain, I would like to introduce Inspector Bayan Kamal of the Palestinian police."

The captain continued to look at Ben. "We should discuss his—"

"We should not make this matter more complicated than it already is. Inspector Kamal is here on my authority. That is all you must concern yourself with. Is that clear?"

She watched the captain stiffen. "If you insist, Pakad."

"Now, I am going to take the inspector to identify one of the bodies. After that I will escort him from the premises."

This time Ben waited for her to take the lead, but he stopped halfway to the row of small Quonset huts and crouched down over the desert floor.

"You said my nephew and the others were archaeologists, Pakad."

Danielle knelt next to him. "Yes. Why?"

"Look at this." Ben moved his hand away from a deep rectangular depression in the ground. "There was a piece of very heavy equipment here."

He rose and moved sideways, never taking his eyes off the ground. Suddenly he crouched again over a second identical depression. Then he was on the move again, finding a third.

"Machinery," he said, looking up. "Something big. I wonder what archaeologists were doing with such a machine."

Captain Aroche stormed toward them, the dirt sounding like ice crystals crackling beneath his boots.

"Pakad, I must insist that you—"

"The inspector was just pointing something out to me, Captain, that's all," Danielle said, tugging on Ben's sleeve. "We'll continue on our business now."

But Ben was staring at the old bedouin who sat in the shade, flanked by two standing Israeli soldiers. "That's the man who found the bodies?"

"Yes," Danielle said. "He was delivering supplies not long after dawn."

"That's all you know?"

"We think his son was one of the camp guards who was killed. Beyond that we haven't been able to make sense of what he's saying; no one speaks his language."

Ben looked at Danielle, then Captain Aroche. "I do."

WITH AROCHE'S RELUCTANT consent, Ben approached the old bedouin and crouched next to him. "I am a Palestinian policeman," he greeted in a vernacular of Arabic his father had taught him as a child. "I am here to help you."

The old man did not acknowledge him.

"I am told your son lies with the dead here. So does my nephew, I think."

The old man's eyes came to life. He reached out and grasped Ben's forearm, mumbled something.

"Can you tell me what happened here?"

"We arrived just after the sun came up," Ben translated when the old man spoke. *"We come with supplies every other day. My son got us this job, because my son . . ."*

Ben stopped when the old man broke down and dropped his face into his hands. Ben shimmied closer, grasped his shoulder gently.

"I'm very sorry about your son."

The old man didn't look up, just pointed toward one of the bodies covered in plastic on the camp's perimeter. A guard. *"I find him like that. See him, but I touch nothing!"*

The old man rose, crying now. Tears followed the deep furrows lining his ancient face, a face that looked like baked leather.

"He lies there, staring at the sky, at God," Ben translated in between the sobs, standing back up. *"He cannot see me."*

"You found no one alive."

The old man shook his head.

"Fourteen—that's the total number of the camp personnel?"

The old man nodded once, still looking down at the ground.

"A dozen Americans?"

"And two of my people," the old man said. *"My son,"* he continued, holding up two fingers, *"and one other. Here because they knew the land and the people. Good with a gun too. Paid well. Too much. Not worth it."*

The old man kept repeating that phrase, shaking his head violently until Ben held both his shoulders. The thin bones felt brittle beneath his grasp, the skin stretched loosely over them beneath the folds of his loose clothing.

"What were the Americans doing here?" Ben asked, glancing up briefly at Danielle. "What were they looking for?"

"Don't know."

"What about your son?"

"My son never told me; I can't say that he knew. He was just a guard and his English was not good enough to understand everything they said." The old man thrust a trembling finger toward the cave opening where two Israeli soldiers stood guard with Galil machine guns dangling from their shoulders. *"Up there. They find something up there just the other day. But my son, they never let him go in. That's what he tells me."*

The old man's sobs consumed him and he buried his face in his hands, sinking once more to the ground. After a few seconds, one of his hands began clawing at the earth, raking the dusty ground as if it were to blame for his son's death. The bedouin's hand froze with a handful of dirt that sifted slowly through his fist as he peered into Ben's eyes. Ben looked back and saw more than grief now, something new added to the mix:

Fear.

"Always they come to the desert to look for something to change history. Always they leave lucky to find a few artifacts. I don't know if these had found anything."

"Ask him how long the American team had been here," Danielle suggested.

"Almost five months in the desert they spend exploring new caves and old. Only a week have they been in this place."

"When was the last time you saw your son alive?"

"Everything was fine. Everything was good. He was being paid very well, more money than most of us ever see."

"When was the last time you saw your son alive?" Ben repeated.

"Two days ago."

Ben returned his gaze to Danielle and the Israeli captain. "That means they all could have been killed anytime in the past forty-eight hours."

"The level of rigor mortis and the temperature of the bodies indicate closer to twelve," Danielle told him, much to Aroche's dismay.

The bedouin began speaking again, clacking off words rapidly as his hands clenched the air before him.

"He says there had been threats," Ben translated. "That his son told him the Americans were thinking about adding more security."

Ben stopped and waited for the old man to catch his breath. "Who do you think did this?"

The old man fought back more sobs before responding.

"This is a holy place, a powerful place. Many claim it for their own and wish no trespassers, interlopers, or infidels to disturb its purity . . . or uncover its secrets. But I, I think this was a robbery. A tribe in search of riches the Americans pulled from the earth. The last time we spoke, my son told me they had found something valuable. I have crossed paths with many tribes in my time that would kill to steal such a thing. The jackals of the desert, who appear by night and vanish by day."

"Bedouins," Danielle surmised.

"We should have a look in that cave for ourselves." Ben turned away from her, toward the huts, before she could protest. "But I want to see my nephew first."

CHAPTER 5

THE BODY OF Ben's nephew lay on a cot in the second of the four prefabricated huts, MOTEL SIX, equipped with corrugated tin sides and roofs, and canvas flaps covering the front and rear. The Israeli soldiers had used white toe tags to mark the bodies with the identifications believed to belong to each. As Danielle hovered back by the entrance, Ben slowly pulled a plastic sheet down to reveal the corpse's face.

"I don't recognize him," he said, his voice cracking. "A young man's face changes so much in five years. I never saw him with a beard before. He always looked so young. . . ."

"When was the last time you did see him?"

"I missed his high school graduation, missed a lot of things."

Danielle met Ben's eyes and tried to remember what that had felt like before. "You can go now. Call your family. Help with the arrangements."

"Not yet," Ben said.

* * *

I CAN HANDLE this myself," Danielle insisted as Ben moved toward the two dead bedouin guards covered by plastic on the camp's perimeter.

"You missed those depressions made by some kind of tripod in the ground."

"Meaningless probably," she said irritably.

"All the same, you may miss something else."

"Look, Inspector, I called you here to identify your nephew's body. That and no more."

"After three weeks . . ."

"What?"

"That's what it took for you to call me after we hadn't spoken for three weeks," Ben said and continued on past her toward the guards who had been felled first.

Drawing closer, he saw the plastic covers had been staked into the scorched earth to prevent them from being blown off. Ben pulled one of the stakes free and drew the plastic away to reveal a body lying as it had been found: on its stomach with a wide pool of dark, dried blood staining the earth beneath the guard's head.

"Shot from behind at close range," he said to Danielle, who had knelt down next to him. Ben noticed something dark and metallic hidden by the guard's splayed left arm, continued to talk to cover his intentions. "Low-caliber bullet. Professional."

"Not likely to be the work of marauding tribesmen," Danielle said, aware of the caustic stare being cast their way by Captain Aroche.

Ben shifted his weight forward and eased his hand nearer the corpse. His palm closed over the metallic object. He felt several recessed buttons and, finally, a thick circular protrusion.

A lens . . .

"If it was bedouins," he said, noting Danielle's attention was still fixed on the wound as he pocketed the object, "this could have been the result of a feud between that tribe and the one which claimed this as its territory."

"Bedouins don't have territories."

"True enough, Pakad. But to avoid trouble archaeological teams are best advised to hire the members of one tribe to protect against incursions from others. It's been this way among the bedouin for hundreds of years."

Danielle stood up, shaking her head. "This doesn't have the look of a tribal dispute."

Ben rose and followed Danielle to the body of the second guard and again stripped back the plastic. This man, he saw instantly, had been shot in almost identical fashion. The pool of blood looked to be almost the same size.

"Interesting," said Ben, trying to remain detached. He had been at enough crime scenes to know the victims had to be regarded first and foremost as bearing evidence. He couldn't afford to let emotion creep in, had to remain objective and professional. It was easier when the bodies were stiff and cold, their blood dried into the ground. Much different when the scene was fresher, each sight and smell chilling. Ben could remember crime scenes in Detroit, before he'd returned to Palestine, where he'd had to put plastic bags over his shoes because the blood was still wet and spreading.

"What is?" Danielle asked.

"The way the bodies fell indicates they were facing opposite directions, fifty feet apart."

"Doing their jobs," she said. "While you are doing mine."

Ben ignored her. "Close enough to hear even a silenced gunshot at night. Unless they were killed at the exact moment." Ben rose and brushed the dirt from his pants. "Now, let's go have a look at the rest of the bodies."

Danielle stood determinedly in his way. "You've already seen the only one you have a right to."

"My nephew's death gives me a right to see anything I want here."

"Perhaps I made a mistake by calling you."

"But I'm here now and I'm not leaving."

Danielle took a deep breath. "All the victims were killed as your nephew was, with single bullets to the head. In bed, on narrow portable cots, as they slept. In all cases, the killings were neat, quick, and extremely efficient. Carried out within seconds of each other, by all indications."

"There was no evidence of a struggle in any of the tents?" asked Ben.

She shook his head. "Nor have we been able to find a single gun fired in self-defense."

"Enough killers to enter all four tents simultaneously."

"The generators had ample supplies of gasoline and were not running when the first troops arrived," said Danielle.

"The killers could have been waiting in the hills for the power to be turned off, Pakad," Ben theorized. "That was their cue. Not like marauding bedouins to exercise such patience, is it?"

"Or thieves," Danielle added, "since there's no indication that any of the tents was searched, much less ransacked."

"Professionals, then. But professionals kill for a reason." Ben fixed his gaze on the cave opening. "Perhaps we'll find it up there."

Chapter 6

THE GOAT TRACKS worn in the cliff face were steeper than they looked, too narrow to allow climbers to ascend side by side. Embarrassed, Danielle followed closely behind Ben as he started to climb.

"Why are you doing this?" she said, not hiding her frustration over his behavior.

"Don't want your fellow Israelis to think we get along, do you?"

Dirt and stones crunched underfoot, and Danielle slipped a few times thanks to her smooth-soled boots in her attempt to keep up with Ben. She had never seen him this driven before, this obsessed. She wondered if there was anything she could do to stop him.

"That's far enough, Pakad Barnea!" She was halfway to the cave entrance when she heard a voice from below, sounding gravelly and slightly out of breath.

Danielle stopped and swung round, muttering, "Great," under her breath. Then, "Now you've done it," just loud enough for Ben to hear.

"I said that's far enough, Chief Inspector Barnea."

Danielle looked down to see Commander Moshe Baruch, operations chief of Israel's General Security Service, or Shin Bet, standing at the base of the hill. A bear of a man, Baruch was flanked on both sides by several equally towering men dressed in plainclothes stretched taut over their frames. His face had a dark, almost Neanderthal look to it; slightly recessed with the eyes set far back in his head. The knees of his dark uniform were scuffed and stained with dirt, evidence he had already made at least a cursory inspection of the scene.

"I heard you, Commander," Danielle yelled down to him. Baruch had been her direct superior during her short-lived transfer to Shin Bet several years before. He had taken an instant disliking to her and later Danielle learned that a formal reprimand Baruch had received from her father, an army general, had stalled his advancement and short-circuited his plans for a career in the military. "I was only wondering why you would waste your time coming out here on a case assigned to National Police. I don't suppose it's to wish me good luck with my investigation."

"Whoever called your office made a mistake. I am here to relieve you."

"The mistake must be yours. This crime clearly falls under National Police authority."

"This American archaeological team was here under the protection of the Israeli government, Chief Inspector. That makes this a matter for the government, and not a civilian agency."

"Protecting the Americans was the government's responsibility, Commander. Now that you've failed, it becomes ours."

"I've spoken to Commissioner Giott. He disagrees."

"I'll wait to hear that from him myself, if you don't mind."

"Very well. He wishes to see you immediately upon your return to Jerusalem." Baruch's huge, dark eyes fixed on Ben. "You may want to inform him about the unauthorized presence of a Palestinian on the scene of an Israeli investigation before I do."

"Inspector Kamal was summoned on my request to act as translator," she insisted, hoping Ben would keep quiet. He stood sideways on the steps, as if on the verge of continuing up to the cave in spite of the Shin Bet commander's arrival.

"Yes," Baruch said smugly, "I'm sure he was. Now take him and leave before he does any further damage."

"Damage?"

Baruch advanced up the steps, swallowing them with his boots, stopping when he was a handshake's distance from Ben. "I would appreciate the item you removed from the guard's possession." And he extended a meaty hand past Danielle, ignoring her.

"The *bedouin* guard, you mean," Ben said to Baruch.

"Just hand over what you took."

Ben kept his stare locked with Baruch's as he reached into his pocket and extracted the tiny video camera he had palmed. "That guard didn't seem to have much use for it anymore," he said, feeling Danielle's burning gaze upon him.

Baruch accepted the camera but left his hand in place, not breaking the stare. "The disc too, please."

Ben frowned and produced a single recording disc from the same pocket. "It must have fallen out."

You're lucky baruch didn't arrest you," Danielle said when they got back to her Jeep. A thin film of desert dirt and dust had turned it a pale oatmeal color, including the windows.

"I was half surprised you didn't beat him to it."

"I'm sorry about your nephew . . ."

"Thank you."

". . . but it doesn't give you the right to remove items from a crime scene." She tried to soften her tone, make it seem less harsh. "When were you going to tell me about the camera?"

"I wasn't. Under the circumstances."

"I'm starting to regret extending you the courtesy of that call."

Ben looked at her. "The nights you were supposed to come to my apartment, I sat by the phone waiting for you to call."

"You could have called me."

"I did. Kept getting your answering machine, but didn't want to leave a message you probably wouldn't return. When you finally answered, I hung up."

Danielle remembered the call that had awoken her in the early-morning hours, certain it was Ben even then. She had just fallen back to sleep after vomiting in the bathroom.

"I was so relieved you were all right," he continued, "I almost didn't care you never showed up."

"I'm sorry. I'll explain, but later, not now. I have to figure out how to respond to Commander Baruch's charges."

"Be prepared for more," Ben said.

After climbing inside, he reached into his jacket pocket and removed a mini-disc identical to the one he had handed over to Moshe Baruch.

"What's that?" Danielle asked.

"I hope your former commander enjoys listening to 'Frank Sinatra's Greatest Hits—Volume One.' "

She looked at the disc in Ben's hand. "You're telling me *that's* the disc that came from the camera? You're a damn fool, Ben."

"So turn me in."

Danielle slammed the door behind her, the sun-baked upholstery singeing her skin through the fabric of her shirt and slacks. She turned on the engine and pressed a knob that sent a stream of washer fluid across the windshield. The wipers swirled the collected dirt into a streaky paste that only worsened her view.

"How did the commander know the bedouin guard had a camera, Pakad?"

Danielle tried the windshield washer again with little improvement.

"Baruch must have been keeping a very close eye on that American archaeological team, yes?" Ben rolled the disc around in his hand. "And perhaps this will tell me why."

CHAPTER 7

BEN HAD BEEN staring at the phone in his office for what seemed like hours, going as far as reaching for it but never quite picking it up.

"I have something terrible to tell you, my brother...."

The news of his nephew's death had to come from Ben, in spite of their relative estrangement over the five years Ben had been back in Palestine. It was seven hours earlier in Detroit, roughly eight o'clock in the morning. His brother Sayeed and his sister-in-law might barely be out of bed.

Putting off the call only gave Ben more reason to stew over Danielle's increasingly cold behavior toward him. It had made him realize with frightening clarity how much he had grown to depend on her. Palestine might have been his homeland by birth, but she was the only person with whom he had forged a meaningful relationship since returning. He recalled a trip they made together to Yad Vashem, the Holocaust Memorial outside Jerusalem he had never visited before. The walk through the eerie darkness, listening to the soft haunting chant of the names of the murdered and then viewing the horrifying memorabilia, had left him shaken and speechless. Danielle had taken his hand but he barely felt it until they were outside.

To Ben that had been a defining moment of their relationship, because Danielle had introduced him to an intensely personal and painful part of her world and her life. She had kept hold of his hand for a very long time after they left, the gesture as important as any intimate moment they had shared. Ben hadn't wanted her to let go and now found himself clinging to the memory. The longer his own people refused to accept him fully, the more dependent he had become upon her friendship and her love. Contemplating the loss of both terrified him, left him as chilled as the corridors of Yad Vashem, and made it even harder to summon the courage he needed to contact his family back in the States.

Fighting the hammering of his heart, Ben forced himself to lift the receiver and bring it to his ear. The dial tone sounded and he began to dial.

"Inspector Kamal," huffed an out-of-breath Palestinian police officer who had appeared suddenly in his doorway, "Captain Wallid says you are to come to Baladiya Square at once!"

Ben looked up, distracted. "What?"

"It is an emergency! Please, come quickly!"

Ben hung up the phone, the call to his brother left uncompleted.

JUST THIRTY-ONE YEARS old, Captain Fawzi Wallid had become chief of the Jericho police district thanks in large part to Ben's efforts nearly a year before. To reach him after leaving the Municipal Building, Ben had to fight through a crowd of people pouring from the popular shopping square, eyes peering back over their shoulders as if expecting some predator to strike. Ben pushed his way forward, badge clipped to his shirt the way he used to do in Detroit.

Captain Wallid, a short, squat man with a prematurely old face and ruddy complexion, was waiting at the rear of the crowd. "Over here, Inspector!" he called, and Ben veered toward him. "We have a hostage situation," Wallid continued, cupping a hand around Ben's shoulder. "A crazy man has already wounded a woman with a sword and two others are trapped. You're the only one on staff with experience in such matters."

Still numb from the pending call to his brother, Ben let Wallid lead him forward.

"Listen to me!" he heard a voice bellow from the center of the outdoor marketplace. "Stay back or I'll kill her!"

They neared a ring of policemen standing with pistols and rifles drawn at the front of the crowd. In the street before them, Ben saw the sword Wallid spoke of and then the man wielding it precariously close to a woman lying at his feet, already wounded. Two other women cowered beneath a nearby kiosk, a mere lunge away for the swordsman.

"Ordinarily," the chief of Jericho's police department explained, "we would handle things in a more traditional manner, but the Oasis Casino has brought an influx of tourism to the area and my orders are to avoid anything that might discourage that trend. Shootings are bad for business."

"So are dead hostages."

Wallid shrugged. "All the same, I would be in your debt, Inspector, if you try to defuse the situation peacefully."

Ben nodded, yanked his pistol from its holster, and handed it to Wallid. Then he removed his jacket before he started forward, so the perpetrator could see he was unarmed.

The man's sword, he noted as he approached, was a Turkish Kilij, an especially effective weapon developed near the end of the fifteenth century. The blade was straight for most of its length, then curved sharply inward to amplify the power of the razor-sharp edge. Ben also saw that this sword had a string dangling from its wooden handle, a price tag attached to the other end, no doubt; it was likely the wielder had picked it up from a nearby stand that sold battle-tested souvenirs.

"Listen to me!" its wielder ranted again. "I am here to help you, to save you! I have seen the devil. Do you hear me? I have seen the devil and he walks among us!"

Ben stopped twenty feet away. The man looked older than his voice indicated, in his sixties at least and few of those years had been kind. His arms were sinewy where once there had been layers of muscle, his face gaunt and ashen. He wore a kaffiyeh that had loosened enough to reveal a head bald except for two sides of matted silver hair. His eyes bulged as though he were hearing other voices at every turn.

The woman at his feet lay on her side, facing Ben's direction. Her expression was a mix of shock and terror. Her right shoulder had been sliced, and some of the blood had dripped onto the street. The swordsman turned his gaze on the fallen woman, and Ben chose that moment to step forward far enough to draw the man's attention upon him.

"Stop!" the madman ordered, eyes narrowing as he extended the sword in a knobby, skeletal hand. It shook in his grasp. "You! Have you seen the devil too?"

"Why don't you tell me what he looks like?" Ben replied, holding his hands in the air to show he meant no harm. If he could distract the madman long enough, the pair of women beneath a fruit stand might be able to escape. But there would be no such effort from the wounded woman lying in the center of the street who remained at the swordsman's feet.

"He looks like all of us," the madman answered finally. "That is how he gets away with his work. We see him and don't realize it. But I have seen him twice now. I remembered the mark he carries on his flesh."

"What mark is that?"

"An upside-down red cross on his forearm. His disciples who wear the mark lie in wait for the weak to pass by so they can snatch them away. They can hide from most, but not from me!" The madman's eyes bulged, looking like golf balls squeezed into his skull. "Show me your right arm! Do it now! Roll up your sleeve! Come on, quickly!"

He lurched forward with the sword, and the two women trapped beneath the fruit cart shrieked in terror.

Ben did as he was told, showed the man his bare arm even

though the sword was very close to striking distance. He watched the madman's wild eyes narrow and focus.

"See," Ben said, "no upside-down cross."

The man's gaze relaxed. "Show me your other arm too."

Ben rolled up the sleeve on that arm as well.

"Full of tricks, they are," the madman said, satisfied after checking Ben's left arm. "Can't blame me for checking. You never know, do you?"

"No, you don't."

"The devil's a sneaky bastard, he is. But he can't fool me, not someone who's seen him before."

"When was the first time?"

The old man lowered his sword to waist level and maneuvered sideways until he was straddling the wounded woman. "I'll kill them all until there are none to haunt me," he raged and brought the sword overhead. "It's the only way."

Ben took a step forward to distract him. "Tell me about the first time."

The sword trembled in the madman's hand. He drew his eyes off the woman and back to Ben. "I was just a boy. He tried to recruit me into his forces. I should have known, though. Even then, I should have known."

The madman sank to his knees, his sword clanking against the pavement, just inches from the wounded woman's leg. Ben crouched down before him. He glanced quickly at the women pinned beneath the fruit stand and used his gaze to signal them to slip away. He watched them begin to slide out, before returning all of his attention to the madman.

"I thought I was free of him. *After all these years, I thought I was free!* But he has returned." The madman's crazed eyes became desperate, pleading. The sword flapped before him like an ornament as he spoke. "I must warn everyone before it's too late because, you see, his time has come." The madman pointed the tip of his sword at Ben. "Have you seen him too?"

"Yes," Ben said in a tone meant only to placate the madman. But an electric shock jolted his spine as he remembered the night he'd come home in Detroit six years before to find a killer dressed in his family's blood. The memories were especially clear in the wake of seeing the body of his nephew just a few hours earlier. "Yes, I've seen him."

The madman lunged back to his feet. "Then you can help me find him."

Ben stood up slowly, careful to keep his hands in clear view. "I'll help you, but first you must give me your sword."

"I'll be defenseless without it." The madman's eyes bulged again. "He sent you, didn't he? This is a trick, a damnable trick. He's full of tricks." And he raised his sword once more over the wounded woman. "She is one of his tricks. Check her for a knife, if you don't believe me. Check her for the knife she would have used to kill me!" The madman stopped briefly, as if waiting for Ben to do just that. He continued when Ben remained still. "The devil must have thought I wouldn't recognize one of his legion, you see, but I have been waiting for the time of testing for so long, I was ready at every turn, just as I am ready *now*!"

And Ben watched the sword start downward.

CHAPTER 8

I WOULD LIKE to apologize for the confusion in the desert, Pakad," National Police Commissioner Hershel Giott said as Danielle approached his desk.

"Commander Baruch had no right to assume jurisdiction," she fumed, feeling the anger building in her anew.

"The situation is a bit more complicated than it seems."

"It's our case, Rav Nitzav. We should not have given in so easily."

Giott looked grim. "Please, sit down so I can explain."

Even rising out of his chair at her approach was an effort for him. Danielle moved to the front of his desk, trying to swallow down the thickness that had settled in her throat. The health of the head of the National Police had begun to fail him just after he announced his own retirement six months before, having agreed to stay on only until a replacement could be found. Now, with that day looming very close, Danielle realized exactly how much she was going to miss this man who was as close to a mentor as she had ever known.

She could have lived with that more easily, if life hadn't cheated Giott so badly. He had made plans to travel, finally having the time and desire. But then his wife had taken ill, and the ravages of age caught up with him as he struggled to care for her. Danielle knew his wife had cancer even before Giott confided in her, nearly breaking down when he explained the relentless deterioration of the woman with whom he had spent more than a half century. There would be no traveling for either of them now. The commissioner's entire existence was confined to a modest two-story home in the Jerusalem suburb of Har Adar.

"Your wife?" Danielle posed tentatively.

Giott frowned sadly, adjusting the yarmulke on his small round head. "The same. Good days and bad," he said, even though Danielle knew there were only bad at this point. "They are preparing to announce my successor. Two weeks more and he takes over officially. I would like you to be my guest at the ceremony."

"Thank you, Rav Nitzav." She fidgeted in her chair. "But I would like to discuss the murders in the desert."

"We are discussing them, Pakad." Giott's eyes darted to the door, making sure it was closed. "My leaving the National Police presents some unique opportunities for those willing to seize them. Positions opening up that have not been available for some time. High-ranking positions, Danielle, like *tat nitzav* or even *nitzav*. Do you see what I am getting at?"

"No," she said impatiently.

"I have been asked to recommend officers for the positions of commander and deputy commander. I would like to recommend you."

Danielle felt warm, as if the chair's leather had begun to suddenly sizzle.

"No woman has ever held either position," Giott continued. "But you were the youngest woman ever to attain the rank of chief inspector, weren't you? Who better to take the next step up in the National Police hierarchy."

Danielle had always dreamed of attaining such a position,

but thought the possibility remained years away. To hear Giott discuss it now, today, raised prospects as exciting as they were mind-boggling. A dream come true. Until she thought of the obstacle standing in her way.

"So the last thing we need at this point," he continued, "is a dispute with Shin Bet. I thought it prudent to exercise discretion this morning. After all, Pakad, it is only one investigation." His gaze hardened. "But there is another problem: your relationship with the Palestinian."

Danielle had to search for her breath. "Ben Kamal."

"I'm afraid that will sour the minds of many on you."

"That was not the case when I was ordered to liaise with him in pursuit of a serial killer, or when our joint investigation led to the end of a white slavery ring."

"Times, I'm afraid, have changed. You have continued to maintain contact with this Palestinian, have you not, Pakad?"

"Professionally," Danielle managed.

"What about socially?"

"We're friends, yes, colleagues."

Giott eyed her cautiously. "There are rumors that the two of you are considerably more than that."

Danielle lurched up from her chair and felt the familiar dizziness overcome her. She sank back down, a deep throb building between her ears.

"Are you all right, Pakad?"

"Fine."

"Some water, perhaps, a piece of fruit?"

"No, thank you." She held tight to the chair's arms. "It's just that my personal life is no one's business, Rav Nitzav."

"I'm afraid in this case it is. Given the difficult times you have experienced in the past year or so—your father's death, losing your baby—I am not trying to judge you. No, your personal life only becomes an issue when it raises red flags that could adversely affect your career."

"My dealings with Ben Kamal have done wonders for my career."

"In your current position," Giott agreed. "But for a person considering advancement . . ." He shrugged his narrow, bony shoulders. "If you are truly interested in attaining an appointment to such a high-level position, you must break off all contact with this Palestinian, both professionally and socially. Such contact is good public relations, and I know it has proven effective. But it does not make good politics."

"I'm not a politician."

"As a chief inspector, you don't have to be." Hershel Giott gave her the fatherly stare she had known so well for so long. But the stare was weaker now, the eyes behind it less potent and powerful. "When I walk out of this building for the last time, Pakad, I want to feel good about what I leave behind. Not just the state of our police force, or the person who replaces me in this chair, but also the people I care about. I worry what will become of them when I'm gone, when others of different judgments and political persuasions are left to make decisions." Giott sat back and folded his arms. "You understand the kind of man of whom I am speaking?"

"Yes," Danielle said, thinking of Commander Moshe Baruch's appearance earlier that day at the crime scene in the Judean Desert.

"The solution in your case, Pakad, is to become one of those who makes decisions, instead of one who is affected by them."

"Perhaps I would be better off remaining where I am," Danielle said bitterly.

"There are no guarantees of even that, I'm afraid. My successor, and those to whom he is beholden, might feel threatened by your successes and your celebrity. And right now you are too easy a target for someone who may carry his insecurities in his briefcase. I intend to do everything I can to secure this appointment for you. Call it a payback for your standing up for me last year."

"After all you've done, you don't owe me anything."

Giott's round face looked suddenly small and sad. "I let you down, Danielle. I'd like to make up for that, and I've got precious little time left to do it. But I need your help, your cooperation. Can I depend on you giving it, Pakad?"

Danielle nodded.

C H A P T E R   9

As the blade had begun its descent, Ben launched himself into motion. He managed to cut off the looping strike by catching his shoulder beneath the madman's elbow and felt the worn, brittle bones wrenched on impact.

The blade stopped a mere yard from the wounded woman's head where it dropped from the madman's grasp and clattered against the street. Ben tripped the madman's feet up and took him down hard to the pavement.

"He's back, I tell you!" the madman raged. "You must listen to me before it is too late! *The devil is back!* You'll see!"

Ben held the man down as the uniformed Palestinian policemen rushed forward, led by Captain Wallid.

"Excellent work, Inspector!" Wallid complimented, helping Ben to his feet.

It was nearly four P.M. by the time Ben returned to his office. He took out a form he himself had created for the

Palestinian police force and, at Captain Wallid's request, began to fill out his report on the incident in Baladiya Square.

Having barely started to type on the old IBM Selectric, Ben realized he could put off the phone call to his brother in the United States no longer. He forgot Sayeed's home phone number halfway through dialing and had to hang up in order to reconstruct it in his mind. He finally pressed all the numbers out, his breath growing short as the phone began to ring.

"Hello, you have reached the Kamals . . ."

Ben greeted the recorded message with relief, glad for another respite. Upon hanging the phone up before the message was finished, though, he remembered his brother would probably by now be in his office at the University of Michigan, Dearborn, where he was a professor of earth sciences. Ben ran his hands over his face, glad he couldn't remember his brother's number there. Ben's mouth was dry and tasted sour, and the back of his shirt had soaked through with sweat. His flesh seemed coated with the same murky film that had covered Danielle's Jeep and he carried the musty scent of the desert on his clothes. Worse, his shoulder ached where it had taken the brunt of impact in deflecting the mad swordsman's blow. Perhaps he should get it looked at in the clinic or, at least, fetch himself some ice.

No! Prolonging this call is only making it worse. . . .

Ben fished his address book from the top desk drawer and flipped through the pages in search of his brother Sayeed's number at the university. It had been so long since he'd called, he forgot where he'd written it and located it squeezed into a dog-eared page in the middle. He dialed the number hoping for a prerecorded message again.

"Professor Kamal," he heard instead.

Ben swallowed hard.

"Professor Kamal," his brother repeated.

"It's Bayan, Sayeed."

Now it was his brother's turn to be silent. Their relationship had soured well before Ben's return to Palestine, when Ben had fallen in love with and married an American woman.

Sayeed found this to be such an affront to the Palestinian culture it had become increasingly difficult to maintain cordial relations with him. He had insulted Ben's future wife at a family dinner, and Ben had left with her before the first course was complete. Now he remembered so clearly the disappointed look on his then young nephew Dawud's face in the window as he drove away.

"I almost recognize your voice," Sayeed said finally.

"I'm sorry."

"Don't bother."

"No, there's something else, something else I must tell you. The reason I am calling you."

"Go on." His brother's voice sounded more impatient than concerned.

"It's about your son. It's about Dawud."

"What about him?"

"Something . . . there's been . . ." The words kept catching in Ben's throat, as if a net kept holding them back.

"Dawud's in graduate school at Brown University," Sayeed said, "and doing quite well. Studying under the famous Martha Joukowsky."

Ben felt the net release, something different clutching his words. "Now?"

"His second semester."

"I don't understand."

"Why are you calling me, Bayan? Why are you asking about Dawud?"

"Where is he now?"

"I just told you."

"No, Sayeed, I mean *today*."

"You're not making any sense."

The receiver felt stuck to Ben's face. "Listen to me. I saw Dawud earlier today. In the Judean Desert."

"That's ridiculous."

"He had been killed, my brother."

Silence.

"Sayeed?"

"What is this madness, Bayan?"

"Not madness. I saw his body."

"Today?"

"A few hours ago. He was killed last night."

"I received an E-mail from him this morning."

"What?" Ben managed after a pause.

"It was waiting when I got to my office. Usually, he sends them to the house but I guess—"

"You haven't spoken to him."

"I just told you—"

"I mean over the phone."

"No."

Ben ran his free hand over his face. "He never told you he was coming to Palestine?"

"No, because he's in school. At Brown."

Ben let himself hope there had been some mistake, some terrible coincidence. Kamal, after all, was a popular name, and so was Dawud. Considering the large Arabic population in the Dearborn area, another young man with the same name could have easily been enrolled as well. That would better explain why he hadn't even recognized the body in the desert as that of his nephew in the first place.

"I'm telling you, my brother, you have made a mistake," Sayeed insisted.

But Ben still wasn't totally convinced he had. "Call him."

"Excuse me?"

"Call Dawud at Brown University. Get in touch with him. I pray you are right about me making a mistake."

"I am right. I'm sure of it."

"Then call me back, my brother," Ben said, calmer, "after you have . . . reached your son."

Sayeed Kamal sighed. "Very well. . . ."

"Just one more thing, Sayeed. What was Dawud studying at Brown University?"

"Archaeology," Ben's brother told him.

CHAPTER 10

WELL, MS. BARNEA," the doctor said, entering the examining room with a folder open before him, "I have the results of your blood work."

Following her meeting with Hershel Giott, Danielle had barely made the doctor's appointment she had rescheduled from that morning, slowed further by the typically awful Jerusalem traffic. Through the agonizing stops and starts in the narrow hilly streets, her thoughts returned to the opportunity Giott had presented her with.

But what would happen once the commissioner learned what the doctor was about to confirm for her now?

The biggest impediment standing in the way of her promotion, Giott had said, was her relationship with Ben Kamal. Because he was a Palestinian. Because she had been associated with him so often in the media during the course of two other high-profile investigations. They were often regarded as a team and neither had done much to dispel that. The proponents of Oslo and Wye had used them as a symbol for the vast potential of peace. The trick, in Giott's mind, was to take advantage of this notoriety, while at the same time defusing the political powder keg Danielle's opponents in the National Police could use against her with the more conservative elements.

For a time she had not known where her relationship with Ben was going. She fought what she was feeling and honestly believed she could win. Originally, they had tried their best to make it work and failed, and both had moved on. Then she had met a man who wasn't like Ben, but at least was Israeli, and Danielle found herself not so much wanting him as desperately wanting to be pregnant. She lost the baby a month after she had last spoken with this man and, soon after, fate had thrown her and Ben together again.

This time Danielle had lacked both the strength and desire to turn away from him. The only time she felt secure and content was when they were together. She didn't think of pregnancy again; it was the furthest thing from her mind. But the nights they managed to share became the happiest times of her life. She felt free, her true feelings no longer denied, for Ben Kamal was the only thing that could even remotely fill the emptiness that had plagued her since the miscarriage.

Then she had missed her period—not terribly unusual, the doctors had forewarned her. But she found herself waking up nauseous almost every morning and purchased a home pregnancy test. Never used it, afraid of the results.

What have I done?

Danielle should have felt thrilled by the possibility she was pregnant again, only the reality of the circumstances intruded. She had made this appointment with her OB-GYN, needing to know and too much a part of her hoping the signals her body had been giving her were wrong.

The doctor leaned against the table atop which Danielle sat, dressed in a thin gown that made her feel cold. She tried not to shiver.

"Congratulations," he said with a smile. "You're pregnant."

Danielle forced herself to smile back.

CHAPTER 11

THE OASIS CASINO lay in the desert outside the town of Jericho, just across the highway from a refugee camp. Some of the camp's residents worked on the construction crews that had built the sprawling complex, thanks to money raised solely by Palestinian investors.

Ben surveyed the grounds of the new casino, envisioned as the first leg of the largest tourist resort ever to be established in the Middle East. Before it was finished, the Palestinian Authority expected to pour at least $150 million into a project meant to draw tourism to the fledgling state. Today the steel shells of two high-rise hotels cast shadows over the limestone-faced casino. Construction of a conference center had begun as well.

Farther in the distance, Ben could see the area where a golf course had been staked out. He'd heard that the Palestinian consortium behind the complex had finally relented and retained Israeli irrigation experts to help design the course and figure out how to keep the sprinklers flowing, water being a scarce commodity in the West Bank. Similarly, today the parking lot was full of Israeli tour buses packed with a multinational crowd. Since the casino's opening, though, Israelis themselves by far remained the dominant customers, the irony of their fattening thin Palestinian pockets lost in the gambling craze.

Ben flashed his identification at the main entrance and went into the casino in search of Nabril al-Asi, head of the Palestinian Protective Security Service. He found the colonel on a raised walkway overlooking the huge floor of slot machines, their levers lashed downward as fast as players could feed in the tokens or coins.

"Come to try your luck, Inspector?" al-Asi said, smiling when he saw Ben approach. The colonel had jet-black, wavy hair sprinkled with gray that gave him a distinguished and dignified look. Though in his early fifties, his skin and teeth were flawless, and he bought his suits from the same private tailor in Tel Aviv who serviced Israel's top officials and businessmen. Italian mostly, although lately he'd developed a liking to the American designers Hugo Boss and Joseph Abboud. He reminded Ben of the actor Omar Sharif, though al-Asi claimed not to have seen any of Sharif's movies.

"Yes, but not on the machines. Besides, Palestinians aren't permitted to play."

"Those lucky enough to have foreign passports can. See, your dual American citizenship can finally be worth something!"

"What about you, Colonel?"

Al-Asi shrugged. He shifted sideways, changing the fall of the pants of his expensive Italian suit. "I, like all other simple Palestinians, must be content to watch."

"Is that what you're doing here?"

"In a sense. You see, the casino's opening has lured a number of—what should I call them?—expatriates back into our midst. President Arafat is most concerned their presence could prove disruptive. I, on the other hand, informed him that it's nothing a little winning can't solve."

"I could play some numbers for you," Ben said.

"Strange, isn't it?" al-Asi asked, ignoring his offer. He

clasped his hands behind his back and moved slowly down the elevated walkway, Ben staying by his side. "Before us lies everything that Muslim tradition abhors. Alcohol, gambling, even men and women mixing among one another. So the Authority responds by banning all Palestinians, denying us pleasures everyone else is free to enjoy."

"Few of us have money, anyway."

Al-Asi slapped his hand on the steel rail and leaned forward. "An empty gesture, then. Across the road, four thousand refugees watch as at least that number of players disembark every day. The men who helped build this place are not even permitted entry to the parking lot."

"Perhaps someday, Colonel."

"The Authority planned a trip to Las Vegas for us to learn about casinos firsthand."

"How was it?"

"I didn't go. My wife wasn't allowed to accompany me."

"Were you taking a stand?"

"Just being practical. It would not be safe for her here with me so many miles away." Al-Asi's face took on a rare somber look that quickly faded. "Now, what has brought you to this den of impropriety, Inspector?"

Ben slid the mini-video recording disc he had taken off the guard in the Judean Desert from his pocket and gave it to al-Asi.

The colonel regarded the disc closely, squinting one eye as if inspecting a piece of jewelry. "I don't think I've ever seen a chip like this. . . ."

"It's a mini-disc."

"What music group?"

"A *video* mini-disc."

"Of what?"

"That's what I need to find out."

Al-Asi returned his attention to the pit below, where lines of players stretched before the slots and the crowds waiting for a seat at the blackjack tables were three deep. "I doubt you'll be able to find a slot machine that will take it."

"I found it in the camp of the murdered American archaeologists."

Al-Asi pursed his lips speculatively. "I wasn't aware you had been assigned to the case."

"I wasn't. Not formally anyway. Pakad Danielle Barnea called after learning one of the victims was my nephew."

Al-Asi reached out and touched Ben's arm. "You have my condolences, Inspector."

"Thank you, Colonel."

"But I am surprised to hear that Pakad Barnea is involved in the case."

"She was briefly, until Shin Bet replaced her."

"I know of Shin Bet's interest."

Ben tightened his stance. "You . . ."

"My Israeli counterpart informed me of their intentions."

"Shin Bet?"

Al-Asi frowned. "One of their many agencies. They have almost as many as we do."

"You gave them permission?"

"They weren't asking for it."

"Did they say anything else?"

"Lots about the prospects of an international incident and doing our best to avoid it." Al-Asi rolled the mini-disc in his hand like a silver dollar. "I get the feeling this might lead to them being disappointed."

"It came from the camera of a bedouin who was working as a guard at the Americans' camp."

The colonel raised his eyebrows at the clear meaning of Ben's words. "And, of course, the Israelis on the scene missed it."

"They accepted a reasonable facsimile."

Al-Asi turned back to the floor. "And you said you weren't a gambler, Inspector. . . ."

"I'd like to learn what's on the disc, Colonel."

Al-Asi gave the disc one last gaze before handing it back to Ben. "Not the kind of technology bedouins are likely to use, is it?"

"Unless they happen to be working for the Israelis," Ben

said over the clank of slot-machine levers being pulled and the clatter of chips being swept off blackjack tables into cavernous drop drawers. "How much did you know about what they were up to, Colonel?"

"I knew they were digging. I love to see foreigners chasing their tails in our desert." Al-Asi's tone sobered a little. "Seeing them murdered is something else again."

"Precisely the reason why I thought it best to keep this disc. I was hoping you'd arrange permission for me to view it."

"On one of the computers at the Palestinian Authority Headquarters."

"Yes."

"No," al-Asi said, shaking his head. "Even if we have equipment that can play this, it's a safe bet it was donated by the Israelis and, thus, not to be fully trusted."

"What's the alternative?"

Al-Asi paused to drink in the sounds of chips and slot-machine levers before responding. "I'll have to make some arrangements. I'd get to it right away, but as you can see . . ." A shrug completed the colonel's thoughts as he gestured with a hand toward the domain beneath him.

"Your surveillance."

"The reappearance of former freedom fighters can make for difficult complications."

"I understand."

The colonel looked hesitant all of a sudden. "There's something else we need to discuss, Inspector. In fact, I was going to call you." He pulled an envelope from the coat of his suit, careful to tug the fabric straight again. "I received this report yesterday. It concerns your brother Sayeed in America."

Ben removed three stapled pages from the envelope and read them quickly, emotionlessly.

"This is the third such report in as many months," al-Asi said when Ben seemed finished. "Apparently his dealings with these unfortunate elements of our culture have escalated to an unacceptable degree."

Ben flipped through the pages quickly, gazed back at the colonel when he was finished.

"I have not taken any action yet, Inspector."

"Thank you."

"It's the least I can do, out of respect for our friendship. One cannot have too many friends, though apparently he can have too many brothers. But you understand I must act on this at some point."

"I understand."

"Unless, of course, some unexpected intervention preempted any action on my part."

Ben returned the report the colonel had provided. "Can you give me a few days to work something out?"

"A few, yes, especially in view of your nephew's death. I have plenty of other concerns to keep me busy for at least that long. It's a good thing for you so much of my attention is currently being directed here to the Oasis." Al-Asi's eyes widened. "In the meantime, why don't you spend some time in the casino? I'll even arrange a stake, so you can take advantage of that American passport that makes you extremely privileged among the rest of us humble Palestinians who are not permitted to play."

The colonel turned from Ben when a casino manager wearing a tuxedo approached.

"Your winnings, sir," the man said, and handed al-Asi a neat stack of dinars.

"Thank you," replied the colonel, sliding them into his pocket.

CHAPTER 12

WE MUST TALK, Pakad," Hershel Giott said tensely, a thin hand fastened around Danielle's elbow as he led her across his office.

She had returned to National Police Headquarters, debating if and when to tell her superior the truth, only to find Giott in a state of agitation, with something else on his mind.

"While you were out, I received a call from Commander Baruch."

Danielle sat down.

Giott took his chair as well, gingerly. "He says your attitude bordered on insubordination to a superior officer earlier today."

"I don't work for Shin Bet. He isn't my superior officer."

"Baruch is a well-respected department head, all the same."

"Not by me, he's not."

"Your family has a history with Baruch, doesn't it? Your father, I believe."

"That was many years ago, and the bastard got what he deserved."

"You're getting defensive, Pakad."

"It was Baruch who was on the defensive in the desert, Rav Nitzav, because he knew he didn't belong there. That jurisdiction should have remained with National Police."

Giott raised an eyebrow. "The commander also provided more of the specifics of your rendezvous. The presence of your Palestinian friend, for example."

"I needed a translator," Danielle lied.

"We have people on staff to provide such services."

"Not for native bedouin dialects."

"This was an unfortunate misjudgment on your behalf, Pakad, because it provided Commander Baruch with just the kind of ammunition he can use against you."

"Let him."

"Don't be naive. Commander Baruch has suddenly become very interested in the day-to-day operations of National Police. That includes the appointment of my successor and and that successor's accompanying senior support staff. I can neutralize his influence to a degree, but if we give him reason to make a stand neither of us will come out the better for it. Am I making myself clear?"

"Yes, Rav Nitzav."

"Do you want an upgraded position?"

"Very much," Danielle replied.

"Enough to choose your footing more carefully, Pakad?"

"Not if it means kowtowing to a bastard like Commander Baruch."

"That's too bad, because the costs of defeat with a man as powerful as Commander Baruch on the other side will be extreme. There will be nothing left for you to go back to. You will be left without a position anywhere in government and I'm afraid you'll find the private sector considerably colder and less inviting for someone with your kind of experience."

Danielle felt a tightness inside her chest. In that instant

she saw herself as Giott, and others no doubt, saw her: a woman in her mid-thirties, which made her too old to be a wunderkind any longer and too young to be considered a secure part of the old guard.

"The way to get what you want," the commissioner of the National Police continued, "and avoid what you don't, Danielle, is to compromise. Say things you don't entirely mean. Do things sometimes your heart is not into. But always with a greater goal in mind."

Giott's tired eyes blinked slowly, the sternness gone from them. Yes, he knew Danielle well, knew her better than anyone and certainly better than she knew herself.

"That goal could be as simple as self-preservation, or as complex as career advancement. Either way," Giott said, his voice winding down the way a toy doll's does when its batteries run low, "it pays to have your enemies believe you are doing exactly what they expect of you. Now, Pakad, I would like your assurance that there are no other surprises, nothing else you are holding back from me."

Danielle took a deep breath.

CHAPTER 13

JERICHO'S NEWEST CATHOLIC church was located on the town's southern outskirts amid neat rows of white stone houses, exactly one mile from Ben Kamal's apartment. He had walked that distance in the fading heat of the late afternoon, already looking forward to the evening coolness that would greet him in the walk back.

Strange how in the five years since his return from America, he had never gotten used to the heat, wishing he could treat it as he had back in Detroit: unwelcome but easily avoidable with air-conditioning always a dash away, life lived between cool cars and cool buildings always with the hum of fans whirring at the edge of his consciousness. But there was no escaping the heat in Jericho, no respite of air-conditioning except in the hotels, popular restaurants that catered to tourists, and now the Oasis Casino. The heat was a reminder to him of exactly where he stood, and how little he could change it.

A run-down, abandoned mosque had provided the home for this church, one construction phase leading to another

under the careful tutelage of Father Mahmoud Faisal, or
"Father Mike," as he was known to his English-speaking
faithful. Just over sixty, Father Mike was a round-faced,
pleasant-looking man with a bald dome and hair like black
wire sprouting from both sides of his head. His family had
immigrated to America at the same time the Kamals had, just
before the Six-Day War in '67, but he hadn't returned to
Palestine until the mid-1980s when he came back to establish
his own church. Lured home by the fiery nationalism of the
intifada.

Father Mike was working in the garden today—planting
or weeding, Ben couldn't tell which. Ben grabbed a spade
from a rusted wheelbarrow and joined the priest crouching
in the dirt.

"If it isn't my favorite parishoner," Father Mike greeted.

"Not because of my attendance on Sundays, obviously."

"Just blame the Israelis, like everyone else. They have become tougher than ever at the checkpoints. My parishoners
often spend their Sundays waiting in long lines to be turned
back." Father Mike gave Ben a longer glance. "But at least
you come prepared to work."

"Call it my penance," Ben said, waiting for Father Mike
to tell him what to do with the spade.

"Penance is prescribed, not volunteered."

"What about anticipated?"

Father Mike looked up from his work and studied Ben.
"Feeling guilty about something, my son?"

"Are we calling this the confessional?"

"It'll do, so long as you keep turning over the dirt before
you as you speak. I want to get the new flower beds in
today."

"I thought you were painting."

"That's tomorrow. I'll expect you to come by for more
penance. Then it's the stone wall the week after that."

"Perhaps you've chosen the wrong line of work."

Father Mike frowned at Ben's clumsy work with the
spade. "Especially since the study of ancient Latin and Aramaic, especially Aramaic, was my original avocation. Not

much demand for a translator these days." Father Mike reached down and held Ben's hand still for a moment. "You'd better talk fast before I have to redo that entire section."

"My nephew, the son of my older brother, was murdered."

Father Mike fixed his face in a tight frown. "In America?"

"No, here. In the Judean Desert. He was part of an American archaeological team that was all killed. I . . . saw his body."

"What a terrible thing."

"I called my brother. He didn't believe me."

"Denial." Father Mike nodded. "Not unusual in such tragic situations."

"It was like talking to a stranger. He didn't know me well enough to trust my word. He didn't think I knew my nephew well enough to be sure."

"Was he right?"

"Yes," Ben conceded.

"So who are you angry with, your brother or yourself?"

"We've only spoken a few times since I came back to Palestine, and our relationship was strained even before I left the United States."

Father Mike went back to turning the ground with his hands, inserting tiny bulbs lovingly into dirt that would turn to dried clay by week's end. The sun and heat had flushed his face red and drew spiderwebs of blue veins to the surface of his cheeks.

"I get the feeling there's something more you want to tell me."

"I arrested a man earlier today," Ben responded without hesitation. "He told me he had seen the devil."

"Is that a crime?"

"He also wounded a woman with a sword. I think he had gone mad. Said he recognized the devil from years before. Right now I want to believe him, I want to believe he really did see the devil."

Father Mike laid his tools down. "You'd like the devil to be real."

"Do you blame me?"

"It's not my job to dispense blame. I leave that to someone else."

Ben didn't seem to hear him. "First my wife and children killed back in Detroit, and now my nephew here in Palestine. Maybe the devil's been following me around. I even told the man I arrested this morning that *I* had seen him too. Was I lying, Father?"

Father Mike brushed his hands off on his baggy work pants. His blue eyes seemed to lighten. "You've seen evil. You've seen violence. You've seen hate." Father Mike nodded. "Close enough to the devil, that's for sure."

"Everything changed for me that night my family was killed. Sometimes I forget how much. Today, in the desert, made me remember." Ben let the words trail off, but suddenly the memories turned vivid on him, like still shots unfolding in rapid fashion. The serial killer known as the Sandman coming at him with a knife, soaked in the blood of his wife and children. Ben putting bullet after bullet into him, wondering now if you could really kill the devil. "I don't know what I came back to Palestine looking for any longer," he continued.

Father Mike nodded, as if that made sense to him. "Those who have walked in the darkness have seen a great light."

"What's that?"

"A proverb from the prophet Isaiah."

Ben smoothed the dirt before him with his hand. "I don't think I see his point."

Father Mike pushed himself to his feet. Ben could hear his knees crack, gazing up at the older man as he spoke. "Maybe Isaiah was saying that light can best be seen from the darkness. Picked out and followed like a beacon to lead you out. I don't think you've seen that light yet, Ben. But if Isaiah was any kind of prophet at all, then eventually you will."

"I don't suppose he was a good enough prophet to say how long it would take."

* * *

BEN WAS AWOKEN by the sound of banging on his apartment door. His alarm clock read one A.M., and he had been sleeping fitfully, racked by dreams of his family back home. His brother had not called back, allowing Ben to still cling to the hope that the body in the desert had not been that of his nephew at all.

Ben threw on his bathrobe and wobbled to the front door. He had barely started it open when the door was forced inward, staggering him backward. A sea of uniformed figures swept into the room, all at once swallowing and holding him still. He heard words being exchanged rapidly in Hebrew, then a new voice in English. A woman.

"I think you have something that belongs to us, Inspector."

CHAPTER 14

Y OU KNOW WHO we are?" the same woman
asked after the Israeli soldiers had transported him to a building somewhere in the West Bank, blindfolded in the back of
what must have been a van.

Ben's vision cleared slowly. He was in a large, square
room surrounded by Israeli soldiers. His legs and arms were
bound to a chair. Around him the bare walls were made of
cinder blocks and the smells of gasoline, dried oil, and rubber
from a pile of discarded tires hung in the air. He could see
dark splotches of grease and motor oil on the floor beneath
a trio of mechanic's lights that hung from the ceiling, providing the room's only light. They must have taken him to
a vehicle storage dump, abandoned after control of the area
had passed to the Palestinians. The windows had been
boarded over and the only door Ben could see was a garage
bay set on rusted metal runners.

"I asked if you know who we are!" the woman repeated
and walked around from behind the chair to face Ben.

She had short brown hair, neatly styled. She would have

been attractive, if not for the nasty scar that ran down the left side of her face like a zipper.

"Yes," he managed, through a mouth that had gone bone-dry.

"You understand you are under arrest."

Ben saw the bars on her uniform that identified her as a captain. "On what charge?"

"Suspicion."

"Suspicion of what?"

"Take your pick, it doesn't really matter. We are not required to say."

The woman's boots clacked against the wood floor as she circled Ben's chair again. She was holding a weighted sap down by her hip for Ben to see. Ben knew the routine of such torture, often called *shabeh,* knew its purpose was to inflict as much pain and bruising as possible without breaking any bones or doing lasting damage. There were stories of prisoners being kept in a chair for days, or being confined for weeks in a coffinlike concrete box. Sometimes loud music was used, or deprivation of water, food, and bathroom facilities. All part of what the Israeli officials when pressed referred to as "moderate physical pressure."

"Since you know who we are," the woman continued, "we can assume that you understand the gravity of the situation."

"I understand you have violated the agreement between our respective law enforcement agencies."

"The agreement is rendered void by crimes committed against the state of Israel."

"Is that what you're accusing me of?"

The woman came closer and knelt down until she was eye-to-eye with Ben. She slapped the weighted sap lightly against her own leg. "You stole something belonging to the Israeli government. That makes this a political incident. That makes you a political prisoner."

"What did I steal?"

The woman removed the mini-disc Ben had given to Commander Moshe Baruch of Shin Bet earlier that day. "I think you know that too. Tell us where we can find the real disc, and you will be released."

"And I'm supposed to believe that . . ."

"We will have no reason to hold you, once the real disc is in our possession."

Ben looked around the room, then back at the woman who was holding the sap at eye level now. He weighed his chances, considered his options. "It must have slipped out of my pocket. I lost it."

"At least you didn't try to tell us you hid it in the garden in front of the Catholic church in South Jericho," the woman accused.

Ben felt a sudden chill, recalling how he had eased the disc, now wrapped tightly in plastic, into the dirt of Father Mike's flower beds when the priest wasn't looking.

"We were watching when you buried it," his interrogator continued. "Since we couldn't find it, we had to assume either you had changed your mind, or the priest had retrieved it." She came close enough for Ben to smell oranges on her breath. "We are now satisfied he did not."

"What did you do to him?" Ben demanded, lurching forward against his bonds.

The woman slapped the sap against the outside of Ben's left leg. It smacked the muscle with a whap that made Ben cringe, grimacing through the pain.

"We did what we had to. I'm afraid he wasn't very cooperative, which brings us back to you. The disc was not in the garden, not in the church, not on your person, and not in your apartment. That means you must have hid it somewhere else."

"I hid it in the garden, just where you saw me."

"You're lying."

"I'm telling you the truth!"

The woman struck him lower down, on the outside of the knee. The pain jumped up his leg and Ben winced audibly. "I suggest you find another truth to tell us. Did you view the disc?"

"No."

"Did you give the disc to someone else?"

"No! I told you I hid it in the—"

The sap got Ben in the side of his ribs this time and his breath split apart inside him.

"I am getting tired of this," the woman said. Her face had turned beet-red except for the jagged, zipperlike scar that remained pale, the color washed out of it. "I meant what I said about releasing you. We have great respect for your work, Inspector. We do not relish this assignment, believe me. But we will keep you for as long as it takes us to recover that disc."

"I'm telling you I—"

The woman hit him in the side of the skull before Ben could finish. His head whiplashed to the side and stuck there, the world turned on edge. The pain lingered, digging deep. Ben tasted blood and realized he had bitten into his lip.

"You were going to lie again," the woman accused, an edge of anger creeping into her voice. "From the normal Palestinian, this would not bother or surprise me. But from a Palestinian I respect, I take such behavior as demeaning and degrading of my position, for it shows you do not respect me, Inspector. How am I to take that?"

"I don't really give a shit!"

The woman struck Ben on the side of the face this time, rattling his jaw. His teeth felt like marbles bobbing in his mouth.

"Someone else must have taken the disc," Ben said, the words slurred by his already swelling mouth. "Someone else must have been following me. It's them you should be after! *They've* got the disc now!"

The woman backed up, as if considering Ben's words. Then, suddenly, she snapped the sap in straight and hard, and Ben's world exploded into a breathless darkness.

DAY TWO

Chapter 15

GIANNI LORENZO, CAPTAIN commandant of the Swiss Guard, the elite force charged with maintaining security in the Vatican and protecting the pope, looked up from the report that had been handed to him just minutes before.

"Under the circumstances," the man seated before him elaborated, "we felt it was the safest course of action."

"I quite agree."

"We felt—"

"I understand," Colonel Lorenzo interrupted. "Just tell me what you have learned of the investigation."

Although his formal title was captain commandant, all who led the Swiss Guard held the rank of colonel. The colonel rose and walked to the window of his office in the Palazzo del Governatorato overlooking the vast Vatican gardens. The office was richly appointed with genuine antiques that had weathered the years much better than he. His desk had once belonged to Pope John II. The Oriental carpets that covered the hardwood floors had been in the Vatican since the eighteenth century, when they had been delivered as gifts by returning Christian missionaries. A chiming wall clock had been a gift to a nineteenth-century Swiss Guard commander from the College of Cardinals.

The Swiss Guard seldom exceeded more than a hundred troops, all of them culled from the best ranks of the Swiss military, as had been the case since their origins as guardians of the pope in 1506. But in the wake of World War II the Guard's number and training had been deemed woefully inadequate to fulfill their original function. Traditional guardsmen were fine for securing majestic entrances throughout the Vatican, or for smacking their halberds into the feet of those overly determined to approach the pope on ceremonial occasions. For other duties certain to be required in this new age of violence, though, a different kind of soldier was called for.

So, with the consent of the Curia and at the urging of Pope Pius himself, the colonel's predecessor had secretly reestablished the Pontifical Noble Guard that had been disbanded in the late nineteenth century. Gianni Lorenzo and seven others formed the first graduating class, envisioned as the basis for a clandestine order to be called upon for special assignments and protective services, much like the American Secret Service.

But no one—not the cardinals, not the Curia, not even the pope himself—would ever know how this secret army had actually been utilized, starting that first time in April of 1948. On that day Gianni Lorenzo's predecessor as leader of the Swiss Guard had faced him much the same way he was facing a subordinate now.

I HAVE READ a number of reports on you, Captain Lorenzo. You should take great pride in the success you have achieved. The small group you have been chosen to lead is the first of a new order. As such, something has come up I feel would be best handled by someone with your skills."

Here, his predecessor's eyes had darted toward the manila

envelope torn open on his desk. The very same desk behind which Lorenzo was now seated. Nothing about the room looked any different than it had that first day. It was exactly as Lorenzo recalled a half century before when he saw the envelope was marked "EPHESUS."

"Thank you, Colonel."

In those days, Lorenzo's wide back and shoulders had virtually obscured the entire width of the chair. His thick hair was cut short and roughly combed against the wave of its grain. He had deep, bushy eyebrows that nearly met in the center of his forehead above a set of piercing blue eyes, the message in those eyes clear. The original members of the Pontifical Noble Guard all came from Italian nobility, and Gianni Lorenzo certainly looked the part here fifty-two years ago when his predecessor had first addressed him.

"Your exploits before you came to us are well documented, Captain, especially at Nunzio."

"I was a soldier. I did a soldier's work."

"You performed bravely and admirably. But I am curious as to why you chose service to the church in the years that followed."

"I have strong feelings for the church, Colonel."

"You had planned to become a priest, had nearly completed your studies, yes?"

"Until the war."

"What changed?"

"A priest was not allowed to carry a gun."

"And this was important to you."

"I wanted to serve my country."

"But not God?"

"We were fighting the devil, Colonel."

"Then you came to us afterward."

"To serve the church the best way I could."

"You would do anything to protect the Holy Father and preserve the sanctity of the church, then."

"I swore an oath."

"A soldier's."

"A soldier is what I am, Colonel."

*   *   *

AND SO LORENZO was still a soldier today, his commitment having never wavered, the duty he was now charged with passed on to him over a decade before by his predecessor.

Before the desk that had served countless Swiss Guard commanders well, Major Flave Pocacinni stood stiffly at attention. "We left nothing behind that can possibly lead back to us, Colonel," Pocacinni informed Gianni Lorenzo.

"But you did leave *something* behind, did you not?"

Pocacinni's angular chin came forward as his neck stiffened. "We searched everywhere. The box you described was nowhere in the camp."

"Our information indicates otherwise."

"I am aware of this. I would suggest the information is wrong."

"You understand the depth of our intelligence-gathering apparatus?"

"Clearly, Colonel."

"Its singular purpose and ultimate dedication?"

Pocacinni looked almost hurt, his massive shoulders sinking. "Do you really need to ask me such questions? I mean no disrespect, sir."

Lorenzo sighed. "Of course you don't. The fault is all mine. Please accept my apologies for questioning your loyalty and dedication."

"I did not interpret your words that way at all."

"It's just that, well, there are certain inconsistencies that continue to plague me. The unusually quick response, for one thing." The captain commandant of the Swiss Guard ran a hand down his face, tracing one of the many furrows that had deepened with age. He studied the report again. "Did you have any sense, Major, that something else was going on out there in the desert?"

"I . . . don't understand, Colonel."

Gianni Lorenzo waved his own suspicions off. "Never mind, Major. I think I'm just beginning to show my age. A dozen American archaeologists are found murdered, we should expect such a response from their Israeli hosts."

"I agree, sir."

"All the same . . ." Lorenzo fought to keep his focus, not lapse from the subject at hand. "We would have known if the Israelis had found the box by now."

"As I said, it wasn't there. Perhaps . . ."

"What is it, Major?"

"I was just thinking, sir, that perhaps the Americans realized what they had actually uncovered, before our arrival."

Lorenzo chose not to consider the ramifications of Pocacinni's suggestion. Instead his mind drifted back to another age and another archaeological team in Ephesus that had stumbled upon the very same discovery. That team's inquiries all those years ago had been neither discreet nor restrained. Winston Daws had understood *exactly* what he had uncovered and was unable to contain either his passion or excitement. Daws's attempts to obtain confirmation from a few renowned experts had alerted Lorenzo's predecessor to the famed archaeologist's discovery. That had been the first occasion the secretly reestablished Pontifical Noble Guard had been called to action.

Gianni Lorenzo thought again of the day he had been summoned to this very office by his predecessor to learn the truth, the day that had changed his life forever. From that moment on, he and the rest of the Noble Guard had dedicated themselves to protecting a secret the world could never learn. How many would die if the secret got out, how many lives would be destroyed forever? The inevitable cataclysm that would result was chilling, incomprehensible. There had been no more choice in 1948 than there had been just days ago.

But that did not make the memories any more palatable. Winston Daws's team consisted of two dozen people, many of them mere students in their late teens or early twenties. As a soldier, Lorenzo knew that death never came easily or quietly, and the screams of the two dozen who had been murdered haunted his dreams to this day.

The recent deaths of the American archaeologists, though,

were even harder for him to bear, because he *himself* had caused them by failing to complete his mission fifty-two years ago. The executions of Daws's team were only one part of his charge and he had failed miserably with the other. Of course, he had never shared his mistake, or the circumstances surrounding it, with a single soul, the pain and guilt his to bear alone.

"Colonel?" Pocacinni prodded.

Pocacinni's voice brought Gianni Lorenzo back to the present. "Yes, Major."

"I was just saying that if the Americans opened the box, well, it's possible they could have sent its contents somewhere else prior to our arrival."

The colonel's mind sharpened again. "If that were the case, our sources would have already alerted us. No, Major, the scroll has not left Israel or Palestine. Our people are still in the area?"

"Of course, sir. Six," Pocacinni said, referring to the force of Noble Guardsmen whose numbers had increased only minimally over the years. "I will be rejoining them as soon as my business here at the Vatican is complete, sir."

"Then you must delay no longer."

Pocacinni saluted, then backed away from the desk and started to turn for the heavy wooden door.

"Major?"

Pocacinni stopped and turned back. "Yes, Colonel?"

The captain commandant of the Swiss Guard rose to his feet as well, remembering the days when he had stood as tall and straight as the former soldier before him. "Do you ever regret accepting the charge you were given?"

"Never, sir, not even for a moment."

"You understand that you and those you lead were selected from hundreds, thousands even. You and the others were chosen for this vigil because all of you were deemed the best suited to be guardians of our realm, of our very way of life."

Pocacinni straightened to attention once more. "I was honored then, Colonel. I am still honored today."

"Even after what your duty forced upon you in the past forty-eight hours."

"The pain of a task in no way negates its necessity, sir."

"They will come to you in your dreams, my son," Gianni Lorenzo said softly. "For many years after this, they will come to you in your dreams."

Lorenzo's assertion did not seem to trouble Pocacinni. If anything, he looked more resolute and sturdy. "Then they will understand what it was they had to die for, sir."

CHAPTER 16

BEN WOKE TO a body throbbing with pain. His mouth felt packed with cotton, and he worked his tongue around to find, thankfully, it was just dry and swollen. A few of his teeth were loose, and his jaw felt as though the bone had shifted, clicking when he moved it. His hair was matted to his scalp and forehead by the water the Israeli soldiers must have poured on him in a failed attempt to revive him.

The closet within which he had been held prisoner, still tied to the chair, stank of rust and metal. Not so much as a single sliver of light was able to sneak through a slat in the boards or crack in the wood. Ben could not see his watch and had long lost sense of the passage of time. He kept nodding off, only to come awake with a jolt; out, for what, seconds, minutes, hours? It could have been any of those.

Still, Ben stiffened in the chair and felt his breath wedged tight in his throat when he heard a key rattle in the lock outside. He let his head slump to his chest and pretended to still be unconscious, feeling the soft half-light upon his closed eyelids.

"Inspector Kamal?"

The voice was masculine, clearly not that of his inquisitor.

"Inspector Kamal, can you hear me?" The voice sounded closer. Then Ben felt a hand shake his shoulder gently. "Wake up, Inspector, you must wake up."

Though the man's grasp was gentle, his next squeeze drew an involuntary wince of pain from Ben, who let his eyes come open slowly. A figure stood before him in the thin light radiating from the large room beyond, dressed all in black. A big man with a V-shaped torso and arms like molded steel. The man whipped a hand up and a knife flashed amid his fingers, glinting in the naked light.

"Let me do something about these," he said, and crouched down.

As the ropes were sliced away, Ben could see the garage door in the square room beyond had been raised, allowing sunlight to flood inside, revealing more darkly clothed men. The Israeli soldiers and his female interrogator, apparently, were gone.

"Can you stand up?" the man asked him.

Ben tried to stretch his arms. "I don't know. Who are you?"

"A friend. That's all you need to know."

"What happened to the soldiers?"

"They were called away. Come, let me help you up. . . ."

Ben felt a tremendously powerful arm loop beneath his shoulder and raise him effortlessly to his feet. He stood on his own, but his left leg buckled when he tried to take a step.

The dark man caught him as he bent at the waist. "Easy now. It's not as bad as it feels."

Ben looked up at the man who was supporting him. "It feels pretty bad."

"You must be treated, of course."

"Where?"

"We have a complete hospital facility. You'll see."

"Who's 'we'?"

"You need a change of clothes. We can take care of that too."

This had to be a trick, Ben thought as the dark man ushered him into the room where he'd been tortured. Ben felt a shudder sweep through him but the Israeli soldiers were nowhere to be seen, replaced by these apparent saviors.

He counted four of them inside the building and two more outside once they reached the open door. Dressed in black as well, stiffly vigilant. Some holding guns, others not.

"Watch your step," his escort advised, guiding Ben into the sunlight that burned his eyes. When Ben's vision cleared, he saw the man was missing a neat chunk of his right eyebrow. A birthmark, judging by its pale smoothness.

Ben had heard of this technique before, resorted to when the more harsh forms of interrogation failed. An apparent rescue, dramatic or otherwise, leading the subject to confess all to his saviors. The Israelis were nothing if not persistent. The trouble was Ben didn't have anything to tell them; if he had, he would have told the others long before.

"What time is it?"

"Just after eight A.M."

Outside, a final man clothed in black stood vigil between a pair of American Humvee vehicles.

"See if you can put pressure on your legs now," Ben's escort suggested, sliding out from beneath his shoulder.

Ben tentatively took one step, then another. His legs trembled but held. His hands flopped weakly in search of something to hold on to.

The dark man sighed. "I apologize for the actions of my countrymen."

"What did you do to them?" Ben asked, even more leery now.

"Asked them to leave."

"That's all?"

"This was an illegal arrest and interrogation. I doubt they wanted to draw any more attention than necessary."

"That never stopped them before."

"It stopped them today."

"Actually," Ben said, walking alongside the man in black toward the lead Humvee, "you did."

"Don't worry: you'll be given a chance to return the favor."

CHAPTER 17

"I GUESS I owe you some thanks," Ben said to the dark man, a while after the Humvees had pulled away from the abandoned Israeli storage dump where he had been interrogated.

"You owe us nothing, Inspector," the man said without turning from the road.

"Where are we going?"

The dark man didn't answer, but Ben didn't have to wait long to find out. A half hour into the drive through the West Bank, the convoy passed just outside of Hebron, following signs for "Kiryat Arba." The drive was made along a trio of roads that only Israelis were permitted to travel on, allowing them to move between settlements and cities without ever drawing close to a Palestinian village or even seeing a Palestinian. Palestinians, on the other hand, were forced to use circuitous routes often hours long to cover absurdly small distances—and only if they could secure a pass. The stories of Palestinians losing long-held jobs and missing the funerals of loved ones for failure to secure such a pass were as commonplace as they were tragic, and showed no sign of letup.

Finally, Ben's driver turned off the main route onto a guarded, private road that was smooth and straight in contrast to the constant state of neglect and disrepair of Palestinian roads. An Israeli settlement laid out like a fort appeared at the very end. Heavy gauge chain-link fence topped with barbed wire rimmed all of the perimeter Ben could see. There were a pair of guard towers and a series of buildings that had a prefabricated bunker look to them. Simple beige-colored rectangular structures, so plain they looked ugly.

A pair of armed guards opened the gates manually and Ben instantly saw a number of settlers strolling leisurely about the grounds. The men and boys all wore black pants, white shirts, and yarmulkes atop their heads. The boys sported a neatly curled strip of hair hanging past their temples, the men had beards of varying lengths. The women Ben saw all wore long dresses and head scarves, consumed by their daily tasks.

It was difficult to gauge the number of residents from the surroundings, but not the level of security. In addition to the two guard towers, uniformed men patrolled the grounds in regular grids. Jeeps armed with pedestal-mounted machine guns sliced through the surrounding fields, driving slowly as if expecting an intruder to be hidden behind every tree and bush. Ben also saw what looked like cement bunkers placed strategically about the grounds, rising just enough over the surface for gun barrels to be wedged through their openings. Beyond them, construction vehicles and workers were busy erecting a host of new structures in various stages of completion. All simple and plain, their drab oatmeal shade rendering them virtually indistinguishable from each other.

Ben's eyes fixed finally on a number of men erecting a large apparatus with a tripodal base that reminded Ben of the depressions he had found at the crime scene in the Judean Desert.

"What's going on there?" Ben asked the dark man.

"They're looking for water. Life will be difficult here if

we can't tap into the primary underground supply." The dark man led Ben away. "Now let's get you fixed up, Inspector."

THE COMPLEX'S INFIRMARY was more like a small hospital. Inside the infirmary, Ben's wounds were cleaned and dressed, he was given painkillers and a change of clothes. He used a sink to wash his face and hands. Opened a brand-new toothbrush to brush his teeth. In his exhaustion, the cushioned hospital table looked desperately inviting. But Ben fought back the temptation to lie down and exited the room.

His large, unnamed escort was waiting when Ben emerged and immediately led him back outside toward a centrally placed building marked by a Star of David over the door. Splotches of sweat had begun to soak through the man's shirt, spreading as he walked in the building heat.

The dark man preceded him through the door, and once inside Ben felt as if he had stepped into a wholly different world. Instead of stark white, the walls were beautifully paneled in a light wood. High-back rows forming pews had been laid out neatly before a stunning pedestal platform in stark contrast to the utilitarian and featureless world outside. The platform featured a pair of ornate lecterns and the familiar markings of the ark where the Jewish Torah scrolls were stored between services.

This is a synagogue. . . .

The dark man stopped where the pews began and nodded at Ben to continue on his own before retreating through the entry doors that rattled closed.

As he walked down the aisle, Ben noticed a figure seated in the front row directly in front of the ark. Drawing closer, he could see the man had long salt-and-pepper hair, a yarmulke held to the top of his dome with the help of a clip. His right hand trembled atop a wooden cane marred by dents and chips. He used it to indicate the seat next to him with a tap when Ben approached.

"Sit, Inspector. Sit."

Ben got his first good look at the old man and froze. He wore sunglasses that covered his face to the temples. The glasses and the angle at which he held his head seemed to indicate he was blind. He was heavyset with big, hairy forearms sticking out from his dark, ceremonial robes.

The old man again indicated the empty seat next to him. "You do not wish to join me, Inspector?"

In fact, Ben wanted to sit down more than anything. The inside of his head felt like a bell's clapper was clanging off one side and then the other. He was woozy, unsteady on his feet, and thought he might pass out at any moment. He ran his tongue around the inside of his mouth, found that even his teeth hurt.

"I'd prefer not to, no," Ben said anyway.

The old man cradled his cane in both palms. "Then I suppose introductions are not necessary."

"You're Rabbi Mordecai Lev, head of the Amudei Ha'aretz. The Pillars of the Land."

The Amudei Ha'aretz, the most radical of all Jewish sects, had first appeared on the scene after the Six-Day War of 1967 when they arbitrarily seized Palestinian land in Hebron, claiming they were exercising their historical right to settle there. The Israeli government later allowed them to build the large settlement of Kiryat Arba on vineyards confiscated from a former mayor of Hebron. But this concession did little to either placate or control the Amudei Ha'aretz, who were vehemently against any territorial compromise with the Palestinians and swore they would take up arms if the Israeli army ever tried to evict them from land they believed was biblically theirs.

In fact, Ben knew the Amudei Ha'aretz firmly believed that the *entire* West Bank belonged to Israel and someday would be returned, which meant the eventual banishment of all Palestinians. Extraordinarily few other Jews, fortunately, shared these radical views and the Amudei Ha'aretz had virtually no friends outside of the several thousand in and around Kiryat Arba. Ben had read somewhere that the sect's spiritual leader, Rabbi Mordecai Lev, was building a separate settlement for a few hundred of the most faithful of the Pillars of the Land, but had no idea of its precise location until today.

"I may have saved your life this morning, Inspector," Lev said pompously. "It would serve us both if you kept that in mind. I ask only a small favor in return."

"A favor?"

"I believe you have something that belongs to me," Mordecai Lev said. "A video recording disc."

Ben gave the old man a long look, forgetting again it could not be returned. "Commander Moshe Baruch of Shin Bet believes, on the contrary, it belongs to him."

"And his Israeli goons would have killed you for it. You will find me infinitely more hospitable."

"Have you forgotten that I'm Palestinian, Rabbi?" Ben asked acerbically.

"I ask that we put our differences aside for the time being."

Ben bristled. "I cannot put aside the fact that you and the Amudei Ha'aretz do not believe Palestinians are entitled to our land, *any* land."

"The Bible clearly denotes this land to be part of greater Israel."

"There's nothing greater about the Israel you and your right-wing Jewish fanatics envision."

"I didn't bring you here to discuss religion or politics," the old man snapped caustically. "Tell me where I can find that disc and you can be safely on your way."

"It's gone."

"Is that what you told the soldiers?"

"Yes, because it's the truth."

Lev took a deep breath and his features relaxed a bit. "What would you say if I told you it was in your best interests to give the disc to me?"

"I'd want to know why."

Rabbi Lev tapped his cane on the floor a little harder. "Sit first. Come, you owe me that much in exchange for freeing you from your captors."

Ben reluctantly took a seat next to him in the pew, but still kept his distance.

Mordecai Lev turned slowly toward him, sightless eyes focused nowhere. "Are you a religious man, Inspector?"

"No, Rabbi."

"Religion for the Amudei Ha'aretz, of course, is everything. The secular world bears no meaning for us. Neither, in fact, does the outside world. We do not serve the army or the government. We serve only God as we await His coming. You do believe in God, don't you?"

Ben swallowed hard. "I used to."

"You are a Christian Palestinian, I'm told," Rabbi Lev said, not disapprovingly. "And being a Christian, at the very least you must believe in the existence of Jesus Christ as the son of God, the Messiah."

"To tell you the truth—"

"We believe in the Messiah as well, Inspector. In fact, we have dedicated our lives to His eventual coming. It will happen here, in the West Bank, and that time is fast approaching."

"How'd you make the Israeli soldiers who interrogated me leave?"

Mordecai Lev continued to ignore Ben's remarks. "The old gospels hold the signs and warnings. They have predicted the world as it has unfolded, almost to the day. But the writings of Him taking His word to the world were lost long ago to the ages. Writings that contain the clues to His coming. We must prepare ourselves. We must be ready to do His bidding and stand by His side. That day is soon."

"What does this have to do with me?"

"Nothing, not directly anyway. It has everything to do with the disc you came to possess."

Ben thought briefly. "How did you even come to know the disc existed?"

"That is not your concern."

"Maybe not. But I know the Bedouin guard with the camera almost certainly made a number of other tapes as well, and if you know about this one, my guess is you've very likely already seen them."

"As I said, that is *not* your concern," Lev said.

"But why should it concern *you*, Rabbi? Why bother if whatever happens outside your settlement means nothing to the Amudei Ha'aretz?"

Rabbi Lev turned again to the front of the synagogue, where the ancient Torah scrolls were stored. "What were the Americans looking for in the Judean Desert?"

"I don't know."

"What if they were looking for one particular thing, Inspector? What if they actually *did* find it?"

Ben thought of the cave he and Danielle had been on the verge of entering when Moshe Baruch had appeared. "The proof would be on that disc. That's what you're saying."

Lev nodded slightly. "That's why they had to die, Inspector. To protect the secret, to keep the Amudei Ha'aretz from the truth."

"What secret, Rabbi?"

"Where is the disc, Inspector?"

"It's gone, I told you."

"Then you must help us find it."

"Why should I?"

Lev's lips quivered. "Because you are in grave danger, Inspector, and we are the only people who can save you."

C H A P T E R   1 8

DANIELLE AWOKE TO the smells of breakfast and sounds of her brothers jabbering away with her father. For an instant, just an instant, the illusion lingered at the edge of her dream, and then consciousness dawned, stealing it away. The power of those brief moments amazed her, how they could set everything right, making her feel warm and good until reality intruded.

The dreams were especially potent at the times she was under the most stress and the latest had been no exception. She lay in bed wondering what would happen when Hershel Giott, and the protective shroud he cast over her at National Police, were gone. Her celebrity was fleeting, forgotten in the months that had passed since her name had again made headlines. Danielle remembered she had wanted to melt into the scenery around her, and now that quest for the ordinary might well contribute to her undoing.

She lay in bed fading in and out of sleep, snippets of scenes from her lost family rotating with those featuring Ben Kamal. For the past few months, their relationship had been the one thing that made her truly happy. She had even begun believing they could live like this forever, free of both formal commitment and the recriminations it would undoubtedly bring. But her pregnancy had changed all that. For a time after she realized, she debated whether to tell Ben at all, or tell him the baby was someone else's. Why bother? He would know she was lying, would know the baby was his. More than that, he *deserved* to know, deserved the truth. The truth was something that Danielle had run from long enough. She had been running from lots of things.

Too many, Danielle thought as she lunged out of bed. *But one less before the morning was out. . . .*

SHE FOUND HERSHEL Giott in the bakery shop around the corner from National Police Headquarters, seated in one of the two tables tucked against the window. A long line of people holding paper numbers waited their turn to order as Danielle squeezed past them.

"Some coffee, Pakad?" Giott asked, looking up from his freshly baked roll. He always drank it black and the small steaming pot smelled strong.

Danielle took the chair across from him. "We cannot let Commander Baruch run roughshod over us, Rav Nitzav."

"We had this discussion yesterday."

"But didn't finish it. We gave in too easily," she insisted. "Because we were scared."

"There is a big difference between fear and caution, Pakad."

"Not in this case, since either allows Commander Baruch to dictate our actions. Don't you see? We're giving him more power, not less, when his agenda is not about to change anyway. We're fools to think it might, both of us."

"You're talking about confronting Commander Baruch head-on. Those who have tried that in the past have come out the worse for the effort."

"He's hiding something," Danielle insisted, the luscious smells of the bakery suddenly making her very hungry. "He was involved in that dig team's work much more than he can afford to admit. My guess is he will want to avoid confrontations at all costs."

Giott weighed her words, flecks of his roll dropping back to his plate as he held it. "There's nothing more we can do."

"I think there is," said Danielle.

CHAPTER 19

MORDECHAI LEV SETTLED as far back as the wooded pew would let him and rested both hands on the head of his cane. "You are aware of the Dead Sea Scrolls and other prominent finds made in the Judean Desert," he continued.

"The Scrolls anyway, yes," said Ben.

"We of the Amudei Ha'aretz have been looking for other similiar scrolls for years, scrolls that may finally give us the information we have long sought. All our best analyses of the ancient texts tell us the coming of the Messiah is not far away. We believe the Americans were looking for the scrolls, or a single scroll perhaps, that would foretell exactly where and when this was going to occur. And, we believe, they found it."

"You're saying that's why they were murdered."

"To protect a secret our common enemy would much prefer never to be revealed."

"And is this 'enemy' the reason you've moved a segment

of the Amudei Ha'aretz to what looks more like a fortress than a settlement?"

"Our people must be protected, especially now."

"Those concrete bunkers I saw were built recently, Rabbi. You expected this, didn't you?"

"As I told you, the time of His coming is almost upon us. The Americans were killed because they uncovered the ancient scroll foretelling where and when. They may have recorded this on the disc you stole, making that disc the only means we may have left to learn the answers we must learn."

"And if I can't get it back?"

"Then you will be of no value to us."

Ben leaned forward so he could better study the old man's ever-blank expression. He had grown used to reading people by their eyes, using a person's gaze as a barometer of his thoughts and intentions. But the dark glasses that covered Mordecai Lev's sightless eyes made this impossible.

"Are you threatening me, Rabbi?"

"We do not believe the killers found the scroll at the site, Inspector. That can only mean it was too well hidden or already shipped somewhere else for safety. In either case, we would like you to find it for us."

"You have an entire government at your disposal," he said, finally.

"Who? The army? Shin Bet? We trust them less than we trust the Palestinians. We are a pain in all their asses. They would like nothing better than to be rid of us and the political problems we cause. If I told you what they had offered for us to give up this settlement . . ." He shook his head.

"You turned them down."

"Because the West Bank belongs to Israel, and so it will belong to Israel again. This is a mere moment in time, a flicker that will fade quickly when the true history is written."

"A history that doesn't include the Palestinian people."

"You can't change that, Inspector. The Messiah is coming and He is coming here to the West Bank, to the land of Judea and Samaria you may dwell on but never call your own."

Ben rose and felt instantly light-headed and woozy. "And in spite of that, Rabbi, you picked me to do your work for you."

"As I said, it is for your own good."

"But you haven't told me why."

"You aren't ready to hear yet."

"That's not good enough."

"It will have to be."

"You know, you're right." Ben stood before Lev on his wobbly legs. "I think I'll leave now. If you want to have me killed or returned to my Israeli inquisitors, go ahead."

Lev made no move whatsoever. "Speaking of Israelis . . ."

Ben studied the old man again, trying to penetrate what lay behind those dark glasses. "What, Rabbi?"

"Your friend Chief Inspector Barnea is up for a very important promotion. I assume she has told you."

"Get to the point."

"If you help us, we can take steps to assure that this promotion is hers."

"And if I don't?"

Lev remained silent, tapping the floor slowly with his cane.

CHAPTER 20

I HAVEN'T BEEN able to reach Dawud," Ben's brother said over the phone in a scratchy, weary voice.

Ben had found the message waiting for him upon reaching the Municipal Building in Jericho and had phoned his brother back instantly. Mordecai Lev had Ben driven back to his apartment, where all he wanted to do was collapse in bed. But he couldn't fall asleep, no matter how hard he tried. By ten o'clock he gave up and drove to police headquarters after taking a hot shower.

"Tell me what was going on in the Judean Desert," Sayeed Kamal continued finally.

"An archaeological dig. Large scale."

"Dawud never would have signed on to something like that without telling me."

"When was the last time you spoke with him directly?"

"Ten days ago."

"From Brown?"

"Yes." Then, with desperation lacing his voice, "I don't

know. I can't be sure. He called me. He said he was in his apartment near the university."

"Have you been able to reach anyone else at Brown, someone who might have known what he was up to? This adviser of his, perhaps."

"Not yet. This isn't like Dawud, not like him at all."

"Dawud lied to you because he was ordered to. The phone calls, the E-mails, you've been receiving—all engineered to assure you had no reason to believe your son was anywhere but where he said he was for the past five months."

"Why was he killed, Bayan?"

"I don't know."

"But you'll find out."

In that instant they were brothers again. Before Ben's marriage to a woman Sayeed did not approve of. Before his return to the West Bank. An image of them playing baseball together for the first time in Dearborn's Fordson Park flashed through Ben's mind.

"Yes, Sayeed," he said, "I will find out."

Y O U   W A N T   M E to what?" Captain Fawzi Wallid, the chief of police in Jericho, asked after Ben had finished his proposal. His office always smelled of the flowers adorning his desk in a simple vase, the scents varying by season and his wife's choice of plantings.

"Assign me to the case of the Americans murdered in the Judean."

Wallid hedged, fingered one of the pockmarks that dotted his face. "The Israelis have jurisdiction. You are asking me to violate policy, Inspector."

"Whose policy, Captain? The Israelis *assumed* jurisdiction on land that is now ours; we did not yield it."

"All the same, the ramifications of conducting an official inquiry . . ."

"Who said it had to be official? It's our territory. At the

very least we should have a liaison assigned to keep track
of the investigation's progress."

"And you're volunteering."

"I have some free time."

Captain Wallid gave Ben a long look. "The Palestinian
Council delegate in charge of internal security called to com-
pliment our handling of the incident in Baladiya Square yesterday."

"I'm glad."

"We turned a negative situation to our advantage."

"We could do the same thing in this instance, *sidi*. Imagine
if the Palestinian police under your command were able to
solve these murders before Israel's Shin Bet."

Wallid's eyebrows flickered. "An interesting prospect indeed, Inspector."

CHAPTER 21

WHAT IS THE meaning of this?" Moshe Baruch of Shin Bet demanded when he saw Ben enter the zone that had been cordoned off with sawhorses and yellow crime-scene tape fluttering in the wind.

"The meaning of this," Ben said, "is that the Palestinian police has decided this crime took place on our land. While we do not insist on taking over the investigation, we do insist on being made a part of it."

"And what makes you think I will go along with this?"

"Because you want to avoid a formal complaint being lodged with your government about the kidnapping of a Palestinian police officer last night."

"And who was this officer?"

"Me."

"I know nothing about that, Inspector."

"As I'm sure the official investigation into the matter would reveal."

Before Baruch could respond, his eyes widened and peered over Ben's shoulder. Ben turned and saw Danielle Barnea entering the scene just as he had, looking as surprised to see him as he was to see her.

"I should have known you would be involved in this together," Baruch hissed. "Beware, Pakad. Your Palestinian friend's presence here represents bad judgment; yours represents severe insubordination."

"Parkad Barnea is here at my request to act as liaison," Ben told Baruch, still looking at her. "I'm sure you understand the rationale, since unlike our Security Service, the Palestinian police maintains no official relations with Shin Bet."

"You should listen to him," Danielle added. "I don't think you want the kind of mess a formal jurisdictional dispute might lead to."

"You have enough problems already, Commander," said Ben.

Baruch rotated his simmering gaze between them, fixing ultimately on Ben. "So what do you want?"

"To inspect the crime scene, for starters."

"You already made use of that opportunity yesterday."

Ben turned toward the cave opening, still guarded by a pair of Israeli soldiers. "You interrupted us before we'd finished."

THANK YOU," DANIELLE said softly as they walked toward the goat path with two more Israeli soldiers clinging to their shadows.

"Just like old times, eh, Pakad?" Ben tried to joke.

Danielle managed a smile. "All too much so, it seems. What happened to your nose?"

"Baruch's men last night—men and one woman, that is."

"Woman?"

"With a scar down her cheek," Ben said, drawing a line down the left side of his face.

Danielle nodded. "Shoshanna Tavi."

"Know her?"

"We were in the Sayaret together."

"Apparently, she learned her trade as well as you."

"Even better," Danielle said, tilting her head back toward Baruch. "She's his mistress."

THE TRIANGULAR ENTRANCE to the cave was just over six feet high. Rocks and stones had been piled on either side.

"I'm sorry about yesterday," Danielle said as they climbed the steps of the goat path.

"You were considerate enough to inform me about my nephew. That was all I had a right to expect."

"From a colleague."

"Yes."

"I'm sorry I couldn't be more than that for you yesterday."

"What about the last three weeks?"

Danielle hesitated. "We need to discuss that. Tomorrow night."

"At my house?"

"No, mine. I'll cook dinner."

Ben took this as a hopeful sign. She had cooked dinner for him only once before, and it had been one of the high points of their relationship. Ben remembered feeling comfortable crossing into Israel for the first time. Even the border guards seemed to have a different attitude toward him.

Danielle had served pressed chickpeas with garlic and olive oil called hummus, along with pita bread and olives to start. The main course was kibbee, a Mideastern dish of ground lamb and pine nuts his mother used to make, and grape leaves stuffed with rice and beef. For dessert they had fresh fruit and honey cake.

What Ben recalled most about that night, though, was not the meal so much as the smells that filled Danielle's spacious Jerusalem apartment. Warm and spicy smells of food cooking on the stove and in the oven that lingered in the air well after the meal was done. Scents that left a lump in Ben's throat because they defined what home was all about and what his had not smelled like in a very long time. It was the kind of thing you got used to living without until something made you realize how much you missed it. That night Ben left Danielle's fully believing their life together had a chance to succeed. He supposed he should have felt happy about the change of heart from her recent behavior Danielle's repeat invitation might have indicated. But the somber look in her eyes quickly tempered his optimism.

"How could a cave like this go uncharted for so long?" Danielle asked before he could take his thoughts any further.

Ben looked at the rocks and stones stacked before either side of the six-foot-high entrance. "Judging from those piles, my guess would be that the cave had probably been sealed by a rock slide decades, even centuries ago. This team must have come equipped with the kind of magnetic resonance devices capable of detecting an opening beyond."

"They cleared it themselves."

"One stone at a time, by the look. Tedious work, but necessary to ensure none of the contents inside would be disturbed." Ben tried to picture his nephew participating in the painstaking task and could bring to mind only the inquisitive, smiling boy he had last seen more than five years before. The beard and close-cropped hair on Dawud's college ID photo made him look so much older, not a boy anymore.

Danielle gazed back at Ben as they neared the entrance. "People lived in caves like this for refuge during several of our ancient wars."

"I didn't know you were such an expert, Pakad."

"On war, or seeking refuge, Inspector?"

"Take your pick."

On Baruch's orders, the soldiers standing guard stood aside to let them pass through the entrance. Once inside Ben and Danielle switched on the flashlights they had brought with them, a good thing since the light saved them a costly misstep onto the cave floor's steep downward grade. Ben considered the sad likelihood they had just retraced steps made by his nephew dozens of times, perhaps tied to the reason for his and the others' murders.

The cave consisted of two primary chambers with a total

length of thirty feet and width of just under eight. A gap in the far wall indicated a trail, dangerous and steep, that led into the deep underground recesses of the underlying structure of the rugged hillside.

Closer to the front, several trenches had been cut through the thick debris that covered the cave floor, going down three feet in some places and two in others. Clearly the archaeologists had found evidence of human habitation in the form of ashes, burnt logs, and the remains of what looked like some kind of porous material that had once been ropes or mats.

"They just left their finds like this?" Danielle asked, feeling chilled by the cave's surprisingly cool temperatures, a sharp contrast to the heat building outside. A musty smell clung to the air.

"This doesn't qualify as much, nothing substantial and maybe not even worth preserving. But they probably reached the level where most of this was found only four or five days ago, would have picked up where they left off yesterday."

"And what about this?" Danielle asked, and aimed her beam at a much shallower and smaller depression in the cave floor just beyond the larger trenches.

Ben knelt down and used the length of his arms for crude measurement. The depression was barely a foot deep and two feet square.

"Judging from the smoothed edges, I'd say they pulled something out of this," Danielle said, leaning over Ben's shoulder.

Ben ran his hand along the outline of the depression. "But it doesn't fit with the rest of these artifacts."

"How can you tell?"

"Well, everything else they uncovered dates back to the first few centuries A.D. Something found this shallow would date back a century at most and probably considerably less than that. From an archaeological standpoint, it would be worthless."

"But whatever it was, they dug it out."

"Clearly."

"Then let's see if we can find where they put it."

CHAPTER 22

THE ARCHAEOLOGICAL TEAM had placed their finds in airtight metal and plastic cases that were then stored in the luggage compartment of one of the three Land Rovers. The vehicles themselves looked to be decades old, untouched by rust thanks to their aluminum bodies but covered in dings and pockmarks. Baruch assigned a trio of soldiers to shadow Ben's and Danielle's every move, the commander himself remaining at a distance discreet enough to appear disinterested while always being able to keep his eye on them as well.

Each case had been neatly catalogued with finds made at different junctures of the five-month expedition. Ben and Danielle started with the case reserved for finds made in this location, labeled "Area 6." Ben unlatched the lid and raised it.

"Like you said," Danielle recalled, sliding up alongside him, "nothing of value."

They stared together at a layer of rocks that had been

packed into the case. Danielle reached in and took one in her hand, testing its weight.

"Maybe they know something about great archaeological finds that we don't," she said.

The rocks varied in both size, shade, and design, looking as though they had been plucked randomly from the earth. Ben eased a few aside to check if anything lay beneath the single layer.

"What do you think those numbers mean?" Danielle asked him, noting the presence of numbers scrawled on white adhesive tape to each of the rocks.

"I don't know," Ben said and continued to rummage through the container.

"I think they're labeled sequentially," Danielle pointed out as she continued checking the rocks.

Ben wasn't paying attention. "I guess they've already removed it from the scene. . . ."

"What?"

"Whatever the Americans took out of that shallow depression we found in the cave. Baruch must have taken that and everything else, besides these rocks."

Ben leaned farther into the Land Rover's cargo bay to unlatch the next case back. It, too, contained a collection of rocks and nothing more.

"Same labels as the first case," said Danielle, giving them a quick look.

Ben moved on to a number of the other storage cases, finding all to be similarly packed. There was an urgency to his motions, as if finding so little in each container made opening the next one more vital.

Danielle leaned into the Land Rover with him after he had finished checking the sixth, lowering her voice so the Israeli soldiers hovering nearby couldn't hear. "In the years since the Dead Sea Scrolls were found, the Judean Caves have been plucked pretty clean. It's possible there was nothing for Baruch to take from here, even if he had wanted to."

"Did you look around the site when we got here, Pakad?"

"Briefly."

"Notice anything missing?"

Danielle thought for a moment. "The cargo trucks that were here yesterday. . . ."

"So obviously there was *something* Baruch must have wanted to remove from the scene."

"It wouldn't take two trucks to transport whatever the Americans found in that cave."

"Another inconsistency."

"Another?"

"The killers were professionals, yes, Pakad?"

"Unquestionably."

"And yet they made no effort to disguise their prowess. They could have, if they'd wanted, with little effort too. Leave the scene more in a shambles. Create the illusion there was some resistance. Use more than a single shot to effect the kills, or even use knives instead of guns."

"The killers didn't care, obviously. They were simply completing a task in the most efficient manner possible."

"Which brings us back to motive: something stolen we have no way of identifying."

"Maybe nothing was stolen at all. Maybe the motive was political," Danielle suggested.

Ben turned his eyes skeptically. "Archaeologists?"

"*American* archaeologists operating on an Israeli visa. That could have upset some of the locals after the land was transferred to Palestinian control."

Ben gestured dramatically around him. "We're in the desert, Pakad. There are no locals. We should be focusing instead on what few clues we have: those three depressions I found in the ground yesterday, for example. Something heavy resting on a tripod."

"Probably meaningless."

"Then why did someone fill them in?"

They stared at each other for a long moment, the tension between them growing again.

"And why do the Americans' storage bins contain only rocks?" Ben challenged.

"Like you said, the team hadn't encountered much luck at their other five sites either."

"But here we know they at least pulled something from that shallow depression up in the cave. Where is it? Why was Commander Baruch so interested in whatever the Americans were up to out here?"

"I don't know," Danielle said.

"I wonder if this might tell us," Ben said as he quietly stuffed a rock he had pilfered from the storage bin labeled "Area 6" into her pocket.

CHAPTER 23

THE FORENSICS LAB was located in the first cavernous sublevel of National Police Headquarters in Jerusalem. The air felt cool and antiseptic, the bright lighting an effective substitute for the lack of windows. As a detective, Danielle was well acquainted with the various personnel who worked among the computer monitors and test tubes. She knocked on the entrance to a cubicle belonging to a technician wearing a white lab coat and thick glasses and whose curly hair had receded from the crown of his scalp.

"Hello, Isser."

Isser Raskin didn't look up from his computer screen.

"Interesting case, Isser?"

He turned his gaze upon her over the monitor. "*New York Times* crossword puzzle, actually. I get it off their Web site."

"What's a four-letter word for 'stone'?"

"Rock."

"Exactly," Danielle said, and produced the rock Ben had taken from the murder site in the Judean Desert.

"Is it my birthday?" Isser asked, taking it.

"Tell me everything you can about that and we'll see about a gift."

Isser rotated it in front of his Coke-bottle lenses. "Is this a murder weapon?"

"Not directly."

"It has a number on it, 5-6-1. What does that mean?"

"I was hoping you could tell me."

Isser held the rock even closer to his eyes. "I can't make out any blood or fiber residue."

"Looking at it under a microscope won't change that. I was hoping for a more mundane analysis."

He frowned. "Then you should have taken it to the geology department at the university."

"It's part of an investigation."

"Logged?"

"Not yet."

"Evidence?"

"Eventually, perhaps."

Isser looked disappointed. "If it were a hammer with skull fragments, or a piece of skin in need of DNA matching, or even a flattened-out bullet requiring forensic reconstruction. But a rock . . ."

Danielle backed up until she was halfway out of the cubicle. "Then it shouldn't take up too much of your time."

"What exactly am I looking for, Pakad?"

"I'll settle for whatever you find."

WHEN DANIELLE GOT back to her office, the door was open. She entered, figuring she must have forgotten to close it earlier, until she saw a pair of scuffed brown boots propped up on the edge of her desk.

"Hope you don't mind me making myself comfortable," a man said. He was wearing a cowboy hat that he removed to reveal a mop of thick wheat-colored hair that was whitening along the temples.

Danielle noted the visitor's badge hanging from his neck. "As a matter of fact, I do."

The man eased his boots back to the floor. "Name's John Paul Wynn. My friends call me J. P." He leaned forward and extended his hand, but Danielle didn't take it.

"What are you doing in my office?"

"You left the door open, ma'am, and that's an absolute fact. A woman should really be more careful about things. Could have been a bad guy waiting when you came back."

"Maybe it was."

Wynn's accent was clearly American, not quite Deep South, but more likely the West. Wyoming or Montana probably, Danielle guessed. He was ruggedly handsome with a tan that looked to be applied permanently on his skin like dye on leather, and his face shared the same parchmentlike consistency. Too many furrows and crevices for a man who couldn't be out of his thirties yet. His eyes were a piercing shade of blue.

"Do all Israeli women talk like that?"

"No, I'm more polite and reserved than most."

Wynn looked her over, not bothering to hide where his eyes were going. "I think I could get used to that kind of attitude."

Danielle glared down at him. "Only if you get the chance."

Wynn glanced around, nodding. "Got your own office, a fancy title . . . You good with a gun too?"

"I don't think you want to find out." Danielle gave the badge dangling from his neck a longer look. "Your pass lists my office as your destination, so I'm assuming you've got a real reason to be here."

"Actually, I was hoping a regular detective would get assigned to me."

"A *regular* detective?"

"You know, a man, being that I never worked with a woman cop before and this isn't the best time to change."

"Feel free to request someone else."

"I was told you were the best." Wynn smiled confidently and started to reach for a pack of Marlboros in the lapel pocket of his shirt. "Mind if I smoke?"

"Yes."

"Gonna chop off my hands too, ma'am?"

"I might start lower, Mr. Wynn."

Wynn reproached her with a wry wave of his finger. "Now I told you to call me J. P. . . ."

"No, you told me *your friends* call you J. P."

"Just thought I'd jump past the obvious, ma'am."

"Then why don't you tell me what it is you're doing here?"

Wynn stuck a cigarette in his mouth but didn't light it. "Thing is, ma'am, I've done plenty of work on behalf of your country. One of the people a bit in my debt was kind enough to make a call on my behalf."

"To arrange a meeting with me . . ."

"Your boss, actually."

"You saw Commissioner Giott?"

Wynn nodded. "Just came from his office. He thought we might be able to help each other out with a couple things."

"And why would he think that?"

"On account of what I do," Wynn said, as if it were something Danielle should have already known.

Danielle leaned back against her desk. "Which is?"

Wynn closed both his hands around the brim of the cowboy hat now resting on his lap. "Well, ma'am, it's a little hard to say."

"Give it a try."

"I find things. Things that are lost and been that way for a whole lot of years, hundreds or even thousands sometimes. So many that in lots of cases people forgot they existed or didn't believe in them to begin with."

"A fortune hunter," Danielle concluded.

"Actually, *treasure* hunter'd be a more accurate way of describing myself." Wynn turned his mouth down at the corners, lengthening the lines that punctuated his face even farther. "You can see why I didn't want to get into this off the bat. Gives you the wrong impression, that I'm just here to make a buck. Women think that way."

"You lay claim to lots of fortunes, Mr. Wynn?"

Wynn flicked his unlit cigarette into the trash can with a

quick twitch of his fingers. "I'm getting the impression that you've never heard of me."

"That's right."

"Guess you don't have much call to read or watch television."

"Not enough to know you, apparently."

"*People* magazine, the *National Geographic,* a couple of *Datelines,* a bestseller—my audience is mostly men, so I guess I shouldn't be surprised when a woman's never heard of me. Left my résumé upstairs with your boss, if you want to check it out."

"Was Commissioner Giott impressed?"

"He said to touch base with him before we left."

Danielle looked at the phone and then back at Wynn. "Where are we going?"

Wynn rose from the chair and blew some air from his mouth in a slight whistle. "I'll give you the whole story on the way."

"Start now," Danielle said.

He wedged his thumbs into the pockets of his jeans. "It's like this, ma'am. Your country's lost its share of antiquities over the years, and I've been able to return the ones I've been lucky enough to track down." Wynn's bright blue eyes twinkled. "That's where I made most of my friends over here and why your boss put me on to you after he learned you and me might be after the same thing."

"And just what is that, Mr. Wynn?"

"What got those archaeologists killed in the Judean Desert, ma'am." He stood up and flashed her a wink. "Now, call me J. P."

CHAPTER 24

BEN FOUND NABRIL al-Asi in the Oasis Casino once again. Just one o'clock in the afternoon and the colonel looked as dapper as he had the previous night; unchanged virtually, except for a fresh suit. Only this time he was standing before one of the one-dollar slot machines and had just yanked the lever down to no result when Ben stopped by his side.

"We've had complaints about these," he reported, sliding another token into the slot. "Apparently the Israeli tourists aren't winning enough. I've been asked to investigate." He jammed the lever down again to the same results. Al-Asi shook his head unsatisfactorily. "Yes, I do believe this one may have some problems," he said, moving to the next machine in the row with a token already in his hand. He finally looked at Ben before sliding it home. "You have the look of a man who's lost his stash, Inspector."

"A lot more than that. I was arrested by Israeli soldiers last night."

The colonel frowned as this machine came up as empty

as the last one. He readied another dollar token, but didn't insert it. "The joint command was not informed."

"Nor would they ever have been. I believe Commander Moshe Baruch of Shin Bet was behind it."

Al-Asi's face wrinkled, as if he'd swallowed something sour. "And yet here you are standing before me now."

"My release was secured by others, also Israelis."

"Merely saving me the bother. Who were these other Israelis?"

"Members of Rabbi Mordecai Lev's Amudei Ha'aretz."

"A messianic cult also known as the Pillars of the Land," said al-Asi, pushing his token toward the slot. "Not particularly well known for rescuing outsiders. I have a rather thick file on Lev."

"Not someone I thought the Protective Security Service would bother investigating."

"We didn't; the Israelis did." The colonel jammed down the lever. "They merely passed the information on to us."

"Why?"

The machine came up empty and al-Asi shook his head again. "They hoped we'd take care of Lev for them: his file had been doctored to make the good rabbi quite the enemy of Palestine."

"Isn't he?"

"He believes in the eventual destruction of our people, Inspector; he has no plans to bring it about himself. Why bother when you have God on your side?"

"The Messiah, actually. That's what his people are waiting for."

Al-Asi played another dollar, to the same results. "We're all waiting for something, Inspector."

"I have another problem, Colonel: that miniature recording disc I told you about yesterday."

"The object of last night's interrogation, no doubt."

"Yes."

"After they searched that church garden and found no trace of it, eh, Inspector?"

Ben's eyes widened. "How could you know that?"

"Because I had you followed too," al-Asi said, and reached into the left-hand pocket of his elegant taupe suit. He emerged with some stray chips he sifted through before coming up with the silvery disc Ben had showed him yesterday. "Just to be on the safe side."

Utterly shocked, Ben took the disc gratefully from the colonel's grasp.

"I know how their Commander Baruch works. Very predictable."

"His mistress, Shoshanna Tavi, conducted my interrogation."

"I know her work too," al-Asi said, the glibness gone from his tone. "A few years ago, after Baruch falsely blamed me for the demise of two of his agents, he dispatched Tavi to my house outside Ramallah to apply for a job as a maid. For payback, you understand."

"What did you do?" Ben asked, caught off guard by the colonel's rare mention of his personal life.

"Hired her, of course. By the time she reported for work the next day, we had moved." Al-Asi turned away from Ben and squeezed another token into the slot machine. He viewed the results with disdain. "So I'm aware of what Captain Tavi wanted from you, but I'm not aware of what Lev and his Pillars of the Land wanted."

"The same thing."

"Interesting."

"He's waiting for the Messiah, Colonel. He thinks that disc might help him figure out the final details of His coming."

"Even more interesting."

"Lev believes the Americans were killed because they found a scroll containing specific references to the Messiah's appearance. Where and when, all that sort of stuff, buried inside that cave over the camp."

"Seems like a pretty thin motive."

"I don't care what the motive turns out to be. Something got my nephew and those other Americans killed, and I'm going to find out what."

"I figured as much," Al-Asi said with a twinge of regret

in his voice. He inserted another token and drew the lever down. "So I've arranged for you to view your disc. . . ."

Before he could continue, though, the machine locked on three gold bars, and change began to spew from a slot in the bottom.

"Well, I think I can report that this machine is in perfect working order," al-Asi said as the coins pooled about his feet. "Who knows, Inspector, maybe this is our lucky day."

CHAPTER 25

From national police Headquarters, J. P. Wynn drove his rental car toward urban West Jerusalem, where the Knesset, the Israeli parliament, was housed.

"Where are we going?" Danielle asked him.

"Don't like surprises, do you?"

"Remember that gun you asked me about?"

"Sure."

"I've got my hand on it now."

"I only wish." Wynn glanced over at her. "Been to the museum lately, ma'am?" he asked, gesturing out the windshield at what Danielle recognized as the Hill of Tranquility. A complex of buildings forming the Israel Museum hugged the hillside.

"I seem to attract relics on my own."

After parking in the museum lot, they passed through a security checkpoint and entered a circular building called the Shrine of the Book, topped by a white dome. Inside it was dark and cool, almost subterranean, to capture the atmosphere of the caves in which the Dead Sea Scrolls were found in 1947.

"I love places like this," J. P. Wynn said. "See, my whole life's been about bringing the past and present together. Salvaging stuff from one generation so another can understand it better. Sure, I've made more than my share of money, but I can also walk into just about any museum in the world and show you something that I recovered."

"What about this one?" Danielle asked him.

"Not in this particular building," Wynn replied meaningfully. "Not yet, anyway."

They walked along a ring of exhibits displayed in glass cases, heading toward the largest a small tourist group had just vacated. Danielle recognized a selection of the Dead Sea Scrolls housed and illuminated within.

"The Jews who wrote the Scrolls hid them in a waterproof pouch made of sheep hide before burying them," Wynn explained, sounding like a tour guide. "That's what saved the parchment from turning to dust. Stuff's brittle as hell, very little moisture content."

Danielle's gaze followed his into the case, passing her eyes over the neatly arranged manuscript that had been written either in an offshoot of Hebrew or Aramaic, she couldn't tell which.

"The Jews took refuge in caves all over the Judean Desert and left much of their legacy behind. Some's been recovered, some lost forever, and there's a little bit still waiting to be found, like what those dead Americans must have uncovered."

She turned away from the glass toward him. "And what got them killed, according to you."

"Oh, it got them killed, all right, and with good reason."

"What reason?"

"Money and lots of it."

"What did they do, strike gold in the middle of the desert?"

Wynn flashed a smile that looked inordinately white in the murky spill of the light. "As a matter of fact, they did."

* * *

HOW ARE YOU with the Old Testament, Chief Inspector?" he continued.

"Pretty good. Especially the parts about sinners and miscreants."

"Tell ya the truth, the closest I come to a Bible these days is in the night table of my motel room. I'm talking about Exodus, Moses, the Jews leaving Egypt—that part."

Danielle nodded. "Sure, but it's been a while."

"Mount Sinai?"

"The place where God gave Moses the Ten Commandments and the stone altar where the Israelites worshiped the golden calf."

Wynn held a hand up. "Stop right there. That's it."

"The golden calf?"

"Gold in general, hundreds of pounds of it. The gold your forefathers took out of Egypt. From what I—and other treasure hunters—have been able to piece together, it was buried at the base of Mount Sinai."

"But Mount Sinai's never been found or positively identified."

Wynn nodded. "That's the point, ma'am. Most people, just about all, hear the word 'Sinai' and think of the desert. Desert's right enough—it's the direction they've been getting wrong for years. I've been pursuing the theory that the Israelites actually buried their gold somewhere in the Judean Desert."

"You think the murdered Americans found the lost gold of Exodus, Mr. Wynn?"

"They were as sure as shit looking for it, ma'am, and now they're dead. Got a better reason to kill for than a fortune?"

"Then you're here after the money too. Here it is, I had you pegged as a pimp when all you are is a prostitute."

The remark stung Wynn, his mouth twisting in displeasure. "The truth is I got enough greenbacks to fill a field, but it's all just manure to me compared to the lost gold of Exodus. We're talking about the greatest archaeological relic left for man to find, and I intend to be the man who finds it. Figure that'll make a great legacy, maybe lead a big-time actor to play me on the big screen someday." He grinned at her. "You can be my date at the opening, if you start calling me J. P."

"Save money and just bring your ego."

Wynn ignored her this time. "You've been to the site, ma'am. Care to tell me exactly what it was you saw?"

Danielle tried to picture the American students uncovering the treasure at Area 6 and carrying it down out of that cave she and Ben had explored. But the task involved logistics much too monumental to undertake in the brief time they had been there.

"They didn't find any gold in the Judean."

"Maybe not the gold itself, ma'am. . . ."

"What then?"

"A map. A map detailing the route the Israelites took that got them to the Judean in their wanderings, with a big X marking the spot where they left their gold on the way."

Danielle recalled the small, shallow trench the Americans had dug in the cave. Could they have found such a map inside it, perhaps concealed in some kind of case or box?

"You're holding something back on me, ma'am."

"I'm a woman, remember? We tend to keep secrets."

"I was under the impression your boss told you it was in your best interests not to keep any from me."

"He told me to use my best judgment. That's what I'm doing."

Wynn nodded, relenting. "If we knew what those Americans found up there, we'd be a long way toward knowing what got them killed."

"Too bad we don't," Danielle said, thinking of the video mini-disc Ben Kamal had kept from Commander Baruch and then lost himself.

CHAPTER 26

BEN PARKED HIS Peugeot near a trio of ancient produce trucks at the entrance to the olive groves in the Jordan Rift Valley, just as Nabril al-Asi had instructed several hours earlier.

"The man who has the equipment you need is named Ari Coen," the colonel had explained as several Oasis Casino workers struggled to collect his slot-machine jackpot off the floor. "He is expecting you."

"An Israeli?"

They had walked away from the slot machines slowly, a portion of al-Asi's winnings jangling in his pockets.

"Not much of one anymore. Call him an expatriate now. Suffice it to say he fell into extreme disfavor with his own people when the Israeli police learned the true nature of his business. He had no choice but to leave the country."

"If he came to the West Bank, he didn't leave the country."

"Appearances, Inspector, are everything. The Jordan Rift Valley is another world entirely."

"You took him in?"

"Coen used to be part of Israel's intelligence community. We thought he could be of service to us by teaching us some of the tricks of the trade. He asked only that he be allowed to continue his more recent trade."

"Which is?"

One of the casino managers caught up with al-Asi and handed him the sack stuffed with the rest of his winnings.

"Better that you see for yourself," the colonel said. He pulled an envelope from his jacket pocket and handed it to Ben.

The envelope felt thick, overstuffed, and Ben tried not to consider its contents.

"Give it to Coen when you get there," al-Asi had said.

No sooner had Ben stepped out of his car amid the olive groves that stretched as far as the eye could see than a man with a shotgun slung from his shoulder appeared from a road at the entrance to the fields.

"We are expecting you," he said, without asking Ben who he was or requesting some identification. The man simply turned and walked off, expecting Ben to follow. Clearly al-Asi had followed through on his promise to alert Ari Coen of Ben's impending arrival. But what was an Israeli expatriate doing in the Jordan Rift Valley?

Ben walked along a high chain-link fence covered with thick vines that squeezed through the openings. The man with the shotgun was waiting in a Jeep just around the corner. Ben climbed into the passenger seat and the guard drove off down a road cut between the neat rows of sprawling branches that smelled of ripening olives. As they drew farther into the rich jungle, though, another smell greeted Ben's nostrils, one he had to pull from way back in his memory to recognize.

Early in his career as a Detroit cop, when he was working narcotics, he had got to know the thickly pungent scent of unharvested marijuana and hashish very well. That was what he was smelling now. And almost immediately he began to recognize the familiar stalks and leafy brush he had seen in their unrefined form years before in his other life.

Before Ben could reformulate his thoughts, a small white house appeared in the midst of the grove, probably well camouflaged from the air by the surrounding foliage. The driver pulled up a bumpy road and stopped in a circular drive set before an enclosed porch filled with wicker furniture. Ben had just started to climb down when the front door opened and a slender man stepped out from the shadows within.

"I am Ari Coen, Inspector Kamal."

They shook hands and Ben found Coen's grasp to be limp and disinterested. The Israeli wasn't just slender; he was almost sickly thin, his hair tied into a thick ponytail that was strangely unbecoming. He looked dull, almost glum—anything but flashy. A man who had carefully constructed his own box, only to find himself trapped within it to the point where his sallow skin looked untouched by the hot Mediterranean sun.

"Let's go inside."

The house was furnished in almost tropical fashion. Spanish tile adorned the floors. The ceilings and walls were finished in stucco. Large windows looked out over the olive grove in all directions, bathing the house with light that made Coen squint. Framed pictures of a woman and four children at various ages covered the top of a closed piano and a writing desk with a whitewash finish. The sweet smell of Israeli oranges filled the air.

"I think you have something for me."

Ben handed over al-Asi's envelope and Coen eagerly tore it open atop an elegant rattan console table. Inside were photographs, dozens of them, all picturing the same woman and children captured in frames throughout the open first floor.

"My wife and children," Ari Coen said, arranging the pictures neatly before him. "I haven't seen them since my relocation. They think I'm dead, along with everyone else in Israel including the authorities, who would come after me otherwise. It was either that or prison." Coen went back to arranging his pictures. "Who knows, maybe I made the wrong choice. This is the only way I get to see my family, thanks to Colonel al-Asi's assets in Israel." He touched a few of the pictures tenderly and backed away from the table. "If you don't mind, I'd like to make this quick. Colonel al-Asi told me you had a disc you can't read."

"I assume he knows what you're doing out here."

"What do you think, Inspector?"

"You grew this shit in Israel, didn't you, until the authorities found out?"

"Actually, I only distributed it; I've stepped up in the world since coming here." Coen finally closed the door behind him. "The Palestinians leave me alone, so long as I lend some assistance to the colonel from time to time on matters pertaining to Israeli intelligence."

"Anything else?"

"I'm not allowed to sell or distribute in the West Bank or Gaza. That was the colonel's condition."

Coen led Ben down a short atriumlike hallway drenched in sunlight from a large skylight overhead. They came to a door in the back of the house that he unlocked by punching a combination into a keypad mounted on the wall. The door snapped open, revealing an array of computer terminals, printers, and fax machines. Two of the monitors flashed to tell Coen he had E-mail. One of the faxes had a stack of pages piled up in the tray. Clearly this was the nerve center of his operation, orders and reports coming in from who knew where.

Coen pressed a button on the wall and shades Ben hadn't even noticed before closed enough to keep out any direct light. The Israeli moved to a computer set by itself in the corner, its screen dark until he flipped a switch on its rear and sat down.

"Let me have your disc," Coen said, extending a hand back toward Ben. He inspected it briefly once Ben gave it to him, clearly impressed. "Nice workmanship. Strictly state of the art. Now let's see what we've got here. . . ."

Coen inserted the disc into a customized slot, frowning as he watched the screen flash to life. "We've got a problem."

"What?"

"The contents are encrypted."

"How big a problem is that?"

Coen brushed some stray wiry hair back with his hands. "Insurmountable, if Colonel al-Asi hadn't asked for this favor."

"And since he did?"

"I want to keep getting my pictures," Coen said, almost bitterly, and Ben understood at once how cramped the box Coen had made for himself here truly was. "The disc is Israeli?"

"That's my assumption, yes."

"Then not a very big problem at all. I'm aware of the sequencing they use in their coding. I'll need a day, two at the most."

"Can you make me a copy?"

Coen's eyes flashed suspiciously. "It'll be encrypted too."

"That's all right."

"I'll call you when I have something, Inspector."

"I'm not going anywhere."

"Neither," said Ari Coen, "am I."

CHAPTER 27

W HEN DANIELLE ARRIVED back at her office from the Israel Museum, her computer screen was flashing with an E-mail message from Isser Raskin in the forensics lab to contact her immediately. She picked up the phone and dialed his extension.

"Yes," he answered.

"It's me. Your favorite investigator."

"Not anymore," Isser said, not returning the joviality in her voice.

"What did I do now?"

"I don't like being the brunt of jokes."

"I don't understand," Danielle said, serious herself now.

"That rock you gave me, the one labeled 5-6-1, was it some kind of a test to see what I'd tell you?"

"What about the rock?"

"You said it was part of an investigation."

"It was, is."

"An investigation *where*?"

Danielle saw no reason not to be forthcoming. "The Judean Desert."

"Not unless the Judean has changed continents."

"Excuse me?"

"The rock you left me wasn't a murder weapon, and it didn't even come from Israel, if my analysis of the sodium, magnesium, and sulphur levels are correct, and you know they are."

"Then where did it come from?"

"The United States," Isser said flatly. "Specifically, the Texas Panhandle."

You're telling me this American archaeological team was bringing items into the desert, not taking them out," Danielle said to Isser Raskin, minutes after speaking to him on the phone.

"That's what my initial analysis of your rock would seem to indicate, Pakad."

"Seem? You sounded more definitive before."

Isser held the rock Danielle had taken from the crime scene in an open palm. "There are certain features of this that are indeed consistent with what you would expect to find in the Judean Desert. But the core structure, trace elements, and general composition clearly place its origins somewhere else entirely."

"Only Texas?"

Isser stole a gaze at his computer monitor. "Also parts of California, but the Texas match is much more complete. There are also indications that this is a subtundra rock, meaning it was pulled from beneath the ground," Isser said, tilting his Coke-bottle glasses up at her.

"And that number, 5-6-1?"

Isser shrugged. "Your guess is as good as mine when it comes to that. It could relate to the order in which the rocks were recovered or packed, or . . ."

"Or what?"

"No, Pakad, it wouldn't make any sense, at least not until I can conduct some more tests." The technician's face grew tentative. "Is that a problem?"

"Why would it be?"

"Because I was under the impression that the murder of

the American archaeologists had been removed from our jurisdiction. That the investigation belongs to Shin Bet now."

"Not entirely."

Isser continued to hold the rock. "Can I assume from your answer that you are pursuing the chain of evidence?"

"Only if there is one, Isser. You could find no blood or fibers on the rock—you said so yourself. So clearly it's not a murder weapon and may have nothing to do with the crime at all."

Isser didn't look convinced by Danielle's words at all. "I've worked with you before, Pakad. You see things nobody else does."

She thought of snatching the rock from Isser's hand before this went any further. "So what is it you want?"

Isser laid the rock back upon his cluttered desk. "As I said, to run more detailed tests on our friend here."

"Without formal authorization?"

"Unofficially. Filed mistakenly in a different case file."

"Is this a favor?"

"If you're onto something," Isser told her, "I want to be part of it."

Danielle looked around his cramped cubicle, trying to remember how long, how many years he had worked within it. "Okay, I think I understand."

"It can't hurt to consult, can it? And if something breaks, I expect you will take care of me, provide just compensation for my services."

Danielle backed up a little, spreading out the tension that had risen between them. "You know, Isser, I may be up for a promotion."

"So I heard. And how can they deny it to you? You are the most recognizable figure in the department with a blue-chip family history. I'd say it was a lock, Pakad."

"And what is the next position in your scale?"

"Shift supervisor. Perhaps field investigator."

"I think you would excel at either." Danielle moved to the cubicle's doorway, letting Isser Raskin keep the rock. "Come visit me in my new office when you have some time."

Isser smiled slightly. "I'm sure we'll be seeing each other well before you move, Pakad."

CHAPTER 28

BACK IN JERICHO, Ben found Father Mike on a ladder painting the ceiling of the portico that fronted his church.

"Father?"

The priest looked down, eyes gaping in surprise, and Ben saw the white paint flecked across his brow. He started down the ladder so fast he stumbled on one of the rungs and nearly fell.

"I didn't know if I'd ever see you again," the priest said gratefully.

"I'm sorry, Father."

Father Mike held him by the shoulders at arm's distance. One of the priest's eyes was swollen and a cheek was bruised.

"You don't look much better than I. But thank God you're all right. Thank God they released you."

"I never should have involved you in this."

"They were actually rather polite, for Israelis. Only hit me twice. I guess I shouldn't have vouched for your character.

They were looking for some kind of disc in the garden, were rather insistent that I had taken it." Father Mike released Ben, still eyeing him fondly. "So how did you manage such a brief captivity?"

"Ever heard of Rabbi Mordecai Lev?" Ben asked.

"Of course. Leader of some crackpot Jews, the Pillars of the Land, who live outside of Hebron and have dedicated themselves to waiting for the true Messiah."

"He's the one who secured my release."

Father Mike narrowed his eyes in concern. "You should be more careful of the company you keep."

"I didn't have much of a choice."

"He must have wanted something from you."

"Everybody does, it seems."

"Be careful with this one, though," Father Mike warned, his mouth taut and fixed. "His vision is extreme and singular."

"He's blind, Father," Ben said, trying for a laugh.

Father Mike didn't even smile. "Even worse. The Amudei Ha'aretz pursues one thing and one thing only. No one and nothing else matters. As far as they're concerned, the rest of the world can go to hell."

"While they wait for the second coming."

"Actually, the first according to them. Their entire existence is rooted in the belief that they are waiting for the one true Messiah, just as ours is founded on the concept of new and eternal life stemming from Christ's resurrection."

"I didn't say I believed Lev," Ben said.

"Then you must be even more careful. When the Messiah comes, only the believers will be spared. Nonbelievers will perish in pillars of fire, brimstone—"

"The biblical Apocalypse."

"According to the Amudei Ha'aretz, yes. They don't like other Israelis any more than they like us."

"Christians or Palestinians?"

"Either. Both. Take your pick."

Father Mike wiped the paint from his face with a handkerchief. His fingernails were brittle and splotchy patches of his hands were dry and scaley. "What does Lev want from you, Ben?"

"He believes the murdered American archaeologists may have found a lost scroll detailing the Messiah's appearance."

"So the Amudei Ha'aretz can be there waiting when he appears."

"I gather that's the plan." Ben hesitated. "Is it possible?"

"Lost scroll? That's a possibility already proven by the existence of the Dead Sea Scrolls, which actually speak at some length of the Messiah's coming. But as for another scroll that foretells the specifics . . ." Father Mike shook his head. "No, I don't think so."

"I see."

"Walk away from them, Ben."

"I did."

"Good. Now grab a brush."

Ben stared down at the paintbrushes soaking in turpentine. "What if I agreed with Lev, Father? About Christ not being the son of God."

Father Mike held his hands stiff by his sides. The wiry hair on the sides of his head seemed to extend straight out. "Are you going to pick up a paintbrush or not?"

"You haven't answered my question."

"Why do you come here and help me with my chores, Ben?"

"I enjoy our talks."

"Here in the church?"

"Yes."

"The church *is* Christ. You can't separate them. You come here and make His house better, it's your own way of trying to stay close—as close as you can, anyway. You haven't lost your faith, Ben; you just can't see it right now."

"I haven't been able to see it for a very long time."

Father Mike studied him closely, his own features relaxing. "So you want Lev to be right to make things easier for you. If Lev's right, you don't have to challenge yourself anymore and I need to get myself a new assistant."

"What if both of you are wrong, Father, you about your

Messiah and Lev about his? I see people trusting that faith will make them stronger, and make them well, and bring them happiness. But at the end of the day they're still weak, sick, and miserable."

"And the next day they will try again anyway. That same faith is often what sustains them, allows them to persevere."

"No. Nothing changes and believing it could make things even worse."

"You want me to tell you what kind of God could have taken your family the way He did?"

Ben's lips trembled. His mouth felt full of paste. "Yesterday, seeing my nephew, brought it all back, made it feel like that happened yesterday too." He tried to take a deep breath, but failed and felt his throat begin to thicken, as if he had swallowed paste. "My family suffered, Father, they suffered horribly. It's tough for me to believe in anything after that. And the truth is I don't want to believe."

"The problem is you don't want anyone else to believe either."

"Because it creates a false security. Be a good Christian and God will look out for you. . . . But He *doesn't,* even if you are. It's a lie, and if people don't come around to realizing that, life will continue to hurt a lot more than it should."

Father Mike stood there very calmly, then smiled. "Just as I told you yesterday. This is your walk in the darkness, Ben, and out of it will come a great light. You'll see."

"I've already been walking a long time, Father, and it just keeps getting darker."

CHAPTER 29

HERSHEL GIOTT WAS looking grave when Danielle appeared before leaving for the night. Danielle thought at first he was ill, until she saw his eyes clearly when they turned upon her.

"Thank you for coming up, Pakad."

"What's wrong, Rav Nitzav?"

"Our strategy in dealing with Commander Baruch has backfired somewhat. His response to your reappearance at the crime scene in the Judean this morning was a formal letter of reprimand he insists be included in your file. . . ."

"Let him. I have a response for him too."

"You didn't let me finish. He is also charging you with complicity in the theft of some recording disc by the Palestinian Kamal. Did you forget to tell me about that?"

Danielle flirted briefly with denying any knowledge of the disc, decided the lies, of omission and otherwise, had to stop here. "It wasn't your concern."

"And the Palestinian's presence at the crime scene today is not my concern either?"

"I didn't know he was going to be there."

"According to Commander Baruch, you are working as Kamal's liaison." Giott's tired eyes grew stern. "I warned you about the costs of associating with your Palestinian friend. I thought I had made myself clear."

"Perhaps it was Commander Baruch you should have warned me about."

"I thought I had done that too."

They stared at each other, the silence nearly unbearable for Danielle. She slid a little closer to her mentor's desk. "It's you Baruch's coming after, isn't it?" she asked finally, realizing.

Giott cupped his face in his trembling hands. "These are difficult times, Pakad," he said, words slightly muffled. "The last of us who saw the birth of our nation are nearing the end of our usefulness. That in itself would not bother me if the generation about to replace us had learned anything from our lessons. They want everything black and white. They don't see the gray."

"They accuse you of the very same thing."

"We were that way in the beginning, all of us, because we had to be. Our survival depended on it then, just as continuing the illusion while learning to compromise permitted us to ultimately thrive." Giott took his hands away from his face and looked up. "It is the art of compromise that escapes Baruch and the others who would seek to wipe out much of what we have done. Is he after me, Pakad? Yes, I suppose he is, because of what I represent. To destroy that, though, he must also destroy those who have learned the lessons he has not." Giott's tired eyes bore into hers. "Like you."

"Unless we destroy him first," Danielle said, voice cracking through her parched mouth.

"Easier said than done."

"Perhaps that American fortune hunter you sent down to my office can help us."

"How?"

"He claims he knows why his countrymen were murdered in the Judean. If he's right, and if we could solve this crime for National Police before Shin Bet has a chance to, then . . ."

"An unlikely and dangerous scenario, Pakad."

"You didn't let me finish, Rav Nitzav. If our investigation were to show that Shin Bet knew more all along than they were telling . . ."

"We would have something to hold over Baruch's head. But what makes you think such a thing?"

"An archaeological team with virtually nothing to show for five months work, for one thing. The fact that Baruch was keeping very close tabs on them, for another."

"That video disc the commander spoke of?"

Danielle nodded. "Our proof."

Giott's face tightened as he considered the prospects. "A precarious game we are playing, Pakad."

"We have nothing to lose, Rav Nitzav."

BACK IN HER office, Danielle checked her voice mail and found a message from Isser Raskin, the forensics technician with whom she had left her rock.

"I've solved your mystery, Pakad, and you're not going to believe it. . . ."

His excited voice trailed off and Danielle found herself pressing the receiver tighter against her ear.

"Anyway, Pakad, I found strong traces of hydrocarbons on that rock of yours, and if it really did come from the West Bank . . . I'd better finish this in person. First I want to reconfirm these tests in an outside lab. Come see me first thing tomorrow morning, and I'll fill you in."

Danielle listened to the time stamp and checked her watch; she had missed Isser by only minutes, would have to wait until tomorrow to find out whatever it was he had uncovered about her rock.

She erased the message and hung up the phone very slowly.

CHAPTER 30

I T W A S D A R K by the time Ben left Father Mike's after helping him with the rest of the paint job. Given the hour, the priest offered him a ride home, but Ben politely declined, looking forward to the exercise and the time alone.

He had started taking walks in Detroit after his family was slain. Walked long hours into the night when sleep refused to come or his dreams brought his family with them. He had moved into a hotel immediately after the murders, and then a small furnished apartment that smelled of Lysol and other people's memories. He found himself wanting to be anywhere other than that apartment. Sometimes he would walk so far and so heedlessly that he actually found himself lost. Other times he would walk himself into exhaustion so by the time he got back home, at least he'd be able to sleep.

His family had been murdered in the spring, and he remembered how cool and clean the air felt outside in contrast to that within his house. But tonight in Jericho, walking to his apartment from Father Mike's, the air was dry and stale. Parts of it seemed to stick to his skin in the form of the ever-present dust shed by the buildings and the ground, and the only breeze he felt was in his imagination. The air smelled sour, as though it had gone bad, and Ben regretted his decision not to accept Father Mike's offer of a ride.

He squeezed through a construction site that had left a gaping hole in the street. Workmen had slung long boards across the chasm and left them in place for their return to work, whenever that might be. In Jericho, construction projects continued in dribs and drabs, only as money became available to complete them.

He had just passed a flashing yellow warning beacon when he heard the dull hum of a car engine behind him, a rare sound since Palestinians almost never drove at night out of fear of being stopped by a random Israeli patrol. Ben figured this must be one of those patrols and readied his identification as he turned.

An old sedan switched off its one working headlight and continued to approach him. Ben resumed walking and eased his hand to his pistol, unsnapping the safety strap on his holster. He closed his hand on the grip as the car picked up speed, its hum growing louder.

Ben continued to walk, not turning until he heard the sedan's tires screech behind him. He swung and fired in the same motion; twice, as the sedan roared at him. Both shots missed badly and he dared not chance another, turning to run instead.

The sedan closed the gap quickly, bumper nipping at him when Ben veered down one of Jericho's narrow alleyways. He heard the sedan screech to a stop and leap into reverse, single headlight switched on again and struggling to find him in the darkened alleyway. He ran, tipping over trash cans in his wake and hearing the car bashing them from its path as it gave chase.

Ben reached the next through street and glanced back long enough to see the sedan still in pursuit. He sliced onto another alley even narrower than the last. Too narrow to accommodate the car's width he thought. But the sizzling grind of metal told him the driver had refused to let that deter him.

He looked back to see the car coming in a shower of white-hot sparks, left to right alternately as it bounced from side to side. Ben tried a few more shots, missed badly again, and rushed on with precious ground lost.

Damn Moshe Baruch! he thought, fully believing the commander's mistress, Captain Shoshanna Tavi, must be behind the wheel. Here to finish the job because Ben still hadn't returned the video disc.

He saw the rickety fire escape, left over from when the Israelis had occupied this section of Jericho, almost too late to leap for it. Out of reach he thought until his hands caught on the lowest rung and he jerked his feet up just before the sedan would have run him over. It careened beneath him, and Ben dropped down awkwardly behind it, his back raked deeply by a jagged piece of steel when the lowest section of the fire escape dropped with him.

He hit the street hard, his back on fire, as the sedan wailed to a halt that blew sparks from both sides. The driver sped backward, Ben noting absurdly that both the car's rear lights were burned out. He steadied his pistol on the rear window and fired, two more bullets wasted before his next three shattered glass in a series of soft pops.

He leaped up and grabbed the ledge of a one-story building. His foot lashed outward and kicked the driver's side mirror as the sedan sped past, out of control now.

Ben leaped down, not daring to take any more chances. He thought he saw a figure desperately reaching across the seat to grab the wheel when he opened fire, three of his last five shots punching through the windshield. A fourth must have hit the radiator, because steam came billowing forth in great gusts.

Baruch obviously insisted it look like an accident this time. Too bad it didn't work. . . .

The sedan coasted backward, both twisted and torn sides grinding against the alley walls, steam continuing to pour from the grill. Ben snapped a fresh clip into his pistol and stepped warily forward. He watched the car coast to a halt on an odd angle, engine wheezing in fits and starts. The horn suddenly began to blare.

There was not enough space on either side to negotiate, so Ben leaped up on the hood with his gun aimed toward the already shattered windshield. He had to mount the roof in order to peer inside the car, and the sight of two still, bloodied bodies made his stomach quiver.

Neither was Shoshanna Tavi; the passengers were both men. Hard to say whether bullets or glass had done the damage, but neither was moving nor, it appeared, would ever move again.

Ben leaned in farther, hoping to find some clue as to their identity. He brushed across the driver and his arm fell away from the wheel. A torn and tattered sleeve slid aside to reveal a splotch Ben first thought was blood but, in the spill of the flickering lamps from the adjoining street, realized was something else altogether:

A tattoo of a red cross, upside down.

CHAPTER 31

DANIELLE SQUEEZED HER Jeep Cherokee between two subcompact cars in her apartment parking lot. The Jeep was the wrong vehicle to have in Israel, especially Jerusalem, given the ancient city's narrow streets and even narrower parking spaces. With the driver's door able to open only a third of the way, Danielle barely had enough room to squeeze out.

In a few short months, she wouldn't be able to squeeze out at all.

Danielle knew she should eat once she reached her apartment on the third floor, but her stomach felt unsettled again, just short of nausea. She should have expected this, of course, should even have been grateful for it, although that didn't make her constant bouts with sickness any easier to bear.

Danielle was sweating by the time she climbed the two staircases and approached her apartment. A wave of dizziness swept over her and she had to lean against the wall for support.

Something shuffled behind her door. She snapped away from the wall, suddenly alert again, her breaths coming in short, quick bursts.

What had she seen?

Nothing, probably. What *could* she have seen? The lights, after all, were off inside the apartment, so how—

Wait! That was it: streetlights streaming in through her living-room window pushed a thin swatch of light under the door. And for a moment, just a moment, that swatch had disappeared.

As if someone had shifted position inside, suddenly and briefly blocking the light. A flicker of movement that was more than enough to alert her.

Danielle backed up toward the staircase, her nausea forgotten, adrenaline having pushed it aside. She backed all the way down into the foyer, made sure the main door didn't slam, and padded back to her Jeep. She climbed in as fast as she could and closed the door behind her to shut out the light. Then she pulled her cell phone from her shoulder bag and dialed her own number.

Three rings, then the answering machine picked up.

Danielle waited until the message was complete, keyed in her access code, and then pressed "6" to activate the room monitor feature.

A few seconds passed. She couldn't hear much, hardly anything at all, but those seconds were enough to convince her of one sound:

Breathing. Soft, shallow, and muted breathing. The breathing of someone very much under control while awaiting her return. At least one person, though something told her there were more.

Danielle eased her keys into the ignition and turned on the engine. Leaving the lights off, she backed slowly out of her cramped space and kept her eyes on her living-room window as she drove off into the night.

CHAPTER 32

BEN CONTINUED TO stare at the upside-down red cross that extended down the dead man's forearm.

The madman in Baladiya Square had described the very same tattoo yesterday afternoon, called it the mark of the devil!

His thoughts a jumble, Ben rolled down the rear of the sedan to the street. The right side of his back exploded in pain. He recalled being raked by the lower edge of the fire-escape ladder and drew a hand to the spot, feeling a warm sticky patch of blood through his ripped shirt. It hurt to walk and he staggered out of the alley, suddenly unsure of his bearings.

"His disciples who wear the mark lie in wait for the weak to pass by so they can snatch them away. They can hide from most, but not from me!"

The madman's eyes had been filled with terror when he had said that, the sword trembling in his hand. But what if he wasn't mad at all?

Ben finally headed on again in a daze and quickly realized

he was in a completely unfamiliar neighborhood. Trembling now, he could smell the coppery scent of his own blood clearly and grew more light-headed with the passing of each block. He felt his feet moving, the rest of him following along, in and out of the patches of light provided by the sporadic functioning streetlamps. He thought he heard footsteps a few times behind him, but when he turned there was never anyone there. At last he realized he had somehow found his own street, his small apartment building just up ahead.

Up the walk, key in the door . . . Taking it by the numbers as his breath slowly returned.

Pushing open the building door when a hand grasped his shoulder.

SORRY I STARTLED—" Danielle cut her own words off when she got a good look at him. "My God, what happened?"

"You're a day early. It's only Tuesday." Ben's knees gave out as he tried to smile. He remembered the floor coming up fast, not striking it, and then feeling himself in her arms.

"Easy now," Danielle said. "I've got you."

"We were supposed to meet at your apartment," Ben babbled. "You were going to cook dinner."

"That's tomorrow."

She half carried him to his second-floor apartment, working the key into the door while somehow still holding him up. Ben didn't realize he was walking again until they were inside and Danielle was steering him for the couch. She eased him down onto it as gently as she could. Ben felt a surge of pain shoot up his spine at the same time a flash exploded before his eyes.

When he came to, Danielle was still there or, more likely, had come back: she was holding what looked like a first-aid kit in her hand now.

"Lie still," she said, opening the kit on a table she had dragged closer to the couch.

"What are you doing?"

"You've got a nasty wound on your back. Needs stitches, eight or nine at the most."

"That's all?"

"Well within my limit."

Ben took a long look at her medical kit. "The way we've been getting along lately, I think I should be concerned."

"The alternative is a long wait at the clinic."

And then he saw the hypodermic in her hand.

"Relax, Inspector. All soldiers in the Sayaret receive medical training equal to the best emergency technicians."

He winced from the sting of the alcohol. The numbness came almost instantly after she shot home the Novocain.

"You won't even have a scar," she promised. "I'm good at this."

"Lots of practice?"

"On cadavers."

"Wishful thinking on your part, maybe."

"Just lie still. . . . That's it. Can you feel this?"

"What?"

"I just pinched you."

"Did it hurt?"

"The Novocain's kicked in. Don't watch if you're squeamish. . . ."

Ben watched her remove a needle and a spool of stitching from her kit, then turned away.

"You really should be more careful at night, Inspector," Danielle said, threading the needle.

He felt a slight prick when she eased it into his skin, pinching the sides of the wound together. "I was. It didn't matter."

"Who was it?"

"There were two of them, and the attack wasn't random." Danielle stopped her work and Ben turned to look at her. "They came after me in a car."

"Baruch's people again?"

Ben recalled the tattoo of the upside-down cross on one of the dead men's arms and shook his head. "I didn't have the pleasure of seeing Captain Shoshanna Tavi dead behind the wheel."

"You killed both?"

Ben nodded.

"Shouldn't you call someone?"

"Finish the operation first." Ben kept his head turned away from her work, imagined the thin nylon being threaded through his skin. "Two weeks you don't come, and this week you show up a day early."

"There was someone inside my apartment," Danielle said deliberately. "I called you, and when there was no answer, I drove here as fast as I could."

"Be nice if we could get along this well when our lives aren't being threatened."

"I thought of that too."

Ben winced. "How you doing back there?"

"Almost done," Danielle said, and pulled a small scissors from the kit. "So if Baruch's people weren't behind all this, then who was?"

Ben's thoughts veered again to the mark of the red cross on his assailant's forearm. How could he explain the connection with the crazed rantings of a madman to Danielle?

"I don't know. Someone else who wants the disc probably, or that rock I gave you. Learn anything about it yet?"

"Nothing that makes sense." Danielle snipped the stitching and applied a tight dressing. "I think you'll live."

Ben gingerly pulled his shirt back down over his side. "What about a prescription?"

"I'm fresh out."

"I'm not: there's wine in the kitchen," he said, and started to stand up.

Danielle eased him back down. "Not so fast. Allow me."

"In that case," said Ben, "bring two glasses."

CHAPTER 33

BEN CALLED PALESTINIAN police head-
quarters to report what had happened when Danielle went to
fetch the wine. Captain Wallid and all other ranking officers
were out, so he was put on hold while the desk clerk scurried
to locate the watch commander. There was a click and then
a dial tone, signaling he'd been cut off.

Ben hung up the phone and gazed at his furnishings, so
meager when compared to those in Danielle's apartment.
Most of his possessions had been purchased before Israeli
duties had made many items prohibitively expensive and created a flourishing black market. With peace, if it ever truly
came, would come free trade and a boon for both Israeli
merchants and Palestinian consumers. It was ironic to Ben
that the most militant forces against peace remained the Hamas radicals and the black marketeers. More than once he
had wondered if they might actually be the same people or,
at least, partners in a twisted conspiracy.

Danielle returned with a bottle of wine she had pulled
from the top of a small rack on the kitchen counter.

"How's this one?"

"My best. A modest label from an Israeli vineyard Colonel al-Asi gave me as a gift for my fortieth birthday."

Danielle placed two glasses on the table next to her still-open medical kit. "You're getting old," she said, and worked the cork out with a soft pop.

"Not as old as I feel right now. What should we drink to?" Ben asked as she poured.

Danielle filled her glass only a quarter of the way and stopped it well short of her mouth. "The fact that you know more than you're saying."

"About what?"

"About who attacked you and who was waiting in my apartment."

"I don't know anything," Ben conceded, "not for sure."

"And if it was the same people who killed the Americans in the desert? Your nephew?"

"Then I would say it makes us even."

"What?"

"You think there's something I'm not telling you. I know there's something you're not telling me." He leaned forward but stopped short of reaching for Danielle's hand. "You don't have to wait until tomorrow anymore."

Danielle gazed at her untouched glass. "Wine makes me sad."

"Don't change the subject."

She seemed far away, listening to other voices Ben couldn't hear. "Tasting it reminds me of the holidays. What I don't have anymore. I taste it and for just a second I can smell my mother's cooking and see the table neatly set, my brothers and father sitting in their chairs arguing. I want to go back to that more than anything in the world. But I can't. There's no way. I have to realize that."

"For you it's the taste of wine, Pakad. For me, it was the smell of blood. It brings me back to the moment I walked into my house that night six years ago. I smelled it from downstairs and I knew. I tried to tell myself it wasn't too late as I charged up the stairs, but I knew. I knew. . . ." Ben's voice trailed off, then resumed, quieter. "Seeing my nephew's body yesterday brought it all back to me. And you know the worst of it? Not recognizing him. He was a stranger to me in so many respects. And when I finally started remembering him growing up, I remembered him playing with my children and all the other memories flooded in."

"I understand."

Ben stared vacantly into space. "Then understand that if those were the men who murdered him tonight, I'm glad I killed them. And if more of them were inside your apartment, I'll kill them too."

"You don't think I can take care of myself?"

"On the contrary, I understand you're up for a major promotion."

"Your friend Colonel al-Asi tell you that?"

Ben decided not to tell her Mordecai Lev had given him the news, posed as a threat. "Yes," he lied.

"Anyway, the commissioner has decided to recommend me for a promotion to one of the top positions in National Police."

"Then we have found something to toast," Ben said and started to raise his wineglass again.

Danielle left hers on the table. "Not yet, because Commander Baruch and others are determined to see I don't get it. They want to punish me."

Ben pulled back a little. "For being on close terms with a Palestinian?"

"And they can go to hell for all I care."

They exchanged a smile for the first time in longer than either could remember, and Ben felt a flutter in the empty hollow of his stomach, unable to take his eyes off her. He quickly drained half of his glass, but it was no use. His heart was hammering against his chest and his breath was suddenly short.

Ben knew what was going to happen next, and somehow the inevitability made it even more thrilling. He could never remember more pleasing seconds than the ones that passed before they reached each other. In that moment, Ben had everything in the world he needed to believe in right in his arms. The rest of his life vanished in the long kiss they shared before sinking to the Berber rug that thinly covered Ben's stone floor.

Tonight they seemed to need each other more than ever, and together they went far away to a place so removed from that room and time that the very color and fabric of reality seemed to change. Ben felt he was somewhere in a different world and he clung to Danielle to hold on to this place he never wanted to leave. He could feel his heart still pounding, but realized he was barely breathing as was she. A window shade rattled. Outside a horn blew. Still joined, though, they heard neither, insulated from all except each other and the peace that brought them. Ben felt light, the whole time as if he were floating. Reluctant to come down and closing his eyes so he wouldn't know the floor when it touched him again.

When he finally opened them, Danielle was starting away from him, toward the ceiling. He reached out and felt her stiffen under his touch.

"Do you regret what we've done?" she asked, still not looking his way.

He stroked her gently. "Yes, because I nearly pulled my stitches out."

Danielle turned onto her side to face him. "You know what I mean."

"You're the only thing in my life that means anything." Ben pulled his hand away. "What's gotten into you? You never needed to ask before. Too much wine, that's my excuse," he said, looking at her untouched glass. "What's yours, Pakad?"

"I'm pregnant."

SHE HAD HOPED telling Ben would be a relief. Instead she felt herself sag, the burden increased. She longed to be able to snatch the words away from him, get her secret back so she could be spared the task of telling him what else was on her mind.

Danielle continued studying his face in the near darkness of the room. His eyes were like a child's, confused and hopeful at the same time. They had walked a very fine line these last few months, finally succumbing to the urges both had managed to repress with the help of their mutually divisive cultures. They had realized, admitted, that they were happy only with each other. It wasn't all the time, one night a week at most. Almost always here at Ben's apartment since the checkpoints leading into Israel had become increasingly difficult for him to negotiate.

Until two weeks ago when Danielle first realized she was pregnant.

They slept together in Ben's bed but did not make love again that night. They awoke on separate sides to the warm sun lapping at their faces. She knew she had to tell him the decision she had come to. It wasn't fair to put the discussion off any longer, especially after last night.

"Ben," she had started when the phone rang on his nightstand.

"What?"

He waited several rings, watching her swallowing hard, before he answered it. "Hello."

"Kamal?"

"Yes."

"It's Ari Coen. I've had a look at your disc. How soon can you get up here?"

DAY THREE

CHAPTER 3 4

WE CAN TALK on the way," Ben said as they walked down the stairs of his apartment building.

"It can wait," Danielle insisted.

"I meant about what we each learned yesterday after we left the desert. What did you think I meant?"

"Nothing. Go on."

Danielle knew Ben could sense something was wrong, but he couldn't know what, not yet. She harbored no thoughts of a happy life shared with a man she knew she loved, because there could be none of that, for both their sakes. Indeed, no Israeli had ever married a Palestinian and maintained the kind of position she now openly desired. In fact, most Israelis who dared break such a cultural taboo had ended up as outcasts in their own country. Pariahs accepted by neither side. Danielle would no longer be a Barnea, not in her eyes or Israel's. This was one time she couldn't have it both ways, the delicate fence she had straddled on the verge now of toppling her off to one side or the other.

What would her father think of this ultimate ignominy,

especially now that the baby afforded Danielle the opportunity to preserve the Barnea name? If she raised him alone, that is.

But there was more, something she felt down deep and could admit only to herself. Danielle had felt it first when she and Ben had made love, and then later while she lay awake next to him through the night. Suddenly her need for him seemed depleted, as if all her emotion had been turned inward toward her baby. What Ben had given her, the security she could find nowhere else, the child would replace—was already replacing.

It wasn't fair; she knew that, even as she knew she couldn't change what she felt.

"An American showed up in my office yesterday and shed a different light on the situation," Danielle said after they had set off in Ben's car.

"An American connected to the dead archaeologists?"

"Not directly. He's some sort of famous fortune hunter."

Ben managed a smile. "Then what is he doing in Palestine?"

"Searching for the gold that according to legend the Israelites left out in the desert."

Ben eased up on the accelerator pedal and a car behind them blared its horn.

"He thinks that the Americans figured out where it was," Danielle continued. "At least uncovered the clues they needed to find it."

"In that cave . . ."

"Yes."

"Do you believe him?"

"I believe he's holding something back."

"Just like you are," Ben said.

Danielle knew she couldn't put this off until tomorrow night. "We need to talk about the baby."

"Go ahead."

"I think it would be best if I . . . I think we should consider having me raise him alone."

Danielle could see the genuine hurt on Ben's face. "Oh," he muttered.

"I've been giving this a lot of thought."

"I see."

"And trying to be realistic."

"I don't think that's realistic," Ben said, his voice as flat as the road ahead of them.

"I'm not saying I don't want you to be a part of the child's life," Danielle tried, hoping to soften the blow she had inflicted.

"Aren't you?"

"It makes the most sense, everything considered."

"I don't think so. *I* know what it's like to grow up without a father."

"So he should grow up and be like you. An outcast among his own people, *both* his peoples, which makes it twice as worse. Is that what you want?"

"I want a chance to make sure the same thing that happened to me doesn't happen to him. But that's not what this is about, is it? The truth is that it would be a lot easier for me to face renunciation from my own people, than you. After all, I've already been ostracized, haven't I? For all intents and purposes, I'm a man without a country, so how hard would it be to face the recriminations of marrying an Israeli?"

"I don't think we'd be happy together, not like this."

"Because you still have a world beyond me you're not ready to give up. And you know something? You're right. I probably wouldn't want to give it up either. I only have one question: why did you tell me about the baby in the first place?"

"It would still be yours."

"And, once in a while, I could sneak across the border to spy on him. If I'm not arrested on the way."

"We can make arrangements."

"So long as they're kept secret. Secret codes, how about pictures sent regularly to a post office drop? Maybe a Web site on the Internet, so I can talk to him that way."

"Ben—"

"No, stop. Everything you've said is right. It makes sense and I don't want to argue anymore. We've got work to do and that seems to be the only time we really get along, doesn't it? Just let me hold on to that as long as I can."

Danielle didn't respond and Ben kept his eyes locked on the road before them.

ARI COEN HAD men waiting at the entrance to his property to again escort Ben to the headquarters of his operation. A slight delay occurred when those men found he wasn't alone, and Ben had to speak to Coen personally over a walkie-talkie to set things straight.

"They think I'm dead in Israel, Inspector, remember?" Coen reminded. "And you bring an Israeli policeman here? I should have you both killed."

"That might make Colonel al-Asi cut off your supply of pictures, don't you think? And, believe me, Chief Inspector Barnea doesn't have many more friends in Israel than you right now."

There was a pause.

"Maybe I should have someone take the disc back to you, forget we ever met in the first place," Coen said finally.

"No problem. I'll just ask Colonel al-Asi if he can recommend someone else who can decipher it for me."

"All right," Coen relented. "Let's get this over with."

AT HIS HOUSE, the Israeli expatriate was clearly rattled by Danielle's presence. He kept tugging at his ponytail as he led them to his office. Since it was morning, the shades were open, allowing sunlight to pour through the windows and fill the room until the day grew too hot.

Coen turned a computer monitor to an angle from which both Ben and Danielle could watch. "The encryption code was fairly basic," he explained, "just as I expected. Definitely

Shin Bet. Mossad would have taken me another day to crack at least."

"It's clear," noted Danielle, "Shin Bet was determined to keep track of those Americans."

"And you're about to see why," Coen said.

Although he permitted her to be present for the viewing, Coen had posted a number of armed guards within sight of the room's windowed walls, wanting Danielle to know they were there.

"Here we go," Coen said, and the picture caught on the disc came to life in brilliant focus on the monitor.

"What the hell is this?" Danielle couldn't help but ask.

She just beat Ben to the question. He had expected to see any one of many things captured on the disc, but what he found himself watching was like none of them. The picture started to bounce a little as the bedouin guard who had been working for the Israelis reangled the camera. Steady enough, though, for Ben to make out a twenty-foot-high assemblage of pipes and rigging. A pair of the Americans stood in the center of an apparatus, looking on as the piping bore deeper into the ground. The tripod upon which the machinery was placed looked exactly like the one he had seen at Mordecai Lev's settlement, except it was considerably larger.

"The depressions I found at the crime scene," Ben noted. "Heavy machinery sitting on a tripod base. . . ."

"Listen," Coen added, reaching for the computer's volume control.

He turned it up and a powerful rumble began to emanate in stereo from the machine's twin speakers.

"I don't know what all this means exactly," Coen said, sounding dumbfounded, "but it looks like they're drilling for something."

"I've never heard of an archaeological team using a drill before," Ben noted.

"That's because the closest these Americans got to archaeology was their local museum."

"What?"

Coen froze the screen briefly. "You're looking at a geological survey team, my friend."

Ben looked at Danielle, unsure exactly what to think.

The murdered Americans were geologists, not archaeologists!

But what had they been looking for in the middle of the desert?

"They were drilling a thousand feet down," Coen continued.

"A *thousand* feet?"

"By the look of the rigging, yes. I briefly served in the Israeli army's engineering department."

"Could they have been drilling for water?" Ben asked, recalling the explanation for the presence of a similar apparatus at Rabbi Lev's.

"Why would they bother? Water might be the most valuable resource of any to Palestinians, but not to Israelis, and according to you, they're the ones behind the Americans' presence. Why would Israelis care about finding another water source in the West Bank? Besides, you wouldn't need a drill this elaborate if you were only looking for water."

"There's another problem," Danielle began. "When I arrived after the murders took place, the entire apparatus had been disassembled. There wasn't any sign of it."

"Thanks to the soldiers who were first on the scene?" Ben asked.

She nodded. "Under orders from someone else, someone who didn't want anyone finding out what those Americans were really up to in the Judean."

Ben moved closer to her. "All this equipment must have been inside those trucks we didn't get to see at the site," he said. He continued to search for his nephew on the screen but the young man must have been out of camera range. "Your friend Commander Baruch arrived at a very convenient moment."

Danielle kept her eyes on the screen. "In time to have everything removed before anyone else could investigate what was really going on."

"Speaking of which, I think you'll find this especially interesting," Coen pronounced. On screen the pair of men in the center were overseeing the process of withdrawing the piping apparatus from the ground. Coen froze the screen when they were finished, worked an X over the spool's very end and with his mouse, and clicked. The computer zoomed in for a close-up of a softball-sized object that looked like a closed mouth, lined on both top and bottom with steel prongs that might have been teeth.

"That's a diamond bore drill," Coen explained. "They must have been going deep all right, through plenty of rock and shale." Coen swung his chair around and accidently struck the keyboard. The screen returned to normal, picking up exactly where it left off. "I want to know what this is about. If it's something that can help me buy my way back into—"

"Freeze the frame!" Ben said suddenly, leaning over his shoulder.

Coen hesitated, then did so with a touch of a key.

"Now back up, slowly."

Coen regressed the picture one frame at a time, a click for each pass until Ben said, "Stop!"

On screen the angle had changed to include the mouth of the cave. A pair of shapes, smaller and less distinct in the distance, seemed to have just stepped out onto the goat path that led back to the ground.

"Zoom in on them," Ben instructed, planting his finger over those two shapes.

Coen worked the keyboard, finally clicking his mouse as Ben waited anxiously. An instant later a man and a woman filled the screen in a grainy image. The man looked to be in his early twenties with dark features and a scraggly growth of beard: Ben's nephew, Dawud.

"Can you sharpen it?" Ben asked, swallowing hard.

"Hold on." Coen worked a sequence of keys until the machine beeped. "That's the best I can do."

"It's good enough," Ben told him. For what seemed like a very long time, he stared at the screen in silence, imagining his nephew still alive. If he had known the boy was here, could he have prevented this? Could he have at least tried? But there was something else on the screen that had claimed his attention, and he slid aside so Danielle could see. "Take a look, Pakad."

She leaned in close to him and tightened her gaze on what Dawud Kamal was holding.

CHAPTER 35

THE OBJECT WAS slightly smaller than a shoe box, light enough to be cradled in a single arm, and made of what looked like some kind of wood. The poor quality of the picture made it difficult to tell anything else for sure.

"It looks like a container of some kind," Ari Coen noted.

"Is there any way you can tell when this part of the disc was made?" Danielle asked, sliding closer to Ari Coen.

Coen pressed the key that displayed the time and date on-screen.

"Two days before the Americans were killed," she calculated.

"But if these Americans were geologists, why would they bother with what was in that cave?" Coen wondered.

Ben looked at his nephew holding a box uncovered in the cave, while below ten other members of the team used a diamond bore drill to explore the ground. He couldn't answer Coen's question. Maybe the Americans were both archaeologists *and* geologists. Or maybe they were something else entirely.

"That box is the key," Ben said, thinking out loud.

"To what?" asked Coen.

"Their murders."

"It could just as easily have been whatever they were looking for with that diamond bore drill," Danielle argued.

Ben's expression didn't change. "How long had they been in the Judean, Pakad?"

"Over five months."

"At how many sites prior to this one?"

"Five."

Ben's eyes returned to the screen. "There was only one thing different about Area Six." He focused on the box his nephew was holding. "And we're looking at it."

"We don't know that."

"We know that the box is gone."

"So who has it?"

"A better question," Ben suggested, "is how anyone else knew it was there."

"The Americans must have been in contact with the outside world, probably through a satellite phone."

Ben nodded. "Then they could have made some calls to inform people of what they had found."

"Say they weren't sure what it was yet."

"But they had a very good idea it was important. They'd need confirmation, at least help in identifying it."

"So who would they call?"

"Their phone records might tell us," Ben suggested.

"They might," said Ari Coen, "but they probably won't. Those satellite phones can be easily equipped with automatic scramblers and rerouters that don't leave any trail. Believe me, I know."

"Well," Danielle resumed, "our mystery box wasn't among the specimens found at the dig, but those numbered rocks were."

"We need to find out what made them so special," Ben said.

Danielle looked back at the screen, remembering how certain she had been that J. P. Wynn was holding something back from her. "And that's just what I'm going to do."

CHAPTER 36

GIANNI LORENZO, CAPTAIN commandant of the Swiss Guard, eased the old man in the wheelchair slowly along the shaded lanes of the Vatican gardens. Tourists were able to see a large part of the gardens from the tour buses that snail along the main roads outside the complex. But, as always, Lorenzo clung to the nearly hidden paths in the wilder parts of the garden near the north wall. The overgrown weeds and vines formed a protective shroud, concealing them from all who passed or stopped to look in, perhaps in the hope of catching a glimpse of the pope himself. Lorenzo knew this was his predecessor's favorite part of the gardens, and spring was his favorite season.

His predecessor was in his nineties now, already crippled by arthritis when a stroke utterly incapacitated him two years earlier. His last official action had been to promote Gianni Lorenzo to colonel and appoint him as his successor against the strident objections of the Curia board. After all, all previous captain commandants of the Swiss Guard had been Swiss army officers and, almost always, members of the corps themselves. But his predecessor, under the circumstances, had felt that Gianni Lorenzo was the best and only man for the job.

Lorenzo had no idea how much his predecessor was aware of now, or even if he was capable of enjoying these trips past the small stone fountains and statues, unchanged through the ages, he had once so loved. Lorenzo looked upon it as another duty to be accepted with grace and dignity, but he didn't feel up to the task today.

Two of my men were killed last night, having failed miserably to complete their assignment. How could things have gotten so far out of control?

Lorenzo continued to move his predecessor's wheelchair along the path that led to neatly arranged rows of flower beds and the sound of splashing fountains. Sometimes the old man would fidget and moan as they drew closer to the clearing, perhaps afraid of relinquishing the security of concealment. Today he was silent and still.

Lorenzo sighed and slowed the wheelchair. "The day all this began you impressed upon me the impact of what the archaeologist Winston Daws had discovered in Ephesus. You convinced me that the discovery required desperate and immediate action, enacted without the knowledge or consent of anyone else in the Vatican. I was honored to accept your charge and journeyed to Ephesus with the other original members of the Noble Guard to complete our mission. And yet I confess today, confess for the first time to anyone, that this mission was never actually completed. I confess that the fault for what we are now facing lies totally with me, and I fear I may have failed you, the Holy Father, and the Lord Himself."

Lorenzo realized he had brought the wheelchair to nearly a complete stop. He doubted very much his withered predecessor could hear or comprehend him. But that made his words no less easy to utter, leaving his mouth dry and pasty.

He swallowed hard. "I confess that in Ephesus all those years ago for a few moments I held in my hands the fruits of Daws's labors and the reason for which his death was necessary. The scroll's parchment was brittle and badly faded, but remarkably preserved considering it dated back almost nineteen hundred years. I could not understand the language in which the ancient words had been written, and so many were blurred I wondered how Daws had managed to string together a context and meaning from the little he had reportedly read. It may have been preliminary, but that made it no less terrifying. I had to assume, as you did, that Daws had shared the contents of his discovery with the rest of his team. As a result, all two dozen had to die.

"But I could not bring myself to destroy the ancient writings. This wasn't just an artifact I was holding, it was an actual piece of history in spite of what its purported message might mean for the future of mankind. I held it in my hands, and knew I could not follow through with my orders to destroy it and chose another way to make sure no man ever laid eyes upon it again.

"I thought my alternative plan would be equally effective and two days later, before returning to the Vatican, I enacted it. No one ever knew. No one ever questioned me, not even you because you believed that my devotion to duty was so total."

Lorenzo realized he was squeezing the wheelchair's handles hard enough to make his hands ache horribly. For just an instant, the colonel thought the old man may have perked up, as if suddenly cognizant.

"I confess my weakness, and my cowardice, for not being able to complete my mission. And I confess my vanity at believing I would always be in a position to safeguard the secret I was charged with protecting forever.

"Forever, you see, did not last as long as I expected. Fifty-two years later, my failure has come back to haunt us all, and the church now faces the greatest crisis it has ever known. I alone realize this and I alone have brought it on. No one else, besides you now, knows how perilously close the very foundations of our faith, perhaps society itself, are to crumbling."

Some drool oozed from his predecessor's lips and Gianni

Lorenzo dabbed the corners of his withered mouth with a handkerchief. The old man offered no guidance in return, no blessing.

The captain commandant of the Swiss Guard started the wheelchair on through the garden once more. "Last night we failed in our attempts to execute two people who have drawn uncomfortably close to the truth. We will not fail again. This I promise."

CHAPTER 37

DANIELLE RECOGNIZED THE large complement of vehicles double-parked in front of Jerusalem's King David Hotel as government issue. That told her something was wrong even before she entered the building.

She had driven to the hotel in hopes of persuading J. P. Wynn to finally divulge everything he knew about what had transpired in the Judean Desert. When the elevator opened on the fourth floor, though, Danielle saw a pair of casually dressed men standing stiffly on either side of an open door halfway down the hall. She approached, counting down the numbers until she was sure it was J. P. Wynn's door.

At Wynn's hotel room she flashed her identification, but the men still continued to block her entrance.

"What's going on here?" Danielle demanded, trying to peer past them.

Captain Shoshanna Tavi of Shin Bet approached from inside, peeling a pair of latex gloves from her hands. "Nothing that concerns you, Pakad."

Danielle glared at the other woman, let her eyes linger

briefly on the latex gloves Tavi had balled up in a single fist. She was as lean and muscular as Danielle, her appearance little changed since their days in the Sayaret together. The long scar looked like a pale exclamation point amid her otherwise rosy skin.

"Tell your goons here to let me inside the room," Danielle insisted, gazing beyond Shoshanna Tavi now. She could see a photographer busy snapping photos, a second man with a black forensics case probably dusting down the room for fingerprints.

"Then you would be disturbing a crime scene."

"What happened?"

"That is none of your concern."

"Wynn was murdered, wasn't he?"

"As I said—"

"A bullet to the head, just like the Americans in the desert. Yes or no?" Danielle's tone was obstinate, and a little fearful: she couldn't help thinking of the person or persons who had been waiting inside her apartment the night before. Or another pair Ben Kamal had slain in self-defense. No doubt she and Ben were supposed to die last night, just as J. P. Wynn had.

"I wouldn't know about the Americans in the desert," Shoshanna Tavi told her.

"You knew enough to ask Inspector Bayan Kamal of the Palestinian police about a certain disc."

Shoshanna Tavi's scar turned a little paler. "Your Palestinian friend should develop a more cooperative attitude."

"His attitude depends on who he's working with."

"So I've heard," Tavi said caustically, narrowing her gaze. "You really should be more careful about the company you keep, Pakad."

"I was about to give you the same advice."

"Consider it done. Now you can leave."

Danielle held her ground. "Shin Bet has no authority to investigate crimes, unless called in by National Police. Strange you should even be here."

"This American's murder is obviously connected to another crime we are investigating. You said so yourself."

"I want to see the body."

Tavi smirked. "Suit yourself," she said, and stood to the side.

Danielle moved inside the hotel room before Tavi could change her mind. J. P. Wynn lay on his back, covered to the chest in a bedsheet, his eyes and mouth hanging obscenely open. His head had lopped slightly to the right, casting his sightless gaze toward her and obscuring the bullet wound from which a thin trickle of blood had run down the pillow to the sheet. Some of it had stained Wynn's straw-colored hair.

"Shot once in the head," Captain Shoshanna Tavi of Shin Bet droned, coming up behind her, "just like you said."

"Any sign of forced entry?"

"None of your business."

"And what is Shin Bet doing here?"

"I already explained that."

"The why, not the how." Danielle turned to face Tavi again. "Who called you?"

"I'd have to ask the duty officer."

"Strange you're not the least bit curious what I'm doing here, what the American and I were working on."

"Should I consider you a suspect, Pakad?"

"In an investigation over which you have no authority? Feel free."

"I leave such jurisdictional decisions to higher powers."

"I thought maybe you just happened to be lying next to Commander Baruch when he got the call."

"And where did you spend last night, Pakad?"

"Who contacted Shin Bet, Captain?"

"A maid finds the body of a foreign national in a hotel room. The manager calls Jerusalem police and Jerusalem police follow proper procedure and call us. Are we done here now?"

Danielle noticed the plastic Ziploc evidence bags the forensics technician had lined up on the nightstand. "Any shell casing?"

"No."

"None were found at the crime scene in the desert either. Interesting, don't you think?"

"I might, if I were better acquainted with that investigation."

"Of course, I forgot. Commander Baruch must have left that part out over cigarettes."

Danielle felt Shoshanna Tavi brush past her toward the bed. "Anything else you would like to see? I mean, this man was a foreigner and you seem quite taken by them. Here, take a look." She reached the bed and yanked off the bedsheet, exposing Wynn's naked body. The photographer and technician backed away, surprised and embarrassed. "Like what you see, Pakad? After all, your Palestinian friend is American as well, isn't he?"

"But he still has a heartbeat, Captain. Have you checked the chest of the man you've been sleeping with? How about the pictures of his wife and children in the wallet he must leave on the bureau?"

Shoshanna Tavi strode forward, close enough for Danielle to smell stale mints on her breath. "You would be well advised to keep your nose out of where it doesn't belong."

Danielle gazed dramatically back toward J. P. Wynn's naked corpse. "Worried he might hear something?"

"Perhaps something about your visit to a doctor's office yesterday, Chief Inspector?"

Danielle held her ground. "Were you having me followed?"

"Perhaps I had an appointment too."

"I'm sure Moshe Baruch would love to hear about that."

"As he will about yours, after I've had the opportunity to fully brief him."

Danielle gazed one last time at J. P. Wynn, whatever secrets he'd been keeping gone for good. "You haven't asked what Wynn and I were working on," she repeated to Shoshanna Tavi suddenly.

"Why should I bother?"

"You haven't asked, because you must already know."

The muscles of Tavi's jaw flexed. "Watch your back, Pakad."

Danielle was already thinking of how she might learn what J. P. Wynn had kept from her. "Likewise, Captain."

CHAPTER 38

I'M LOOKING FOR the doctor who would have been on duty Monday afternoon," Ben said to Dr. Henri Devereaux, a French physician on loan to the clinic in Jericho from the United Nations Medical Corps.

"I was here Monday afternoon," Devereaux said disinterestedly as he sorted through some charts.

"In the emergency room?"

Devereaux looked up impatiently. "It is where I work, Inspector."

Late last night, a pair of Palestinian police officers had finally checked out the alley where Ben had reported the incident that had left two men slain inside a car. Not surprisingly, the officers had found nothing. The bodies, and the car, had been removed.

But the tattoo of an upside-down red cross on the driver's arm had brought Ben to the hospital to check out the bizarre claims made by the madman he'd arrested in Baladiya Square two days ago. Until last night, he had given those rantings no credence at all. Seeing that red cross, though, had changed everything, especially now that someone had gone to great lengths to eliminate all traces of what had happened.

"A woman would have been brought in with a wound suffered in an attack in the marketplace, Baladiya Square. A sword wound," Ben said. The madman had insisted the woman had meant to attack *him,* claimed she had a knife in her possession.

The same madman had told Ben that he too had seen men with the upside-down red cross on their forearms. He had called them disciples of the devil.

Dr. Devereaux found the chart he was looking for and started down the hall, Ben trailing alongside. "Yes, I treated her myself. A flesh wound. She was lucky."

"Did you notice any . . . distinguishing marks?"

"Like what?"

"A tattoo of some kind."

The doctor shook his head. "Not that I recall."

"You saw both her arms?"

"Saw both. Worked closely on only one. But I don't remember seeing a tattoo on the other either. The patient had suffered fairly substantial blood loss, though, and I was concerned about some residual atrophy in the belly of the muscle. I stitched her up, ordered some tests."

"And?"

Devereaux shrugged, slowing as he approached one of the trauma rooms. "And nothing. She left, walked straight out before she was discharged. I came back to have her admitted and she was gone. Even left her belongings behind."

"Do you still have these belongings?"

Devereaux drew back the curtain. "Ask at the front desk. We'd be happy to get rid of them."

THE BELONGINGS THE wounded woman had left behind were stored in a single plastic bag. Ben peeled it open and turned it upside down atop the counter.

A cigarette lighter and small makeup case dropped out.

Then a knife clinked to the counter between them. Ben laid
the storage bag down and examined the knife. It was a
smaller version of the Jambiyah, the Arab knife of legend.
This one could easily be concealed in a hand, a woman's
hand, when held low near the hip. Show the knife only long
enough to lash out or swipe its razor-sharp blade, and then
be on your way. At any size, including this customized one,
a knife like this had only one purpose: to kill.

Ben didn't expect to find any blood on the blade; the madman in the square, after all, had told him he had struck the
woman with his pilfered Kilij sword before she had a chance
to get him. Nor did he expect to find any fingerprints on the
hilt because a professional would never leave any.

The madman claimed he had grabbed the sword from the
sidewalk stand display and acted out of self-defense, attacking only when the woman was poised to kill him. That made
no sense at all Monday morning.

It made only a little more now.

The madman told Ben the woman had been sent by the
devil, after he witnessed the return of the devil's disciples to
Palestine. Except the woman did not have the mark of the
cross on her arm; at least Dr. Devereaux didn't recall it being
there.

Perhaps the madman could tell him more about that tattoo,
and who might be behind the attempt on both their lives.

There was only one way to find out.

CHAPTER 39

"M URDERED," HERSHEL GIOTT repeated after Danielle had finished relating her experience at the King David Hotel.

"And Shin Bet was first on the scene."

"This Captain Tavi was in charge, you say."

"Shoshanna Tavi," Danielle affirmed. "Why? Is that important?"

"No," Giott said evasively, avoiding her gaze.

"What is it?"

He looked at her again. "Captain Tavi is one of those being mentioned prominently for one of the positions that should be yours."

Danielle swallowed hard, felt something like cold static dance across her flesh. "Shin Bet knows more than they're saying, Rav Nitzav. I'm sure of it."

"Something to do with the murdered Americans being geologists, you think?" he asked her, then continued before Danielle had a chance to respond. "What would geologists be looking for in the West Bank, Pakad, and what could it have to do with rocks?"

She checked her watch. "The forensics technician Raskin is due in shortly. I'll know then."

"But you think Wynn knew."

"Right from the start and it had nothing to do with that cover story he made up about the lost gold of Exodus."

Giott's empty gaze was somewhere else. He looked ghost-white to Danielle today. "The Americans could not possibly have brought in all that equipment without our government knowing, yes?"

"My thoughts exactly."

"Then the government must have been complicit in this from the beginning."

Danielle nodded. "Through Shoshanna Tavi, Rav Nitzav. And Commander Baruch."

"Who was directly responsible for the Americans' security. That is not something he would take on without very good reason. The stakes must be truly high." Giott nodded and his yarmulke slid forward on his scalp, no longer a good fit. He moved it back into place and Danielle felt a hollow pang of sorrow at the degree to which he was wasting away. "This is a most embarrassing situation for the commander, and we can use that to our favor by disgracing him, by revealing how badly he botched this matter."

"You believe he did?"

"Maybe yes, maybe no, but what's the difference? The integrity of National Police is at stake, along with your future." In that instant he looked like the man who had mentored her in earlier years as a detective, time wound backward. "I am committed to preserving that future before my retirement, whatever it takes, so long as we can live with ourselves. And I can live with myself for destroying Moshe Baruch. I cannot live with myself for letting his people take over this office."

Danielle thought briefly. "Destroying him means exposing the truth behind what brought the Americans to the West Bank."

Giott nodded. "I'd say avoiding such exposure was one of the prime directives he was given in this matter. He may survive the ridicule and embarrassment, but he will suffer for it. We will find the commander appreciably weakened, certainly enough to forestall the power play he and others like him are attempting." The commissioner of the National Police balled his hands into two weak fists he held before him. "You will have your new office, Danielle. We will make it so." He leaned forward, a look of optimism lighting up his face. "Find the truth, Pakad, whatever it takes."

FROM GIOTT'S OFFICE, Danielle drove the short distance to her father's grave in a crowded Jerusalem cemetery where the rows between grave markers were barely wide enough to accommodate a single visitor. She knelt over his grave and deposited the customary single rose she had purchased just outside the gates.

"I have news, Father, wonderful news. I'm pregnant again! Remember how I lost the last baby? I know you must, just as I know you'll want to hear about the father. Did he serve the army and his country proudly? Is he a sabra? Does he have relatives who were here at the beginning?

"He is none of those things, Father, but he is a wonderful man all the same. A wonderful Palestinian man. Would you give me your blessing if you were still alive?"

Danielle felt the hot tide of tears forming and tried to fight them back.

"But you're gone, and Mother's gone, and my brothers are gone. All of you left me alone to make these decisions and choices totally by myself. You all died for your country, our country, a country that was always more important than our family or ourselves. So how can I marry this man or raise my child with him, whether I love him or not, when I would be betraying the legacy you died to create?"

The tears came and this time Danielle could do nothing to stop them.

"Tell me it's okay to be weak. Tell me just this once it's

okay to let my emotions control my reason. Tell me I can love this man and still be loved by this country you died for."

A hand touched her shoulder and Danielle swung round breathlessly to find nothing. Just a trick of the same wind that was already tugging at the petals of the rose she had laid upon the marble grave marker. A man's life summarized in a set of years etched below the Star of David.

"I won't let you down," Danielle said, touching it. "I won't let you down."

CHAPTER 40

THE JAILER LOOKED at Ben strangely. "We don't get many police down here."

"Then you should be glad to see me."

The jailer's pockmarked face grew tentative. "I don't know if I can let you in."

"I arrested him. He's my prisoner."

"After they're dropped off here, they become ours."

Ben sighed in concession, slapped his palms lightly on the jailer's desk. "I see. I'll go inform Colonel al-Asi. . . ."

"Wait," the jailer called before Ben could turn around, "I thought you were with the police."

"I am," Ben said. "But I'm pursuing this inquiry on behalf of the Protective Security Service."

The jailer fumbled for the keys. "You will not report this confusion to the colonel."

Ben watched the man finally snare them and slide out from behind his desk. "I see no need."

* * *

THE JAILER LED Ben down the long, colorless hall past cell after cell. The district of Jericho's jail had once been a small hospital, rendered obsolete when the Palestinian Authority built the new clinic near the town center. In the Authority's rush to convert the former hospital to a jail, though, they neglected to include proper facilities for mentally ill criminals who would be served better as patients than prisoners. But there were simply not enough funds available in the budget to pay for the kind of care such individuals required.

Ben tried to ignore the odors of urine and sweat that permeated the hall, then gave up the attempt in the hope that his nose would simply get accustomed to them. A few of the prisoners watched him as he passed. Others cowered in their cells, clinging to the corners of the cold concrete.

"What's the man's name?" Ben asked as they neared the last cells on the hall.

"We don't know," said the jailer. "He hasn't told us yet."

"Have you asked?"

"He hasn't said much of anything, whether we ask him or not."

The jailer stopped at the last cell on the right-hand side. "Here he is."

Inside, the man Ben recognized from Baladiya Square two days ago sat in a corner on the floor, head down and arms cradled around his knees, rocking himself slightly. His stringy hair was wet with sweat and oil, the bald patches of his scalp plainly visible. A mattress lay across from him, but no bed. The water in the sink dripped. A stench rose from the chemical toilet. The arm Ben had wounded in subduing him had been placed in a makeshift cloth sling that was now stained with dirt.

The jailer rattled his keys against the bars to get the man's attention. "Hey! Hey, I'm talking to you!"

Ben grabbed his hand and stopped the jangling. "Open it up and let me go in there with him."

The jailer narrowed his gaze. "You're sure you want to do that?"

"Don't make me repeat myself."

The jailer shrugged, inserted a thick key from his ring into the lock, and pulled open the cell door. "I'll have to lock it behind you," he warned as Ben slid past him.

"Be my guest."

Ben moved deeper into the cell and sat down on the floor across from the man, who seemed oblivious to his presence, still rocking himself.

"Do you remember me?"

The man rocked himself harder.

"We met at the marketplace the other day." Ben twisted back toward the bars and saw the jailer standing there, just within earshot. "Everything is under control here," he called. "You can return to your post."

"Yes, sir," the jailer said and walked stiffly off.

"I am Inspector Bayan Kamal of the Palestinian police," he said to the man before him. "I would like to help you, if you let me."

The man started humming, staring at the floor.

"I didn't believe what you told me about the devil, until I saw a man last night with a tattoo of an upside-down red cross across his forearm."

The man looked up just enough to meet Ben's eyes.

"He tried to kill me," Ben told him. "And now I need you to tell me what else you know before someone else tries again."

The man turned a little, looking away.

"While you are here," Ben started, "who is feeding your cat?"

The man's eyes widened in confusion, then sadness. His features suddenly perked up. He gazed around as if unsure what to do, back-crawling to put more distance between himself and Ben.

"How did you know I had a cat?" he asked, his voice a mixture of suspicion and curiosity.

"The scratches on your arms. The cat must have had a bad day."

"She has a lot of bad days."

"What if you could be released so you can feed her?"

The man's eyes lightened a little. "They think I'm crazy."

"I don't. What's your name?"

The prisoner eyed Ben intently and seemed to relax a bit. "Abid Rahman. And it's not so bad."

"What?"

"You asked me about my arm. It doesn't hurt much anymore."

"I'd like to show you something," Ben said, and removed the Jambiyah knife, encased in a Ziploc bag, from his pocket. "Do you recognize it?"

Rahman's entire body tensed and he pushed himself back almost to the concrete wall. "Where did you get that?"

"Tell me where you've seen it before."

"In Baladiya Square! The woman was holding it in her hand when I attacked her." Rahman's eyes bulged. "Did you get it from her? Where is she?"

"The woman you wounded left the clinic on Monday before they were finished treating her." Ben paused to make sure he had all of Rahman's attention. "She left the knife behind."

Rahman's eyes sharpened, tried not to meet Ben's. "She'll come for me again."

"Not if you are under my protection."

"You would do that for me?"

Ben nodded. "Yes, in exchange for your help."

"Me? How could I possibly help you?"

"I would like to hear more about the day all those years ago you first saw the devil."

CHAPTER 41

*I*T WAS *1948* and *I was just a young boy. Barely into my teens, I think. Yes, because it was just before the first war with the Jews, the Mavtah, that changed our world forever.*

Our village, the village of Bani Nai'm, was poor. We had no money. We sold off what few possessions we had in order to survive. A common tale, I know, but it belongs to me all the same. I was reduced to begging in the streets to feed my family. Sometimes I stole. When I was caught, I was beaten. Once a shopkeeper hit my head against a wall and my memory has been weak ever since.

But the day I saw the devil for the first time remains clear. He came as a lost soul, neither Jew nor Palestinian. He was not familiar with our land and I heard him offering money for a guide. He wanted to go into the desert which I knew well, since our village was located on its edge, and often my father and I would go exploring in the caves.

My father would tell me the stories of our proud history. I think he knew what the future held for us with the Jews and he wanted that history preserved, wanted me to stay proud no matter what happened. So I knew the desert and I led the devil out there, sitting beside him in the passenger seat of his Jeep.

Of course, I did not realize he was the devil then. That came later, though not very much, and I blame myself to this day.

The devil asked me to guide him to the very caves I had explored with my father. You can see my tears now, hear my sobs, because it hurts so much to remember even to this day. I was drawn to him and I'll tell you why: because he was everything I wish my father had been. He was big and strong, with arms that bulged out from his shirt. It was warm, so he rolled up his sleeves, and that is when I saw the tattoo of the red cross for the first time.

I wanted to be big and strong like the devil. My father, you see, was a small man with bad breathing. I had grown out of appreciating him and it had been a long time since he took me to explore the caves. I went with this stranger, became his guide, not so much for the money he offered as to just be with him. Recapture the feeling I had once enjoyed with my father before his breathing got so bad he could hardly walk. I blamed him for that and imagined the stranger was my real father, and he would teach me things I hadn't learned yet.

He was good at making the weak believe in him, and I was weak. I admit that. I see now that is why he chose me. That is how he works, sensing our weakness and preying on it.

I showed him the way into the desert and the whole time he kept one hand on his tightly fastened canvas pack. I asked him what was inside, but he wouldn't tell me. I remember being confused, a little scared. That was the first time I began to wonder who this stranger really was. He told me he was a soldier and I made myself believe him, but I knew he was something much more than that.

We drove deep into the desert, several miles, as the sun began to weaken, and I wanted it to be over, regretted ever coming. The stranger finally stopped the car and we hiked to one of the caves. We drank lots of water, but his canteen never emptied, and it always tasted cold. I remember being scared by that too, but I was so thirsty, I just kept drinking.

Finally we climbed toward one of the cave openings. Inside he asked me to hold his flashlight while he dug. Now I was sure he was a soldier because the shovel he had was the folding kind I knew soldiers carried. He dug a hole and placed the entire pack into it. I remember how careful he was to fill the hole back in. But I never found out what was inside that canvas pack; I was afraid to ask and he never told me. I remember wanting to run when his back was turned and he was busy filling in the hole, because I knew he was going to kill me. And I did run, as soon as night fell. It was several miles back to Bani Nai'm, but I don't think I ever stopped. I knew I had been party to something evil, but I didn't understand how evil until I finally got home to find my mother crying and my father gone. The war with the Jews had begun.

The sorrow you hear in my voice is real, unchanged by the passage of time. I never saw my father again, and I knew it was my fault. I had forsaken him to ride with the devil. So my father died because I stopped believing in him. The devil had taken away what little faith I had left.

I knew the evil one had come to Palestine so the war could begin—I helped him begin it! I don't know what he buried in that cave, but I'm certain to this day that as soon as the last shovel full of dirt covered whatever was inside that pack, the first shots were fired. Life for the Palestinians would never be the same. Our world had changed forever and I had been a party to that, an accomplice.

But in the folly of youth, I thought I could set things straight. I thought if I could dig up whatever the devil had buried, I could end our misery. I never acted, though, until we heard of my father's death. After the funeral, I began venturing into the desert again in search of the cave, carrying only a shovel slung from my shoulder while other boys carried guns. I would go for days at a time looking for the *cave where the devil had buried the pack, believing I could undo what he had done. But no matter how long and often I searched, I could never find the same cave again.*

I thought if I could find it, and dig up what the devil had buried, I could bring my father back. Tell him how sorry I was and how much I wanted him to show me things again and tell me the tales of our people. Sometimes I would wake up at night and the devil would be leaning over me. I would awake screaming and I knew it was the devil's way of warning me not to interfere with his work.

His work . . .

He had destroyed my people, made many of us turn to his evil ways as the only way we could survive. We have lived with violence and hate this long, because we have convinced ourselves it is our only recourse.

Yet I know that somewhere in the desert lies the cave where he buried what could be the only hope of our people. Over the years I have continued to look; less often as I grew older and, lately, not at all.

But I still have the same shovel, always at the ready. . . .

CHAPTER 42

HOW LONG HAS it been since you went to the desert?" Ben asked.

Abid Rahman shrugged. "A few years now. I finally gave up." The gray pallor of guilt that had disappeared during his story returned. His hands began to tremble. "I say to you now that I probably would not have been able to look inside that pack, anyway. I would have been too afraid of what I might find. Maybe that is what the devil wanted me to do all along. Maybe the world is better off I didn't." He looked up at Ben. "Do you think I can go home now?"

"Soon. If you saw the cave again, would you know it? If I showed you the very hole you watched the devil dig, would you remember it?"

"*Inshalallah*. God willing." Abid Rahman suddenly pressed himself against the cold stone wall. "Why? Has it been found? Is that what you're telling me?"

"I'm not sure."

"*Yaa Allah!* You don't know what you have done!"

"I'm not the one who found it."

"But something terrible happened to whoever it was, didn't it?"

Ben felt chilled by the eerie prophecy of Abid Rahman's question, but didn't respond.

"That is the way of the devil, you see," Rahman continued. "He called himself a guardian, I remember that now. The punishment for anyone who invaded his realm would be unspeakable."

"Then you must have been braver than you thought, because you kept searching."

Rahman's face sagged in sadness. "Except I found nothing."

"It might not be too late, Abid, if you'll come with me into the desert."

"Are you foolish enough to believe you can stop the devil?"

"If it's not too late."

"You can't stop the blood. You can only keep it from your own hands. That much I know from my day with the devil."

Ben kept his tone calm and patient. "And you've seen him again."

"The other day. In the village of Bani Nai'm, where I still live. Do you know my village?"

"I've heard of it, but don't think I've ever been there."

"Almost unchanged these many years. Small cement houses and roads full of potholes. We have more electric poles now, and television antennas on many roofs, but a lot of our apricot and guava trees have died. The figs and the pomegranates too. Why do you think that is, Inspector?"

"I don't know."

"I think it's because of the devil. The evil remained after he left, spreading slowly, killing slowly. I think that's what it was. And, you know, I swear, I swear . . ."

"Take your time, Abid."

Rahman steadied himself with several deep breaths. "I swear that after the devil returned the other day, the few good trees our village had left shed their leaves."

"Was it the same man you remembered?" Ben asked.

Rahman shook his head. "He sent his disciples this time. I don't know how many I saw, but they all carried the mark of the upside-down cross on their arms. I was afraid they had come for me, knew my only chance was to finally tell my story and hope someone believed. So I came to Jericho, to the police headquarters, but they must have followed me. I noticed the woman in the square before I ever reached the Municipal Building."

"And you saw these others in Bani Nai'm, on the edge of the desert?"

"Yes."

"More than one of the men you saw had the mark of the cross?"

"Oh, yes."

"And might you remember *when* you saw them?"

"The other day, not long ago, like I told you."

"You remember when we first met?" Ben posed patiently.

Abid nodded tentatively. "In the square. When I thought you might have been one of them."

"You made me show you my arm."

"I still didn't fully believe."

"Because the woman who tried to kill you didn't have the mark either."

"Evil is sneaky."

"But when you saw the men the other day in your village, you approached them, didn't you?"

Abid nodded, very slowly.

"I would like to hear what you said to them."

Abid's eyes flashed, remembrance filling them with excitement. "Yes! Yes! I accused them of my father's death, of the destruction of my people. I asked what more they could do to us, why they had bothered to return."

"This was before Monday."

Rahman looked confused. "When did I see you in the square?"

"Monday."

"Two days before, at least. Yes, it was two days, I'm almost sure."

"Did they seek out your help again? Looking for a guide, perhaps."

"I sought them out this time. 'Why us?' I asked them. 'Why again?' " Rahman's face dropped in sadness. He sobbed, sniffled.

"But you came to Jericho."

Rahman looked up imploringly. "I had to warn people. I had to tell people they had come back, about the horror sure to be coming too while it could still be stopped."

"Would you like to help me stop it?"

"It is what I have been waiting for all my life." Rahman straightened, looking suddenly quite sane. "*Allahu maa asabirin.* God helps those who are patient."

CHAPTER 43

INSTEAD OF WAITING for Isser Raskin to return her call, Danielle went to see him in the subbasement level of National Police Headquarters where he performed his magic in a modular cubicle. By now Isser should be ready to provide the full report on the rock Danielle had given him.

She started to knock on the open doorway of his partitioned office when she saw he was not inside. More, his desk had been cleared off and all of his personal items removed from the walls.

Danielle felt her stomach quake. She leaned against Isser's chair to steady herself and then walked to the office of the department supervisor, barging into his office after a cursory knock.

"I'm looking for Isser Raskin."

The man took off his glasses and glared at her, befuddled. "He's not here."

"I can see that."

"He's been transferred. The instructions came down last night."

"Transferred where?"

"I don't know."

"How can I reach him?"

"You can't."

"Why not?"

"His transfer was to a division of intelligence. Special assignment. Overseas, I believe. He was very happy about it."

"I'm glad." Danielle could feel her heart beginning to pound, a tremor of fear mixing with the frustration that had coursed through her. "But he was handling some case work for me."

"I understand, Pakad." The supervisor turned to his computer. "If you tell me the case, I will see who the work was transferred to."

"Er, I'm not sure he would have had the chance to log it yet."

"Give me something, anything."

"Try Judean Desert."

The supervisor worked some keys. "Sorry, Pakad. Nothing on that."

"How about rock?"

"Just 'rock'?"

"Try it. Please."

The supervisor did as she requested and shook his head. "Sorry."

"Could he have left something for me?"

The supervisor shook his head again. "I'm sorry, I checked his box myself. He left in quite a hurry, though. He must not have gotten around to you, I'm afraid."

"I understand," Danielle said, and stiffly backed out of the supervisor's office.

She retraced her path to Isser's cubicle. She entered and, although feeling she was somehow invading Isser's privacy, began riffling through his drawers.

Except for office materials, all of them were empty. Nothing inside of note.

Including the rock she had given him.

Danielle sat down in Isser's chair and took a series of deep breaths. Her stomach, forever queasy, began to betray her again. She dragged over the empty trash can in case nausea overcame her.

What had Isser said in his phone message yesterday? Something about wanting to get confirmation from an outside source. She could listen to her voice mail and replay it but—

That thought steered her gaze upon Isser's phone. Like hers, it was built with a digital display. She reached to the keypad and hit REDIAL.

A number, unfamiliar to her, appeared on the display. The last number Isser had called before he left the office yesterday.

Danielle jotted it down.

WHAT IS IT that you teach, Professor?"

"Who did you say this was?"

"Pakad Danielle Barnea of the National Police. If you would like to come down to headquarters . . ."

"No," Professor Maurice Bernstein of Hebrew University told her. She had been trying to reach him in vain since late that morning, then finally got Bernstein on the phone during his afternoon office hours. "That isn't necessary. I am a professor of geology."

Danielle felt her stomach lurch again and squeezed the phone tighter, recalling the tape of the Americans at work in the Judean Desert.

"And, yes, I spoke to Isser Raskin yesterday, just before he brought his sample over for me to analyze."

"The rock, you mean."

"Why don't you just ask him all this?"

"He called you for confirmation. I'm doing the same."

She could hear Bernstein sigh. "Where would you like me to start?"

"What does the label on it mean?"

"The rock's a sample," Bernstein droned, as if it were obvious. "The number '561' refers to the depth it was found at underground."

"There were about a hundred other rocks in the case."

"Yes, and I would expect the highest number to have been around one thousand or slightly more."

"That's right," Danielle recalled.

"Increasing concentration of hydrocarbons the deeper they drilled. They stopped when they were sure."

"Sure of what?"

Danielle dropped into her chair as Bernstein told her.

CHAPTER 44

AFTER LEAVING THE jail, Ben had gone straight to the Oasis Casino, where he found Nabril al-Asi at a blackjack table.

"The Israeli tourists have accused some of our dealers of cheating for the house," the colonel explained. "I thought it best I study every one. Pull up a chair, Inspector."

Ben obliged, but waved off the dealer when it was time to lay down his bet. Al-Asi slid a fifty-dollar chip into the box and waited for his cards.

"I need a favor, Colonel."

"Does this concern that matter involving your late nephew?"

"Yes, it does."

"Just one minute," al-Asi said, watching the dealer slide him a queen and then a ten. "No, I don't think this man is guilty at all. Now what can I do for you?"

Ben watched as the dealer took a mandatory hit on fifteen and busted. Al-Asi stacked his winning chip atop his original bet and let it ride.

"I need a prisoner released from jail."

"An exchange?"

"A *Palestinian* jail, Colonel."

Al-Asi received a king first this time. "Who is this prisoner?"

"Abid Rahman. The man I arrested in Baladiya Square on Monday."

"Then why come to the Protective Security Service? Why not just obtain the authorization from that young police chief who is so in your debt for his position?"

The dealer flipped al-Asi an ace and paid him three chips instantly.

"The paperwork would delay things for days," Ben explained. "I can't wait that long."

The colonel left four chips, two hundred dollars, out for the next hand. "I detest bureaucracy, something to be avoided at all costs."

Al-Asi's next two cards were a two and an eight. He doubled down and drew a nine. The dealer locked at seventeen and slid eight more chips against the colonel's pile.

"I do believe you're bringing me luck, Inspector."

"Then you'll do it?"

"I would have done this for you, even if you weren't bringing me good luck. These dealers must be put on notice that someone is watching them. I have many tables yet to visit."

Ben started to back his chair out. "Do you want to—"

"No, this one suits me just fine for now. You're sure you don't want to play a hand or two? I'll back you."

"Another time."

Al-Asi smiled. "Of course. Now tell me what you learned from that disc I arranged for you to view."

"Those Americans weren't archaeologists, at least not all of them."

"Your nephew?"

"I'm not sure, I'm not sure of anything right now."

Al-Asi hit on twelve and drew a seven for nineteen. The dealer flipped over his hole card to reveal an ace and eight, giving the colonel a push. He reached and pulled all but one twenty-five-dollar chip back.

"I was suspicious of them from the beginning, Inspector."

"Why?"

"Because there's nothing of significance left to find in the Judean Caves."

"They were running some kind of tests on the ground."

"The ground is something else again."

"They had set up sophisticated rigging and drilling equipment. The Israeli soldiers must have dismantled it before anyone else got to the scene."

The dealer recorded an instant twenty-one and collected all the chips laid out in a semicircle before him.

"Did you consider doing any surveillance on them?" Ben asked.

"Why bother? Whatever they were doing didn't concern me. I rather enjoyed their little ruse. Playing dumb is one of the greatest advantages we Palestinians have going for us."

Al-Asi lost fifty dollars on the next hand and pushed his chair away from the table. He collected his remaining pile of chips and rose.

"Time to check another dealer, Inspector." He looked at Ben, seeming to see him for the first time. "Now what do you think this man you arrested can add to your investigation?"

"I was attacked the other night by men matching the description he gave me: they had tattoos on their arms, tattoos of an upside-down red cross."

"Have you researched this mark?"

Ben nodded. "No mention of it anywhere I can find."

"The Internet?"

"I haven't tried that yet, no."

"Let me help, then. I've gotten quite good with a keyboard. We used to have to tear fingernails out to get what the Internet gives us now."

"The man who's being held prisoner attacked a woman he claims was about to kill him, Colonel. He claimed she had a knife—I found that knife in a bag of her belongings she left at the hospital."

"And did she have this same tattoo?"

"No, but men who appeared in the man's village a few days before did. They tried to have him killed because he had recognized them."

"From how many years ago did you say?"

"Fifty-two."

Al-Asi straightened his tie. "Not a lot to go on."

"Enough, perhaps, to bring me to the killers of my nephew."

"Who have reappeared after half a century. I imagine they must have their reasons."

"So do I, Colonel."

AL-ASI ARRANGED FOR Abid Rahman's release before the afternoon was out. Now, a few hours before sunset, the former prisoner stood by Ben's side five miles from the village of Bani Nai'm in the Judean Desert as Commander Baruch of Israel's Shin Bet glowered at them both.

"What do you think you're doing, Inspector?" Commander Moshe Baruch of Shin Bet demanded when he saw Ben leading Abid Rahman about the crime scene in the Judean Desert.

Ben looked up past Baruch's barrel chest. "Working with a witness, Commander."

Baruch's gaze narrowed on Rahman, who stood fidgeting, leaning alternately on one leg and then the other. "A witness to the murders?"

"Not exactly," said Ben.

"What do you mean by that?" Baruch demanded.

"He was a witness to something being buried in the Judean Caves many years ago. I believe it was the same thing that led to the deaths of the Americans." Ben hesitated. "That box two of them brought out of the cave. You can watch it all on this."

Baruch's face reddened as Ben handed him the original of the disc Ari Coen had made a copy of. The commander sucked in his breath. His cheeks puckered, as if he were hiding something behind them.

"I should have you thrown off this land right now. . . ."

"From here or the West Bank, Commander?"

"We can start with here."

Ben looked about the site. "I notice you've managed to keep the media away from the scene. Perhaps I should make some calls, see if we can get you on tonight's news. Maybe tell the reporters all about the drilling apparatus you had the army dismantle before anyone else had a chance to see it."

Baruch stood there fuming, motionless. He closed his hand around the small disc. "Make it fast, before I change my mind."

CHAPTER 45

TAKE A LOOK around. Does any of this look familiar to you?" Ben asked Abid Rahman after they walked away from Baruch toward the hillside.

Rahman's eyes slowly panned the site. "I don't know yet. I've got to walk around, get the feel of this place, see if anything I remember strikes me."

Together, they continued along the guarded strip of desert where the Americans had been murdered, shadowed at every step by a pair of soldiers. Abid Rahman didn't seem to be looking for anything at all, but remained attentive, even focused if the lines that had deepened on his forehead were any indication.

He stopped suddenly when the sun hit his eyes, a hand held before his face to partially shield them. Now it was only the sun he seemed to be looking at; wide-eyed, trying not to blink.

"What is it?" Ben asked.

"Wait, please," Rahman said, and held his hand up to keep Ben from drawing any closer. "I remember now. . . ."

"Tell me."

"The way the sun pierces the slope of the hills and bounces off the desert." Rahman's words emerged in a dull monotone, as if a product of shock. "The same way it was when the devil finally found the spot he was looking for. I will never forget the feel of it on my face in that moment, because it was the last moment I would know true peace." He pulled his hand down and looked at Ben. "Here, *sidi*."

Abid Rahman pointed at the cave and headed toward it. With a pair of Israeli soldiers looking on, he hesitated at the foot of the goat path briefly before ascending toward the doorway.

Ben stayed on his heels, not wanting to miss a single word.

"I remember this slope," Rahman recalled, "the opening then just as it is now."

"You're sure?"

"The sun was in my eyes until we were halfway up." They climbed past the midpoint of the path and entered the shadows. "Then it was gone. The view is the same, the hillsides unchanged. But how is it I never found this place before? . . ."

"The devil could have covered the opening with rocks and dirt after you ran away," Ben said, recalling his earlier analysis of the twin piles of debris that the Americans had cleared from the cave entrance. "Covered it to blend in with the rest of the hillside."

Once inside the cave, Abid Rahman plopped to his knees near the shallow depression that Ben's nephew and another of the Americans had located nearly a week ago now.

"The devil wanted to explore the rest of the cave, but it was too close to getting dark," he started. "So he buried it here. I remember him digging this hole."

"You never saw what was inside his pack, though?"

"No." Rahman turned back to the hole. "Tell me, why are all those people outside?"

"Because two days ago, more than a dozen people died here. After they had found whatever you saw the devil bury fifty-two years ago."

Rahman tensed and clasped his hands in a position of prayer. "*Haududallah!* Where is it now?"

"We don't know."

Rahman reached out and grabbed the legs of Ben's trousers. His whole body was trembling. "You must find it, *sidi!* Hurry, before it is too late. Whoever has what the devil buried cannot possibly know of its power!"

"It seems, Abid, that somebody does."

CHAPTER 46

DANIELLE SAT AT her desk, trying to keep down another wave of nausea. Hershel Giott had been in a high-level meeting since her call with Professor Bernstein had ended.

"Oil," the professor had told her. "Wherever that rock came from, the land is extremely rich in oil reserves. One of the richest strikes in decades."

"You're sure?" Danielle had managed.

"The concentration of hydrocarbons on the sample provided me could suggest nothing else."

Oil, Danielle thought now as she waited for Hershel Giott to become available. *That's what the Americans had found in the West Bank and what J. P. Wynn had suspected from the time he arrived.*

Oil . . .

Danielle recalled Isser Raskin's insistence that the rock she had given him for analysis matched similar rocks found in the Texas Panhandle. Israeli geologists, and scientists perhaps, must have uncovered the possible existence of oil in the West Bank. Lacking the technical expertise to probe further, they had hired an American geological survey team and provided them the cover of archaeologists so no one would think twice about their presence in the desert.

After all, the mere existence of oil in the West Bank proved a complicated enough issue even before the issue of ownership entered into the picture. Whose land was it anyway? That part of the Judean Desert had recently been ceded to the Palestinians, but technically it remained under joint Israeli-Palestinian control. So who did the oil belong to? It seemed as if Israel was prepared to claim it as her own, the economic potential too mind-boggling to even consider allowing it to slip away. The Palestinians, of course, would argue for a hefty share at the very least. But it was hard to envision the State of Israel allowing the Palestinians to attain the power and wealth oil inevitably brought with it, which meant Israel needed to find a way to keep all of the reserves for herself.

"Could you tell me where this rock came from, Chief Inspector?" Bernstein had asked her.

"How could it have taken so long for the oil to be discovered?" Danielle responded instead.

"Probably because nobody bothered to look. The truth is there might be far more oil on Earth than we could ever use hidden in places we've never thought of looking. In years past the reserves were buried beneath shale and salt domes far too deep to find. But now we've got the technology to reach down a thousand feet and beyond." Bernstein had cleared his throat. "Now about the location of—"

"I'll call you back later, Professor," Danielle had said and hung up.

So much still remained unclear to her, but what *was* clear was that not only had Shin Bet known the truth behind the presence of the Americans, they were complicit in them being there. Heads would roll if that truth were ever revealed; Commander Baruch's and Shoshanna Tavi's, at the very least.

The phone rang and Danielle snatched it to her, expecting Hershel Giott to be on the other end.

"Rav Nitzav?"

"Excuse me?" a female voice said back to her.

"I'm sorry. I thought it was someone else."

"Yes, well, this is Dr. Petroska's office calling," the woman said, referring to her OB-GYN. "The doctor would like to see you."

Danielle felt the words clog up in her throat. "Is there . . . a problem?"

"I'm sure I don't know. I'm only relaying his message. Could you come down to the office right away?"

"The doctor said right away?"

"As soon as possible."

Danielle realized she was shaking badly. "Yes. Of course. I'll leave right now."

"I'll inform the doctor."

THE RIDE TO the medical building passed in agonizing stops and starts, normal heavy Jerusalem traffic bothering Danielle more than it ever did. Her test results had come back and the doctor must have seen something he didn't like. She was sure of it.

The thoughts she had harbored before, about how the child should be raised, suddenly seemed insignificant. Perhaps Dr. Petroska was going to tell her she had lost the baby. Again.

There were no parking spaces in the medical building lot, and Danielle left her Jeep in a crosswalk rather than search the street. She was halfway to the entrance when she caught the reflection of a familiar face in the glass, everything clear but the scar.

"Please stop and keep your hands where I can see them, Pakad," said Shoshanna Tavi.

Danielle turned to face her. "Whatever this is about, it will have to wait. I have an appointment."

"I know; I'm the one who had the call placed."

Danielle saw a pair of men she recognized from the door

of J. P. Wynn's hotel room approach her from either side.

"And in your haste to get here," Tavi continued, "you must have left your pistol in your bag instead of clipping the holster to your belt. Please lay that bag down in front of you." Tavi made sure Danielle could see the Heckler and Koch nine-millimeter clutched low by her hip. "Now."

CHAPTER 47

SECURITY AT THE fenced compound belonging to Rabbi Mordecai Lev's Amudei Ha'aretz outside of Kiryat Arba had been increased since yesterday. Ben had earlier arranged for Abid Rahman to be placed in "observation" at the Palestinian clinic in Jericho until he could work out something more permanent. Then he had driven straight to the compound, arriving two hours after dark.

He met Lev in the synagogue again, only this time a pair of armed guards stood vigil at the entrance.

"Have you brought the disc?" Lev asked, sitting in the front pew directly before the bema as he had the day before.

Ben dropped a second copy into the rabbi's extended hand. "It makes for most interesting viewing."

Lev closed his hand around the copy, waited for Ben to continue.

"The Americans found something in that cave, all right. It's all there, on the disc, but they weren't archaeologists."

Lev remained silent.

"They weren't archaeologists, Rabbi, they were geologists,

and you knew it from the beginning, because you've been getting copies of the surveillance discs even *before* they reached Area Six. What were they up to, Rabbi? And why did you care?"

"You are letting your imagination get the better of you, Inspector."

"It's that disc that proves those Americans were digging for something other than relics, not my imagination. But, sorry to disappoint you, whatever they found in that cave was buried fifty-two years ago, not two thousand."

Lev's head snapped forward. He felt blindly for Ben and clamped a surprisingly strong hand on his shoulder. "Keep talking!"

"Just before the start of the '48 War, a man stopped at a Palestinian village on the edge of the Judean Desert in search of a guide."

"How do you know this?"

"I found the guide."

Lev's hand dug in deeper, his grasp tightening on Ben's shoulder like a vise. "What did he tell you?"

"The man buried a pack containing a box in a cave on the same site where the Americans were killed."

"They found it, didn't they?"

"Yes, they did; it's recorded on that disc I just gave you."

"They removed it from the cave. . . ."

"Yes."

The rabbi's grip slackened and he began muttering in Hebrew, bowing his head low. "Is there any sign of this box?"

"No."

"Then you must find this box, Inspector. Whatever it takes. At all costs."

"Why should I?"

"Because the contents of that box are as important to you as they are to me."

"But they're also important to someone else, aren't they? Someone who dispatches assassins carrying the mark of an upside-down red cross on their arms."

Lev turned back to the bema and the ark containing the ancient Torah scrolls set at its rear.

"They're the ones who killed my nephew and the rest of the Americans, aren't they?" Ben continued. "They're the reason why you've turned this settlement into a fortress, because they're after the same thing you are."

"No," replied Lev, his dead gaze still fixed on the ancient scrolls of the Jewish people, "they are committed to making sure we never see it, that *no one* ever sees it."

"Why?"

"Because the contents of that box would destroy their world, Inspector, and they can't allow that."

CHAPTER 48

BLESS ME, FATHER, for I have sinned. . . ."

With these words, Gianni Lorenzo began the nightly ritual of feeding his predecessor in the set of rooms that had been specially appointed for his needs in the Swiss Guard barracks just inside St. Anne's Gate. The old man would never eat until it was dark, relying on the sky above the central court-yard beyond his window to tell time since the concept of hours and minutes had long been lost to him. The same window afforded him a clear view of the small, private chapel reserved for use by the Swiss Guard. How many times had the old man gone there to pray, able to share his thoughts only with God? At least Gianni Lorenzo had the old man to confide in, although since his predecessor's stroke their conversations had become increasingly one-sided until Lorenzo was not even sure the old man could hear him.

"It has been three weeks now since my last confession," Gianni Lorenzo said and raised a small piece of creamed chicken to his predecessor's lips. "A thousand times I thought about going back to the desert to right the wrong I committed fifty-two years ago, but I never did and now it is too late."

A slither of chicken and trailing sauce dribbled down the old man's chin. His tongue, pale and withered, emerged to try to swipe at it. Lorenzo wiped the excess away with a napkin.

"And tonight we face the potential ruination of our entire way of life because of me. So I confess to you not only what I have done, but also what I am about to do. Those who have learned anything of the secret we determined to keep must die. I must not let last night's failures deter us. The man and woman, and our other enemies, will not escape, cannot hide—this I pledge."

The old man made a gurgling sound low in his throat. His mouth opened and his lips flapped dryly together. The colonel realized he had inadvertently ceased the feeding and immediately dipped the fork into the bowl on the tray before him. The old man pursed his lips into a narrow slit, all the effort he could muster required to keep them that way.

"The blood will be on my hands. But it will end here," Gianni Lorenzo promised and eased another forkful of food toward his predecessor's mouth.

The old man's lips trembled after he swallowed. His eyes widened and in that instant Lorenzo thought he might be about to speak. But the old man simply belched, hard enough to shift him in his chair.

Gianni Lorenzo pried his predecessor's shrunken, patchwork hands off the rails and took them in his, squeezing lightly. Even a gentle pressure drew a wince from the old man.

"Holy Mary, mother of God, help us to pray as our fathers did. Help us to pray for the poor, wretched souls who know not why they must die before the next day is done."

MORDECAI LEV TAPPED his way down the center aisle of his settlement's synagogue. He smelled the fresh layer of varnish that had been applied to the rows of wooden pews that were identical to those in the synagogue at Kiryat Alba. There were more than were needed to accommodate those currently in residence, but all that was going to change soon enough.

Lev sensed the presence of his visitor as he reached the front row. "Is that you, Commander? I wasn't expecting company."

"I let myself in," Moshe Baruch replied.

"I'm sure you had good reason."

"I need to hear what you discussed with the Palestinian Kamal this afternoon."

"He has no idea of the truth," Lev said, "if that's what you are asking." He tapped his way to the center of the front row and sat down next to Baruch. "I have him believing the missing scroll is all this is really about."

"Pakad Danielle Barhea has learned about the oil."

Lev tightened his hands on the cane's handle. "And if she knows about the oil . . ."

"That is all she knows, believe me. And she has been removed from the scene."

"To keep our secret safe of course, Commander."

"Just a few more days, Rabbi. That's all it will take."

An ironic smile crossed Lev's lips. "We've waited twenty-five hundred years, Commander. I suppose we can wait a little longer."

DAY FOUR

CHAPTER 49

COME ON, WAKE up."

Danielle heard the voice at the same time she felt a series of sharp slaps to her face. She came slowly awake to the sounds of a deafening engine and felt a familiar flutter of motion in the pit of her stomach.

A helicopter, she realized. *But where am I? How did I get here?*

Disoriented, she fought to open her eyes, and when this failed reconstructed her thoughts back to . . .

Lock on to a starting point. The last thing you remember. . . .

It came back along with a dry, sandy feeling inside her mouth. Shoshanna Tavi and two Shin Bet goons had taken her hostage outside the medical building. A drive to a military air base in the desert followed, where she and Captain Tavi boarded a jet.

"Wake up, I said. Come on!"

Danielle had received the first injection just before they took off, her senses dulled almost immediately, even as she screamed at them that it might hurt her baby. They had stopped to refuel somewhere, and sometime after that had landed again to be transferred onto this helicopter.

"Wake up, bitch."

Danielle finally pried her eyelids open and caught Shoshanna Tavi's next slap in midair. "You made your point."

Tavi glared at her as Danielle let go of her hand. "You have shamed our country."

"Really? Am I guilty of kidnapping too?"

"You sleep with a Palestinian, fully prepared now to bring his child into the world, and you accuse me of *anything*."

"Carrying on affairs with public officials to further your own career? I'd say you've got plenty to answer for yourself."

Tavi fumed inwardly. "You are a disgrace, Pakad Barnea. I only wish you could have stayed in Israel, where a more fitting punishment could have been arranged."

"Then why not just kill me?"

"I asked the same question, believe me," Shoshanna Tavi said and turned away.

"You knew the Americans were looking for oil in the Judean all along. But who was it Shin Bet couldn't protect the Americans from?" Danielle challenged. "Who was it that killed them?"

"We don't know."

"But whoever it was killed Wynn too, didn't they?"

Shoshanna Tavi feigned disinterest but something kept her talking. "Word leaked out after we informed the Americans' employer about what had happened. Wynn showed up to sniff around, looking to get rich by picking up where they left off."

"And was killed before he had a chance."

Tavi finally looked back at Danielle. "But not before he used you to help him get up to speed."

"They were waiting in my apartment for me the same night."

"Pity you didn't go inside."

"So you wouldn't have to be here."

"That's right."

"And where are we going?"

"A place where we won't have to worry about you for a while," said Shoshanna Tavi. "Make sure your seat belt's fastened."

Danielle turned her head to follow Tavi's gaze out the window. "Of course," she muttered as the massive shape sharpened before her eyes, seeming to rise from the depths of the sea itself.

CHAPTER 50

IT WAS AFTER midnight when Ben hammered his fist against the front door of the small rectory next to Father Mike's church.

"I'm coming. Just a minute," he heard a voice drawl sleepily.

The door creaked open to reveal Father Mike in his bathrobe, his wiry hair sticking out to the sides. He looked at Ben and tried to smooth it down.

"Little late for confession, isn't it, my son?"

"I need to talk to you," Ben said, pushing past him.

"Why don't you come in?" Father Mike asked sarcastically.

"Close the door."

"What?"

"Close the door. *Now!* Lock it."

Father Mike slid the bolt into place and stuck his hands in his pockets. "What's gotten into you?"

Ben couldn't stop moving, eyes as jittery as the rest of him. "I've been to see Lev again."

"Ah, the mad Jewish rabbi . . ."

"You really believe he's mad, Father?"

"He's a fanatic, Ben. Even the rest of Israel wants nothing to do with him."

"What about his Amudei Ha'aretz, the Pillars of the Land, waiting for the Messiah?"

Father Mike shrugged. "They're still waiting, aren't they?"

"So are we—so to speak, I mean."

"For the *second* coming."

Ben's eyes looked like big dark marbles wedged in their sockets. "What if there was no first?"

Father Mike craned his neck, made a show of checking his watch impatiently. "It's too late for a theoretical discussion on theology."

"It may well be," Ben said.

W H A T   D O   Y O U mean the contents of that box would destroy their world, Rabbi?"

Lev had leaned on his cane and tried to stand up, but Ben had held him down with a hand planted on his arm.

"Where to start . . ." Lev's voice trailed off into a sigh.

"What's wrong with the beginning?" Ben asked him.

The old rabbi worked his jaw nervously from side to side. "In 1948," he said finally, "an archaeological team was working on a dig in Ephesus."

Ben nodded. "Go on."

"That team of twenty students was led by a famous linguist and scholar named Winston Daws. Daws believed he had found the final resting place of the great Jewish historian Flavius Josephus and was looking for proof in the form of lost scrolls and writings. He found a grave that contained a box, Inspector, just like the one I described to you in our first meeting."

Ben felt a slight chill, recalling the taped replay of his nephew carrying a similar box from the cave in the Judean Desert.

"Daws opened it," the blind man continued, "and found

an ancient scroll stored inside, wrapped in some sort of animal skin. It was written in ancient Aramaic, and though
remarkably well preserved, portions of the text had been lost
to the ages."

"Like the Dead Sea Scrolls," Ben interjected.

"More than you realize," Lev said knowingly. "Now, being an expert in ancient history, Daws was able to confirm
the manuscript was actually written by Josephus. But even
though he was a brilliant linguist, Daws had trouble trans-
lating the Aramaic. He had brought a young Jewish scholar
along on the dig just for that reason, and with the scholar's
help Daws made a preliminary translation of much of the
text's early portions. In spite of the holes and gaps in the
scroll, there was enough to tell this scholar he had uncovered
something of infinitely greater impact than the Dead Sea
Scrolls. Before they could go any further in their work,
though, Daws and his entire team were brutally attacked; all
of them killed, except for the scholar, who passed into an-
onymity and might have been better off dead."

Lev stopped and took a deep breath before finishing.

"Because he was blinded."

THEY WERE SITTING at Father Mike's kitchen table
now, the priest's callused knuckles squeezed white around a
cup of coffee. His face looked pale too, except for the red
marks his fingers had left on his cheeks through the course
of listening to Ben's tale thus far.

"Lev was part of Daws's team," Father Mike concluded,
trying to sound indifferent. But a thin layer of sweat had
appeared on his forehead, starting to thicken into beads. "The
one survivor."

"Left for dead by the killers, unable to identify any of
them. Twenty years later, after the Six-Day War, he became
one of the founding members of the Amudei Ha'aretz and
was there when they seized the land on which they currently
reside outside Hebron. Kiryat Arba."

"So now Lev must want to finish the translation he started."

"With good reason," said Ben.

THE KILLERS STRUCK at night," Rabbi Lev had continued in the synagogue. "I had walked out to the perimeter of the camp to relieve myself in our makeshift outhouse. "When I came out, the guards were already dead. I froze and saw the dark shapes of the killers moving about the camp in the spray of the floodlights. I turned to run and felt something like a kick to my skull. There was tremendous pain and everything before me went dark. But I still managed to crawl toward one of the trenches we had dug and dropped in. The dirt and the darkness must have camouflaged me, because they never checked to see if I was alive. I regained consciousness the next morning, thinking it was still dark, not realizing I was blind until I felt the hot sun on my face. Then I knew. I knew. . . . The authorities were already at the site. They heard my screams."

"Why didn't they investigate?"

"They did, but the investigation didn't go anywhere. I hadn't seen enough to help them, and the killers, well, it was as though they vanished into thin air."

"How much of the scroll had you had a chance to study?" Ben asked.

Lev's voice faded, reduced to a dull monotone as he replayed that last day in Ephesus in his mind. "I remember working alongside Professor Daws in his tent. We unrolled the scroll slowly, a little at a time so not to worsen the tears in the parchment that were already present. Much of it was yellowed, with the consistency of dried-out leaves. I used a magnifying glass over the faded portions of the parchment and did my best to fill in the gaps that were illegible.

"According to the portion of Josephus's tale that Professor Daws and I managed to translate, a doctor was waiting in his home the night Christ was crucified. A pair of Roman guards brought a critically injured man to him. His wounds were identical to the ones inflicted upon Christ in all versions of the gospel. But the man was alive—just barely, but alive. It was clear from the scroll that the doctor knew exactly who he was treating, that he was part of some conspiracy hatched by the Jews, the Romans, or a combination of both.

"Somehow they had concocted a plan to make sure Jesus survived the crucifixion. Our interpretation was that things hadn't gone as planned; the conspirators underestimated both the crowds and the severity of the wounds. Something went wrong and their original plan to assure Christ's survival had to be abandoned. In the end, according to the scroll, they resorted to some kind of switch, another dead body replacing that of Jesus before it was placed in the tomb. Think about it!"

Ben was already doing just that.

"This would explain why they blocked the entrance to the tomb. But the replacement wouldn't hold up to thorough scrutiny, so they removed or, more likely, buried his body in the cave itself. They didn't expect Jesus to live at this point, so the problem was moot. Low and behold, though, the doctor performed a miracle. Jesus survived, but left Jerusalem, never to return." Rabbi Lev raised his dead stare to the synagogue's plain ceiling. "You know what this means."

"Those people who claimed they saw Christ later on the road, in a town . . ."

Lev nodded. "Yes, it was the actual man, not the apparition. But much more is involved than that, much more at stake. If the scroll Daws discovered proves Jesus didn't die on the cross, then the resurrection never took place! The very foundations of Christian theology and dogma will crumble!"

"But why should you care? Leader of a group that believes the rest of the world can go to hell."

The rabbi smiled slightly. "Who do you think blinded me, Inspector? Who do you think wiped out Daws's entire team?"

"The church?" Ben posed reluctantly.

Lev nodded. "Just as they killed your nephew to protect the same secret."

"You saw them. . . ."

"Briefly."

"Do you remember . . . a tattoo of a—"

"Red cross, Inspector?" Lev completed, strangely emotionless. "It was the last thing I saw, before I turned to run, before one of them shot me in the skull and left me for dead. The bullet is still up there." He squeezed his knees with his hands. "You're right; I don't care about their theology. Except proving their Messiah was merely a man will provide the best revenge possible on the people who did this to me. And Josephus's lost scroll contains just that proof."

"Because without the resurrection—"

"Christianity cannot exist, at least as it is defined now. The church will fall into chaos, the same church that did this to me and murdered your nephew!" Lev said, his voice rising as he gestured toward his eyes. "The execution of Christ, considered alone, is at worst a miscarriage of justice, an abuse of power. But the resurrection turns that tragedy into a glorious victory. Without it, Christianity is nothing more than a fairy tale. The concept of redemption, of recovery from sin, crumbles and the foundation of the entire religion falls with it."

"And you get your revenge."

"Help me and you get yours too. They killed your own flesh and blood, Inspector. Recovering that scroll is the best way to make them pay for their sins."

"By exposing the truth."

"It's what you want, Inspector, what you've wanted for some time."

"How can you know that?"

"Because I know you."

CHAPTER 51

AN OIL RIG," Danielle said, mostly to herself.

Shoshanna Tavi snickered, crinkling the lower edge of her scar. "Not just an oil rig. This is the Ulysses GBS," she said as the chopper sank toward a massive oil platform anchored in the seas of the North Atlantic.

Danielle shuddered as she recognized icebergs dotting the waves and fields of ice covering the nearby land masses. She guessed that the land was a part of Newfoundland, just off the Grand Banks. But she had never seen or heard of anything like the platform Tavi had called the Ulysses GBS. It spired over seven hundred feet at its highest point, rising out of the sea upon five concrete modules that made it look like some kind of robotic monster constructed by an alien race.

The chopper bucked and squirmed in the biting wind. Danielle could feel that wind's frigid snap every time it pasted the chopper with its power.

"Put this on, if you don't want to freeze." And Tavi tossed her a waterproof winter parka from under her seat.

Danielle draped it over herself like a blanket, unwilling to remove her safety harness for the time it would take to pull her arms through the coat. The helicopter continued to battle the swirling winds as it hovered over a concrete landing grid. She thought her ears were ringing, then quickly realized the sound was a combination of the gusts butting up against them and the powerful wave swells nearly a thousand feet below.

"This must be the place those American geologists called home," Danielle surmised, almost shouting to carry her voice hardly four feet.

"At least the company they worked for. We're about to land on the largest oil rig ever, constructed over three billion barrels of oil just waiting to be sucked up."

"And how many barrels are there in the West Bank?"

"A bit too early to tell, I'm told."

"What did the Americans think?"

"Fifteen billion conservatively, making it the fourth richest field the planet's got to offer." Shoshanna Tavi said that with pride, enjoying the fact that she was privy to so much more information than Danielle.

They touched down at last with a final jolt and Danielle could hear the rotor blade rotating down.

Tavi unfastened her seat belt. "I don't expect you'll have call to try anything stupid way out here."

"I was thinking about making a phone call."

The woman from Shin Bet shook her head. "Sorry." She tightened her parka around her body and pulled up the hood. "You better put yours on too, if you want to be alive come nightfall; the windchill's below zero and today's as warm as it gets."

Shoshanna Tavi yanked open the doors to the chopper's rear compartment and Danielle gasped as she felt the sting of the frigid air against her face. Coming from the dry heat of the desert, the wet cold of the North Atlantic's Grand Banks seemed to freeze her breath. She knew the water temperatures could drop to thirty degrees and the wind gusts routinely topped seventy miles an hour.

"I'll avoid walking near the edge, if you don't mind," Danielle said, as she climbed out.

Shoshanna Tavi barely glanced back at her. "Suit yourself. I'm a patient woman."

Chapter 52

FATHER MIKE DABBED at his forehead with a napkin, a fresh layer of perspiration rising as soon as he was finished. "A wives' tale, a myth that's made the rounds for centuries, only never before associated with Josephus."

"That's what I thought," Ben told him.

"Then you must also find the historical inconsistencies and contradictions to be rather extreme. *Hundreds* of witnesses were still about when Christ was removed from the cross. *Dozens* watched him laid out in the tomb, and the cave was guarded *continuously* for the period until his body was found missing."

"Guarded by whom, Father?"

"Roman soldiers, of course."

"And if they were part of this conspiracy?"

"The rock placed before the cave entrance weighed upward of a ton. Not something that could simply be moved in the dark of night to remove, or even bury, the body of this supposed imposter, as your rabbi friend alleges."

"Unless there was another way out. A tunnel, a secret passage . . ."

Father Mike leaned forward, the steam no longer rising off the coffee cradled between his now-white hands. "Did the fanatic Lev say that?"

"No. I was just thinking out loud."

"My God, man, whose side are you on?"

Ben said nothing.

MORDECAI LEV HAD taken a deep breath to settle himself. "Daws cabled word of our discovery to select experts all over the world. He wanted to have his authentication, and subsequent translation, confirmed on-site to avoid all possible accusations of forgery or possible hoax." The old rabbi's shoulders sagged. "Forty-eight hours later, everyone except me was dead. No trace of the box containing the scroll was ever found. It was thought to have been destroyed by the killers, who had been sent to make sure the world never learned of its contents." Mordecai Lev shifted in the pew closer to Ben. "And now you have heard a tale about a man burying just such a box in a cave in the Judean Desert."

"A man with the tattoo of an upside-down red cross on his arm. In 1948," Ben noted.

The rabbi nodded, dead eyes staring ahead. "The man your witness remembers from his boyhood could have come to the West Bank from Ephesus, intending to bury the box somewhere it would never be found again . . . but then the Americans came and dug it up."

"And proceeded to make the same mistake Daws did: they must have contacted outside experts to inform them about what they had found."

"It is doubtful they were sure. But someone tied somehow to the church who was listening was sure enough, someone determined to make certain the secrets hidden in that ancient box were never revealed, no matter what it took."

"Including mass murder."

"The church had done it once before, Inspector. Why not again?"

"The same force both times . . ."

Lev nodded. "You've seen their work firsthand. They will kill anyone who draws close to the secret they may have been protecting for almost two thousand years. That means me." Lev reached out and felt for Ben's shoulders. "That means you." He almost smiled. "Unless we reveal the truth first."

"Perhaps they destroyed the scroll for good this time. No more chances."

Lev shook his head demonstratively. "They would not have tried to kill you the other night, if they had nothing more to fear. No, Inspector, the killers did not find the box at the murder scene. It is somewhere else. Someone else has it."

"And you want me to find it for you."

Lev pulled his hands from Ben's shoulders. "For me, Inspector, and for yourself."

F ATHER MIKE PATTED his forehead again, using a balled-up, soaked napkin to keep up with the sweat.

Ben's voice grew distant. "The old rabbi knew me well, Father, as well as I know myself."

"What do you mean?"

Ben's stare sharpened a little. "He knew about my family back in Detroit and my nephew here. He knew about me losing my faith, that I didn't have much to believe in anymore."

"Because you chose not to."

"I think he knew that too, maybe most of all. After what happened to my wife and kids, I didn't want to believe in anything because if there is a god, if God is real, then how could He let something like that happen? My children suffered, Father, and no one in your line of work has been able to justify that to me."

Father Mike let his napkin fall to the table. "Faith isn't about justification."

"Then what is it about?" Ben started trembling as he spoke, the memories vivid and ugly. "If good people die terribly, how can we believe in anything faith alone teaches us? How can we believe in God?"

"This is what Lev knew about you. . . ."

"Yes."

"That you were on a walk in the darkness."

"He didn't phrase it that way."

"But it makes you the perfect person to do his bidding for him, because it's your own desire now too, isn't it, Ben?"

Ben spoke with his eyes staring down at the tablecloth. "If I can find that box, and the scroll says what Lev claims it says . . ."

"You'll have your vengeance, both of you."

Ben looked up. "It's more than that. If I can find that box, then things will make sense, because there is no God as you and I, and all Christians, understand Him."

"Then it's a different kind of revenge you want, my son: to punish God for what He let happen to you six years ago."

"What if that scroll is the truth, Father?"

Father Mike slid his chair backward, the legs squeaking against the old stone floor. "Why did you come to me tonight, Ben?"

"I don't know."

"For confession? For absolution?"

"There's . . . something else. Something Lev *didn't* know about."

"What?"

Ben swallowed hard. "I'm going to be a father again." Someone else's voice, someone else's words, but it sounded good hearing them.

"Danielle Barnea?"

Ben nodded.

Father Mike smiled slightly. "And how does that make you feel about God?"

"Pakad Barnea does not want my help in raising the child,"

Ben replied, the pangs of hurt clear in his raspy voice.

"And you accepted that."

"She didn't leave me much choice."

"So you're giving up."

Ben shrugged. "Respecting her wishes."

"And you blame God for your own decisions? He's giving you a second chance, my friend. Can't you see that?"

"He's already taken two of my children, Father. Now he wants to take a third. The joke's on me. You should be laughing it up."

But Father Mike wasn't even smiling. "So you want to find this scroll to get Him back."

"Least I can do."

"Even if it does irrevocable damage to the church, perhaps even destroys our way of life."

"The truth hurts sometimes. Believe me, I know."

"It's your way of life too, Ben. You should consider that before you join forces with Lev, before you make your deal with . . ."

"The devil, Father?"

Father Mike's features twisted into a frown, then went flat again. "Depends on your perspective."

"Yes," said Ben, "it does."

C H A P T E R   5 3

DANIELLE LEANED AGAINST a steel storage shed to buffet herself from the wind on the deck of the Ulysses GBS. She could feel its bite through the parka Shoshanna Tavi had provided, sharp teeth prickling the top layers of her flesh. She tightened the fur collar against her neck.

"You really don't get it, do you, Captain?"

"I guess you're ahead of me again, Pakad."

"Unless you help me figure a way out of this we're both going to die here."

Tavi shrugged her off. "If you don't mind, I'd like to get something to eat first."

Danielle reached out and grabbed her parka, twisting Shoshanna Tavi around toward her. The cold wind numbed her fingers through the Thinsulate gloves she had found in the parka's pockets.

"Listen to me, you ass. We're floating out here in the middle of nowhere. Sitting ducks, as soon as they figure out where I've been taken. They probably already know."

"Who?"

"The same people who killed the Americans in the desert and J. P. Wynn. They tried for me once. They'll try again."

"Here?"

"Yes, here."

Shoshanna Tavi pried Danielle's hands off her jacket and almost laughed. "I didn't know illusions were a side effect of your condition. Look around you."

Danielle jammed her gloved hands inside her pockets and gazed about at the massive structure of the Ulysses GBS. Huge cranelike towers rose in equidistant corners of an inner rectangle of what she imagined as a fortlike structure. Below, huge pointed retaining walls had been erected around the base to protect the complex from the powerful waves of even a hurricane or the thrust of an iceberg.

"This is a floating death trap," Danielle insisted.

"We're not actually floating at all," Tavi said. "GBS, you see, stands for 'gravity-based system,' meaning this rig has a concrete base driven into the ocean floor. We're standing over seven hundred feet up atop more than a million tons." She shook her head. "No, the only way you'll die out here is if I kill you myself."

Danielle gazed at the icebergs floating in the distance, looking like flecks of frosting atop a dark chocolate sea. A pair of large barges zigzagged slowly away from them, heading toward the Ulysses.

"They're just practicing," Shoshanna Tavi said, following her eyes.

"At what?"

"When we get an iceberg alert those barges are dispatched to either blow the berg from its path, or lasso it to change its direction."

"Did you say lasso?" Danielle asked her.

"Just like a rodeo, only with heavy-gauge steel cable instead of rope. Once the barges get hold of a berg, they tow it into a different course so it's guaranteed to miss the Ulysses."

"They practice a lot?"

"All the time, I'm told. You can never be too careful."

Danielle walked away from Tavi, listening to the heavy clank of machinery battle the wind for supremacy. The men in hard hats and cold-weather suits blew misting breath from their mouths as they coaxed oil from the ocean floor several hundred feet below. Its strong, bitter smell permeated the air and clung to everything it touched.

Danielle swung to find Shoshanna Tavi right on her heels. "If you want to be careful, then listen to me, Captain. It wasn't oil that got those Americans killed in the Judean, it was something they found in the cave above the site. A discovery somebody desperately wants to keep secret. That's why they were killed . . . and why we will be too, unless you do something." Tavi reached out to grab her arm and Danielle swiped it away. "I'm a liability now, and so are you because they think we're onto whatever it is they've been trying to keep secret."

Shoshanna Tavi looked as if she almost found that funny. "Do I look like I give a shit?"

"You should; you're in as much danger as I am."

Danielle gazed at the men working nonstop on the levels that spiraled over her. She had the feeling she was trapped in a vast open shaft. The machinery continued to churn and grind, enclosed within covered housings to shield it from the slap of the wind and the water as it pulled oil up through the dark depths below. Just beyond there was a trio of modular seven-story buildings, set in a U, which contained the offices and living quarters for the three hundred workers on board the Ulysses at any time. Three hundred workers who, if Danielle's hunch proved right, were about to come under siege.

Shoshanna Tavi's hand crept inside her jacket. "Just get moving."

Danielle looked at the gun Tavi was ready to draw. "Kill me, Captain, and you'll only save whoever's out there the trouble."

CHAPTER 54

BEN KNEW HE could expect bad news when Nabril al-Asi asked to meet him outside the office, even worse when the colonel was late. He sat sipping strong coffee laced with cardamom in a small outdoor Jericho café that was virtually deserted this late in the afternoon. Checked his pager again, in case he had somehow missed a message from Danielle.

Where is she? What has happened?

They had not spoken since meeting with Ari Coen the day before. Ben had returned home from Father Mike's expecting there would be a message on his answering machine and called Danielle at home when there wasn't. He left the first of a dozen message on both her apartment machine and office voice mail. Tried beeping her to no avail.

After lunch he had finally phoned al-Asi and asked the colonel to see what he could find out. Two hours later the colonel had called back and suggested they meet here.

As he sipped his coffee, Ben finally saw al-Asi's Mercedes pull up to the curb. The colonel climbed out and approached

Ben's canopied table, missing his usual smile but holding a manila envelope in his hand.

"I'm afraid the news isn't good, Inspector."

Ben leaned forward and nearly spilled his coffee.

"Pakad Barnea has apparently disappeared. According to my sources she has not been seen in over a day. Her Jeep was recovered outside a medical office building in Jerusalem, but she never went inside to see any doctor."

Ben's mouth had gone bone-dry. It was hard for him to speak. "That's all?"

"No, I'm afraid not. A man she was briefly acquainted with was murdered two nights ago. Another American. A man named Wynn."

"The treasure hunter she told me about . . ."

"One bullet to the head, I'm told."

"Just like the Americans in the desert."

"Unfortunately, yes." Al-Asi tried to pump some hope into his voice. "But no blood was found in or around Pakad Barnea's Jeep and there were no signs of a struggle."

"They've got her, they must."

"Who?"

"I don't know, I don't know," Ben said and tightened his hands into fists as an empty feeling of despair built up inside him.

"Perhaps I can help," al-Asi offered, sliding his chair closer to the table so he could lay his manila envelope atop it. He unclasped the envelope and removed a single color photograph. "Does this look familiar, Inspector?"

Ben's gaze widened and he snatched the picture from the colonel's hand. "It's the red cross the killers wear tattooed on their forearms," he said, eyes locked on the blunt, wedge-shaped arms that formed the cross. "But it looks different somehow."

"That's because you're looking at it the opposite way. The tattoo makes the cross look upside down."

"The sign of the devil," Ben realized. "The one that Abid Rahman identified from a half century ago and then again last week."

Al-Asi nodded. "But not the sign of the devil at all. This insignia, better known as a cross patee, was used by the Knights Templars almost a thousand years ago."

"What are the Knights Templars?"

"An elite order of soldiers who grew out of a small military band formed by the church to protect pilgrims visiting Palestine after the First Crusade. They actually obtained papal sanction for their order and effectively became the church's private army. The earliest guerrilla fighters, some call them. They originally wore the insignia of a red cross just like this as a shoulder patch and later on the left lapel of their robes."

"And now?"

"By all accounts, they don't exist anymore, at least not in their original form. They continue in a sense as members of the York Rite of the Masons, not soldiers. I believe you can join over the Internet. The annual fee is one hundred American dollars. For that you get a patch, a certificate, and four newsletters a year."

"Obviously, some of them still take their work more seriously."

"Quite. I did some additional checking, contacted a number of my sources with knowledge of paramilitary activities. Apparently the Vatican has been quite active in providing a regular number of elite commandos with specialized training they wouldn't need just to keep order at papal masses. This dates back to the early days after World War II when Pius had real reason to fear for his life. By all indications, he must have recruited soldiers from all over Europe with a strong allegiance to the church and ordered the Knights Templars reestablished to protect him. Placed them under the auspices of the Swiss Guard, in the guise of the defunct Noble Guard, so no one would be the wiser."

"What does killing archaeologists have to do with protecting the pope?"

"Nothing, because someone at the Vatican must have decided that the Knights Templars had another more important role."

Ben could feel the coffee cup cooling between his hands. "Starting in 1948, of course, when they wiped out Daws's team in Ephesus. Then last week they murdered the Americans in the Judean Desert. Protecting the same secret both times, because one of these Knights couldn't bring himself to destroy the scroll Daws found when he had the chance. Buried it for a second time instead."

"Necessitating his return. Or, at least, the return of his successors."

"Too bad we don't know who he is."

As if on cue, al-Asi finally flashed his familiar smile. "Perhaps we do." With that, al-Asi removed a single sheet of paper from inside the same manila envelope. He straightened its folds and handed it to Ben.

"The man in this picture was caught innocently by a journalist in the background of a shot that later ran in *Look* magazine in 1948. Not that anyone really noticed, Inspector. Until now."

Ben could tell the reproduction had been enlarged and very likely enhanced by a computer. It showed a powerfully built man with chiseled features approaching St. Anne's Gate outside the Vatican. The man's rolled-up sleeves revealed the tattoo of the now-familiar red cross along his right forearm.

"You're saying *this* is the man, Colonel?"

"Computers can do miraculous things with faces these days, Inspector, especially with the power and access to databases a man like Ari Coen has. Why, his equipment can take a picture shot in 1948 and use distinguishing facial features to age it indefinitely in the course of the search."

Ben again studied the grainy shot of a sharply angular face dominated by a pointed chin. Even in the black and white shot it was clear the man had olive skin and jet-black hair cropped close to his head. The dark spheres of his eyes seemed to have swallowed all of the whites and his eyebrows almost joined in the center.

"I took the liberty of showing this picture to Abid Rahman, Inspector," the colonel continued. "When the shock finally wore off, and I was able to calm him down, he identified the man in the picture as the same man he escorted into the Judean Desert as a boy fifty-two years ago. Rahman was being sedated when I left."

"Who is the man in the picture, Colonel?"

"His name is Gianni Lorenzo," al-Asi replied, "once a captain in the Italian army and currently head of the Vatican's Swiss Guard."

I WAS ALSO able to locate this," the colonel continued, reaching into a different pocket as Ben held the computer-enhanced picture of Gianni Lorenzo before him. It seemed to tremble in his hand.

Al-Asi unfolded a copy of a newspaper article and handed it to Ben. Ben saw that the logline read "TURKEY" and the date at the top was "April 10, 1948." A photocopying machine had cut off part of the article but the picture was clear enough.

"Courtesy of the London *Times,*" the colonel explained, "and unfortunately the only item they had in their archives pertaining to the Winston Daws expedition."

The picture showed Daws, a tall, strapping man with thinning hair and glasses, standing in the center of the students who had accompanied him to Ephesus, where all but one had died four weeks after this picture had been taken. Daws had his arms around the shoulders of the students on either side of him, young men who at that point had only one month to live. A camera hung from a strap around Daws's neck. Ben tried to pick out Mordecai Lev, the only one to survive, but couldn't even imagine what the leader of the Amudei Ha'aretz had looked like all those years ago.

"I'm sorry I couldn't do better," said al-Asi.

Ben was about to pocket the clipping when a new thought made him return his attention to it. *What if . . .*

"If there's anything else I can do, Inspector . . ."

"There is," Ben told him, looking up from the article. "If you can find a way of tracing correspondence in and out of Daws's camp. Postal records, perhaps."

"What are you looking for?"

"Addressees where Daws may have sent letters, parcels, reports—anything."

Al-Asi didn't look too optimistic about the prospects, but he used his Montblanc pen to make a notation in a burgundy leather notepad. "I'll check."

"Phone records too, from anywhere he was likely to have called from in Turkey."

"It is doubtful such records still exist."

"But you'll try."

"Of course."

"And one more thing: an inventory from the crime scene."

"Again, I doubt the Turkish officials—"

"It was British nationals who were murdered, Colonel. You may have better luck with Britain's Foreign Office or even Scotland Yard."

Al-Asi nodded and made some more notations on the small pad. "And what will you be doing in the meantime, Inspector?" he asked, looking up.

Ben folded the picture of Gianni Lorenzo into threes and stuffed it into his pocket. "Visiting the one man who can help me get Lorenzo before it's too late."

CHAPTER 55

FROM THE CAFÉ, Ben drove straight to Rabbi Mordecai Lev's settlement outside of Hebron, cutting through a barren plain that had once been home to row after row of fertile olive groves. He remembered the groves from his boyhood and wondered what had happened to them. It would have been easy to blame the Israelis, but the truth was Palestinians had probably let the fields fall into deep neglect before abandoning them altogether.

The first thing Ben noticed was the absence of spotters on the roadside, calling ahead to alert the settlement guards of his—or anyone's—impending arrival. He found this strange and was at once alert as he approached the settlement's gate.

The gate was open, blowing back and forth slightly in the breeze. Even from this distance he could see that no one manned the guard towers and the settlement grounds looked empty.

Ben slowed when he neared the open gate, still expecting a guard to appear and ask for his identification. But no one approached his car. The post had been abandoned.

He drove on into the complex.

DANIELLE HAD SLEPT in the cabin through the bulk
of the day. The effects of the sedatives used in her long flight
had taken their toll. To revive herself, she finally began pac-
ing back and forth in the small cabin in which she had been
locked. Judging from the appointments, the cabin must have
belonged to a member of the Ulysses GBS's senior crew.
There was a cot, a cramped bathroom, and a security system
featuring a close-circuit monitor capable of zeroing in on any
part of the platform.

Danielle considered the option of picking the lock and
taking her chances back on deck. Whatever Shoshanna Tavi's
orders might have been to the contrary, Danielle felt certain
the woman from Shin Bet intended to make sure she never
left the Ulysses GBS alive. But she was also just as certain
that the same force that had killed the American geological
team and J. P. Wynn might beat her to the task. Danielle had
nothing to lose, then, but also no plan to pursue at the present
time. She wondered where Ben was now, if he had been any
more lucky than she, when an alarm began to ring.

BEN SAW THE first of the bodies at the same moment
he smelled the bitter stench of cordite and sulphur hanging
unwelcome in the air. There were two corpses lying face-
down in the ankle-high undergrowth. Each had been shot
multiple times. Both their weapons were still shouldered.

Ben pressed on, drawing closer to the completed structures, the smell of gunpowder residue strengthening. He
could see the effects of small arms fire on buildings now,
their concrete exteriors dappled and pockmarked, windows
shattered or fragmented amid blackened concrete. An arm
lay over the top of the nearest guard tower. Clearly, Gianni
Lorenzo's Knights Templars had gone for more than just

head shots this time: they had struck during daylight hours in an all-out attack.

The dry wind whistled, sounding like laughter, and Ben spun about, gun held ridiculously in hand as if it might help him fend off the killers who had been here and gone. He approached a building with drawings pasted across neat rows of windows, children's drawings done in crayon and finger-paint. A few had magazine cutouts pasted into themed collages. Around the artwork, the glass had been shattered randomly, leaving some of the the drawings flapping in the wind.

The first steel door Ben came to had been latched from the outside and buckled outward. The image chilled him, clear evidence that the attacking force had trapped everyone inside before lobbing in the grenades. He didn't have to pry one of the blast-rippled doors open to know there would be no survivors inside, could only hope the children had managed to seek safety in underground shelters Ben was certain the Amudei Ha'aretz would have constructed.

None of the other buildings showed any more signs of life than the first and the closer Ben drew to the center of the settlement, the more bodies he found in the streets. Almost all of those he saw crumpled upon the ground were armed. For these there had been enough time to mount a response to the ambush. Ben could only hope there had been enough time for the settlement's women and children to seek refuge in underground shelters.

The synagogue was directly before him and Ben approached it cautiously.

AT THE SOUND of the alarm, Danielle moved to the security monitor and switched it on. She quickly flipped through the various camera angles, stopping when she came to a long view of the center of the Ulysses GBS. Workers were scurrying in all directions in response to the incessant, shrill alarm. She continued scanning through the various viewpoints, in search of what might have spurred the alarm.

She stopped the screen on a view off the Ulysses east to the water. The huge barges she had seen earlier were heading straight for the platform on a collision course.

Of course! What better way to gain access to an inaccessible oil rig at sea. . . .

Yet whoever was steering the barges could not expect a collision to do any real harm. Nor could they expect to simply board and take the Ulysses from such a disadvantageous position at sea level.

And then the explosions began.

THE DOOR TO the synagogue was still closed when Ben got there. He threw it open and heard it rattle against the frame as he lunged inside, pistol ready.

The synagogue smelled clean, of the fresh leather recently laid over the pews. It looked unmarred by gunfire or explosions. At first glance, there was no trace of damage to any of the structure and even the windows were, for the most part, whole.

When Ben looked closer, though, he saw the bema had been torn apart. The podium had spilled over onto its side, the loose pages of a prayer book scattered across the floor. The ark where the ancient Torah was stored had been ripped open, the ancient scrolls shredded. The paper composing the scrolls had been spread out, strung like toilet paper during an American Halloween prank. The leather covering of the pews, too, had been torn apart. Someone had done it systematically with a knife, by the look of things. Not maliciously and not hatefully either; they had been looking for something, and Ben had a pretty good idea what it was.

He continued on toward the front of the synagogue, half expecting to find the body of Rabbi Mordecai Lev lying there not far from his favorite seat so close to the wrecked bema. Upon reaching the first row, though, Ben found nothing but the old man's cane lying on the floor, covered at one end by a tattered strip of a Torah scroll etched in perfectly aligned Hebrew lettering.

The paper had the feel of parchment, much like the lost scroll of Josephus that Winston Daws had pulled out of the ground over fifty years ago. That scroll was what the killers had come looking for. But they had encountered no more luck finding it here than they'd had in the Judean Desert after Ben's nephew had dug it out of the cave.

Then where was it?

The answer began to dawn on Ben as he stood there.

Of course! he realized. *No one has been able to find the manuscript because . . .*

The synagogue's front door banged open, freezing Ben in midthought. He sank to the floor and ducked under the front pew as footsteps thumped toward him.

CHAPTER 56

DANIELLE FELT THE cabin floor tremble beneath her. She heard glasses from a nearby shelf clattering together an instant before the next series of explosions sent them hurling for the floor. She looked back at the security screen, but the monitor had filled with static and she didn't bother trying for a different view; what had happened on the Ulysses GBS was clear enough to her already.

The enemy had rigged explosives on the barges to explode on impact with the platform. But Danielle knew that was just a distraction to clear the way for an attack now that the killers from the desert had somehow traced her here.

Danielle found a tweezers in the cabinet located in the small bathroom. She bent the tweezers straight and used it to pick the lock on the door, had it open in under a minute. She flung on her parka and moved into the hall, dashing forward into a noxious white smoke that seemed to rise in rhythm with the incessant wail of the security alarm.

Another explosion rocked the Ulysses, a vibration that rose from deep inside the platform. It was just the way she would have planned the attack herself. Create chaos in order to pre-empt any potential defense. The *real* enemy had done its homework.

But Danielle had her own plan. The platform certainly had emergency evacuation procedures and she rushed down the stairs to join the process. The alarm had shut off, replaced by a prerecorded message to follow emergency directions to the proper lifeboats. She reached the deck, still five hundred feet above the water's surface, to a rumble that shook all of Ulysses as the entire structure trembled atop its base. Huge plumes of fire shot out of the structure when oil being sucked up from the sea was ignited by more blasts.

The bravest workers continued scrambling in an attempt to put out the fires and regain control. The swirling winds caught the smoke and spread it like a blanket, obliterating the view of anything farther off than Danielle's own hand before her. The sickening stench of oil gobbled up the frigid, salty air and left its residue across her face in a thick film. It stung Danielle's eyes as she moved toward the edge of the platform, recalling the position of the lifeboats.

Danielle pressed herself against one of the modular structures for guidance and shielded her eyes with a sleeve. She used her free hand to feel her way, nearing a corner when a figure lunged out in front of her.

"Get back where you belong!" Shoshanna Tavi ordered, holding a pistol even with Danielle's face.

"Are you crazy? Don't you see what's happening here?"

"I'll shoot you myself!" Tavi screamed.

Before she could pull the trigger, a stitch of automatic fire clanged off the steel immediately over their heads. Both women went down, still in the sights of a masked gunman charging toward them.

CHAPTER 57

TUCKED UNDER THE front pew of the synagogue, Ben silently drew his Beretta, reluctant to use it for the additional forces the gunfire would be certain to draw. Right now he counted only two sets of footsteps he would have to deal with, if necessary.

But how?

A few feet from him, just within his reach, lay Rabbi Mordecai Lev's cane. He shifted his upper body slightly and snaked a hand out to snatch it before the two new entrants drew within sight.

Ben's hand had just closed on the cane's handle when he noticed something else. At first he thought his eyes were playing tricks on him, but he could see there was some kind of trapdoor built into the bema, revealed when the podium had been spilled over by the killers. Was that how the old rabbi himself had escaped?

The slow pace of the pair that had just entered convinced Ben they were methodically checking each pew; probably in search of Lev, since their initial sweep must have failed to net him. Ben's hiding place would not stand up to such scrutiny and he readied himself to move as soon as the first man drew within his range.

The cane gave him an extra three feet of reach and he intended to take advantage of it, hoping that would help him avoid use of the gun. One of the men walked far enough ahead of the other for Ben to ready the cane like a spear, prepared to thrust it out and capture a leg.

The front gunman's lead foot came down within easy reach of the cane, and Ben quickly looped its curved end around the man's ankle. He joined his second hand to the base and jerked just as the man looked down. The pull yanked the man's leg out from under him. He hit the floor and struck the back of his head hard.

A moment of shocked silence followed from his partner, at which point Ben rolled out from beneath the cover of the pew and landed on his knees. The second man raised his gun and fired once. A curl of wood exploded behind Ben's head. The coughed-up splinters stung his eyes and the gunshot's stinging echo made it feel as though somebody had poured ice pellets into his skull. But Ben managed to get his pistol up and fired, was still firing when the second gunman collapsed.

Ben's first thought was to check both men's right arms for the tattoo of the cross patee, insignia of the Knights Templars. Then he got his first clear look at the one he had shot.

It was an Israeli soldier, barely out of his teens, lips trembling and eyes wide with terror.

What have I done?

Ben abandoned thoughts of escape through the trapdoor and moved to the soldier. He eased him onto his back to check his wounds, ready to scream for help as loud as he could.

He had caught the soldier twice, once low in the thigh and once below the right shoulder. The shoulder wound was worse, bloodier, and Ben tore his own undershirt apart to use for pressure.

The Israeli patrol must have arrived shortly after Ben had

entered the synagogue, alerted by a survivor, perhaps, or just a desperate plea for help over a phone or radio. They hadn't announced themselves, nothing to tell Ben they were anything but the Knights Templars that had attacked the Amudei Ha'aretz settlement, killing indiscriminately.

I need some help here.

Ben pressed the balled-up T-shirt into the young soldier's shoulder wound to stanch the bleeding. But he had little medical training and couldn't stay much longer in any event.

Yes, sir, I shot your soldier. Put two bullets in him. And the other one lying here with the busted-up skull; I did that too.

The kid he'd shot, though, would die without quick work by someone who knew what they were doing. Ben had been so fixated on the soldier's wound he hadn't noticed the walkie-talkie clipped to his gun belt. Keeping pressure on the wound with his blood-soaked T-shirt, Ben pried the radio free and drew it to his lips.

Good workmanship, state of the art, and top of the line—something the Palestinians would not see for a decade or so.

"Man down, man down!" he said into the mouthpiece. "Synagogue, rear quarter of area. I need help here!"

Ben lay the walkie-talkie on the floor and maneuvered the soldier's left hand up to replace his over the T-shirt.

"Say again," the radio squawked. *"Repeat, say again and identify yourself."*

"Keep the pressure up as best you can," Ben told the young soldier. "They'll be here in no time."

"Identify yourself," the radio squawked once more.

Ben pushed himself up from the floor. He moved onto the bema and searched in the dim light for the trapdoor. Up close it was harder to spot somehow, and Ben had actually begun to believe he had merely imagined its existence when his fingers closed on its rim.

He gave it a jerk and the trapdoor snapped upright, revealing a ladder and darkness beyond. Ben lowered himself onto the rungs and eased the door closed before beginning his descent, wondering how long it would be before the Israelis found his escape route and began their pursuit.

CHAPTER 58

LYING FLAT ON her back on the swaying deck of the platform, Shoshanna Tavi twisted her pistol away from Danielle and clacked off several rounds at the onrushing gunman. Impact staggered him and he fired a wild spray into the sky. Danielle hoped that the awareness of a common danger might soften the woman from Shin Bet, desperation having forged an uneasy alliance between them.

But Tavi instead resteadied her pistol on Danielle. Before Tavi could pull the trigger, Danielle jammed a hand under her elbow and jerked the gun away. A single round whizzed by her ear. The gun clattered to the deck out of reach. Danielle used her free hand to smack Tavi in the nose, felt the woman from Shin Bet grab and yank her hair in response.

The oily air had blackened Tavi's face, including the scar that ran down one side like a teardrop. Her eyes were wild and unfocused. Her breaths came in rapid, rasping bursts. With her gun out of reach, she launched a series of blows that Danielle's thick parka easily absorbed. Danielle retaliated with a knee to the other woman's belly and then a fist that snapped Tavi's head backward.

Danielle lurched forward in that same motion, momentum allowing her to slam Tavi's skull against the steel support rail immediately behind them. Shoshanna Tavi's enraged eyes grew glassy and she slumped to the deck. Danielle picked up the pistol from where it had fallen and dragged Tavi with her across the platform.

Tavi came alert and began struggling anew.

"Stop it! They'll see us!" Danielle warned.

But Tavi continued to fight, trying to tear free of Danielle's grasp.

"I'm trying to help you, you stupid bitch!"

Tavi clawed at Danielle's cheeks and Danielle slammed her in the head with the butt of the pistol. She felt something crunch and Shoshanna Tavi instantly went limp, slumping to the grated section of the platform.

Danielle left her there and moved off amid the black swirling smoke that now threatened to choke off her breath. She covered her mouth with a sleeve when she coughed, trying to hide the sound. The wind stung her eyes with oily smoke, and she felt them watering as she pressed on, moving toward the lifeboats.

Before her, she could now make out crewmen working them desperately, fighting the hydraulics that were supposed to lower the covered boats to the sea at the flick of a button. But it looked as if the ferocity of the explosions had crippled the lines and generators, and she could see crewmen outfitted in black-streaked protective jumpsuits trying to release two of the lifeboats manually.

The Ulysses shook again as one of its pipelines ruptured in a huge flume of flame and smoke. Danielle lost her balance and clutched for a cable that tore free of her hand. The deck came up too fast to cushion the fall and she found herself staring at a sky camouflaged by the black smoke, with flames spreading around her. She lay still long enough to see the pair of the lifeboats plunging downward, nothing to slow their descent but the sea, which was like hitting the sidewalk from ten stories. The men inside the boats were screaming when they passed her, and then the wind swallowed their wails and the sickening thuds that would have accompanied their impact with the sea.

Danielle had just propped herself up on her elbows, pulling her legs in to rise, when she spotted the steel glimmer of a submachine gun poking out of the smoke. She steadied Shoshanna Tavi's pistol before her, fought to still the trembling, and fired. Three times, until she heard the plop of a body hitting the deck.

Danielle lurched to her feet and sliced through the oil smoke on a diagonal to the man she had hit. One of her bullets had obliterated his face; she saw that clearly enough as she pried the shoulder strap of the submachine gun free and took it in her own hands. She could feel upon it the warm sweat of the man she had killed. She wiped it clean against the outside of her parka and pressed on.

The Ulysses' deck was slick and wet, and that meant she had to worry about her footing, along with everything else. As the sea air pushed the oil smoke closer to the platform's edge, Danielle saw she had a bigger problem: no lifeboats remained in sight, all having been stripped or lowered from their perches.

Still Danielle continued on, listening to the staccato bursts of machine-gun fire through the wind and crackling flames. All the sounds and swirling smoke conspired to deny her a firm fix on distance and direction.

Drawing closer to the platform's edge, though, she saw something flapping in the wind. At first she assumed it was just a piece of the rig that had broken away, yet closer inspection through the oil smoke revealed it to be an emergency escape chute called a "Sea-Scape." It must have inflated automatically at the first sign of alarm, a twisting, curving plastic form laid out in an interconnected S-pattern. If she climbed in through the top, and followed the handholds, the Sea-Scape would guide her all the way to the surface of the sea, where several of the lifeboats that had dropped from their moorings looked intact.

But the force of the explosions had twisted the Sea-Scape away from the deck, leaving a gaping chasm between it and the top of the chute. Danielle yanked it back as best she could, but it wasn't enough. In the end she would have to use the rope attaching it to the Ulysses to shimmy her way over. Knowing she had only one chance, Danielle leaped up and grasped the rope.

For that moment there was nothing but soupy gray-black air between her and the frigid seas hundreds of feet below. Feeling another explosion rock the Ulysses, Danielle kicked her feet through the air to reach the Sea-Scape.

CHAPTER 59

FOR BEN, THE sensation of moving through the tunnel was that of clawing through a grave, trying to fight his way up from death. Rabbi Mordecai Lev had thought his defenses were impregnable. But somehow the force composed of what Nabril al-Asi had identified as the Knights Templars had gotten through in a sweeping, overpowering action that had placed the entire population of the settlement at their mercy.

The tunnel was lit to the dull glow of sporadically placed naked bulbs, strung together with wire that dangled overhead. Ben heard no signs of pursuit and took that as a sign that the Israeli soldier he had shot must have passed out before he could direct his fellows to the trapdoor.

Ben continued on, no idea of how much distance remained before him. By now his movements had become wholly automatic and he had lost track of how much ground he had covered already. He tried to focus on the bigger picture, what had struck him before. The killers had torn the synagogue apart, because they didn't have what the Americans found at their Area 6 of the Judean Desert. Rabbi Lev certainly didn't have it and neither did the Israelis. Ben wouldn't have even believed it existed if not for seeing himself the box carried by his nephew on the video disc. A disc taped secretly by a guard placed with the team by Commander Moshe Baruch of Shin Bet.

So where was the lost scroll, where could it be?

There was only one possibility, Ben had finally realized, and he was headed there now.

DANIELLE MANAGED TO throw her legs over the top of the plastic escape tube. She clamped down hard and drew the Sea-Scape closer to the rest of her body as her hands clung to the line for dear life. Still bent at an awkward angle, she finally let go of the rope and dropped in, her weight absorbed by the spongy plastic. Her chin slapped the rim, stunning her for an instant, and she groped for a hold on the tube's sides with her hands.

Using the Sea-Scape was like walking down an endless succession of thinly angled, interconnected ramps that stretched all the way to the swirling waters below. The center of the tube was easily wide enough to accommodate her, and she used her arms to brace herself against the sides as she began her descent. She could still see at least two lifeboats floating in the sea. As she watched, though, a huge chunk of concrete fell atop one of the enclosed craft and smashed it like a child's toy in a bathtub, leaving only one intact.

Danielle picked up speed rapidly. She had finally settled into a decent rhythm by learning how to push her gloved hands in against the plastic, when pops began to sound in the tube above her. She knew it was gunfire, well out of range thankfully for the kind of offensive weapons the assault team had brought with them. That didn't mean a lucky shot wouldn't find her, but the Sea-Scape's proximity to the platform further obscured her from view the closer she drew to the sea.

There was another problem, though. A person couldn't

survive more than a minute in these icy waters of the North Atlantic, and that was precisely where she might well end up. Danielle would have to work her way straight from the Sea-Scape to the one remaining lifeboat. She hadn't had time to don an orange survival suit before fleeing, and that would cost her if she miscalculated in the least.

The powerful winds shook the Sea-Scape from side to side, and the angry swells pounded the tail end of the plastic chute in the very spot Danielle would have to emerge. Even then, though, she judged the remaining lifeboat would still be ten feet away. Ten feet of frigid water. Beneath her, Danielle could see chunks of a small ice floe fragmented by the explosions from the sinking barges. She welcomed the flames rising from what was left of those barges for the false warmth they provided, distracting her from the idea of just how cold the water was.

Then she took a closer look at the chunks of ice floating around her. She tried not to think of what all this might be doing to the baby inside her, and instead imagined for a fleeting instant that Ben Kamal was standing beneath her, ready to catch her in his open arms.

She halted just short of the bottom portion of the Sea-Scape and waited until a hefty chunk of the iceberg approached, on a trajectory that would take it between the chute and the lifeboat. Danielle dropped down to the ice as soon as it was beneath her. It felt rock-hard and slippery, but she managed to dash across it, leaping the final two yards across the cold, black sea onto the plastic cover shielding the deck of the one remaining lifeboat.

Clutching the cover with one arm, Danielle found the zipper and drew it open. Then she dropped through onto the lifeboat's deck.

BEN EMERGED FROM the tunnel a quarter mile from the grounds of the settlement. Despite his haste, he made sure to close the hatch after him and cover it with dirt.

He headed south through the fading heat of dusk. He came

upon no trace of humanity until he reached the outskirts of yet another Amudei Ha'aretz settlement in the midst of construction well beyond the original Kiryat Arba. Ben thought he recalled that this was to be part of a major expansion effort throughout the West Bank undertaken to placate Israel's hard right, appease them for the many land concessions made of late. One of those was the stretch of the Judean Desert that included the spot where the Americans had been murdered, the spot where Ben was now headed.

At the work site, he noticed a pickup truck bearing a construction company's markings in Hebrew and climbed quietly into the cab. Construction workers lingered within easy view, seeming in no particular rush to get the day over with, and Ben stayed low beneath the dashboard until he found the truck's keys sitting atop its console. He eased them into the ignition and turned the engine on. Then he pulled casually away, the nearby workers noticing just as he reached up to adjust the rearview mirror.

UPON CLIMBING INTO the lifeboat, the first thing Danielle saw was a neat stack of survival suits wrapped in plastic piled in the corner. The small boat bobbed mightily atop the swells as she stripped the plastic off and climbed into one of the suits, finding instant comfort in its thick warmth. The material felt rubbery and smooth, and Danielle quickly located the pull tabs used to ignite the air pockets layered at chest level in case she fell overboard.

She moved to a chair set before the steering wheel and pressed the craft's starter button. It resisted at first, but then cranked to life. Danielle eased the throttle forward and the boat tore through the sea, leaving the Ulysses GBS in its wake.

CHAPTER 60

WHAT THE AMERICANS had called Area 6 in the Judean Desert now looked strangely empty. Other than the large cargo trucks that were anomalously still present, all the equipment had been removed.

Ben parked the pickup as close to the cave entrance as he could. A pair of Israeli soldiers approached, looking bored. The truck's white Israeli license plates led them to let their guard down long enough for Ben to get his pistol drawn and on them before they could reach for their rifles.

He used rope from the truck's rear bay to tie the soldiers up, leaving them leaning against the tailgate. He found a shovel in the truck and a flashlight as well, and hurried up the steps of the goat path leading to the entrance. It would be dark soon and he didn't want to be caught inside without light. He might be here awhile; after all, he wouldn't be leaving until he found what he had come for:

The mysterious box containing the lost scroll of Josephus.

Inside, the cave was dim and murky. Ben looked around him, waiting for his eyes to adjust to the semidarkness. It *had* to be here, he thought again, and began to dig in an area slightly back from the spot where his nephew had originally found the box. Rabbi Lev's people didn't have it, Gianni Lorenzo's Knights Templars were still looking, and the Israelis hadn't even known it existed, interested only in covering up the truth of the Americans' mission.

The minutes passed. Dusk descended outside the cave. Ben intended to dig here until dawn and beyond, if that's how long it took, even if it meant venturing into the deep, unexplored recesses of the cave about which Abid Rahman had warned him.

The validation of his own being seemed at stake, and he went about the task with a maniacal energy indicative of a man not only with something to prove, but something to gain. He *wanted* Christ to just be a man, wanted to change the way people thought about God. To prove that he had been right all along in abandoning his faith. There was no great light at the end of the darkness; that was the joke the prophets and priests had been playing on man for centuries. The darkness just kept going and a faith soon to be revealed as baseless kept man walking through it toward nothing.

Ben felt the grime of the cave sticking to his face, the sweat acting like glue. As he continued to dig, flecks of dirt danced in front of the flashlight's beam. He had laid the flashlight on the floor of the cave, readjusting it every time he moved on from one aborted hole to another, certain his nephew had *reburied* the box in this very cave for safekeeping. The last place anyone would think to look.

Ben's shoulders were aching terribly but he wouldn't stop, *couldn't* stop. Hot, dry dust coated his throat, making it hurt to breathe. It felt like he had swallowed glass and nearly gagged a few times, each cough making the pain worse. His hands had started to hurt too now, his strength ebbing but not his determination. There was no longer any pattern or order to his work; he simply dug in places he hadn't dug before, refusing to let himself be denied. His nephew would have wanted to protect his discovery, take precautions, hide it where no one would expect.

What if...

Ben shuddered.

Of course!

He adjusted the flashlight beam toward the front of the cave and moved to the shallow depression he and Danielle had examined two days ago, the depression from which the box had originally been lifted by the Americans.

Ben sank his shovel into the bottom of the small trench and worked the blade around, removing only thin layers of dirt at a time at first before picking up the pace. He was down six inches when the shovel struck something hard.

Trembling, he abandoned the shovel and dropped to his knees. Then he plunged his hands into the deepened hole and cleared the rest of the dirt aside with his fingers.

The box lay before him, caught in the dim glow of the flashlight beam. Clay-colored dirt was matted to its surface, the steel latch having no more than a simple peg worked through its slots. Ben pried the peg gently free and lifted the box toward him.

As the box tilted, something shifted inside it, clacking hollowly against the box's sides. Ben suddenly felt out of breath.

He wasn't sure how long he sat there with the box cradled in his lap. He maintained enough presence of mind not to open it for fear of what a sudden rush of air might do to its fragile contents. Ben stuck the peg back through the latch to reseal it.

A wave of dizziness swept over him. A bright light burned his eyes and he was certain he must be about to pass out.

But a second light joined the first, followed by a third. Voices he couldn't understand exchanged words and then a large figure stepped through the cave's entrance into the spill of the new light.

"I'll take that," said Commander Moshe Baruch.

CHAPTER 61

EXHAUSTED, DANIELLE CLUNG for life to the boat's steering wheel. The powerful swells had lashed her lifeboat across the sea, swallowing it only to spit it out again. A heavier craft, one with less buoyancy, would have certainly been lost. But this craft's balance, together with her skill as a pilot, allowed her to ride out the thrashing and harsh spray rising off the waves.

Still, the sea seemed on the verge of finishing the killers' work for them. Pulverized, the boat was taking on water at an alarming degree by the time she reached calmer waters.

Suddenly a spot of land appeared on her right, its rocky shoreline illuminated by shafts of moonlight sneaking through the clouds. Danielle tried to turn for it, but the steering wheel fought her every inch of the way. It took all her strength to manage the task and even then the lifeboat's engine finally gave out a quarter mile from shore, just after she had fired a flare into the night.

With no other choice, Danielle dropped off into the sea in her survival suit and felt strangely warm, her body heat trapped within to keep her from freezing to death. She pulled both emergency cords and the suit inflated with a quick burst of air that left her able to do little but float on her back.

The survival suit could give her ninety minutes in these conditions, and Danielle wondered if she could reach the shore in that time. She managed to flap her arms a bit, paddling to make use of the currents. She landed on the sand of the shoreline with plenty of time to spare but in no condition to celebrate. Her time at sea had left her motions slow and lethargic, her muscles seeming to have lost their elasticity to such a degree that she could hardly walk or raise her arms.

Danielle released the air from her suit and collapsed atop the rocky shore, safe from the waves and still warmed by her space-age suit. Come morning, she would rely on whatever warmth the sun gave up to revive and recharge her.

The first boat came well prior to that, though. Danielle saw its light sweeping across the shore well before she heard its engine above the crashing waves. She sat up and tried to wave her arms, found she couldn't muster the strength. But the crew must have seen her, because they dropped anchor and came ashore in a dinghy.

As soon as she saw the eyes of the two men who had arrived she knew. This was no rescue party that fortuitously had happened to be in the area; these were members of the same assault force that had destroyed the Ulysses GBS just to keep their secret safe.

Danielle had summoned her own executioners to her!

She found enough strength to twist to the side and grab a jagged rock, ready to use it on the first man who reached down for her when a heavy boot clamped down painfully on her wrist. Danielle cried out and tried to thrash free.

She saw another man draw a heavy-caliber pistol from his belt and steady it straight on her.

CHAPTER 62

BEN WAS TOO dazed by fatigue to hand the box over right away. Instead, wordlessly, he tucked it tighter against him, almost as his nephew had in the recording made of the box's discovery.

Baruch had come a little closer to him. "Inspector Kamal, I advise you not to make things any harder than they already are. We know you took the two guards on duty here captive. And you are also suspected of wounding two Israeli soldiers at the settlement of the Amudei Ha'aretz." His voice cracked a little. "Am I to conclude you had some part in the massacre that occurred there as well?"

"How many?" Ben rasped.

"What?"

"How many were killed?"

"I don't know. We found dozens hiding in underground bunkers. Children mostly."

Ben breathed a sigh of relief for that much and looked up, but his voice still sounded as if someone had scraped sandpaper across his vocal cords. "How did you know I had been there?"

"The shirt we found pressed into that soldier's wound had your name inside it."

"Because I tried to save him."

"You are a mass of contradictions, Inspector. I must also assume that you stole the vehicle parked outside an Israeli construction site, and now you have violated a crime scene and removed what may be material evidence."

"Would you like me to put it back?"

"I would like you to give it to me and then I am going to place you under arrest."

Ben could have done many things, responded in many ways, at that point. But he only smiled, not budging.

"Must you make this difficult, Inspector?"

More silence.

Something kept Baruch from approaching any closer. "I will contact your people immediately, do what we can to avoid making this a bigger incident than it is already."

Ben lifted the box to his face, as if to examine it closer. "Do you have any idea what's inside?"

Baruch shook his huge head, looking almost pleased. "You still haven't realized what's really going on here, have you?"

"I know enough. Plenty."

"Not even close."

"What have you done with Danielle?" Ben demanded.

"I don't know what you're talking—"

"Yes, you do. Did you have her killed? If you did, I swear I'll kill you too."

Two other men finally joined Baruch inside the cave, fingers close to the triggers of their Uzi submachine guns.

"Give me the box, Inspector."

Ben looked at the gunmen, then back at Baruch. The scene, him kneeling before them, was almost laughable. He handed the box toward Baruch, who snatched it away before Ben could change his mind.

"I wouldn't open that, if I were you, Commander."

A quick nod from Baruch and his two subordinates were on Ben, each taking an arm and jerking him upward. One of his legs had fallen asleep. He couldn't put any pressure on it and when it buckled, the Israeli on that side kicked him in the shin.

He was still limping when he finally emerged from the darkness of the cave between the two men from Shin Bet where another four armed men waited. Baruch joined them halfway down the steps, prepared no doubt to officially take Ben into custody, when a phalanx of cars poured down the strip that passed for a road in the desert.

Baruch's men tensed, readying their weapons as the approaching headlights caught them. They split into a wider spread, ready to shoot now.

The arriving cars, five of them, separated into a neat row, coming to a halt abreast of each other fifty feet before the Shin Bet agents. Even in the dark, Ben recognized Colonel Nabril al-Asi's Mercedes at the head of the pack. The back door opened and al-Asi stepped out casually, all by himself.

The men from Shin Bet tightened their stances and steadied their weapons, a few sliding bolts back with an audible *click*. Al-Asi looked unfazed. He fastened the button on his double-breasted suit and walked straight into the armed camp alone without hesitation, seeming to ignore everyone but Moshe Baruch.

Only when the colonel reached the foot of the steps of the goat path leading to the cave did he finally look at Ben. Then he ascended leisurely, past gunmen who followed him with their weapons, and stopping just before he reached Commander Baruch

"Good evening, Commander," al-Asi greeted. He slipped a hand casually inside his suit jacket and came out with a tri-folded document. "This is a court order confirming this to be land duly ceded to the Palestinians and instructing you to vacate the premises upon being served."

Baruch's lips curled back like a dog ready to spring. "We do not recognize Palestinian courts."

Al-Asi quite calmly handed him the document. "This was

signed by an Israeli justice." The colonel's gaze came to rest on the box still clutched beneath one of Baruch's beefy arms. "As such, I'm sure you understand that all objects found on or removed from these premises are the property of the Palestinian people. Yes?"

Baruch inspected the order in the spray of the headlights. The pages crumpled in his hand as he finished reading them. He jerked the box out toward al-Asi's chest.

The colonel latched his hands on it just before impact. "Similarly, Commander, I'm sure you understand that, according to the agreement between our governments, seizing a prisoner on our land requires a writ of cooperation or formal approval. I suggest you turn over Inspector Kamal to me until such time that we can work out his disposition."

Baruch nodded and, with a flap of his hand, signaled the men holding Ben to let him go. Baruch drew himself up to his full height and stormed down the goat path, followed closely by the rest of his men.

Al-Asi and Ben watched them go from the steps, the box still held in the colonel's grasp.

"Thank you, Commander," al-Asi called after Baruch. "Let this go down as a high-water mark in the spirit of cooperation between our peoples."

COLONEL AL-ASI HAD returned the box to Ben as soon as they were seated in the backseat of his Mercedes. But he didn't speak again until Moshe Baruch's jeeps had sped past them. Ben noticed he was fiddling with a battery-operated poker game.

"Our casino management company gave me a few of these as gifts for my children," the colonel said, barely looking up from the small screen.

"Must make them very popular in the neighborhood."

"Unfortunately, other children are not keen on playing with mine. We have parties and no one comes. Their parents apparently know who I am. Was it the same for you back in the United States?"

Ben shook his head. "I lived among other cops. The kids used to argue which of us was the toughest."

"I'd cast my vote for you."

Ben tried to smile. "Even my sons didn't."

"I meant right now, Inspector." Al-Asi went back to his video game. "We are thinking of adding these to the Oasis Casino, on a much bigger scale, of course. I thought it best to give one a try before I render an opinion."

"And what do you think?"

"I'm still trying," al-Asi said, waiting for his hand to lock digitally into place. He folded the hand without betting after it came up without even a pair.

"Is that the only gambling you've done tonight?" Ben asked him wryly.

"You are speaking of the court order I obtained signed by an Israeli judge. He's quite a customer at the Oasis, one of the casino's best. A fifty-thousand-shekel marker, all of it used." Al-Asi's stare didn't waver. "I was able to clear the slate."

"You're a remarkable man, Colonel."

Al-Asi gave the electronic game a closer look. "You know initially the Israeli courts forbade their citizens to patronize the Oasis. Gambling is illegal in Israel, after all. They were afraid of being labeled hypocrites until a few judges, like our friend, came to their senses. A good thing, as it turns out. Ironic that the same Israelis who have bulldozed our homes are now losing theirs to us."

"We need to get going."

"Where to, Inspector?"

Ben cradled the ancient wooden box, thinking of Danielle. "I've got a delivery to make."

DAY FIVE

CHAPTER 63

DANIELLE WAS DREAMING of her family. Her father presiding over a Sabbath dinner Friday night, while her mother made trip after trip from the kitchen, seldom sitting down for longer than a minute at a time. She was on one side of the table next to her younger brother Yakov, her older brother Jonathan directly across from them. Both dead now.

In the dream Danielle felt the same peace and security she had known on nights like that. But tonight's dream was even better because two new faces had joined the table. Danielle had a baby in her lap, snuggling against her breast, smelling sweet and soft. And next to her sat Ben Kamal, chatting and smiling with her family in the dream as he never would have been able to in reality. He reached over to stroke his child's head and grinned. Danielle kissed him lightly on the lips, holding as tight as she could to the serenity of that moment as if she knew it would end when the dream did.

Why couldn't things actually be this way? Why couldn't

her family still be alive, ready to accept the man she loved into their lives?

How can I expect them to when I'm not ready to accept him into mine?

She awoke with that thought on her mind, remembering the moment she had lain on the rocky island shoreline fully expecting to die. The gunman looming over her had been ready to fire when two spotlights suddenly blazed onto the scene.

A pair of fishing boats had arrived in clear view of the shore within seconds of each other, alerted by her flare. The fishing boats pulled up on either side of the craft that had anchored first, shining their twin spots on the shore before the trigger could be pulled.

Men shouted out in bullhorns using broken English. Danielle's would-be killers had no choice but to proceed with their apparent rescue. They carried her onboard their boat, and the fishing boats, both having picked up other survivors of the Ulysses, followed the smaller craft to St. John's Harbor in Newfoundland, where the docks were lined with dozens and dozens of media representatives come to cover one of the greatest sea disasters of all time.

Upon carrying Danielle onboard, her captors had drugged her, leaving her too woozy to either escape or call attention to herself. And, much to her dismay, they had kept her drugged ever since. Danielle had only a few moments of lucidity interspersed amid the dreams. Worse, the pleasant security those dreams brought made her reluctant to see them end, the chemical haze they provided infinitely preferable to reality.

But reality was all that could save her now. No one even knew where she was. Her captors were professionals not open to negotiation, even if she were in a position to manage it. She realized she must force herself to concentrate on escape, use strength of will to push the drugs out of her system, or at least negate their effect.

She came awake earlier than they must have expected this morning and found her arms and legs strapped to the bed.

She had just begun trying to work herself free of her bonds when a key rattled in the lock and the door opened.

Danielle closed her eyes, pretending to be unconscious. She recognized the pair of men who entered from the stench of stale sweat mixed with the residue of sea spray. They seldom spoke in her presence, but this morning she heard them exchange a few words while pulling one of the straps binding her arms free.

Italian! They are speaking Italian!

It took all of her will for Danielle to keep her eyes pinned closed, continuing the illusion that the sedatives were still doing their job. Nonetheless, she felt her arm jerked harshly out from the strap and her shirtsleeve peeled back.

In that instant, the last moment before a fresh supply of the drugs would be shot into her vein, Danielle contemplated trying to overcome these two now. She did have one hand free, after all, and the element of surprise lay on her side. Her legs and other arm, though, remained strapped to the bed. Impossible to maneuver enough to overcome any captors, much less ones this professional.

Danielle felt the sharp bite of the needle being jabbed into her forearm, twitching as its contents pumped home to swim with her blood. The world around her turned to pillowy cotton again. Whereas before she hadn't opened her eyes, now she *couldn't*. The sensation was that of floating lazily. Stretch your arms out and swim with the wind.

And the two men were speaking in Italian again.

We must get the boat ready—something like that. *Just one more hour and she will be . . .*

Danielle lost the rest of the words in her mind, lost everything, and drifted away.

CHAPTER 64

IN PREPARATION FOR our landing at Rome's Leonardo da Vinci International . . ."

Ben Kamal listened to the flight attendant's instructions repeated in English, Italian, and Hebrew. He tightened his grasp on the leather satchel he had held in his lap the whole of the flight from Tel Aviv. There had been one stopover in Athens, but Ben had remained on the plane. The delay had been maddening for him, the sixty-minute interval spent wondering if men in dark suits were going to board the plane and spirit him off before anyone noticed. He didn't breathe easily again until they were bound for Rome, and then his gaze remained shifting and furtive, forever scrutinizing all the new passengers who had boarded.

He would have to stow the satchel under the seat in front of him for the landing, but his eyes would never leave it. Inside was the ancient box containing Josephus's scroll that his nephew had first dug up and then reburied in almost the very same spot. The box itself was unremarkable, bled of color and showing signs of decay from its long years beneath the earth. It was cracked in several places and the simple latch had swollen, no longer a neat fit. It felt light and delicate in Ben's hands, prickly with the splinters from the spots where the wood had peeled away.

The papers Colonel al-Asi had provided allowed him to effortlessly negotiate Customs and Immigration and emerge into the warm sun outside Leonardo da Vinci International. There Ben boarded an express bus to Vatican City. He had intended to take a cab, but the sign posted on the bus's front proved too inviting and eliminated any need to wait in the long taxi line.

As it turned out, he had to wait inside the bus instead, though he fortunately had a seat all to himself until just moments before the bus set off. Once again he tucked the satchel atop his lap for safekeeping through the duration of the drive. He noticed a team of young Gypsy pickpockets working the passengers standing in the center of the bus and, since he was clearly a foreigner, feared they might target him. Traffic was congested this time of day, so it took thirty minutes before the bus discharged its passengers at the head of St. Peter's Square, the ceremonial beginning of the Vatican.

But Ben bypassed the lavish square, frequented by thousands of tourists at any time during the day, in favor of the Porta Sant'Anna, an entrance to the nonpublic areas of Vatican City. It was here that the picture Colonel al-Asi had found of Gianni Lorenzo had been taken. A number of Swiss Guardsmen, outfitted in their lavish blue uniforms, stood guard behind a steel-bracketed gate, occasionally posing for a photograph snapped by a tourist from the sidewalk.

Ben slid up to the gate as soon as there was an opening and leaned close to the steel, giving the nearest Swiss Guardsman a slight smile. "Excuse me, I'd like to see the captain commandant of the Swiss Guard," he said innocently, tucking the tote bag close to him, and hoping the man spoke English.

The guardsman shook his head slightly, as if he didn't understand. "Signor?"

"The colonel of the Swiss Guard—Gianni Lorenzo. I'd like to see him."

Now the guardsman returned Ben's smile. "The captain commandant is not available to tourists, signor."

Ben made himself looked surprised. "Oh, I'm not a tourist, I'm an old friend."

"Do you have an appointment?"

Ben nodded. "No, but please tell Colonel Lorenzo that Winston Daws is here to see him."

CHAPTER 65

DANIELLE AWOKE TO the sensation of being at sea again. The sudden jolt of a boat being kicked up to more speed got her stirring.

But not very far.

At first, she thought she couldn't open her eyes. Then she realized her eyes were open, but she couldn't see anything, because there was nothing to see. She was in some kind of box, but a quick run of her hands along its sides told her it was made of a thick durable plastic instead of wood or metal.

Her mind cleared little by little and Danielle continued to feel about the edges of the box, searching for a seam or a break, a place where she could wedge her fingers through and pry it open. She found none. Instead, all she could feel was the boat's thin hull smacking against the waves.

They were taking her back to sea, planning to drop her body among all the others lost when the Ulysses GBS had gone down. What was one more to be identified someday when it finally washed ashore? By the time the fish and parasites got done with her, no one would know the difference.

Danielle fought to clear her mind, consider the predicament with a soldier's cold precision. The fact that this was a small craft meant there could only be a few of the enemy onboard. Their plan would be to throw her over the side after reaching a predetermined point. They would have to open her tomb to do so, of course, and that was when Danielle would strike. If she was lucky, one or more of the men might be occupied when she made her move. If she got really lucky, there would be something within reach she could use as a weapon.

Danielle could feel the small boat riding the sea harder, each thump sending her thrashing about her confines with no way to brace herself. She thought of Ben, of the look on his face when she told him she was pregnant. How happy he seemed, until she had told him of her plans for the baby.

Ben, Danielle said out loud as the boat continued to slam over the waves.

C H A P T E R   6 6

WOULD YOU LIKE me to remain, Colonel?" asked the Swiss Guardsman who had escorted Ben up the stairs to Gianni Lorenzo's elegant office in the Government Palace.

Lorenzo looked from Ben's eyes to the satchel tucked beneath his right arm. "That won't be necessary."

"Of course, sir," the guardsman said and stood rigidly until Ben had closed the door behind him.

"Does he have a tattoo of a cross patee on his arm, Colonel Lorenzo?" Ben asked, unable to disguise the bitterness in his voice.

The captain commandant of the Swiss Guard continued to size him up, then pulled back the sleeves of his robe. "You mean like this, Inspector Kamal?"

"I see I don't have to introduce myself," Ben said, and craned his neck to better see the tattoo. The front of the large, wood-paneled office was dark and he could barely make out the design burned into Gianni Lorenzo's arm. The thinning of his muscles had folded the blunt edges of the cross around his forearm, nearly obscuring them in the wrinkled patches of skin.

"You should be dead now," Lorenzo said.

"I apologize for disrupting your plans."

"The fact that you used the name Winston Daws to gain entry means you must know far more than I had thought."

"I also know about your foray into the Judean Desert fifty-two years ago, Colonel. And I know what you left behind."

Lorenzo tried very hard not to look surprised. "My compliments, Inspector. May I ask how?"

"A boy guided you into the desert. All these years later, he still remembers that day quite clearly."

Lorenzo shook his head regretfully. "I should have killed him then."

"I'm sure you would have, if he hadn't run away. Your mistake was ordering him killed last week. If you hadn't, I probably wouldn't be here right now."

The colonel's eyes fell again on the satchel Ben still clutched to him. "Then it is a good thing I did. He must have led you to what lies inside that bag."

"Neither of you, it seems, can escape the past. But the past is what all this is about, isn't it?"

"Show me what you have in your bag, Inspector."

Ben withdrew the box from his satchel and angled it so Lorenzo could see the name "Flavius Josephus" in Hebrew letters carved into the top. "Why didn't you destroy the scroll after you killed Winston Daws, Colonel?"

Gianni Lorenzo's eyes bulged at the sight of the box, viewing it with an odd mixture of longing and distaste, as he focused on Flavius Josephus's name. "Because I couldn't. I felt it would be . . . a sin."

Ben couldn't believe what he had just heard. "You had just supervised the murder of two dozen innocent people."

"They were no longer innocent, Inspector, not from the time they found that box and opened it."

"Casualties of war—is that what you prefer to call them? Is that how you rationalized it?"

"I'm afraid I did—I still *do*. Casualties of a war that has been raging unchecked for centuries. A war spearheaded by those who would stop at nothing to see the church destroyed." The colonel's eyes never left the wooden box. "You are holding the means to do that in your hands, Inspector, just as Winston Daws did fifty-two years ago."

"You're not giving the church enough credit, Colonel."

"Some of us can't afford to take chances."

"Then I guess I'm lucky to be standing here alive. Puts me in very rare company."

Gianni Lorenzo retreated into the center of the sprawling office, his feet padding onto the thick Oriental carpet. An unseasonable cold snap had kept him from opening the office windows as of late, leaving the room with a musty scent that reeked of age. The stink of the terrible things men had been dispatched from here to do.

"If you know that, Inspector, why have you come to me?"

"To make a trade."

"A trade?"

Ben nodded, slowly. "The contents of this box in exchange for the life of Pakad Danielle Barnea of Israel's National Police force."

"We do not take hostages, Inspector."

Ben followed the leader of the Swiss Guard onto the carpet. "You better hope you did this time, Colonel."

"I believe I was briefed on her, on all the unusual Israeli activity."

"Unusual? A dozen Americans were killed! What did you expect them to do?"

"For archaeologists, not nearly this much."

"No, Colonel. Only two were archaeologists," Ben told him. "The rest were members of a geological survey team."

The colonel kept his mouth from dropping, but his lips quivered and his eyelids began to flutter.

"You didn't know," Ben realized. He found himself surprisingly calm and cool, as if the emotion had been sucked out of him. "Just as you couldn't have known one of those killed was my nephew. That makes you responsible for his death. And I'm going to tell you something else. Danielle

Barnea is pregnant with my child. If anything happens to her
. . . well, I believe the Bible has much to say on such things."

A tremor of fear slid onto Lorenzo's expression. "Have
you come here to kill me, Inspector?"

"I have something far worse planned, if you don't coop-
erate with me. The archaeologists were with the geologists
purely for cover. They weren't supposed to find anything.
I'm sure uncovering this scroll was as big a surprise to them
as it was to you."

"But they must have known what it was they had dug up;
they contacted experts."

Ben regarded Gianni Lorenzo coldly, knowingly. "It was
those experts who contacted you, wasn't it?"

The colonel nodded. "The first links in the chain."

"Well, your chain's unraveling and so is your world." Ben
took a step closer, then another. "But I can help you with
both, Colonel. I can help you erase the mistake that has
haunted you for most of your life." He held the box out
casually. "Destroy the contents of this box and you need
never worry again about anyone finding proof that Christ did
not die on the cross, that the resurrection never happened."

Ben's final statement seemed to inflame Gianni Lorenzo.
He stormed forward and for an instant, just an instant, Ben
recognized the young man who fifty-two years before had
murdered two dozen innocent men. "Let me see that!"

Ben twisted away from Lorenzo and backpedaled. "Not
yet. Not until you tell me about Danielle Barnea."

"All right, all right. We rescued her at sea."

"What?"

"Our people traced Barnea to an oil platform in the Grand
Banks where the Israelis brought her."

"Oil," Ben repeated.

"That's what those American geologists must have been
looking for," the colonel said blankly. "It didn't make sense
before, but now . . ."

"And I think we can safely assume they found this oil,
Colonel. Everyone else believes that's what all this has been

about. They don't know something much more valuable is at stake."

"The scroll!"

"No—Danielle Barnea." Ben found his feelings for her were stronger than ever, in spite of their estrangement, in spite of her intention to raise their child without him. If anything, that made him want and need Danielle all the more. Perhaps this was his way of proving himself to her. "First you arrange for her release," he continued. "First you bring her to me. Then you get the scroll."

A cold hardness settled over Lorenzo's expression. "Look around you, Inspector. For all your cleverness in getting this far, you are hardly in a position to make demands."

"Because you could just have the box taken from me."

The colonel simply nodded.

Ben shrugged and extended the box out in both hands. "Then go ahead. Take it."

Gianni Lorenzo removed it from his grasp almost gracefully, held it at arm's length as he walked toward the edge of the carpet to his desk. He laid the box down atop the polished wood top and worked open the latch, thinking of the other two times he had held it in his hands. Looking up after seeing the inside, his expression was a mix of disappointment and rage.

"It's empty!"

"Of course, it is," Ben said.

"Where is the scroll?"

"Where is Chief Inspector Barnea?"

"You bastard!"

"Such language, Colonel Lorenzo. Isn't that another sin?"

"Where is Josephus's scroll?"

"It's here. Right in Rome. Only you don't get the scroll until I get Danielle Barnea."

The colonel's lips puckered as he seethed, on the verge of exploding. "That is out of my control."

"Too bad. For both of us."

"I could have you tortured, Ben Kamal. You would talk. In the end everyone does."

Ben's expression remained chiseled in ice. "It might take too long to do you any good." He pulled back his sleeve and checked his watch, exaggerating the simple motion. "You have eight hours. If I do not retrieve the box's contents before then, you will never see them. But someone else will: Rabbi Mordecai Lev. Everything's arranged."

Lorenzo tried to stand his ground, but looked suddenly shaky on his feet. His shoulders stooped, at once bony and withered beneath his robes.

"He will be dead before the scroll ever reaches him, Inspector."

"You already missed your chance at Lev—twice."

"What do you mean twice? What are you talking about?"

"You left him alive at Ephesus, Colonel; blind, but alive."

Gianni Lorenzo clutched the back of a nearby chair for support. "A survivor . . ."

"Unfortunately for you, yes."

"And what does this religious fanatic expect to gain?"

"Religion has nothing to do with his desire to expose the truth," Ben continued. "His crusade, his desire for vengeance, is wholly personal. Just as mine is now."

Lorenzo shook his head disbelievingly. "You should know how this man feels about Palestinians, Inspector."

"Just as you should know how I feel about Danielle Barnea."

"I could make sure you never leave the Vatican alive," Lorenzo threatened, not very convincingly.

"Then I suppose some of your Knights Templars have returned from their latest killing spree in Israel. How many more innocent people have to die, Colonel?"

Lorenzo gave him a long look. "You are not innocent at all, Inspector."

"Kill me and Rabbi Lev will receive the manuscript before tomorrow is out, ammunition much more powerful in his hands than anything you can wield. He has nothing to lose, Colonel. You know what he'll do with it." Ben paused to let his point sink in. "It's up to you, and I suggest you make your decision fast. Otherwise, His Holiness will have a lot of explaining to do."

DANIELLE WAS AS ready as she could be when she heard footsteps, followed by voices, in the cabin. She had been ready since the boat had slowed to a stop and the engine died out. The voices were muffled, muted by her confines. But she felt two of her captors hoist her tomb off the floor and tote the box forward, then up two steps. They set it down again on what must have been the deck beyond and she readied herself to spring as soon as the lid came free.

Danielle flexed her fingers, pushing the blood and strength back into them. She fought to empty her mind, let instinct take over once the lid came free and they reached in for her.

Danielle felt hands rustling against the outside of her tomb. She tensed in nervous expectation, her heart thudding loud enough for her captors to hear and give her away, she was sure.

Then, suddenly, the container was heaved upward, jolting her. The angle changed on a sharp tilt that cracked her head against the top and compressed her lower body toward the bottom.

My captors aren't going to remove me from it! They are throwing the container into the water with me inside!

Danielle felt a thump as her tomb hit the gunwale and held there only long enough for her captors to give it one final thrust.

She was airborne, plunging downward headfirst. The container smacked the water's surface and bobbed briefly before it began to sink.

BEN WATCHED AS Gianni Lorenzo hung up the phone slowly. "I have done everything I can."

"You better hope it was enough, Colonel."

"It will be some time before I hear."

Ben made sure Lorenzo could see him check his watch

again. "You have just over seven hours and fifty-five minutes."

"And if I cannot have Danielle Barnea here by that time . . ."

"Then you will never again see the contents of that box you want so desperately."

"You are a Christian, are you not, Inspector?"

"A Christian who would like nothing more than to expose you and your private army for the wholesale, senseless murders of dozens."

Lorenzo didn't look regretful. "It was done for the sake of preserving the church. I'm sorry you disapprove of my actions."

"I wasn't speaking of just you personally, Colonel, I was talking about the entire doctrine you represent. If your faith is based on a lie, then your followers have a right to know that."

"And you are the man to tell them."

"If it's the truth, why not?"

Gianni Lorenzo gave Ben his longest look yet. "Spoken as if you're seeking vengeance as much as Mordecai Lev."

"You killed my nephew, Colonel."

Lorenzo did his best to look confident, but his eyes blinked rapidly and his breathing had picked up. "And how do I know you really even have the contents of this box to exchange for your Israeli friend?"

"Because I swear I've got them," Ben said. "I swear to God."

CHAPTER 67

BEN CHOSE ROME'S Villa Borghese for their meeting, to take place at nine o'clock that evening. Occupying over six square miles north of the famed Spanish Steps and Via Veneto, the Villa Borghese is made up of cool shady paths, formal gardens, scenic terraces, and numerous fountains and statues that serve as a welcome respite from the noise and bustle of the city beyond. For Ben, those same features would make for excellent cover and hiding on the chance that things went poorly tonight.

He had not yet considered an escape route. He had not even considered what he would do if Colonel Gianni Lorenzo could not produce Danielle Barnea. If she was not in the park tonight, he knew he would never see her again, or the child she was carrying inside her ever, and those were thoughts he chose not to bear.

Lorenzo tried to have him followed from the Vatican. But the swirls of people cluttering the sidewalks and the endless traffic cramming the streets made losing them easy. Beyond that, all those the colonel dispatched were dressed in uniform and none, Ben guessed, were members of the elite Knights Templars.

Lorenzo obviously had more important work for them elsewhere.

Still, Ben waited until dark before returning to Leonardo da Vinci Airport. There, in a square trash receptacle disguised as a planter, he had tossed the contents of the box after placing them in a tightly wrapped, weather-sealed bag. The time limit he had given Lorenzo was based on the knowledge of when those receptacles were emptied every day. Of course there was no copy ready to be sent to Mordecai Lev. But Lorenzo didn't know that and couldn't take the risk that the manuscript might fall into the old rabbi's hands.

Ben had chosen a busy time at which to return to the airport. Busy enough that no one would notice a man picking through a trash can. Ben simply lifted off the squared lid with the planter top and rested it on the floor. Then he dipped his hands into the middle of soda cans, candy wrappers, half-eaten sandwiches, and stray magazines and worked them about in search of the tightly wrapped package he had stowed deep inside.

He found it after only a few seconds of probing. It was sticky and wet, but thanks to his wrapping job, the contents would be untouched and perfectly preserved. He tucked the package into the small tote he had purchased upon entering the airport, returned the lid to its place carefully, and took a taxi back to the city.

BEN WAITED BEFORE entering the park at eight o'clock. It had officially closed at dusk nearly two hours before, meaning anyone entering would at once stand out.

He watched from the shadows across the street, wondering if someone was already inside the park waiting for him to appear as well. He knew he was at his most vulnerable from this moment on because all Lorenzo's men had to do would be kill him and take his tote bag. That would render the exchange superfluous, sealing Danielle's fate as well.

If she was still alive.

Ben wasn't sure what he was waiting for until a gang of unruly teenagers approached the park entrance. One smashed a bottle on the sidewalk. Two others stopped to light cigarettes. Ben heard laughter and swearing. The boys, easily a dozen in their late teens, swaggered more than walked as they turned into the park. He watched a straggler guzzle the remainder of his beer and smash his bottle as well.

From that point, Ben didn't hesitate. He turned his collar up and emerged from his hiding place as if these boys had been exactly what he was waiting for. He raised an empty hand to his lips and whispered into it, pretending to have a radio or walkie-talkie at the ready. Anyone watching in the dark would assume he was just a cop doing his job. The tote bag would have betrayed his disguise, so before walking across the street he discarded it and stuck the package, still sticky with dried soda, under his tucked-in shirt. Then he zipped up his jacket to hold it firmly in place.

Ben entered the park, pretending to follow the gang of teenagers through the umbrella pines growing along the paths that sliced through the gardens. During the day these trees would provide great shade for strollers and joggers. At night, they had the opposite effect of obscuring the already-thin light emanating from sporadically placed ground lanterns.

Ben stayed on the boisterous trail the kids left behind long enough to figure that anyone watching would have already dismissed his presence. He then broke off and headed southwest toward the Pincio and the Moses Fountain located at the bottom of a hill layered with lush, colorful foliage.

He kept himself to the shadows as he drew closer, waiting for any sign of the enemy's presence. Feeling a bit more secure but still wary, Ben decided to hide behind a pair of flowering trees until there was reason to show himself. If Gianni Lorenzo appeared without Danielle, Ben would know all bets were off and that his plan had failed.

With twenty minutes still left before nine o'clock, Ben heard the faint shuffle of footsteps approaching and watched a pair of young men pass by him. They were holding hands, lovers apparently out for a nighttime stroll. Except that their eyes were everywhere but on each other, no matter how much they tried to hide it. This must be Gianni Lorenzo's advance team, or part of it anyway.

The two young men sat down on the edge of the fountain adorned with a statue portraying Moses as a baby wrapped in a granite basket. They kissed lightly, then rose and walked off into the cover of trees and denser brush.

Somewhere in the distance, a clock struck nine and more footsteps clacked atop the walkway. Ben clung to the darkness and held his breath as a single man stopped in front of his hiding place. The man continued on again almost immediately and another set of footsteps followed his. Ben recognized Gianno Lorenzo, accompanied by a smaller figure walking by his side. A figure Ben thought first was a man from the clothes, then realized was a woman an instant before the light caught her face:

Danielle Barnea.

CHAPTER 68

HOURS BEFORE AND half a world away, Danielle's tomb had begun to fill with the frigid water of the Grand Banks when she felt it jerked suddenly upward. The flow of water slowed but the angle tipped her head downward to where the bulk of it had settled. She could feel the tomb swaying and fought to steal what breath she could.

Finally the container was righted and plucked from the water to be hoisted upward in a maddening series of stops and starts.

What is going on? Have my captors suddenly changed their minds about killing me?

Back on the deck, they cut the lid open but Danielle was in no condition to mount the resistance she had considered. Most of her body was still immersed and the frigid temperatures of the Grand Bank seas had numbed her to the point of near exhaustion.

A pair of men, quickly joined by a third, spoke rapidly in Italian, clearly relieved she was still alive. She was yanked from the water and taken below, where her icy clothes were stripped off and replaced by blankets and towels. She realized in all the excitement they had forgotten to bind her hands, but the blood still felt like thick mud in her veins, and the desperate immediacy of escape had passed because, clearly, something had changed. Despite the many blankets wrapped around her, she continued to shake uncontrollably.

They motored fast back toward shore. Danielle at first lacked the strength to dress herself in the ill-fitting clothes the men gave her. She managed to pull them on finally just before the boat docked. The pants sagged on her hips and the shirt was like a tent, material swimming all around her. She used a damp blanket as a coat and was all too happy to disembark into the waiting company of two well-dressed men whose suit coats could not disguise their powerful builds.

One of them explained in decent enough English that she was being returned home, that a ransom for her was being paid.

What ransom? And *who* was paying it?

They did not drug her during the flight by private jet; they didn't have to. Exhaustion and the lingering effects of the icy water had her asleep before the private jet was even off the ground. Danielle didn't awaken again until the wheels smacked the runway, half expecting to look out the window and see Tel Aviv.

Instead she saw Rome's Leonardo da Vinci Airport and felt more confused than ever. Four more men waiting on the tarmac brought her to a car and drove straight for what she recognized as the Villa Borghese.

They escorted her into the park where she was met by another man wearing an ill-fitting military uniform. He was tall and gaunt, with a sharp angular face, and the others treated him with extreme reverence.

"Welcome to Rome, Chief Inspector Barnea," he greeted, taking her by the arm. "I am Gianni Lorenzo. Come, we must hurry. . . ."

She did not resist and a few short minutes later, they entered a large clearing and stopped in front of a lavish fountain. Danielle felt Gianni Lorenzo's grasp tighten on her arm as they turned back toward the path.

"Inspector Kamal? You can come out now, Inspector Kamal."

And Danielle watched as Ben emerged from behind a nesting of trees. She knew instantly he was the reason she was still alive. She should have felt happy, joyous, but a wave of guilt washed over her instead.

Somehow Ben had arranged her release. Ben Kamal, the man she was willing to forsake to preserve her good name and heritage once her baby was born. Danielle looked into his eyes again and saw the relentless resolve, like nothing she had ever seen in them before. Knew he was fighting to save something she had decided to deny him.

The three men who had accompanied Gianni Lorenzo into the park closed ranks around him. Danielle felt him slide slightly behind her and grab hold of her other arm as well.

"Let's get down to business," said Lorenzo, "shall we?"

CHAPTER 69

GOOD EVENING, COLONEL," Ben greeted.

He realized Gianni Lorenzo was wearing a black uniform with enough medals hanging from his left lapel to strain his frame. From the way the pants hung too low and the jacket sagged on him, Ben guessed it was the colonel's old military uniform. Perhaps the very one he had worn when he was sent to train as a member of the Knights Templars on the Swiss Guard's behalf. He was lost in the thick material that had covered his once-powerful frame. He was a skeletal shape in a walking coffin, and Danielle braced before him.

Ben could no longer see the male "lovers" and knew he had to proceed now without a lock on their positions. That posed extremely precarious prospects, but he had no choice at this point, and the good thing was they increased the enemy's number by only two, a total of six when added to the three Swiss Guardsmen who had accompanied Lorenzo and Danielle into the park.

Ben kept his hands in view as he approached Gianni Lorenzo through the spill of the night lanterns. He tried to hold his eyes on the colonel, but they kept straying to Danielle. She looked pale and weak, otherwise okay.

"As you can see, Ben Kamal," the captain commandant of the Swiss Guard said when Ben stopped ten feet from him, "I have fulfilled my part of the bargain." Here, he eased Danielle slightly away from him. "Chief Inspector Barnea is alive, well, and before you. Now, where are the contents of the box you gave me earlier today? Live up to your end of the bargain and hand over Josephus's scroll."

Ben slowly reached under his shirt to extract the well-wrapped bag that had spent the day in the airport trash can.

"Take it from him," the colonel ordered one of his guardsmen.

"Interesting choice of clothing," Ben noted.

"I thought it was fitting."

The guardsman removed the bag from Ben's outstretched hand and started back toward Lorenzo.

"Now, release Inspector Barnea," Ben demanded.

Lorenzo let Danielle go and took the bag from the guardsman. He crouched to inspect the contents of the box he had buried in the Judean Desert fifty-two years before, his hands trembling so much he could barely hold it.

Danielle rushed to Ben. He lunged the last step to meet her and took her in his arms, holding her there briefly before easing her slightly behind him. She was icy cold. He could feel her trembling.

"One of you, bring me a flashlight!" Lorenzo ordered his men.

Another guard approached and held the beam over the colonel's shoulder. Gianni Lorenzo cradled the padded envelope and used his liver-spotted hands to tear away its seal. From it he removed the same animal skin the scroll had been rewrapped in a half century before. Then he peeled away the skin's folds, angling the contents to catch the spray cast by the flashlight.

The colonel's eyes bulged. He looked up from the ground toward Ben, fury brewing in his eyes.

"What is the meaning of this?"

He stormed forward and stopped three feet from Ben and Danielle, then emptied the contents of the dried animal skin onto the concrete.

Dust and tattered refuse emerged, filling the cracks in the concrete. A pair of faded, decaying wooden rods that had once supported the parchment on either side of the scroll dropped out last, clattering at Lorenzo's feet.

"Where is the contents of the box? Where is the lost scroll?"

"That's it," Ben said. "Nothing has been touched."

"What?"

"You just dumped out the lost work of Josephus, Colonel. Exactly as I found it yesterday in the cave where you buried it."

The colonel sank to his knees and began spooning his hands through the thick dust and minuscule fragments of what had been the parchment scroll he had seen only once before.

"What have you done?" he asked, not looking up.

"Not me, Colonel, you. When you returned the scroll to its skin, you must not have closed the ties tightly enough. You let the air of the Judean get to it and after fifty years . . ."

Gianni Lorenzo lurched awkwardly back to his feet, stumbling a little. "Liar! Where is it? I'm warning you, speak now!"

Ben sidestepped to shield Danielle. His eyes met hers briefly, enough to pass an unspoken message.

When I move, move with me.

There were only three men in sight besides Lorenzo, plus the unseen male lovers, giving them a better chance than they had a right to expect. With only six to best, and the dark working for them, Ben felt they could pull it off. The problem was Danielle's condition. The way she looked, Ben doubted she was capable of the quick escape required. And there was a *third* life to consider here, that of their baby.

"My nephew might have suspected what he had found from legend, Colonel," Ben said finally, "but he never could have proved it. So his murder, all the murders, were pointless. And now it's over," he continued, a trace of honest regret creeping into his voice. "You and your faith have nothing to worry about anymore. The evidence that could have destroyed you was destroyed itself. It's finished."

Lorenzo straightened. "Unfortunate. I was hoping to finish this for good tonight. Now the best I can hope for is to eliminate the two remaining witnesses to the truth."

Ben didn't react. "When are you going to let it end, Colonel? Don't you get it? Your Knights Templars aren't needed anymore. No more senseless massacres to hide the truth. No more worrying about something you neglected to destroy a half century ago."

"That may be so," Gianno Lorenzo said. "But still . . ."

He finished his remark in a shrug that Ben interpreted as some kind of signal. He had looked toward Danielle to give her his own sign when the nearby brush ruffled and footsteps sounded against the pavement.

The gang of street toughs Ben had followed into the park emerged from all angles, surrounding them.

I've played right into Lorenzo's hands, goddamnit!

Up close, Ben could see they weren't teenagers at all; just men made up to look like them, so no one would notice such a large group entering the park. Lorenzo had been one step ahead of him all along!

The captain commandant of the Swiss Guard was smiling when Ben returned his eyes to him.

"Let us go, Colonel."

"I can't do that. I'm sorry."

"At least the woman, then. I gave you what you want. It's over. We can't hurt you. Nobody can."

Lorenzo didn't look at all remorseful. "I'm afraid we can't take that chance. I swore an oath half a century ago to protect and preserve our faith at all costs. Eliminating you is a small one, Inspector. I am merely—"

Pop . . .

Ben heard the sound at the same time the figure next to Lorenzo twisted into the old man, collapsing. The colonel lost his balance under the strain and fell beneath the body, his hands coming up coated in something dark and wet.

"Blood," he mouthed, dumbfounded.

With the sound of a second pop, another figure snapped upright, a huge cavity in his chest briefly visible before darkness closed it and the figure crumbled. At the third muffled shot, Ben crashed into Danielle and took her hard to the pavement. Even pinned beneath him, he could feel how slow and lethargic whatever she'd been through had made her.

"What's going on?" she managed.

More shots sounded and the third and fourth bodies fell almost simultaneously as the rest of Lorenzo's men whipped out their weapons and swung desperately about.

"It's a sniper," Ben said, perplexed by the identity of their savior as he gazed up into the darkness of the Pincio, the original hill of gardens.

Sure enough, the next time he heard the popping sound, a brief flash accompanied it. Whoever was up there was damn good, using a semiautomatic scoped rifle instead of the often still preferred bolt action, based on the rapid succession of shots.

The colonel's soldiers had recovered enough from their shock to see the last muzzle flash as well, turning in unison, it seemed, toward the Pincio. Three more of the guards dressed as street toughs went down in rapid succession before the rest mounted a crazed charge up the hill. If nothing else, this allowed two of the guardsmen who had accompanied the colonel to the park to drag him out from beneath the first fallen body and lead him to safety.

"Come on," Ben said, yanking Danielle to her feet with him.

"No!" Lorenzo screamed to the men enclosing him protectively. "Stop them! They'll get away!"

The guardsmen held their ground and turned toward Ben and Danielle. Before they could move, though, another shot rang out in the night and the head of one of the Swiss Guardsmen exploded, showering blood and brains all over the colonel. He spun one way, then the other, before a host of his men took him down to the pavement and covered him once more.

"Now!" Ben implored.

"We'll be shot!"

"If he wanted us, we'd be dead already."

"Then—"

Ben didn't give Danielle a chance to finish her thought. He latched on to her arm and drew her away with him. She lumbered more than ran, every step heavy and thick, still stuck in the wrong gear as if the proper wires had been disconnected.

"Faster!" he ordered, and she did her best.

Screams had replaced the silenced shots they were too far away to hear now. Ben had known a few snipers in his time, back in his days with the Detroit police. Enough to understand they were a breed unto themselves, literally one in a million for the reflexes, instincts, eyesight, and plain resolve it took to do their job. He remembered witnessing one put a bullet through the eye of a drug addict who'd taken hostages in a school. The addict had emerged from the building with a kid clutched in either arm, holding them in front of him. The shooter had maybe an inch to spare on either side and had still taken the shot, nailing it dead solid perfect. Whoever was on the hill must be at least that good, probably better, since the role he had given himself here required multiple shots, mere microseconds spent retargeting before pressing the trigger again.

"Who was it back there?" Danielle rasped when he at last let them stop. She dropped her hands to her knees to catch her breath. "Who saved us?"

"I don't know," Ben said. "I don't know." He held her by the shoulders. "But he won't get them all. We've got to get out of here."

CHAPTER 70

BEN AND DANIELLE rushed through the park, sometimes mistaking the rattle of branches shifting in the wind for the rush of footsteps toward them. There were no sounds of pursuit, no other noise at all. Behind them, even the shrill sound of screams had passed, evidence the sniper had either completed his work or been killed himself.

Danielle felt herself coming back to life during their dash, her mind clearing. She concentrated on moving as fast as she could, struggling against the fatigue that threatened to overcome her.

Ben led the way through a nest of buildings housing various museums, circling round the Giardino del Lago, or Garden of the Lake. The water bounced the reflection of the moon and lantern light off its surface, making the night seem much brighter here. They came to a thick line of trees, and Ben yanked Danielle off the path into their covering darkness.

"What's wrong?" she whispered.

"I don't know. I think I heard something. I can't be sure.

But we've got to get out of here—I know that much. Hurry, this way!"

The gates to the park's zoo, Giardino Zoologico, were closed but not locked. Ben led the way in, making sure to relatch the gates from the inside.

The earthy scents of the many animals and pungent stench of manure hung in the air. The night gave up reflective signs pointing the way toward the antelope, wolves, giraffes, tigers, and elephants. Some of the animals were stirring in their enclosures, making noises that were fine for Ben and Danielle, since it would help mask any sound they made in the course of their escape.

"This has got to lead to a road on the other side of the park," Danielle said softly.

"And an exit."

They continued on, leery of every shadow and sound. But Ben felt free, almost weightless. They were back together again, with only each other to depend upon. For these moments anyway, the world that had come between them didn't matter. The decision Danielle had made didn't matter, although every time Ben thought of that, he let himself hope she would change her mind.

What else do I have to do to prove myself?

Was that why he had come to the Vatican? Did he fear more for his unborn child than Danielle when he learned of her fate? Ben could no longer make the distinction.

They were well past the lions' den when he heard a few of the big cats growl, a deep rumble coming from the back of their throats, ominous enough to freeze time. Ben gazed back briefly.

"They're coming," he whispered to Danielle, sweeping the scene again with his eyes, following the sounds of traffic. "There's a street directly before us, just on the right. A ten-foot fence, no gate."

"We can make it," Danielle assured him.

"Topped with barbed wire."

"Take your jacket off," she advised, already removing hers. "Cover your hands with it."

Reaching the fence meant risking a dash to it in a flat open space, no matter which route they chose. The shortest cut directly between a pair of night-lights placed atop buildings, and that was the one they opted for.

Ben and Danielle ran from the darkness into the light, springing onto the fence with their jackets ready to save their hands from the barbed wire. The gunshots started as they reached the top and spilled over, grasping the wire with their covered hands. Ben felt the sharp prods dig through the fabric and tear into his palm. He yanked his grasp off and went flying, sprawling to the ground with a sickening thud, his breath pouring from him.

Danielle dropped down next to him. "Are you shot?"

"Just cut," Ben gasped.

Fresh gunfire burst from inside the zoo, figures darting forward as they fired.

"We've got to move!" Danielle wailed, helping Ben reach the main road, where he fought to get his breath back, doubled over with his hands on his knees.

They could hear heavy feet clanging off the fence, coming fast in their wake. Ben had just eased himself from Danielle's grasp, both of them searching futilely about for their next move, when a dark car screeched to a halt on a diagonal before them.

"Get in!" ordered a voice from behind the wheel, a voice that was somehow familiar to Ben. "Quickly if you want to live!"

A bullet slammed into the car's quarter panel. Another shattered its rear window. Ben pulled Danielle with him into the backseat, slammed the door hard.

"Stay low!" the driver ordered. "And keep your heads down!"

The voice grew more familiar to Ben with each word. But only when the driver swung to check on them, and Ben got his first clear look at the man's face, especially a birthmark marring his left eyebrow, did he remember where from:

This is the man who a week ago saved me from the Israeli

soldiers on Mordecai Lev's behalf! He is a member of the Pillars of the Land!

The Israeli screeched around a corner.

Ben saw the long black rifle with infrared scope affixed to its bore propped on the front seat next to him. "You were the one shooting in there!"

"Yes, I was. I followed you here on Rabbi Lev's orders."

"Lev?"

"He still wants the lost scroll, Inspector, the story that cost him his eyes."

"It's gone," Ben said as he clutched Danielle's hand, afraid to let go lest she slip away from him again. "Reduced to dust."

"Not entirely," the big man said confidently.

"What do you mean?"

The man weaved his way through a traffic-snarled street, nearly colliding with a dozen vehicles before he sped through an intersection just as the light turned red. Certain that they weren't being followed, he slowed the car and looked back at Ben.

"Winston Daws took pictures, Inspector. Somewhere there is still a record of everything."

DAY SIX

CHAPTER 71

HOW NICE TO hear your voice, Inspector," Colonel al-Asi greeted when Ben reached him on the cell phone al-Asi had provided prior to his departure for Rome.

Lev's sniper continued to drive on through the night as Ben spoke, ever aware of the view in the rearview mirror. He introduced himself as Asher Katz. He had dark skin and the kind of hard glare to his eyes that Ben had come to know all too well. Katz kept his hair short, but it had turned tangled and knotty from the sniper's mask he must have worn while perched on the hillside back in the Villa Borghese. Hair grew wild from his ears and nose as well, and his eyebrows were thick and curly, except for the fleshy streak through the left one Ben recalled from their previous meeting in Israel.

"You sound tired, Colonel," Ben continued. His hands continued to ache from the antiseptic stored in a small first-aid kit Katz had provided. Ben had done his best to apply gauze bandages, but they wouldn't stay on. "I'm sorry I woke you."

"You didn't; I'm at the casino. The Israelis are complaining that the roulette wheel is rigged. So far everything seems to be in order. Do you have a favorite number?"

"Why?"

"Never mind, Inspector."

"Have you learned anything else about Winston Daws? Some kind of report listing his personal effects catalogued on the scene in Ephesus, maybe, or any records of correspondence?"

"Of course I have. But tell me first how is Chief Inspector Barnea?"

Ben looked across the seat. "Right here beside me."

"Truly wonderful news. Once I found out . . . In any case, may I conclude that congratulations are in order? What is it the Jews say? *Mazel tov!*"

"Thank you, Colonel," Ben said, feeling the familiar clog in his throat.

"I told you about my children," al-Asi continued. "After the last birthday party when no one showed up, I changed their names so they don't become targets and can have friends. I hardly ever see them anymore. It is a terrible thing when we must live that way."

"Yes, it is."

"It was the Israelis who caught on to a Hamas plot against my youngest boys. They'd be dead now otherwise. Good people to work with, the Israelis. Very reliable and responsible, but also very stubborn. I keep that in mind in all my dealings with them. You would be well advised to do the same thing," al-Asi added.

"I've learned that much, believe me. What about Winston Daws, Colonel?"

"Let's start with the inventory recovered from the site of the murders in Ephesus. What is it you were specifically interested in, Inspector?"

Ben recalled the camera dangling from Winston Daws's neck in the picture, along now with Mordecai Lev's recollection of the shots Daws had taken prior to the massacre. "A camera."

"Hold on a minute, I have the list right in my pocket. The

Turkish police were not very helpful, but you were right about Britain conducting their own investigation. . . . Here it is. A camera, you said."

"Yes."

"Unfortunately," said al-Asi, "no camera was found among Daws's personal effects either. I'm not surprised. Gianni Lorenzo is nothing if not thorough."

"But Winston Daws could still have taken pictures of the scroll he uncovered and sent them away before he was murdered. Which brings me to the correspondence coming in and out of the camp. . . ."

"The British must have come to the same conclusion, Inspector: they found that a mail shipment did go out between the time Daws made his discovery and the time his team was murdered. None of the addresses were logged anywhere, so that turned out to be a dead end."

"Phone calls," Ben said, feeling his hope slipping away.

He could almost see al-Asi nodding on the other end. "The British were able to trace several made by Daws prior to the start of his final expedition, and a few during it. But none of those he spoke with reported receiving any pictures."

Ben knew it was gone now, any hope, just wanted to be home. "More dead ends."

"Not quite, Inspector. You see, the British authorities were only interested in following up calls going to Britain. I, though, was able to learn that Daws had a sister in the United States. Outside of Boston, actually."

Ben felt his hope slip back in, rejuvenated. "Brilliant, Colonel. How?"

"I read a copy of Daws's obituary. That's all."

THE SISTER'S NAME was Florence," al-Asi continued. "I was able to trace phone calls made by Daws to a number in Lexington, Massachusetts. The number has been disconnected. All I have is an address."

"Good enough."

Al-Asi hesitated on the other end of the line. "It's been over fifty years, Inspector. She couldn't possibly still live there."

"But it's a start, Colonel. And that's all we've got."

CHAPTER 72

"You don't have to come with me, you know," Ben said to Danielle. Katz had stopped the car to make contact with someone close to Mordecai Lev, leaving them alone in the backseat. "Katz is going back to Israel. You can go home with him."

"And why do you have to go to America?"

"To find Daws's pictures, if they still exist. You know that. This is my fight now."

"What makes it *your* fight?"

"Lorenzo and his private army of Knights Templars killed my nephew. I don't know if I can ever expose them, but with those pictures I can expose the truth they're trying so desperately to protect."

Danielle waited for a moment before responding. "So who are you really trying to hurt?"

"I just told you."

"No, you didn't. These pictures could change the way people think about religion, the way they think about God."

"The world has a right to hear the truth. Let everyone

make up their own minds, be their own judge, instead of being suckered and played for a fool."

Danielle remained silent for a moment before responding. "It's not the church you're trying to punish, Ben: it's me. By getting yourself hurt or killed and leaving me the blame if I leave you alone."

"This has nothing to do with you, Pakad."

"It has *everything* to do with me!"

"Because of the oil?"

"It's what your nephew really died for. Billions and billions of barrels of it. One of the greatest strikes in modern history."

"Which Israel wanted to keep secret from the Palestinians, of course," Ben said bitterly.

Danielle nodded. "A job given to Moshe Baruch, who had me taken to that oil platform where I almost died."

"You'll find Baruch in Israel, Pakad, not where I'm going."

"That's the point! You said so yourself: the Amudei Ha' aretz were watching the Americans all along. That means Lev and Baruch must be in this together. And it also means Lev knew all along what those Americans were really doing in the Judean."

"Why would Mordecai Lev care about oil being found in the West Bank?"

"Whatever the reason, he and Baruch can't afford to have its existence made public. You wanted to know why I have to go to the United States with you? Because we both know about the oil and I'm in as much danger as you are." She hesitated. "That means the baby is too."

"Are you including me in a discussion about his welfare, Pakad?"

"If he's going to live, if *we're* going to live, it's because of whatever's waiting for us in America. Baruch and Lev can't afford to let either of us come back with the truth, and neither of us can make it back alone." Danielle's voice became softer, almost pleading. "The only way we can beat them is together."

Katz climbed into the car and closed the door behind him. "Are the two of you ready?"

THE SUBURB OF Lexington, Massachusetts, was located thirty minutes from Boston's Logan Airport. Ben and Danielle's flight arrived on schedule early Saturday afternoon. Exhausted, they both slept soundly during the entire trip. Colonel al-Asi had arranged a rental car for them which was waiting in the special Hertz Number-one covered area of the lot.

Lexington, Massachusetts, maintained a rustic, colonial feel that was true to its roots. The main road leading through the town was lined by old houses in comfortable yards with low fences people could talk to each other over. The commercial center was laid out around an old-fashioned common where parking remained hardly a dollar for the whole day. The promenadelike rows of shops and stores were finished in painted wood or brick facades. If it wasn't for the cars and the fancy equipment in stores like Starbucks, it could have been a hundred years ago here.

They had to stop and ask on three separate occasions for directions to the address Colonel al-Asi had provided for Florence Daws, finally realizing why they couldn't find it: it didn't exist anymore. The building that had once occupied that address and several others had been razed decades earlier to make room for the expansion of the commercial district. The Town Hall was closed on Saturdays and no one in any of the stores currently occupying the land knew anything of what had become of the building that used to be here.

Ben and Danielle split up to better canvas the area. They agreed to meet in an hour's time in a Starbucks that to Danielle looked identical to the Starbucks that had recently opened in Tel Aviv. The second shop on Ben's list was a Waldenbooks tucked into the center of a tight nest of shops. When none of the employees could provide information about the building that had once occupied the nearby square, he turned his attention to finding a local history book that might. He was repeating his request to a young clerk chewing a huge wad of gum when a woman in the next aisle overheard him.

"You're talking about the Monsignor Alley School," she said, peeking over the top shelf.

"School?"

The woman nodded. She looked to be in her early fifties, wore thin glasses and an inviting smile. "A sad day for many of us when they razed it in '72. Still, enrollment was down and the church couldn't afford to keep it open. The alumni got together to try to save it, but we—"

"We," Ben interrupted. "You attended the school."

The woman nodded again. "Grades one through six, a thousand years ago."

"Ever come across a woman named Florence Daws?"

She laughed. "I should say so. She taught grades four and five, as tough as they came. We all loved the way she talked. The boys made fun of it."

"Her British accent."

"That's right. We had trouble understanding her at first."

"You didn't keep in touch with her by any chance, did you?"

"No," the woman said, somewhat sadly. "We lost track of a lot of people after the school closed. That was three years before the town bought the property. But Florence Daws shouldn't be too hard to find, I'd expect, if she's still alive. Just ask at the church."

"Church?"

"The First Parish," the woman acknowledged, smiling reflectively. "It's just down the street. She was the assistant pastor there."

CHAPTER 73

At THE FIRST Parish Church, a rough stone building with the look of an ancient castle, a young paster remembered meeting Florence Daws only once. So far as he knew she had taken up permanent residence at Mountain-view, a rest home located well west of Lexington amid the Berkshire Mountains. He believed she was still alive.

It was a long but pleasant drive to the Berkshires down the Massachusetts Turnpike just over the border into New York State. Danielle and Ben stopped in town and asked for directions, after which they quickly found the rest home by following the signs for the Tanglewood music community. A long gravel road led to a circular driveway adjacent to a small lot designated for nonresidents. The home's grounds were full of flowers and trees, the lawns beautifully mani-cured. The air smelled of lilacs and fresh-cut grass.

It was so quiet Ben was afraid to speak above a whisper. Danielle had suggested he proceed alone at this point. Too many strangers might startle the old woman—Ben had already concluded that Florence Daws might well be over ninety by now.

A woman sat behind a reception desk just inside the entrance, and Ben noticed the walls were all outfitted with handrails.

"May I help you?"

"I wonder if I might be able to see Florence Daws."

The receptionist looked at him suspiciously. "You're not a relative."

"No."

"A friend?"

"Ex-student," Ben said, smiling. "I won't say friend, based on the grades she gave me."

"Your name?"

"Ben Kamal."

The wariness slipped from the receptionist's expression, replaced by a smile. "Let me buzz the floor and see if she's able. If you'd like to sit down for just a moment . . ."

Ben took a seat in a small reception area and paged absently through a magazine, while the woman spoke into the phone.

"Mr. Kamal," she called when finished.

Ben rose from his seat and approached the desk again.

"You can take the elevator to the fourth floor. Someone at the desk there will be able to help you."

UPSTAIRS, BEN WAS ushered to the last room on the right-hand side of the hall. The door was open and the sweet scent of just sprayed air freshener, a flowery scent, drifted into the hall.

"Pastor Florence?" the duty nurse said from the doorway. "Your visitor is here."

The nurse smiled as Ben slipped past her. The flowery air freshener might have made a dent in the room's staleness but couldn't disguise all of it. Pastor Florence Daws sat in a wheelchair by the window, which was closed in spite of the radiant day beyond. A pink shawl was wrapped around her shoulders, revealing gray hair combed to thinly cover a number of bald patches.

"I never had a student named Ben Kamal," Florence Daws said in a surprisingly strong voice, not turning from the window.

"I lied downstairs."

"What's the truth?"

"I'm here about your brother."

She looked at him for the first time. One of her eyes was coated with a milky paste, the other sharp and dark blue. Her skin had the fragile texture of thin wrinkled paper. "You're not old enough to have been a student of his either, so don't bother lying upstairs too. How old are you?"

"Forty."

The old woman tried to scoff at him and ended up coughing. "My brother was dead before you were even born."

"Some of his work may have survived him."

With great effort, Florence Daws spun her wheelchair around to face Ben. "That work cost him his life." Her voice cracked when she tried to raise it. Her hands looked like flesh-tinted bones atop the wheel mounts. "For what? For nothing."

"Yes, I know," Ben said, thinking about his nephew and another dig. "He was killed in Ephesus."

"Is that what you've come about?"

"Have others come?"

"Not in a long time. They were the only ones who did come for quite a while." Her one eye widened sadly. "I wish you really were an ex-student of mine. . . ."

"So do I; I might have done better in school."

"Where are you from?"

"Dearborn, Michigan."

"And originally?"

"Palestine. The West Bank. I moved back there five years ago."

Florence Daws leaned forward in her wheelchair. "You came a long way to see me about a man you never met."

"I'm here about the film he sent you from Ephesus, just before he was killed."

The old woman's lower lip dropped, her mouth lingering open to reveal dentures as shiny and white as pearls that looked misplaced amid the rest of her face. "No one's ever asked me about that before."

Ben felt a wave of excitement wash through him. He knew there was hope now. Even with the contents of the box gone forever, the scroll reduced to fine dust, he might still uncover proof of Winston Daws's discovery.

"It was the greatest find of his career," he resumed. "He sent you those pictures to preserve it in case something happened to him."

"That's not what he said in his letter, Mr. Kamal. He said in his letter I should hide the pictures forever if something happened to him, so no one else would be hurt. He was scared. In my letter back I begged him to go home to London." Florence Daws looked down at her lap, then up again. "He never read it."

"Did you follow his instructions?"

"I shouldn't be talking to you about this. . . ."

"Your brother deserves the credit long due him for this discovery. He deserves a legacy."

"My brother studied history, Mr. Kamal. He had no desire to become a part of it."

"He became part of it when he was murdered fifty-two years ago, Pastor Daws. Do you remember what you said to me a few minutes ago?"

The old woman's mouth dropped a little more. Ben could hear her breathing now, a thin wheezing sound.

"You said, 'For what? For nothing.' Do you really believe your brother died for nothing?"

"You don't . . . you don't think he did?"

"I don't think it has to be that way. I think we can still make it right."

"How?"

"He was killed because of what he had found in Ephesus by men who've been protecting their secret ever since. Your brother uncovered that secret. It's in the photographs he sent you."

The old woman's lips came together, trembling. "I did what he told me. It was just two rolls of film. His letter said to have it developed and hide the pictures where no one would ever find them, to forget they existed until I heard from him again." Her voice sank. "I never did."

"Where did you hide the pictures, sister?"

"I tried to forget," she said dryly, the words separated by a light cracking sound in her mouth. "All these years . . ."

"For your brother, Pastor Daws. This is the last chance you'll ever get to help him. Where are those pictures?"

Florence Daws swiped her tongue across her lips and began to speak.

CHAPTER 74

THE OLDEST BAPTIST Church in the country?"

"It's actually called the First Baptist Church in America, dating back to 1638," Ben explained to Danielle just outside the car. "That's where Florence Daws was transferred just after she received the package from her brother. Eventually, she came back to Lexington, but the pictures stayed where she hid them."

"And, after all these years, you think they're still *there*?"

Ben shrugged.

THEY RETRACED THEIR route down the Massachusetts Turnpike, this time heading toward Providence, Rhode Island, where the First Baptist Church in America was located. Reaching Providence an hour after nightfall, Ben and Danielle found themselves battling snarled traffic in streets congested by a festival called "WaterFire" that had drawn thousands of people to the downtown area. Danielle finally squeezed their car into a space on a steep hill not far from the church they were seeking.

Ben took over the lead once they reached the majestic white wood building. They found one side entrance open during tonight's festival activities. Once inside, Ben led the way up a set of stairs to the auditorium, where services at the church were actually held, toward the sounds of an organ softly playing.

Originally constructed in 1775, the auditorium reflected the generally plain New England meetinghouse style. It was laid out in a simple eighty-by-eighty-foot square with white walls, clear windows, and minus any crosses, statues, or icons. The fluted columns that rose above twin aisles on either side of the pews had been carved to look like classical pillars. A balcony brought the seating capacity to over twelve hundred, a staggering number for colonial times. Of these seats, though, none were occupied.

A number of the first-floor pews were numbered and private, dating back to days when they could be rented or purchased. A simple latch held them closed and many were adorned with small hidden drawers set before cushioned bench seats where personal items like eyeglasses belonging to the original pew occupants could be conveniently stored.

Ben stopped before the pew numbered 95, as Florence Daws had instructed, and lifted the small latch to open the waist-high door. It swung inward and he entered, leaving Danielle to watch as he quickly located the drawer and crouched down before it.

The drawer slid out smoothly on its dovetail joints, and Ben lay it on the cushion behind him before working his hand into the space revealed. He felt around briefly, finally feeling the shape of the envelope Florence Daws had taped to the wood of the drawer's ceiling. Remarkably, that tape had withstood a half century and at least one major renovation. Ben pried the envelope free and brought it to him, wiping away the dust and flecks of stray paint. The clasp was of the string-tie variety and the string broke as soon as he tugged on it. The flap came free and he eased the contents out from inside.

The snapshots looked small and simple, the colors rich and the focus sharp on section after section of the scroll archaeologist Winston Daws had unearthed in Ephesus fifty-two years before. They were neatly ordered, and Ben was careful not to disturb them as he made a rough count of just over fifty pictures.

Even if he had been able to read the Hebrew or Aramaic in which the scroll was written, the words were too small to make out to the naked eye. A magnifying glass or, more likely, a microscope would eliminate that problem, although he could only hope Daws's ancient camera was able to capture all of the faded writings scrawled on ancient parchment that had now withered into dust.

Danielle looked on behind him but Ben barely felt her presence. In his hands, he felt certain, was the means to prove the religion he had once believed in was based on a sham. Could Christianity survive the revelation of Christ's surviving the crucifixion? Ben didn't know, didn't care. But these pictures he held in his hands could explain why so many innocent people, including his nephew, had been killed by Lorenzo's renegade faction of the church.

Ben tucked the envelope into his pocket and eased himself in front of Danielle to lead the way up the aisle. They took the staircase back to the first floor of the church, where a man and a woman had just walked outside into the night.

A scream sounded as Ben and Danielle started to follow them through the door. Ben barreled outside ahead of her, saw the man crouched over the fallen body of his companion.

"She's bleeding," he muttered, his hand wet with blood. "I think she's been shot. I think somebody shot her."

People rushed over from the sidewalk to see what had happened. In the midst of the commotion, something caught Danielle's attention, just a flutter that was there and then gone. Wasting no time, she grabbed hold of Ben and dragged him back into the darkness cast by the shadows of the church building.

"The gunman thought it was me," she said softly. "I was supposed to be the one shot."

"*What?*"

"And you right after me."

"Gianni Lorenzo's assassins wouldn't have waited until we were outside."

"No, but *Israeli* assassins would."

Ben twisted her around so he could scan the area around them. "I warned you about coming with me, I warned you!"

"Let's just get away from here, all right?"

Ben nodded and started to retreat farther back into the shadows.

"No!" Danielle grabbed hold of his arm. "This way, where there are *people*!"

She took the lead down the church walk and joined the mass of strollers heading for the sounds of the nighttime festival. The air was crisp and cool and laced with the pungent aroma of wood smoke drifting up from Providence's downtown area, where the masses of milling people were headed.

"How could they have found us?" Ben asked her.

"I don't know. A leak. Somewhere."

"Impossible."

"Is it? Asher Katz knew we were coming to America. And why."

"But Katz is loyal to Mordecai Lev, and Lev wants the pictures as much as I do."

"Which explains why the Israelis waited until we had the pictures in our possession before they struck. They were acting on the orders of Moshe Baruch."

"Who is somehow connected to Lev," Ben finished.

"Exactly. Oil, everything comes back to oil."

"But why would *Lev* care?"

"I don't know, but Moshe Baruch does and he can't take the risk that I'll tell the world about the secret operation he was running."

"Lev doesn't care about the oil and Baruch doesn't care about the scroll."

"That's right."

"So what brought them together, Pakad? What are they really after?"

"We'll have to make it out of here to find out, Inspector."

They continued downtown toward ever thicker masses of people strolling the streets, often, it looked like, getting stuck in logjams of pedestrian traffic. The tight clusters were trying to weave their way along a complex of trails built into the bridge of walkways that crisscrossed the downtown district. The scent of wood smoke grew stronger while the harmonic strains of music sharpened.

"We've got to stay in the crowd, follow the flow to escape," Danielle instructed.

That flow took them onto a grass-covered park toward a mass of people gathered before a troupe of mimes performing on the steps of a monolithlike war memorial statue. Ben and Danielle swept behind the crowd as they applauded.

The tightest clusters of festival patrons, offering the best camouflage, moved in both directions down a walkway at the river's edge. Ben realized the strange and haunting strains of music had their origins down here as well and moved with Danielle to join either of the flows.

Drawing closer, they saw the black water shimmering like glass, an eerie orange glow emanating from its surface. Boaters and canoeists paddled leisurely by. A water taxi packed with seated patrons sipping wine slid past, followed in the water by what looked like a gondola straight from Venice.

But it was the source of the orange glow reflecting off the water's surface that claimed Ben's attention. He could now identify the pungent scent of wood smoke as that of pine and cedar, hearing the familiar crackle of flames as he and Danielle descended a set of steps onto a promenade that ran directly alongside the river.

Before them a line of bonfires that seemed to rise out of the water curved along the expanse of the Providence river walk. The source of those bonfires, Ben saw now, were nearly a hundred steel baskets, or braziers, of flaming wood moored to the water's surface and stoked on a regular basis by black-shirted workers in a square pontoonlike boat.

The twisting line of flames seemed to stretch forever into the night, concentrated mostly in the opposite direction. Ben and Danielle continued to walk among the crowd, keeping the knee-high retaining wall on their right. Kiosks selling food, beverages, and souvenirs had been set up above the river walk on streets and sidewalks, offering excellent cover for any gunmen who were about.

Ben felt a ripple in the crowd behind them, slight yet distinct. Someone forcing their way through, disturbing the uneasy rhythm the flow had found. He turned in time to see the barrel of a silenced pistol being raised just behind Danielle, its shiny black steel struggling to shimmer in the darkness, close enough to touch. Ben latched on to the gun and jerked it aside, before he could clearly see the person holding it.

A bullet coughed downward and a teenage boy nearby yelped in agony as he fell to the ground. The hot steel of the barrel burned Ben's skin but he held on fast as Danielle swung round too and found herself face-to-face with their assailant. She saw the scar first, a long, pale strip illuminated by the glow of the flames.

Impossible!

It was Shoshanna Tavi.

CHAPTER 75

DANIELLE HAD NO time to consider how it was possible the woman from Shin Bet had managed to survive the ordeal upon the Ulysses GBS. She lashed out with a fist that struck Shoshanna Tavi in the side of her head. Tavi staggered sideways, stunned by the blow, enabling Ben to tear the pistol from her grasp. His angle was better than Danielle's and he used it to grab Shoshanna Tavi by the shoulders, then thrust her over the concrete retaining wall into the shallow river below.

The patrons of a water taxi peered over the side at Tavi's drenched form as they passed, without missing a sip of their wine.

Danielle snatched the pistol from Ben's hand and stuffed it into her jacket. "She won't be alone. Come on," she ordered, reversing their original direction and heading toward the downtown center of Providence, where the clutter of pedestrians was much thicker.

They quickened their pace, aware significant attention had now been drawn to the area and perhaps even to them. They pushed through the crowd as best they could, afraid of being separated, crossing the street against the command of a local policeman who thankfully did not stop them.

They followed the heaviest congestion of people with the fire to the other side of the street and banked right along the route where the urns of flames wove in curving fashion atop the river. The river walk narrowed slightly, and the clutter of pedestrian traffic tightened further, slowing their pace to a crawl past a series of outdoor dining tables set upon a restaurant patio just above them.

They continued on beneath the overhang of a bridge, tensing in the darkness that obscured all those around them. They emerged to the sight of a water taxi approaching, this one less full than the other they had seen.

"Sit down, please. Hey, you're not allowed to stand up!"

The urgent words of the water taxi's pilot drew their eyes back toward it in time to see a male passenger yank a machine pistol from beneath his jacket. He opened fire instantly, spraying bullets toward Ben and Danielle, who both dove to the cold surface of the inlaid brick walk, flesh pressed against the brick and mortar as bodies toppled all around them. Screams rang out and people struck by flecks of rock launched by stray bullets wailed wildly that they'd been shot.

Ben and Danielle stood up again and pushed their way forward through the now-panicked crowd. In the chaos people were shoved off the river walk onto a large, flattened construction site on the right, or toppled into the water on the left.

Ben and Danielle surged on, pushed by the momentum from the rear, unable to slow up even if they had wanted to. The loud sounds of an approaching motorboat made them think the police had come to quell the uproar, until fresh submachine-gun fire spit from below, fired from the pilot of the motorboat that had drawn even with them while they ran.

Danielle drew the pistol from her jacket and fired back, her single shots clacking in absurd rhythm with the barrages sent up from the river. The braziers along the river became fading blurs of light as more bystanders dropped in their tracks around her and Ben. Danielle could now smell the odor of gasoline mixing with the wood smoke, indicating she had hit the boat's gas tank with one of her bullets.

She and Ben sprinted slightly ahead of the motorboat, and one of her last shots shattered its windshield and punched the glass backward at the pilot. The man stripped his hand from the wheel to comfort his face, and the motorboat listed out of control, smacking into one of the braziers that ignited the spilled gasoline. A *poof!* followed and the boat was suddenly in flames.

Before Danielle could relax, she saw a figure pushing toward them through the crowd. Recognizing him as the same man who had shot at them from the water taxi just moments before, Danielle steadied her pistol and fired.

The soft click of the trigger told her the gun was empty. The moment froze in time with an awful reality. The man was angling his gun through the crowd and there was too much space to close before he fired. Suddenly, though, a powerful explosion blew light and heat across the river, fanning the urns of flames lining its surface. Danielle remembered the motorboat catching fire and realized it must have finally exploded.

All at once the gunman ahead was engulfed by a fresh surge of panic spreading through the crowd and lost his grasp on his pistol. Ben watched him stoop to retrieve it and spotted a loose steel chain, part of a barrier between sidewalk and water. He tore it from its iron posts as the man surged forward with pistol in hand again. Ben swung it out and caught the gunman across the face before he could fire, then whipped it back and struck him a second time, snapping his head around in violent fashion. The man had barely begun to crumple when the crowd swallowed him.

Ben grabbed Danielle's hand so they wouldn't be separated as they hurried on, heading toward the end of the alley of lights at a sign reading WATERPLACE PARK. Sirens were wailing steadily now, fire and additional police personnel trying to pinpoint the source of the chaos and closing fast.

Ben and Danielle reached Waterplace Park amid a huge

mass of people charging up cement steps with benches leading to a grassy knoll. At the top was a restaurant called the Boathouse that led onto a street. There, revolving lights in white, blue, and red were plainly visible. Other WaterFire patrons had actually been forced off a stage platform into the river itself, where they splashed about frantically, while trying to figure out how to pull themselves back up.

Ben and Danielle had just reached the steps when a number of men in civilian clothes appeared at the top of the grassy hill, pushing against the flow as their eyes swept the surroundings.

"More Israelis," Danielle recognized, already starting to retreat. "The goddamn bitch Tavi! We won't get twenty feet."

"What's the alternative?"

Soaring above all the other sounds came the staccato beat of a helicopter. It seemed to be descending directly for them until it veered toward the construction site adjacent to the river walk they had passed fifty yards back.

Danielle watched the chopper drop from view as it banked to land. "*That's* the alternative," she told him.

Ben followed her as they renewed their efforts to push against the masses that were flooding up the hill to escape. The going was easier once they reached the river walk again and began to retrace their route past the braziers. Abandoned gondolas and water taxis drifted in the water beneath them as panicked patrons waded or swam through the dark murkiness broken by the glow of the flames. Ben and Danielle clung to the water side, close to the edge, and kept their pace steady.

They drew even with the construction site in time to see the helicopter land and a trio of what must have been local dignitaries pile out. Ben and Danielle skirted the freshly poured foundations and rushed into the spray of dirt and pebbles coughed up by the chopper's rotor wash. They actually passed the two men and a woman who had just arrived, reaching the helicopter before the pilot was ready to take off again.

Ben sped beneath the rotor blade and yanked open the chopper's side door. The pilot swung to find Danielle aiming her empty pistol dead on him.

"You're going to take us for a ride," she instructed flatly and gestured for Ben to climb in first.

The pilot tried to push him out. "What are—"

Danielle reached across Ben and stuck the pistol under the pilot's chin. "Get us out of here or I'll fly this thing myself! Now!"

The pilot returned his attention to the controls. Danielle settled into her seat and reached outside to close the door. As the chopper lifted off the ground, though, a hand from the darkness below latched on to Danielle's belt and yanked mightily. Before she could respond, both her feet and most of her torso were hanging out the door, bringing her almost even with the figure of Shoshanna Tavi.

"Keep going!" Ben ordered the pilot as he grabbed hold of Danielle's left arm. The Israelis would be closing on the construction site by now, having seen what happened. Land and they were dead.

"Are you nuts?"

"Do it, if you want to live!"

The pilot continued working the throttle, the chopper fighting him for every inch of air, starting to spin while Danielle's feet dangled off the ground. Tavi had wrapped one arm around the helicopter's right landing pod for support. Ben could see her clothes were soaked with water, her hair a tangled mess of knots and ringlets. Even hanging outside, she smelled pungently of wood smoke.

The chopper continued to climb sluggishly, while outside Shoshanna Tavi fought to yank Danielle all the way out and dump her to the ground. Danielle kicked and flailed to free herself, but the blows did nothing to deter Tavi's efforts.

"I've got you!" Ben screamed, holding on to Danielle with all his strength. He managed to get his other arm wrapped around the seat's safety harness and felt his muscles stretched to their absolute limit.

Despite Ben's grasp on her arm, Danielle felt herself slip-

ping even farther and launched a series of strikes to Shoshanna Tavi's scarred face. Tavi swallowed each thumping
blow with a grimace, continuing to tug on Danielle with one
arm, keeping her remaining hand wrapped like a snake
around the landing pod.

Ben had to lean through the door to keep his hold on
Danielle now. But the angle and the wind shear gradually
tore her from his grasp. She managed to grab the same pod
Tavi had hold of and curled her arm around it similar fashion
as Ben finally let go and hoisted himself back up into the
chopper. Tavi flailed at Danielle and locked a hand around
her belt. In response, Danielle drove her elbow down into
the hand, hammering it as hard as she could.

The back of Tavi's wrist buckled. She cried out from pain
and relinquished her grip. Danielle was at last free and used
the opportunity to kick out with a foot, bringing it up and
around in order to catch Tavi in the head. Her aim was
slightly off, but the blow still cracked into Tavi's temple,
stunning her.

That gave Danielle the instant she needed to grab the other
woman's hair. She jerked Tavi's head violently backward,
feeling something crunch and crackle inside. Tavi's grasp
came free of the chopper, and she groped desperately for any
part of the pod to grab hold of.

As Tavi looked up, Danielle stared straight into her hate-
filled eyes and lashed out again with her feet. Shoshanna
Tavi's arms flew backward, flapping as if she were trying to
fly, in the last instant before she disappeared into the darkness below.

THEY'LL BE WATCHING every airport, you know,"
Danielle said after Ben had lifted her back into the chopper.
"We'll never get out of the country."

But he had already turned toward the pilot. "Take us to
the nearest airport," he ordered over the engine sounds.

"Didn't you hear what I just said?" Danielle demanded.

"I've got an idea."

"They'll have us on a watch list. We'll be flagged as soon as we try to fly out of the U.S."

"We're not leaving the country, not yet anyway."

"So where *are* we going?"

"Home," Ben said softly. "Home."

DAY SEVEN

CHAPTER 76

DANIELLE DRIFTED OFF to sleep almost as soon as Ben headed their rental car onto Route 94 toward Dearborn from Detroit Metropolitan Airport.

"We're going to *my* home," Ben had elaborated the night before. "The place where I grew up."

"What good will that do us?"

"You'll see."

Ben hadn't been back, and had corresponded very little with his family, in the five years since his return to Palestine. Now he was coming home in the midst of the tragic death of his nephew, a death that so far as he knew still remained unconfirmed by authorities in Israel.

Ben had only vague memories of his family's original move from Palestine to the Dearborn area. He remembered they had stayed with friends for a time, before settling in the South End, near the Ford Rouge Assembly Plant, where his father worked for over a year before politics called him back to his homeland. Ben attended the Salina School and remembered walking with friends to the Arab bakeries on Warren

Avenue for *kanahef* pastry. The Rouge River was very close to his house but no one was allowed to swim in it because even back then the river was polluted.

Later he played football at Fordson High School, where he graduated with honors. But his father never saw him play or graduate, because he was assassinated shortly after his return to the West Bank. Ten years after his father's death, Ben enrolled in the University of Michigan, just as his older brother had done before him.

Ben was still in high school, though, when his family moved to a two-family house on the north side of Dearborn south of Warren Avenue near Patton Park. His mother lived on the first floor to this day, but his brother and uncle had relocated to their own homes a few blocks away; his brother to an old Victorian with a detached garage on Coleman Street, which was where Ben was headed now.

But ten minutes out of the airport he passed the turnoff for the home where he had lived with his wife and children in the Copper Canyon section of Detroit. On impulse, he began to slow at the next exit that would allow him to double back on the Southfield Freeway west of Rouge Park. The name "Copper Canyon" appeared on no map and was coined thanks to the large numbers of police officers who resided in the area. Residency requirements mandated that all Detroit police officers live within the city limits, so the kind of enclave Copper Canyon became should have been expected.

But that hadn't stopped a serial killer known as the Sandman, for his penchant for striking at night while his victims slept peacefully, from paying his fateful visit six years ago.

Ben was on autopilot from there, kept telling himself one more mile, one more block, but it was already too late. He knew he was headed to a place he recalled in emotionally polarizing extremes. The good and the bad, the tragic and the wonderful, the beginning and the end. Ben's heart was hammering against his chest by the time he turned onto Warren Avenue, and continued to the house on Chatham Street where his family was murdered.

Barely breathing, Ben parked across the street and stared

at the house. Danielle had still not awoken but here, right here anyway, she seemed not to exist for him. He was back in the past on the night the Sandman had come and worked the front door open with his locksmith's tools.

Ben climbed stiffly out of the rental car. His hands and feet feeling almost tingly, he walked straight up to the door and rang the bell. Part of him hoped no one answered. Another part knew he'd find a way into the house if that was the case.

A woman opened the door, eyeing him suspiciously. "Yes? Can I help you?"

In that moment Ben realized the house didn't even look like his anymore. The paint color was different, the trim had been changed, and looking over the woman's shoulder, he could see the entire downstairs had been remodeled. A wall taken out, a divider installed. Stools instead of chairs were set around a central island in a kitchen that now extended into a large family room. The only thing that seemed the same was the front door that had still been open when Ben arrived home that night.

"I was wondering," Ben stammered finally. "You see, I used to live here, and I was wondering if I could just have a look inside."

The woman continued to regard him with suspicion.

"I was, er, I am a police officer. Ben Kamal."

She seemed to relax a little. "We bought the house from you."

"I'm sorry, I don't remember. . . ."

"You didn't come to the closing. Everything was pre-signed."

"Oh."

"But I know what happened. I'm very sorry."

"It was a long time ago."

The woman opened the door all the way. "You wanted to look around."

Ben hedged. "It's all right. I . . ."

"No, please. Come in. I hope you don't mind what we've done to the place. . . ."

"Not at all," Ben said, and the words felt like thick marsh-mallows sliding up his throat to be forced from his mouth.

The truth was he did mind, minded because it didn't look at all like his house anymore. *Everything* was different, even the steps he had raced up all those years ago, already sensing he was too late.

They lay before him now, a straight hike into his past atop blue carpeting instead of the beige he remembered. But the house smelled the way he remembered it. The light dimmed to the same hue it had been that night.

Not looking back, Ben started up the stairs.

DANIELLE WOKE UP to her own scream. It wasn't unusual, happened often in fact, always to find herself alone. What was unusual today was that something felt *wrong* about being alone. She awoke disoriented and stiff and quickly re-alized she was in a car, rapidly recovering her bearings now.

Where was Ben? That was what felt wrong. He should have been here, in the driver's seat. And the car should have still been moving.

Danielle tried to collect her thoughts but the dream chased her down again. This particular one was a replay of the day the cramps and pain had come not long before she noticed the bleeding. She'd gone to the doctor fearing the worst and got it after being admitted to the hospital. But the worst thing about the dream was that her baby was always alive in it. The doctors were wrong. Her baby was right here in bed with her. Just look for yourself.

The dream today, though, was different because the baby was nowhere to be found in it. There was only the cramps, pain, and blood come back to ruin her again. Instead of Ben, the shape of Moshe Baruch, commander of Shin Bet, had been looming over her hospital bed, grinning. She thought he might be holding her baby, holding it hostage, but the dream ended with a scream before she could see clearly.

Ben hadn't been there in the dream and he wasn't here

now. Slowly Danielle began to realize where he must have driven and reached for the door latch.

HIS LEGS HEAVY and mouth dry, Ben retraced his path from six years ago. Afraid to hold his eyes closed too long, lest the visions return with the events of that night being replayed. It did seem darker all of a sudden, and then the rich blue of the carpeting suddenly looked like the beige his wife had chosen for the hallways and stairway. He looked down at his right hand, expecting his gun to be there. He saw it for an instant, quivering like a mirage in the desert, before he closed his hand and felt nothing in his grasp. Still he squeezed until his fingers ached, as if he were trying to roust himself from a dream.

It didn't work. He kept walking. Almost to the top of the stairs when the sharp stench of blood hit him. Ben smelled it, saw it, remembered shooting the man who spilled it a dozen times before he fell. He wavered and grabbed the banister for support.

"Are you all right? Can I get you something?"

He looked down the stairs and saw his wife standing there in her white nightgown, the same one she'd been wearing when the Sandman had stabbed her and draped it over his own clothes. Then it wasn't his wife anymore; it was the woman who owned the house now, whose name he didn't know.

Ben shook his head, continued on. He needed to do this, live it, all on his own. The real walk in the darkness wasn't into the unknown or the mystical, it was into the past, into the very depths of his own soul. He had relived this moment so often, trying to change it in his mind, make it end differently. Yet the stairs were smaller than he remembered them, and not as steep. And at the top there was no stench of blood or white-shrouded figure with knife in hand ready to pounce. His imagination did not produce them. The past failed to give them up.

Ben stood there for what seemed like a very long time,

beneath the lazy spin of a ceiling fan that hadn't been there six years ago. The shadow of its blades danced against the wall, but that was as close to seeing a ghost as he got. The rooms on the right his children had slept in were neatly made up, empty. The master bedroom where he had found his wife after stepping over the Sandman's body was drenched by the afternoon sun.

Ben wondered what he'd expected to see, what he *wanted* to see. It was just a house, after all, occupied by strangers who had washed it clean of his memories.

A cold wash of anxiety surged through him. He felt like an intruder in someone else's world, not just their house. His past belonged here no more than he did.

"Ben."

The voice from the bottom of the stairs made him shudder. He turned slowly, expecting to see his wife again, dead these many years.

Ben looked down to see Danielle standing there instead.

"Ben?"

He didn't remember going to her. There was only her arms sweeping him away from this place to somewhere different when they embraced. And for that moment, just that moment, they felt inseparable, their lives irrevocably and wondrously intertwined.

Even after the moment faded, replaced by the cold harshness of reality, Ben still clung to Danielle, wishing it could be like this forever and knowing it couldn't.

CHAPTER 77

BEN HEADED BACK down Warren Avenue into Dearborn, trying to plot a course that would take them past St. Bernadette's Church, to his brother's house. He remembered now that the church had closed in '97; his mother had told him in a letter. Warren Avenue was considerably more commercial than he remembered, lined with shop after shop featuring signs in both English and Arabic. He marveled at the number and diversity of the stores that had been added, especially compared to streets back in the West Bank, where the poor economy had forced many shops to close altogether or open for only short hours.

He passed Fordwood Park and Woodmere Cemetery, where his father was buried and his nephew soon would be. The neighborhoods looked remarkably unchanged. Arabic men and women strolled about or worked in their yards. Children knocked a soccer ball about. Others crisscrossed the streets on their bicycles, paying far too little attention to the traffic signals. It could have been Palestine, except for the neatly shingled homes with side yards of grass instead of dust. There was no mistrust in the eyes of those he drove past, no longing or hurt. The neighborhood's children threw baseballs instead of rocks and lived without fear of soldiers coming to disperse them with rubber bullets. It was the world he had left in the hope he could make a difference in another one.

Had he? It seemed not. Even so, that hadn't left him longing for this world again. Instead, if anything, it was Palestine he missed, as dusty and fear-filled as it might be. The ever-changing dynamic that seemed to cheat progress at every turn while refusing to deny hope.

"My brother lives just up this block," Ben explained to Danielle.

"Did you tell him I was coming?"

He smiled at her. "I told him I was bringing a friend."

THEY HEADED UP the walk together, skirting the collection of children's toys strewn across the lawn. One bike with training wheels and two without them. A skateboard. Strange how that stood out in Ben's mind, that and the training wheels. Children rode bikes in the West Bank too, but he did not remember ever seeing training wheels.

In that instant Ben understood more clearly than ever why his father had moved his family here, and how difficult it must have been to go back when the aftermath of the Six-Day War left his world in tatters. His departure and subsequent death had left a hole in Ben this return was finally helping him to understand. Filling it was as much as anything the reason why he had returned to the world of his birth in the first place. Doing what his father had done to better understand the legacy left him.

A six-year-old boy whose father kissed him good-bye at the airport in 1967 and never came back again.

Ben's own boy was almost the same age the night the Sandman had struck, neither man able to see their son grow up. He had that much in common with his father but had found little else over the years.

Ben climbed the steps onto a small porch and knocked on the door. Inside his family would still be observing the formal grieving period over the death of his nephew, everyone gathered in the *midafeh*, the room where guests would be received.

Ben knocked again and this time his brother Sayeed opened the door, his face ashen, his tie poorly knotted. Sayeed reached out; to embrace him, Ben thought, until his brother seized him by the lapels and dragged Ben in far enough to slam him up against the wall.

"Where is my son? Where is he?"

Ben made no move to resist. "I'm so sorry." A tight group of family members clustered behind his brother in silence. Ben scanned their faces, shocked at how little he remembered any of them. The five years he had been away might as well have been a lifetime; in many ways, it had been.

Sayeed's grip slackened, but he didn't let go. "I still haven't spoken to anyone in Israel. No word on when they will send me Dawud's body. No one answers my questions, no one returns my calls." His eyes fell on Danielle. "Is that why you have brought this one here, Bayan? Does she know something?"

"She is my colleague, Sayeed. We pursue the same enemy."

"We know who she is," a woman's voice chimed in, and the crowd parted to reveal Ben's mother. "We recognize her from all the pictures." Hanna Kamal stopped beside Sayeed and laid a hand over his arms, gently prodding them off Ben. "It is not your brother's fault," she said, trying to sound soothing. "He did not bring this misery upon us."

Sayeed finally let go, and Ben hugged his mother for the first time since he had left to return to Palestine. She seemed even shorter than he remembered and her hair looked grayer, thinning in patches.

His mother eased Ben away and turned her eyes on Danielle. *"Beitna beitek.* Our house is your house."

Danielle smiled tightly back. She continued studying the faces of those around her, Palestinians all. There were few times, if any, she had been in the company of so many Palestinians at once, at least as the lone Israeli. Raise her child with Ben, and she doubted that even these would accept her.

She could see much of Ben in both his mother and brother. Sayeed was taller, darker, but not quite as broad with the same thick wavy hair. His mother shared Ben's eyes and the ever-present glint of questioning in her expression. A subtle strength and power behind a veil of somber self-assurance.

Ben's mother grasped his hands in hers and started to lead him forward, toward the living room. "You will tell us everything and we will figure out what to do together."

Ben let her drag him a few steps, then held his ground as gently as he could. "I need to speak with Sayeed alone first."

CHAPTER 78

SAYEED LED BEN outside and into a detached garage. Ben stood with his back to a wall of neatly placed screwdrivers, ratchets, and wrenches. His brother faced him from the covered fender of a classic MG sports car he was in the midst of restoring. The garage smelled of fresh tire rubber and car wax.

"Have you swept this place lately?" Ben asked Sayeed.

"I'm sorry its cleanliness does not meet your standards."

"I meant swept it with electronic equipment for bugs, listening devices."

"Tell me, Bayan, why would someone want to bug me? To listen to my sobs over my son's death, which I cannot even fully mourn?"

"No, because when fugitive Palestinians who have taken refuge in America want to return to their homeland, you are one of the men they contact."

Sayeed stiffened. "Did you come home to share my grief, or am I just part of another case you are working on?"

Ben held his brother's eyes as best he could. "Listen to

me, Sayeed. Danielle and I have come here because we're being hunted by the same forces behind Dawud's death. No way we can use traditional means to exit this country. We need new papers, identities, passports good enough to hold up to any scrutiny."

Sayeed's eyes had turned blank. "How did you find out about . . . my work?"

"I have a friend in Palestine—Colonel al-Asi. He gave me the report he had on you last week, asked me to do something so he wouldn't have to."

Sayeed stood up. "So I have you to thank for my freedom. Is that it?"

"You have Colonel al-Asi's friendship with me, to be more accurate, that and the fact that the men you have helped so far merely wanted to come home."

"I screen those I help carefully. They should have a right to return to their families, don't you think, my brother? A right to go home without being hunted by Israelis like your girlfriend."

The remark failed to get even the slightest rise out of Ben. "Most of the hunting is done by Palestinian authorities now."

"Acting in concert with the damn Jews."

"Sometimes, sometimes not. But, please, this is not the time for us to argue."

"No, it is a time you have returned because you need me to help you."

"I need your help to get to the people responsible for Dawud's death."

"Then let me join you, help you get the bastards. I have friends, you know. I am owed favors by men *no one* in Palestine would dare cross," Sayeed declared fervently.

"Those I am after are much bigger than they. You must believe me."

"Why should I?"

"Because I'm your brother."

"Then tell me the truth about what's going on, what my son died for."

Ben had rehearsed these next words in his mind often, but

they still didn't emerge as planned. "Dawud was part of a team only pretending to be archaeologists."

"But he *was* an archaeologist. I told you that."

"Because they needed one or two for cover. The rest were geologists."

"Geologists?"

"The Israelis have found oil in Palestine."

"Where?" Sayeed asked, his spine straightening.

"In the Judean Desert, near the caves."

Sayeed shook his head very slowly. "Then my son died for nothing. Or, at least, very little."

"Didn't you just hear what I just said about the oil?"

"Yes, I heard you." Sayeed's expression hardened in the garage's dim light. "And what you are saying makes no sense."

Ben shook his head incredulously. "This oil field contains as much reserves as the North Sea and more than the Grand Banks."

"Buried under hundreds, perhaps thousands, of feet of shale and rock. Yes?"

"I'm not sure."

"Assume it is, my brother; otherwise, it would have been discovered long ago. Now, the deeper you drill, and the more obstacles you encounter along the way, the more expensive it becomes to bring the oil up. Measured by the linear foot, and assuming we are talking about a thousand feet—a conservative estimate, believe me—you are looking at up to thirty dollars per barrel of oil in cost."

"You're the expert, Sayeed."

"Then consider that the *price* of oil on the market these days is only *twelve dollars per barrel*." Sayeed seemed on the verge of laughing, but with no trace of amusement in his voice. "So your Israeli friends would be going to all this trouble, and all this subterfuge, to *lose* eighteen dollars on every barrel they bring up."

Ben tried to find an argument to refute Sayeed's logic, but clearly there was none.

"It wasn't oil that brought you back to America anyway, was it?" Sayeed asked. "Wasn't just oil that got my son killed."

"No. It was something much more."

Sayeed turned his palms upward, gesturing for Ben to go on. "What?"

Ben fingered the envelope of photographs that hadn't left his pocket since he recovered it in Providence. "I've said enough."

"I have a right to know, don't you think?"

Ben knew he should have stopped there, but he couldn't help himself. "The Americans, perhaps Dawud himself, stumbled upon a discovery in the midst of their cover: a scroll written by Josephus attesting to the fact that Jesus Christ didn't die on the cross, that the resurrection never happened."

Sayeed seemed on the verge of losing his balance. He reached out and leaned against the classic MG's fender for support. "What happened to this evidence? Did you destroy it?"

"I didn't have to. The years took care of that for me."

"Thank God. . . ."

"But Winston Daws, the archaeologist who originally uncovered the find a half century ago, took pictures." Ben fished the envelope out of his pocket. "These."

Sayeed's eyes widened. He pulled his hand from the MG's fender, leaving in its place a perfect imprint on the glossy finish that began to fade immediately. He started to reach for the photos, then changed his mind. "You're telling me this is what my son died for?"

"The secret they represent, yes."

"Can you, can you get these people who did this thing?"

Ben nodded. "Yes, I think I can."

"And you trust this Israeli woman to help you?"

"As much as I trust anyone." Ben took a few shallow breaths. "I stopped at my old house on the way here. It looks a lot different."

"Nothing stays the same."

"You want to help me, Sayeed?"

"I want to go back to Palestine with you and find the people who killed my son."

Ben reached out and grasped his brother's shoulders. "There's something you can do more important than that."

CHAPTER 79

THEY SPOKE IN a corner of the room by the window, the rest of the Kamal family clearly respecting their privacy.

"Thank you for your hospitality, Umm Kamal," said Danielle. "I didn't mean to intrude."

"It's the least I can do for the woman about to make me a grandmother again," Ben's mother returned, tapping her fondly on the arm. She tried to smile but her eyes teared up instead.

Danielle felt her heart skip a beat, taken aback. How much did Hanna Kamal know? "Did Ben, did he . . ."

Hanna Kamal shook her head before Danielle could finish. "He didn't have to. I could see it on your faces; his a little, but yours mostly. Boy or girl, I don't care. Let it just be healthy. After all we have been through, that much we deserve. . . ."

Danielle felt tears stinging her eyes, couldn't find any words to respond.

"You haven't had children before."

"No."

Hanna Kamal tried to smile again. "Something else a woman can always tell. Just like I can tell my response surprises you."

"It does."

"Of course it does. The fact that you're a Jew and my son is Palestinian, it should bother me, yes? Well, years ago it would have. But it's been a long time since I've seen him happy." Hanna Kamal leaned very close to Danielle and lowered her voice. "My question is how do you feel about it?"

"I—"

"You are troubled," Ben's mother completed for her.

"I lost a baby once before," Danielle said, hoping that explanation would suffice. But deeper, below the surface, saying that to a stranger made her realize how much she missed her own mother, missed her desperately for the private and personal moments, both good and bad, Danielle could share with no one else. Gone for so many years now and the void was still no less easy to bear.

Hanna Kamal flapped a hand between the two of them. Danielle thought she smelled Evian hand cream, the same kind her mother used.

"Is that all? I lost two myself," said Hanna Kamal. "One before my oldest was born, another between my second and third. But I knew losing one would not affect me having others, as it obviously hasn't affected you."

"I'm scared of losing this one too."

"As you will be until he takes his first breath free of your belly. We have a saying: fear for what you cannot control, but control your fear. It gets easier after a few months."

"I barely got that far the last time."

Hanna Kamal nodded firmly. "This time will be different. My son deserves this." She studied Danielle closer, waited for a few of Ben's nieces and nephews to drift away before continuing. "And so do you, from what I understand, even more so."

Now it was Danielle who hesitated. "It doesn't bother you, Umm Kamal?"

"What?"

"The two of us, Ben and I . . ."

Hanna Kamal reached out and took her hand when Danielle's voice trailed off. "We have a saying, Danielle: *Inshalla binnisr, inshalla diddawlah.* It means 'May we meet at the victory, may we meet in our country.' Well, the United States is our country now and our battles are different from what they used to be."

"You've made me feel very welcome."

"*Kull emleeha.* Everything is good between you and my son. That is all that matters."

Danielle almost told her the truth, but couldn't find the words to start. "Thank you, Umm Kamal," she managed softly, instead.

Hanna Kamal let go of Danielle's hand and smiled. "You are the first person to address me as 'Umm' in a very long time, Danielle. My friends here, Palestinian and otherwise, call me 'Mrs.' My grandchildren call me 'Nana.' I've been an American for almost thirty years. I haven't been back to my homeland in even longer than that and wonder if I ever will. So this difference in cultures does not bother me. You know what does bother me? My son being unhappy bothers me. Him being alone bothers me."

"I understand . . . Mrs. Kamal."

"Hanna."

"Hanna."

Hanna Kamal reached over and squeezed Danielle's hand. "My son is troubled, isn't he, Danielle?"

"Yes."

"Always he has been this way, since he was a boy, always a project. He didn't always succeed but he never left anything unfinished. Just like his father. My husband had to go back, to Palestine, and it killed him."

"He had enemies."

"My son has told you?"

"I put things together."

"You are troubled too?"

"Because Ben has enemies as well, even more powerful ones than his father."

"This is what brought you here. . . ."

"And what will take us back."

Hanna Kamal sighed. "I wish you could stay here, both of you. Palestine has already taken enough of us."

"We are going back to do what must be done."

Hanna Kamal's eyes finally filled with tears, her grief overflowing. She turned away from Danielle toward the window. "That's exactly what my husband said before he left."

GIANNI LORENZO ONCE again reviewed the reports lying on his desk. By all indications, Ben Kamal and Danielle Barnea had inexplicably fled to America following their escape in Rome. Clearly something was waiting for them there and Lorenzo felt certain it was connected to Winston Daws and the lost scroll of Josephus.

If Lorenzo's information was correct, they had flown into Boston. After that, what he'd been able to learn became sketchy at best. But no matter. Where they had gone, where in America they were now, was irrelevant. Very soon, inevitably, they would be returning to Israel with whatever they had found.

Seven of his best Knights Templars, under Major Flave Pocacinni's leadership, remained in Israel now still searching for the blind madman, Rabbi Mordecai Lev. Gianni Lorenzo, captain commandant of the Swiss Guard, would join his men there now.

And wait.

MOSHE BARUCH WALKED past the guards he had planted at the safehouse where Rabbi Mordecai Lev was staying. The safehouse was located on the outskirts of the Palestinian village of Abu Dis primarily because it was among the last places enemies of Shin Bet would think to look for someone in the organization's care.

Lev was seated by the window when Baruch stepped through the door, looking out as if he could see. "What have you to tell me, Commander?"

"My people failed. Barnea and the Palestinian got away."

"Can we keep them out of the country?"

"We can try, but Barnea is good, well trained."

"You ignore the Palestinian?"

"None of them worry me with their cleverness."

"This one should, Commander. It would not surprise me if he has figured out the truth by now."

"Impossible, Rabbi."

Lev tilted his head slightly to the side. "You said the same thing about the two of them escaping your people in the United States."

Baruch was glad Lev couldn't see the uncertainty flutter across his features. "In any case, Pakad Barnea is in for a surprise when and if she returns."

"Just make sure the surprise lasts another day, Commander," said Lev. "After that, it won't matter."

DAY EIGHT

CHAPTER 80

Sᴀʏᴇᴇᴅ'ꜱ ᴀʀʀᴀɴɢᴇᴍᴇɴᴛꜱ ᴛᴏ get Ben and Danielle back to Israel were surprisingly simple. He was aided by the fact that an exiled Palestinian delegation out of Cairo had received permission from Arafat himself to attend a meeting of the entire Palestinian Council.

Ben and Danielle would reach Cairo by way of Paris, where, as part of the delegation, they would pose as former exiles in order to reach the Palestinian airport in Gaza. Israeli scrutiny was certain to be intense there, but Ben's brother Sayeed had promised to devise a way to expedite matters for them, calling in favors owed to him by those he had smuggled back into Palestine.

For Ben and Danielle, the early legs of their journey passed for the most part in uncomfortable silence. They had argued mightily back in Dearborn, and then again while their plane was delayed in New York, about whether or not Danielle should remain behind.

"You shouldn't be doing this. It's too dangerous. You're not thinking of the baby."

Ben watched her expression change in response to his charge. "Yes, I am," she said.

"Do you want to lose it?"

"*What?* How could you ask such a thing?"

"Because that's how you're acting, like you don't want a child at all."

Danielle felt hot tears brewing behind her eyes. "Did I lose the first one on purpose too?"

"Why don't you tell me? It's not just about you this time, though. It's about me too, whether you raise him yourself or not."

The tears began to slide down her cheeks. "Then you should have tied me up and left me in Dearborn."

"So once you lost the child, you could blame me."

"Why don't you go to hell?"

"I've already been there, Pakad, both of us have. The difference is I'm trying to work my way out—I thought I had—with you. But I only found myself in a different one."

Danielle tasted warm salt on her lips. "I guess you're right: I *am* going back, because of you *and* the baby." Her tone sharpened. "Because I don't want to see you dead. Because I intend to do everything I can to keep the father of my child alive."

"Too bad he won't know me as his father."

Danielle lapsed into silence.

Ben leaned back with a sigh.

The plane out of New York's Kennedy Airport, comprising the second leg of their journey, took off two hours late. Another twenty hours remained before they were scheduled to at last land in Gaza, after the rendezvous with the group of Palestinian exiles in Cairo. Ben couldn't even imagine how the journey might go based on the contentious atmosphere with which it had started.

"The truth is," he said finally, glad to change the subject, "I don't even know what we should do once we get back."

"Are you talking about Winston Daws's pictures?"

"I've almost tossed them in the trash a dozen times already. I still might before we get home."

"Why?"

"Because you were right: proving there was no resurrection, that the entire basis of Christianity is a sham, *is* about punishing God, the world . . . you. Show everyone else that they were as much fools as I was for believing."

"What changed?"

Ben gave her a long look as the pilot announced yet another delay. "Nothing—that's the problem. Going home. Seeing my family, my old house. If I keep fighting God, nothing will ever change. But I've got to try to put it behind me. I'm not sure if I can, but I've got to try."

"Does that include me, Inspector?"

Ben tried to wet his lips but his mouth was dry, thanks to the stale, recirculated plane air. "That's your decision, Pakad." He cleared his throat. "Anyway, I'm glad I didn't destroy the pictures, because they might be the only leverage we have once all this is over."

"Leverage over whom? Not the Israeli government, of course, who can't afford to have us running around telling the world they've discovered oil in the West Bank."

"My brother told me the oil was worthless, at least for the foreseeable future. The expense doesn't justify bringing it up."

"That's not the way my government, through Baruch, has been behaving."

"Exactly."

"So what are we missing, Inspector?"

"We know Rabbi Mordecai Lev, for some reason, was involved in the search for oil in the Judean. He knew the truth about the American geologists from the beginning and he was following their progress well before they had unearthed the remains of the ancient scroll. But why would Lev care? Why did he become so involved in a secret operation to find oil everyone should have known was too expensive to pursue?"

Danielle shrugged in response as the plane began to taxi toward the runway.

C H A P T E R   8 1

THE FINAL FLIGHT of their long journey was made out of Cairo in an ancient propeller plane packed with Palestinians. It finally ended with a bumpy, thumping landing on the Gaza Airport's main runway late Tuesday afternoon. Danielle had been uncomfortable and tense since arriving in Cairo. Harsh glances cast at her quickly gave way to the exchange of hushed whispers. Despite her disguise of a dark dress and cloak to cover most of her face, it was clear she stood out. As it was, fortunately, the Palestinians kept to themselves and there was almost no talking in the brief duration of the flight from Cairo to Gaza.

The plane's jolting taxi toward the gate area in Gaza provided a clear view of a troop of Israeli soldiers surrounding the entire airport complex. There were personnel carriers and jeeps present as well, each threatening additional firepower if it was needed. Perhaps most ominously, a few empty trucks were parked on the edge of the tarmac, just in case the Israelis decided to off-load the entire group of passengers onto them as soon as they deplaned.

"Welcoming committee," Ben noted, peering out the window.

"They're expecting us. Apparently, your brother's contacts must not be too discreet."

Ben thought briefly. "If they were sure we were onboard, they would have the plane surrounded already. They must be checking all planes into Gaza as a precaution."

"Which doesn't seem to help us out very much."

Ben felt his neck and spine stiffen. "Our papers are all in order. If it's just a cursory check . . ."

"It won't be. I can assure you of that."

"Those are your people out there, Pakad."

"I'm being hunted as much as you, maybe even more so, Ben. Commander Baruch knows I know about the oil he was ordered to safeguard."

Ben leaned forward in his seat. "Baruch," he muttered, thinking. The only thing Baruch and Mordecai Lev had in common was a hatred for Palestinians and a desire to see them evicted from the West Bank. Might that somehow be connected to their mutually obsessive interest in the discovery of oil in the Judean Desert? And if so, how?

Ben's search for answers was cut short as the plane halted well short of the gate, and he turned his attention to a scene out the window. A pair of Palestinian police cars sat just to the plane's right. Ben was confused until he saw a familiar Mercedes parked behind them. As the plane came to a complete stop, Nabril al-Asi climbed out of the backseat of the Mercedes. Almost instantly, four Palestinian policemen joined the colonel, a pair flanking him on either side.

Inside the plane, a flight attendant opened the main door and waited for a portable stairway to be wheeled into place. After it was secured against the plane's exterior, the colonel climbed the steps and entered, followed by the four police officers.

"Welcome to Palestine, my brothers and sisters," he greeted. "I am Colonel al-Asi of the Protective Security Service and I am here to assure that your trip remains safe and secure." He began walking slowly, dramatically, down the aisle, trailed nervously by the eyes of those he passed on the way. "However, it has been brought to my attention that a very small number of you are traveling with false papers in violation of the agreement signed by our president with the Israeli government to allow your entry into the country." He stopped even with Ben and Danielle. "Therefore, I have no choice but to check your papers so the identities of those not in compliance can be ascertained. I promise to cause you as little inconvenience as possible," he added over the groans of protest and disappointment.

The colonel leaned over and seemed to pick something off the plane floor. He extended it toward Ben with a slight smile.

"I believe you dropped this."

Ben took the object in his palm: a chip from the Oasis Casino.

When Ben looked up again, two of the Palestinian policemen who had accompanied al-Asi onboard had begun the arduous task of inspecting the papers of the passengers, starting in the front. Instead of assisting them, the other two policemen veered toward the colonel in the back.

"Please join these men in the rear galley," al-Asi said to Ben and Danielle.

Ben looked at the way the two men were smiling and realized they weren't policemen at all. "My brother sent them . . ."

"Indeed," acknowledged al-Asi. "It appears I was wrong about him, after all."

MINUTES LATER BEN and Danielle, dressed in the police uniforms previously worn by Sayeed Kamal's two contacts, exited the plane on either side of the colonel. Danielle had tightened her hair into a bun that fit well enough beneath the standard Palestinian police beret. Her disguise would not stand up to close scrutiny, but the Israeli soldiers had remained at the outskirts of the tarmac, content to watch from a distance.

Playing the role of al-Asi's bodyguards, Ben and Danielle settled into the backseat of his Mercedes on either side of him. Then his driver headed off directly through an Israeli checkpoint at the airport exit, slowing only long enough for the colonel to toss the nearest soldier a wave.

At the police headquarters in Gaza City, al-Asi led Ben and Danielle into an empty office where fresh fruit, sandwiches, and drinks were waiting for them on the desk.

"Your brother expected the two of you might be hungry, Inspector," explained the colonel. "So did I."

"Thank you," Ben said. "For everything."

"Thank your brother as well. I could not believe it when those two men contacted me. I have been looking for them for months. Pity I learned only today that they have fled the country once again." Al-Asi turned toward Danielle. "I understand congratulations are in order, Chief Inspector." He extended a hand and shook hers warmly. "You have my best wishes."

Danielle nodded her thanks, afraid to look at Ben.

Ben drained a glass of ice-cold soda and poured himself another. "What now?" he asked the colonel.

"I have fresh Palestinian police uniforms for the two of you to put on." Al-Asi looked toward Danielle. "A problem for you, Chief Inspector, since virtually our entire force is made up of men. However, women have recently begun to serve in a clerical capacity, so we can hope an administrative position with a ranking commander will serve as sufficient cover."

"Me a ranking commander?" Ben asked.

"A disguise, Inspector, nothing more, meant to get you out of the Gaza Strip and back to the West Bank."

"I need to get into Israel," Danielle interjected.

"That may not be wise under the circumstances," al-Asi told her. "You have been placed on the primary watch list."

"On what grounds?"

"Subversive activities and suspected collaboration with Palestinians."

"That's ridiculous! They could never make it stand up!"

"It is merely a pretext to detain you, Chief Inspector. You know better than I how your people work."

"Baruch?"

Al-Asi nodded. "I believe that's a safe assumption."

"He knows I killed his mistress, his handpicked choice to serve directly under the new commissioner. Well, the bastard still doesn't control National Police. If I can get there, to Giott, and explain what was really going on in the Judean Desert, we can bring Baruch down. He's running a rogue operation here the government will never tolerate."

Al-Asi smiled slightly. "Your country's politics amaze me, Chief Inspector. Sometimes I think you dislike each other more than you dislike us."

"You wouldn't be far wrong, Colonel."

IT'S TOO DANGEROUS," Ben argued after al-Asi had left to complete the arrangements.

"You think it's safer for me to stay in Gaza?"

"I agree with the colonel. You're risking too much."

Danielle shook her head. "I've got to get back to Giott."

"Al-Asi was right about the politics, wasn't he?"

"Commander Baruch wants a Shin Bet puppet running National Police. We can't allow that. And this isn't just about me. Hershel Giott helped build National Police from the ground up. It'll destroy him if the force falls into the hands of Baruch and his cronies."

"What can you do?"

"Go public with the existence of oil in the West Bank. An American geological survey team murdered while under the protection of Shin Bet . . . Baruch will be lucky to keep his job for a week."

Ben weighed the impact of her intentions. "And in the process the Palestinian Authority will find out your people intended to steal the oil right out from under us."

"The Israeli government will label it a rogue operation, apologize profusely, and then offer to share the billions of barrels down there in a magnanimous gesture."

"How generous."

"You mean, political." Danielle hesitated. "What about you?"

"It's time to learn the rest of the tale Winston Daws uncovered a half century ago."

Danielle frowned skeptically. "You'll need plenty more than a magnifying glass to read those pictures he sent to his sister."

"And I know just where to find it," Ben told her.

C H A P T E R   8 2

I T   W A S   N I N E   o'clock that night by the time Danielle reached National Police Headquarters in Jerusalem. Even from the street she could see a light burning in Hershel Giott's top-floor office and waited outside a side exit until a pair of off-duty clerical workers emerged. Danielle ducked in past them and entered the building unobtrusively.

She started up the stairs, more nervous than she'd been since the Palestinian police car carrying her and Ben approached the Israeli checkpoint at the Gaza border. Unlike the West Bank, whose long and rugged border was almost impossible to seal, Gaza was surrounded by an electrified fence with crossings for both workers and official or diplomatic personnel. Al-Asi had provided passes for them to enter Israel on police business, handing the passes over with an approving stare cast toward Danielle.

"That uniform suits you well, Chief Inspector."

"Thank you."

"Should circumstances ever require it, please know that a

more proper and permanent change of clothing would be yours for the asking."

"That shouldn't be necessary, Colonel."

"But keep it in mind."

As a result of those passes, the Israeli soldiers at the checkpoint monitored Danielle and Ben only cursorily before waving them through. Ben had dropped Danielle off in Jerusalem before heading back to the West Bank himself.

Now, an hour later, she climbed toward the commissioner's office with the news that could preserve his legacy and her job. She found his door open and, at this late hour, no secretary to bother with.

"Rav Nitzav," she said as she entered, trying to think of where exactly to start when the commissioner's chair turned slowly around to reveal an unexpected hefty shape seated within it.

Danielle felt her heart skip a beat. Her breath caught in her throat.

"Good evening," greeted Commander Moshe Baruch of Shin Bet.

THE OLIVE TREES of the Jordan Rift Valley shook lightly in the breeze as Ben approached the home of Ari Coen. Upon reaching the outskirts of Coen's land, Ben saw additional guards had been posted, armed with automatic weapons instead of shotguns. A few wore flak jackets and had grenades clipped to their belts.

Ben found suitcases stacked in the foyer when he was ushered into Coen's home, after another drive through his marijuana-scented fields. What remained of the furniture had been covered up, much of it having already been removed.

Ben heard Coen's heels clacking against the stone floor a moment before he appeared, looking haggard and worn, stray strands of hair having escaped his ponytail.

"You just caught me," Coen said shortly.

"You're leaving?"

"Apparently the Israelis have learned that the reports of my death were greatly exaggerated."

"Was it my fault?"

"We'll never know, will we?"

"Where will you go now?"

"When you no longer have a home, Inspector, it doesn't matter." Coen waved him forward. "We've got to make this fast; I want to get out of here before midnight."

"You haven't packed up your computer equipment?" Ben asked, falling in step behind him.

"I don't plan to. I'd rather leave it for the Israelis and let them waste their time trying to make sense of everything."

Coen led the way into the computer room. Ben had never been inside its glass solarium walls at night before and the dark world beyond gave the room the feel of a jail cell. True to Coen's words, though, the equipment itself remained untouched, at least for the moment.

"Now," he said. "What have you got for me?"

I REGRET TO inform you that Rav Nitzav Giott has been hospitalized," Baruch said expressionlessly.

"What happened?" The words felt like marbles sliding out Danielle's mouth as she stood rigidly halfway between the door and the big desk that had always dwarfed the small man who had helped forge her career.

"A stroke, I think. He was rushed to the hospital late yesterday. I'm afraid the prognosis is not very good." Baruch rocked the chair forward and stood up the better to face Danielle. "You came here to tell him something?"

"That's between me and the commissioner." Still marbles, but smaller ones now, emerging more smoothly from her mouth.

"Then it is between you and me, Chief Inspector, because I have been appointed to fill this role until a successor can be chosen."

"Too bad Captain Shoshanna Tavi wasn't available."

"Most regrettable, in fact," Baruch said, holding her stare

with a strange lack of emotion. "For now I can only tell you that a permanent replacement for Commissioner Giott is on the verge of being named."

Danielle swallowed hard and remained silent.

"Of course," Baruch resumed, "none of the positions immediately beneath him have been filled, and Captain Tavi's unfortunate demise leaves both available. *Nitzav*, commander, and *tat nitzav*, deputy commander, are still open. Would you be interested in one of those positions, Pakad?"

Danielle understood the game he was playing and the stakes involved. Not even the death of his mistress Shoshanna Tavi seemed to have moved Baruch at all. Danielle realized he had used Tavi in one way, just as he was trying to use her in another.

Baruch strolled out slowly from behind Hershel Giott's desk, keeping his eyes on her the whole time. "I understand your reluctance. You have been an investigator with National Police and a field operative with Shin Bet. But a commander or deputy commander must practice politics instead of forensics. Knowing what to say, when to say it, and to whom. Everything is dictated by necessity with the long view in mind, not the short. Do you follow me, Pakad?"

Danielle remained silent.

"The person chosen for *nitzav* or *tat nitzav* must be someone capable of exercising discretion, of being able to prioritize. That means putting the concerns of the state first, of knowing when to yield. Sometimes it means compromising one's values to work toward a consensus and achieve a greater whole. Are you such a person, Pakad?"

"No," Danielle said finally. "I don't think I am."

Baruch bristled. "That would be regrettable, a terrible waste."

"Like the loss of your military career?" Danielle watched Baruch's face redden as she continued. "I know why my father reprimanded you. I know you executed a Palestinian prisoner in the field. You want to blame my father for never having advanced, go ahead. You want to get your revenge on me, fine. Anything to avoid taking the responsibility yourself, including turning your wrath on all Palestinians." She lowered her voice. "That must be what the oil the Americans found in the Judean is all about, isn't it? You've gone to such great lengths to keep its existence a secret, because somehow you're going to use it against the Palestinians. Right or wrong, Commander?"

Baruch fought to remain calm. "It appears I have misjudged you again, Pakad. I thought there was hope for your future, I truly did. I was willing to overlook your indiscretions and what could be construed as the high treason that you committed in the United States."

"What?"

"You killed an Israeli national who was duly retained to arrange your detention. That leaves me with no choice other than to conclude that the initial reports of your suspected complicity and collaboration with certain Palestinian officials may have some validity, after all."

Baruch seemed to be enjoying every word and phrase he uttered. Danielle almost expected to see him smile. Indeed, he looked like a man trying very hard to hold back his pleasure over holding such a great advantage on her.

"Go to hell," Danielle said, anyway.

Baruch scowled. "You think you know what hell is, Pakad? You don't yet, but you will."

"I already do," Danielle snapped at him. "It's a world where schools are closed for no reason, where men are detained without cause and incarcerated for months without trial. Sound familiar?"

Baruch's face was turning bright red. "It sounds like treason."

"I quite agree."

"I was speaking of any Israeli who would level such charges."

"And I was speaking of the man who helped enact those programs in the West Bank, Commander."

Baruch tried hard to keep himself calm. "Well then, I guess that makes me the devil."

"More than that. I understand Rabbi Mordecai Lev knew

the truth about what was really going on in the Judean Desert as well. That means you must have told Lev everything about the American geologists. You were working with him from the beginning."

Baruch's eyes popped. "Your Palestinian friend, Ben Kamal, told you this, didn't he? The Palestinian you collaborated with. You incriminate yourself with your baseless accusations, Pakad. You are a traitor."

"Who is the real traitor, Commander? What's your connection to the Amudei Ha'aretz? Why bother protecting oil that's useless for the foreseeable future?"

"I'm going to let you leave, Pakad."

"Because you're afraid to arrest me."

Baruch took a menacing step forward, hands held taut by his sides. "I have other plans for you."

"No doubt you do."

"You are dismissed."

Danielle finally backed up for the door. "I'm going to find what it is you're hiding, Commander. And I'm going to destroy you."

THE PHOTOS ARE in good shape, considering their age," Ari Coen said after inspecting the snapshots Ben had produced.

"What happens now?" Ben asked him.

Coen wheeled his chair over to a state-of-the-art scanner. "We digitize each picture and transfer it onto a database. Then we ask the computer to enlarge and clarify the digitalizations, so they can be read. You might even be in for a pleasant surprise."

"Surprise?"

"Well," Coen explained, "fifty years ago the faded or illegible portions of the scroll remained a mystery. Today, even using photographs, the computer will be able to see what we can't and fill in many of the blanks. That should yield a much more complete translation than anything Winston Daws could ever have come up with."

The process went surprisingly fast. Coen was careful to keep Winston Daws's snapshots in the precise order in which Ben had handed them to him. The scanner screen could accommodate three at once, and Ben listened to the quiet whir of Coen's computer as it accepted the material. He watched the pictures gather shape on the monitor, Coen moving on to the next series only after the screen flashed DIGITALIZATION COMPLETE.

There were fifty-four snapshots in all, accounting for eighteen separate digitalizations for the computer to complete. Ben had no idea how many of these Daws had actually translated with Mordecai Lev's help to begin the story that had led to his death; he would not know that until he found someone to finish the job, so the story would be complete.

"Now," Ari Coen said, gathering up the pictures in a neat stack before sliding over to the printer, "let's see what we have here. . . ."

CHAPTER 83

I HOPE THESE prove worth it, Inspector," Coen said as he handed Ben a stack of fifty-four pages, one for each of Daws's pictures.

Because the photos had been of different sections of a scroll, there was some overlap of contents, the end of one page often repeated at the beginning of another. But the writing was surprisingly legible, except for those blurred areas even the computer could not enhance.

Ben studied the top page. "I can't read the language. Is it Hebrew?"

"Aramaic, I think. Long dead. Not many around who can even translate it anymore."

"I know somebody," Ben said, flirting with a smile.

Coen switched off his color printer. "Then this might be your lucky day."

HERSHEL GIOTT LAY in a hospital bed in the intensive care ward of Jerusalem's Hadassah Hospital, so many tubes and wires running in and out of him that the machines had to fight for space around his bedside. It was all Danielle could do to look at her mentor as tears brimmed in her eyes.

She had maintained a daily vigil over her father after his stroke until he gradually wasted away and died. That day had brought relief with it until the reality that she was alone had sunk in. Her mother dead, both brothers, and finally her father. She learned she was pregnant only a few weeks later, looking upon it as a gift from her father as well as God. But then the gift was cruelly torn from her and with it, perhaps, the opportunity to live the life Israeli women were supposed to. And yet she realized it had been a good thing for her in the end, forcing her to look more deeply into herself and decide exactly what it was she wanted out of life.

Now, standing at her dying mentor's bedside, she could feel a life growing in her again. A second chance, perhaps her last chance. The baby all that mattered, the baby and its father who might be dead soon too unless she could do something to prevent it.

Before her Hershel Giott stirred, but Danielle recalled the doctor's words that he continued to lapse in and out of consciousness without ever regaining lucidity. How much she wanted to say to him, but time had run out as it always seemed to. Once again she had fooled herself into believing there would always be another day, only to be disappointed. Maybe someday she would learn.

Giott's eyes fluttered and he mumbled something. Danielle saw that his parched lips were wedged together by dried spittle. She lifted the water cup from his bedside, made sure the top was tightly on, and eased the straw into his mouth. The old man's throat pursed and writhed, working hard to suck in some liquid.

After all he has done for me, Danielle thought, *this is the best I can do for him.*

The water began dribbling down his chin and she pulled it back, drying the droplets with a tissue.

Water . . .

Something began to dawn on her while she stood there

with the plastic cup in her hand, the water swirling about inside it.

Water . . .

A resource more valuable than oil in the landlocked West Bank that drew eighty percent of its supply from the Eastern Aquifer beneath the desert.

Oh, my God . . . of course!

At last she understood the basis for the unholy alliance that had been forged between Rabbi Mordecai Lev and Commander Moshe Baruch. The reason why oil in the West Bank was so valuable to them . . . and why they needed to keep its existence a secret from everyone else.

Because this wasn't really about oil at all.

Standing over Hershel Giott's bedside, Danielle began to tremble. It was as though her mentor had revealed it all to her, one final gift to remember him by.

Ben, she thought, realizing the true scope of what they were facing. *I've got to find Ben. . . .*

Y OU REALIZE THE value these have," Coen said, handing Ben a large manila envelope.

Ben squeezed the fifty-four pages inside and fastened the clasp. "They're not the originals."

"But, according to you, they still tell a story no man has ever heard. Think about that."

"I have. Too much."

"You should do something about your conscience, Inspector."

"Like you have?"

Coen shrugged. "All I have to believe in is money, and one thing I've learned since leaving Israel is that money isn't enough."

"Why don't you go home?"

"Did it work for you, Inspector?"

An alarm began to sound through the house.

"Intruders," Coen said. "We've got to get you out of here," he added, and surged ahead of Ben toward the door. "Hurry!"

Outside, the staccato bursts of gunfire could clearly be heard. Overhead the distant whine of jet aircraft was getting louder.

"Take my Jeep," Coen said, tossing Ben the keys as they rushed out of the house. "It's your only chance."

"You should do something about your conscience too."

Coen started to retreat back inside. "I've been here before. Just get the hell away and tell Colonel al-Asi I'll contact him from wherever I end up."

Coen disappeared inside before Ben could say thank you. He turned and sprinted toward the black sports utility vehicle parked in the semicircular drive set before the house.

Ben had just climbed behind the wheel when the first explosions lit up the sky, followed by the spreading glow of fire as a section of Ari Coen's marijuana crop burst into flames.

Napalm! The jets were firing napalm!

Ben revved the Jeep's engine and spun it back down the drive, tucking the envelope with the digitized pages of Josephus's lost scroll under his jacket to protect it. A hundred yards down the road, the bright lights of an Israeli army armored personnel carrier nearly blinded him, and with no place else to go, he turned off into the fields, where he knew the Israeli soldiers would not follow, since the napalm would reduce them to smoldering ash in a matter of minutes.

The Jeep bucked through the thick stalks that surrounded him on all sides, separated by only yard-wide rows between the plants. He could hear the screech of incoming rockets and felt the Jeep jostled each time one struck. A few times it seemed the tires were actually lifted off the ground, more so with each strike, and Ben realized he was literally racing the fire-breathing rockets across Ari Coen's land. He could feel the sweat soaking through his shirt. The envelope containing the pictures and pages was already wet, and Ben desperately feared they were going to go the way of the original scroll.

Lost. Gone forever.

He couldn't let that happen.

The flames reared up in his rearview mirror, and Ben gave the Jeep more gas as twin rockets exploded on either side of him. All at once the flames briefly enclosed the vehicle, until the Jeep sped out of them only to encounter yet another series. This time a wall of fire lay directly in his path, and Ben burst through it feeling the heat start to sear him and watching the paint peel off the Jeep's hood in the glow of the flames around him. It felt as though the air were being sucked out of his lungs. The steering wheel was scorching beneath his hands. The back window exploded and a hot gush of wind, followed closely by a finger of fire, singed the back of his neck.

Ben screamed in desperation and stamped the accelerator pedal all the way to the floor. He had found hell and half expected the demons of his past to scratch at the car as he tore past them.

But there was only the return of an endlessly black night and a sudden cool wash of air welcoming Ben back to the world he gratefully surged into.

DAY NINE

CHAPTER 84

BEN LEANED AGAINST the door, pounding it again and again.

"I'm coming! I'm coming!" a weary voice called from inside. Father Mike finally flung the door open and regarded him with a shocked expression. "What the hell happened to you?"

Ben leaned against the doorjamb for support, showed Father Mike the envelope in his left hand. "How well do you remember your Aramaic?"

FLAVE POCACINNI WATCHED with piqued curiosity as the priest ushered a man he recognized as Ben Kamal into the small rectory attached to the Jericho church. Pocacinni had been at his post, nestled amid refuse in a narrow alley between two buildings across the street, for twelve hours now. From this distance, even through his miniature binoculars, Pocacinni could not tell whether Ben Kamal was carrying anything on his person.

He dialed a number on his digital phone and spoke as soon as it was answered.

"This is Pocacinni, Colonel," he said to Gianni Lorenzo. "He's here."

THEY SAT AT the kitchen table, the envelope between them, Ben guzzling water from a glass he kept refilling from a pitcher.

Father Mike touched the envelope with a finger, stopped short of grasping it. "So the legendary lost scroll of Josephus exists, after all. . . ."

Ben finished draining another glass. "Just a copy, I'm afraid."

"What's the difference? You have the proof you wanted."

"I don't know what I have. I need you to tell me."

Father Mike hesitated, eyes rotating between Ben and the manila envelope. "I could destroy this right now."

"You won't."

"Why?"

"Because you want to know the truth as much as I do."

"Do I?"

Ben shoved the envelope across the table at the priest. "Yes."

FATHER MIKE RETURNED to the table wearing his reading glasses with a yellow legal pad and pen in hand. A single bulb, hanging from the ceiling, provided a thin shaft of light that extended barely beyond the reach of the table.

Ben watched him flipping through the pages, making notes on the legal pad as he went. Some sections of the scroll's contents took longer to go over than others. A few, as Ben suspected, must have indeed been indecipherable based on the way Father Mike referred to them on his pad.

Time lost meaning; the hours passed with the pages and the notes. Ben nodded off in brief spurts that ended as more pages were flipped and more notes taken. Father Mike never looked up, never seemed to move anything other than his eyes, hand, and pen across the pad. He showed no reaction at all, lost in a scholar's indifference yet obsessed by the task. Ben left him to that task in silence.

With the last page flipped, Father Mike continued to hold his gaze downward, his attention rooted on the notes before him as if he had disappeared into the story they told. Ben watched him flip his notes back to the first page. Father Mike removed his reading glasses and rubbed his eyes. When he finally looked up, his face was blank.

"I don't know if you're going to like this," the priest started.

CHAPTER 85

THE OLD DOCTOR heard heavy feet sloshing through the mud before he saw the two shadowy figures lugging a third between them.

"I've been waiting since sundown, Captain," the doctor said, holding the door open. "Hurry up and get him inside."

The soldiers carried the man into the dim glow cast by the room's oil light. They smelled like the rank and spoiled street muck that coated their feet. Perspiration, strong and salty, glistened on their brows and dropped from their cheeks. The trail of blood that had speckled the mud in their wake followed them across the stone floor.

"Lay him on the table," the doctor ordered. He closed the door behind him and made sure all the shutters were latched. "He is still alive, I presume?"

"We wouldn't have bothered, if he wasn't," the captain replied, straightening the unconscious man's legs upon a heavy wood table matted with straw that crackled under his weight.

"A fool's errand, nonetheless," the doctor said, approaching the table with lantern in hand.

"We all have our orders." The captain frowned. "To follow whether we approve of them or not."

"I'm not a member of your Roman guard."

"You are a citizen, all the same."

"But not a miracle worker." The doctor moved his lantern closer to the prisoner and ran it along the length of his body, stopping at his head, where plum-colored blood soaked the table in a widening swatch. "Do your superiors really expect to get away with this?"

"They have no choice."

The doctor looked up from the prisoner and swallowed hard. "And this has no chance."

"Just do your part. What happens afterward is not your concern."

"And if I refuse?"

"My orders are to kill you."

The doctor laid a goatskin bag containing his instruments on a stone pedestal within easy reach of the table. "Then I suppose I should get started."

He lifted a pot from the open flame where he had set it long before to boil and placed it too on the pedestal next to a rag. Next he removed the first instrument from his bag and inspected it in the dull glow of the oil light.

"All the same, Captain, even if this works it will change nothing."

"You'd better hope it does," the captain said grimly, "for all our sakes."

FROM WHAT YOU'VE told me, that was as far as Winston Daws—and Lev as a young man—got in their translation," Father Mike explained after he had finished paraphrasing the first part of Josephus's tale. "Because so much of the scroll was illegible, and because they lacked the equipment they needed, they assumed the patient was Christ and the doctor had been ordered to save him."

"And the Knights Templars struck before Daws and Lev could get any further."

"If they had," Father Mike said. "If they'd been able to . . ."

"What?"

Father Mike's face was grim, or perhaps just weary. "You really want to know?"

"Why wouldn't I?"

"Because you may not like what you hear, Ben," Father Mike said and picked up his paraphrased translation of the story where he had left off.

THE DOCTOR MOVED a circular instrument over the prisoner's right palm. The hand was dirty, but otherwise unmarred by blood or wound. The doctor started to lower the point of the instrument toward his flesh, then stopped and gazed again at the two soldiers from the Roman guard.

"I'm much more used to treating wounds, not inflicting them."

"This man had been sentenced to die anyway," the captain said matter-of-factly.

"So I am to be his executioner."

"It is a better way to die than what we had planned for him: he raped and murdered a child."

The doctor grimaced.

"Does that make your job any easier?" the captain wondered.

"Not when his greatest crime is the resemblance he bears to—"

"Please get on with it, Doctor."

"I swore an oath, Captain."

"So did I. Now hurry."

The doctor adjusted the nearest lantern slightly before proceeding. He aimed his round-edged instrument directly for the center of the prisoner's palm, felt a brief tug of re-

sistance as it pierced the top layer of flesh before the impetus carried its razor-sharp tip effortlessly through bone and gristle until it emerged through the back of the prisoner's hand. Hesitating not at all, the doctor moved to the other side of the table, readjusted the lantern, and repeated the process on the prisoner's left hand.

"What next?" the doctor asked as twin pools of blood ran down the table from the matching wounds, dripping to the floor.

"His skull," the captain replied, drawing an imaginary line across his own upper brow.

"The crown of thorns . . ."

"And a spear wound in his side. I will show you exactly where when you pull up his shirt."

"You don't have to."

The doctor moved around to the rear of the table to work on the prisoner's skull as instructed with a different instrument, but found both his hands shaking. He fought to squeeze the blood back into them, trying to remain detached.

"When I was first contacted, I thought . . . I thought . . ."

"You thought what, Doctor?"

"That you were going to bring Jesus himself here. That you took him down alive from the cross and wanted me to save him."

The captain laughed. "That would be quite impossible."

"Why?"

"Because he was dead when we took him down, a day ago now."

"Then what—"

"His body disappeared from the cave we placed it in." The captain gestured at the prisoner on the table. "That man is our replacement."

"BUT THE ROMAN guard was too late," Father Mike continued, looking up at Ben. "According to the scroll, by the time the soldiers brought this nameless prisoner to the cave to replace Jesus, the disappearance of his body had already been discovered."

Ben felt numb all over, grateful when Father Mike paused so he could collect his thoughts. But his mind was still floundering in the short moments before the priest resumed.

"It was a conspiracy, Ben, one of the oldest of all time. Once Christ's body was found to have vanished, the Jews concocted the plot and paid the Romans to carry it out. The tale Josephus tells goes into some detail concerning that."

"What about the resurrection?" Ben managed to ask.

Father Mike held the reconstructed pages in both hands. "The tale these tell ends before that time. It does not prove Jesus rose from the dead, but neither does it disprove it." Father Mike's eyes sharpened, seeming to glow in the room's shadow-draped light. "But He vanished from the tomb, Ben. You have found the clearest, most direct proof of that ever uncovered. Congratulations."

Ben sat there, struck by the irony. In his obsessive desire to prove Christ had been nothing more than a man, he might well have proven quite the opposite. If there had been any explanation for his body vanishing, other than the long accepted gospel, then why would the Jews and Romans have bothered staging so elaborate a conspiracy? That could only have been concocted out of fear in the wake of their misdeed, misjudgment, and overreaction.

Ben rose from his chair and walked to the kitchen's single window set over the sink. He gazed out into the darkness in search of answers the light had yet revealed. His journey had brought him to a different end than expected, and he didn't know what to make of it yet.

"Ben."

He saw Father Mike's reflection in the glass next to him.

"Ben."

Father Mike reached for him and spun Ben around, their positions exchanged, the red dot that would have landed on Ben's forehead lodging on Father Mike's instead.

"*No!*" Ben screamed, barreling into him as glass shattered behind his ear.

Impact took them both into the kitchen table that tipped over, spilling its contents to the floor. Ben landed atop Father Mike and separated himself as more gunfire peppered the room.

"They're here," he muttered.

"Who?" the priest asked, his face wide with terror.

"The Knights Templars, the Israelis—I don't know." Ben's mind was whirling. His eyes traced the pages of the manuscript that had scattered across the floor. Then he slid away from Father Mike and began collecting them. Glass popped and crackled the whole time and he felt the slivers raining onto him.

"We've got to get out of here!" Father Mike called to him.

"No, *you* have to get out of here; it's me they've come for."

Finally satisfied he had gathered all the pages, Ben crawled back to Father Mike and pressed the floppy disc that contained the manuscript and Daws's original pictures into his hand.

"What am I supposed to do with these?" the priest asked.

"Hold on to them for safekeeping. Can you make your way out through the back?"

Father Mike nodded.

"I'm going to head into the church, hopefully draw them in after me. As soon as you hear voices, get out of here and don't look back. Okay?"

"I hope you know what you're doing, my son."

"Keeping you alive, and that manuscript intact, are good enough. The best I can hope for. Now, just get ready!"

CHAPTER 86

BEN SHOOK THE glass off his back and crawled into the short hallway connecting the rectory to the church. He stayed on the floor when he reached the church hall, mindful of the large windows lining the walls.

The scent of sawdust mixing awkwardly with that of fresh paint was sharp and pungent. He continued to crawl, drawing even with a fireplace still aglow with fading flames when the faint echo of a gun bolt being drawn back froze him, even before the shadow of a man loomed overhead. Ben looked up.

A face as expressionless as death gazed down. The man gestured with his silenced submachine gun for him to rise. Ben did as he was ordered, clutching the now-wrinkled pages tight to his chest.

The front door burst open and more gunmen entered in single file, fanning out as they surrounded Ben, keeping their weapons poised on him. The last man through the door wore an ill-fitting military uniform that sagged on his frame, the excess cloth billowing slightly.

"Hello, Colonel," Ben greeted Gianni Lorenzo. "Welcome to Palestine."

It all seemed so absurd, so ironic. Here he was about to die for a discovery this man and others had killed to protect, unaware that the contents of the scroll actually affirmed, even validated, their beliefs.

"I believe you finally have something for me, Inspector Kamal," Gianni Lorenzo said, holding his ground.

Ben joined a second hand over the manuscript and began to laugh. The Knights Templars looked at each other and then to their commander for guidance.

Before he could provide any, though, a burst of automatic fire ringed the church, digging divots from the wall nearest Lorenzo. The Knights Templars took cover instinctively. Ben dove behind one of the pews, while the colonel held every inch of his ground.

"Is that you, Chief Inspector Barnea?" Lorenzo called.

"Have your men drop their weapons," Danielle ordered from the cover of the altar.

"I can't do that, Chief Inspector."

"I'm not giving you a choice."

Ben caught sight of the Knights shifting positions, trying to better their angles toward the altar. What was Danielle doing here? Why had she taken such a risk?

"Can you hear me, Ben?" Danielle called to him.

"Yes," he said from his covered position behind the pew.

"Listen to me, you were right about the oil, about Lev and why he cared about it so much. Because this isn't about oil at all; it's about *water*," Danielle explained, stating what she had realized in Hershel Giott's hospital room. "Lev's going to use the oil to poison the water coming into the West Bank!"

THE PAGES FELT suddenly heavy in Ben's hands. His knees shook, then tightened beneath him.

Water . . .

The most precious commodity of any in the West Bank

by far. Two underground aquifers alone were responsible for supplying the West Bank with all its water, and the Israelis maintained extremely tight control over both of them. Poisoning the much larger Eastern Aquifer with oil was as simple as it was unthinkable, the results sure to be catastrophic.

To all but Mordecai Lev and Commander Moshe Baruch, that is. Two extremists joined in an unholy alliance by a common goal. Ben should have known when he saw a virtually identical drilling apparatus set upon the land of Lev's newest settlement; in place to find water, not oil. No settlement, Asher Katz had explained to Ben that day, can survive without water.

Neither can a people.

"Lev and Baruch are going to force the Palestinians off their own land, turn this entire region into a desert, a wasteland!" Danielle resumed as the Knights Templars continued trying to better their positions. "That was their plan all along."

And there was no time and no way to stop Lev, Ben added in his mind, nothing at all any of them could do. Unless . . .

Ben sucked in a deep breath and bounced up from behind the pew, holding the pages of what had been Josephus's scroll over his head. "This is what you want, Colonel!" he called to Lorenzo. "This is what you've killed to protect for over half a century!"

Lorenzo looked suddenly unsure of what to do. "Give it to me."

Ben lurched backward until he could feel the dull heat of the dying flames behind him. "You should have listened to me before, Colonel. But you would have killed us in the Villa Borghese, whether I handed over the manuscript or not. I won't make the same mistake this time."

With that, Ben hurled all but the first ten pages of the manuscript into the fire. Instantly the flames lifted upward, gratefully swallowing the paper.

Lorenzo surged forward, stopped when he saw the pages had already blackened and shriveled. "What have you done?"

Ben held out the first part of the manuscript toward him.

"Don't worry, I saved you the best part. Here, take it."

Lorenzo looked at the pages, but didn't take them.

"Only the scroll doesn't tell the story either one of us thought it did, Colonel. In fact, it tells pretty much the opposite. Proves Christ wasn't a man, after all."

Lorenzo's eyes bulged and he snatched the pages from Ben's outstretched hand.

"You won't find the proof in those, though," Ben continued. "That comes later, the pages I burned."

Lorenzo flipped through the pages quickly, growing incensed. "You damn fool."

"Don't worry, Colonel, I can get you another copy. But first you have to help me."

"Help you *what*?"

"Stop Mordecai Lev. He's your enemy too and I know where he is. Help me stop him from poisoning the West Bank's water supply and the rest of the pages are yours."

"You could be lying. Again."

Ben gestured toward the pages Lorenzo was holding. "Have those translated, Colonel. Then tell me I'm lying."

Gianni Lorenzo hesitated. "You're sure you know where we can find Lev?"

"Yes." Ben nodded, turning toward the altar and Danielle. "I am."

CHAPTER 87

Fʀᴏᴍ ᴛʜᴇ ᴄʜᴜʀᴄʜ in Jericho, the strange convoy drove straight to the Judean Desert, stopping near the site where the Americans had been killed ten days before. The convoy parked its cars behind a hillside, and Lorenzo sent a scout team on ahead. Twenty minutes later, he approached Ben and Danielle with what they had found.

"You were right, Inspector: the area around the cave is crawling with armed men—Israelis, according to my scouts."

"Baruch's people," said Ben. "And the trucks I told you about?"

Lorenzo shook his head. "No trucks of any kind in the area."

Ben nodded. "Because whatever was inside them has already been off-loaded, soon to be put to use." The process of transporting the equipment Lev needed deep underground must have been completed within the last day or so, Ben figured. With Commander Moshe Baruch of Shin Bet in charge of security, fear of being discovered had never entered in. "Can you handle Baruch's men, Colonel?"

Lorenzo looked from Ben to Danielle. "While the two of you . . ."

"Deal with Lev," Ben completed.

"You believe he's in that cave?"

Ben recalled Abid Rahman's mentioning the fact that this particular cave swept deep down into the subterranean layers of the mountainside along a precarious trail. "I'm sure he is."

Lorenzo frowned. "Very well, then. My men will deal with the guards, creating safe passage for you to reach the cave."

"Do I have your word, Colonel?"

"You have God's word, Inspector."

With that, Lorenzo grouped his Knights Templars together to give them their orders.

"We'd never be able to stop Lev without him," Ben whispered to Danielle, reading her mind.

"All the same, it's like making a deal with the devil."

"Maybe the real devil's in that cave, Pakad."

Lorenzo returned to them moments later, his men having already slipped away across the desert to carry out their part of the mission.

"They'll signal us when their work is finished," he reported.

Ben checked his watch and found it was just after three A.M., leaving another two hours of darkness. He had just glanced at his watch again thirty minutes later when Lorenzo received a call over a palm-sized walkie-talkie.

"The route into the cave is clear. My men will watch your backs just in case." Lorenzo grabbed Ben's arm before he could move away. "Make sure you come out of this alive, Inspector. I want the rest of that manuscript."

Ben waited for Lorenzo to let go, then turned to Danielle. "Let's go, Pakad."

"Go with God, Inspector," Lorenzo said as they started down the hill for her Jeep, where they had left their weapons and equipment.

Upon reaching the vehicle, Danielle opened the front door and leaned inside the front seat to grab their pack. Just as her hand closed upon it, Ben latched a handcuff onto her wrist and fastened the other end to the steering wheel before she could swing back toward him.

"What the hell are you doing?" she demanded, yanking mightily on the cuffs.

"I'm sorry, Pakad," Ben said, and reached past her for the pack.

"What's wrong with you?"

"Nothing. Absolutely nothing."

She groped for him with her free hand as he pulled the pack out. "Let me go!"

Ben shook his head. "I can't do that."

"Why, for God's sake?"

Ben's voice remained icily calm. "You told me the child would always be mine too, even if I can't really be a father to him."

"I know what I said."

"Then understand that I'm doing this for him. To give him the best chance to survive, no matter how he is raised."

She tugged on the handcuff and the metal rattled against the steering wheel. "For God's sake, let me go!"

"I am," said Ben.

CHAPTER 88

THE LAST STRETCH to the cave was across open desert. Ben could sense the presence of Gianni Lorenzo's Knights Templars about him, lying in wait in case more of Mordecai Lev's Amudei Ha'aretz, or men from Shin Bet dispatched by Moshe Baruch, showed themselves. The Knights had already hauled away the bodies of those killed in the initial attack. Other Israelis, currently out patrolling the perimeter, could probably be expected, and the Knights would handle those as well. They had come for Winston Daws on a night like this, the American geologists on yet another, and who knew how many others in between. All in the name of God. All toward keeping a secret that did not need to be kept.

Ben raced up the steps of the goat path leading to the cave and yanked a flashlight from his pocket once he was inside. Ben recalled how this particular cave swirled downward and guessed the Americans had included that in their report. Rabbi Lev would likely seek out the lowest point and drill down as far as he could before dropping in an explosive.

The rest would unfold with inevitable precision. The shale above the oil would rupture. The pressure would force the reserves upward into the land. Within months, weeks even, the oil would seep into the primary aquifer servicing the West Bank and poison it for years, perhaps decades. With their water supply tainted, and no other source readily available, two million Palestinians would be forced from their homes. The West Bank would become a wasteland, true to Lev's—and Moshe Baruch's—mad vision.

Before pressing on, Ben removed a pistol and a Heckler and Koch submachine gun from his pack as well. Then, submachine gun shouldered behind him, he began following the serpentine cave path he had only glimpsed the previous times he'd been here. The going was tough in places, all of it downhill and much of it very steep. Ben's trek was complicated by the fact that he was trying to move silently and didn't want to shine his flashlight too far ahead for fear of alerting Lev and whoever else had accompanied him into the cave.

The angle of descent changed to almost a sheer drop all of a sudden, and Ben fell onto his buttocks, sliding down the grade. He felt his skin lashed by rocks and stones and lost his grip on his flashlight that crashed somewhere below. He tried desperately to stop himself, but succeeded only when the grade leveled off once more. The back of his head struck something at the last and he touched it to find the wet stickiness of blood already matting down his hair. He felt dizzy and sick to his stomach, and tried to find some bearings in the darkness. He had quite literally entered Rabbi Mordecai Lev's world now.

Afraid he'd pass out if he waited any longer, Ben pulled himself back to his feet and trudged on, wobbling from side to side. He felt ahead with his hands that were already scraped and battered raw by his scrabbling fall. It grew colder, but he couldn't tell if he was shaking as a result of the temperature drop or the concussion he had likely suffered at the end of his fall.

Finally Ben heard the steady hum of machinery nearby.

Not very loud, but enough to snap him reasonably alert again. He pressed himself against the wall and snailed on, choosing his footing with extra caution since a slip this close to whatever awaited him was certain to give his presence away to anyone present.

The dim glow of lighting gradually sharpened as he crept forward. Ben swung the Heckler and Koch submachine gun around before him. His heart hammered against his chest, his breath suddenly short, and he tried to steady himself by thinking of Danielle.

Danielle . . .

If nothing else, she and the baby would come away from this safe and alive. He took great comfort in that, resigned to whatever else might happen.

The light ahead brightened and now Ben could hear words exchanged in Hebrew, hushed beneath the steady whir of machinery. He readied his submachine gun and stopped just before a large gap between two shiny rocks that led into a large flat area, perhaps the lowest point of the cave. He pressed against one of the rocks and peered around it.

Dressed in his dark ceremonial robes, Rabbi Mordecai Lev stood bowed in a position of prayer in the spray of powerful hydrogen vapor lights that had been set up around the cave floor. They illuminated the whole interior space from its high ceiling to its rough, stony floor. Nearby, a generator feeding power to the lights hummed loudly. In a slight depression before the rabbi, meanwhile, a pair of his followers had just finished removing a drill bit, twelve inches in diameter, from a mechanically operated cable attached to a winch that stretched a dozen feet up into the air. At their feet, a neat circular hole had been bored in the cave floor, likely descending hundreds of feet to the shale and bedrock that had concealed the oil for these many years.

Ben watched one of Lev's men remove a cone-shaped explosive called a shape charge from a black case and attach it to the cable in place of the drill bit. The other man moved to the winch's control panel, both his hands busy programming instructions that rendered the gun holstered on his hip useless as well. Besides Lev, these were the only two in sight.

Ben stepped down into the open area and steadied his sub-machine gun before him. "Stay where you are."

The two men tensed, stopping just short of going for their pistols.

Lev swung in Ben's direction. "Inspector Kamal, is that you?"

"You lied to me, Rabbi."

"The world is full of lies, Inspector. Have you brought me the scroll?"

"Tell your men to move away from the winch."

"I'm afraid I can't do that."

Suddenly the man on the left drew his pistol. Ben dropped into a crouch and fired, pulling the trigger and holding it until both men had been hit. Impact hurled them backward, almost out of sight, and left the explosive device to sway harmlessly over the hole it had been destined for.

"It's over, Rabbi," Ben said, advancing straight toward him.

Ben heard stones shift behind him and spun. He saw a figure lunging at him from a dark corner of the cave. Before he could bring his submachine gun around, a shovel struck Ben square in the middle of the back and pitched him forward. His submachine gun clacked across the cave floor as he dropped to his knees, then fell face first to the hard cave floor. For a long moment he couldn't feel his legs, and when the feeling came back they were numb. He looked up as the large figure of Asher Katz reached down and stripped the pistol from his belt, tossing it aside.

Katz took a single step back and aimed his own subma-chine gun straight down on Ben.

CHAPTER 89

N O ! " LEV ORDERED, sensing Katz's intention as clear as though he had sight. "I want him to see. I want him to bear witness to the end of his people and the return of Judea and Samaria to Israel. Is he alone?"

"Yes," Katz reported, and slid slightly away from Ben. "There's no one coming behind him."

"As I expected."

Through the pain, Ben fought to turn his gaze on Rabbi Lev as Katz took the place of the dead man at the winch's controls. A flip of a single switch on a small panel was all it took to send the cable descending into the dark hole drilled to accommodate the shape charge now attached to its end. It looked as though the cave floor were swallowing it, one rapid gulp at a time.

Rabbi Lev removed a transistorized detonator from his pocket and held it reverently before him. "When the cable stops its descent, it will be time to return this land to its rightful owner. We will await that moment together, Inspector Kamal."

"Go to hell."

"The very place you have been these many years, and where your people will go when they leave the land of Israel." Lev continued to stand reverently, placidly. "The Palestinians at last will be vanquished, and at the same time my vengeance against an even older enemy is achieved."

"You're wrong, Rabbi." Ben could feel his strength returning as the machine's whine steepened. "Daws's scroll doesn't tell the story you were expecting at all. Quite the opposite. It proves there *was* another Messiah before the one you're waiting for and His name was Jesus Christ. Sorry to disappoint you."

Mordecai Lev's face twisted into a scowl beneath his dark glasses. His body trembled.

"You can kill me," Ben said quite calmly. "You can blow up the oil and poison our water, but you still don't *win,* Rabbi, because the entire basis of the Amudei Ha'aretz's existence is a lie. Do you hear me? A lie!"

Lev stumbled forward, tripped, and started to fall. Asher Katz lurched to catch him, his attention turned away from Ben.

Ben wasn't sure where he found the strength to lunge, couldn't be sure his legs would even work when he needed them. But he managed to crash into Katz as the bigger man supported Lev with both hands. All three of them tumbled back to the cave floor. The detonator skittered across the dirt, coming to rest yards away from Lev.

A loud *click* followed as the cable reached its preprogrammed end, the explosive now within blasting distance of the shale protectively sheathing the oil.

Mordecai Lev, sunglasses stripped off, rummaged about the ground for the detonator, fanning his hands desperately through the dirt. His elegant robes soiled now, a tear in one of the shoulders.

Ben locked on to Katz and rolled with him across the cave floor. Katz tried to free up his submachine gun but wasn't able to do so with Ben pressed against him. They exchanged wild blows, none having very much effect until Katz fastened his thumbs on Ben's throat from beneath him. Their bodies came to a halt against the winch, the angle improving Katz's leverage.

Ben felt the cartilage lining his windpipe begin to give, crackling audibly. He tried to strip Katz's grasp off, tried to pound his way free with no success. Then, as Mordecai Lev continued to flail about the ground behind him in search of the detonator, Ben latched one hand on to the cable and found enough slack to twist it around Katz's throat. The big man could still breathe, partly at least, until Ben stretched a hand up and pressed the button that started the cable rising out of the ground again.

The slack was taken up instantly and Katz's grasp on Ben was stripped away. The force of the cable rising jerked Katz to his feet and slammed him against the machine's housing. His face purpled and a low gurgling noise began to emanate from his throat. Katz's extra weight, though, tripped the machine's automatic shutdown circuit. The cable ground to a halt again, leaving Katz to strangle to death, his feet twitching madly.

Ben swung back toward Mordecai Lev just as the rabbi's right palm grazed the steel of the detonator. His fingers closed on it and he raised it before him in trembling hands, feeling for the button.

Ben tried to lunge, but his legs betrayed him and he found himself half crawling, half lurching across the cave floor. He threw himself through the air, screaming as Lev's thumb finally found the button.

Ben saw it compress, saw the red light flash on.

"No!"

But no explosion sounded in the earth beneath them. No rumble shook the cave.

Ben crashed his shoulder into the rabbi and sent the detonator flying again. It landed well back in the darkness, and Ben moved stiffly toward the winch's control panel. He untangled the cable from Asher Katz's neck and pulled his corpse down from the steel housing. Then Ben activated the controls to bring the shape charge back up. The winch began to whir and the cable climbed smoothly from the ground. Soon the explosive would clear the surface, preserving the Eastern Aquifer.

"God help me!" he heard Mordecai Lev scream. "God be with me!"

Ben swung to see that the old rabbi had found the detonator again. Holding it before him, Lev ran his thumb about the metal housing once more until he found the button and pressed it a second time.

A low-pitched rumble shook the walls. The floor quaked and nearly tore Ben's feet out from under him. The winch apparatus spilled over atop Asher Katz's corpse. Ben swung round one last time to see Rabbi Mordecai Lev standing with his arms raised toward the heavens in his scuffed and filthy robes.

Then Ben launched himself toward the cave path rising back to the entrance as the world began to crumble around him.

DANIELLE FINALLY GAVE up calling out for help, abandoned the futile effort to free herself from the steering wheel. She jammed keys to the Jeep into the ignition and gunned the engine. She used her free hand to shift into gear and tore across the floor of the Judean Desert, heading for the cave.

The hand Ben had cuffed to the wheel slowed her, but only slightly. Danielle aimed the Jeep straight for the steps of the goat path leading to the cave entrance. She switched on her high beams to help pierce the night and floored the gas pedal.

BEN RUSHED UPWARD through the darkness, coughing up the grit and dust that had spilled down his throat. He could feel the walls and roof of the cave collapsing around him, its structure compromised when the explosive charge had detonated too close to the surface. The pervasive black air before him gave up little view, and at times the steep increase in grade had him slipping back downward no matter how much he struggled to drag himself on. Yet, somehow, he fought to keep going, still believing he could make it out until the opening in the path before him started closing up, sealed by the time he reached it. Earth and stones began to pile upon him and he coughed dryly, spitting up dirt.

Trapped . . . No way out . . .

Ben pushed his palms desperately against the new wall before him and felt the world itself slipping from his grasp.

DANIELLE NEVER HESITATED, increasing her speed as she thumped up the steps of the goat path. Her high beams stretched for the sky as the heavy tires struggled up the incline. The Jeep bucked and rocked, but nonetheless climbed for the opening.

She had just realized the entire hillside around her seemed to be shaking when the Jeep slammed through the cave's entrance. Falling rocks pounded its hood, shattered its windshield. The cave was disintegrating before her eyes in the spill of the Jeep's headlights.

BEN BELIEVED HE saw a light. Just a sliver of it shining through the very top of the wall before him, but still enough to give him hope. He brushed the sand and dirt from his eyes and pulled himself to his feet. Stretching his hands upward, he found the opening and began to claw the soft dirt of the wall away. The more he clawed, the more light streamed in until, finally, the gap was wide enough to squeeze himself through.

Ben emerged on a crumbling incline. He inched along on his stomach, hands raking the dirt and stones. He pulled himself over a rise in the cave and the light grew almost blinding. Ben's watery, dirt-clogged eyes focused enough to see the nose end of Danielle's Jeep wedged through the entrance to the cave.

Her eyes bulged when she saw him leap onto the hood through a shower of rock and dirt and grab hold of the lip. She instantly shoved the powerful engine into reverse. The Jeep shook mightily, then freed itself. It plummeted down the steps sideways, Ben shed from its hood on the first of two rolls that left the Jeep lying inert on the driver's side when it hit the bottom.

"Danielle!" Ben screamed, dragging himself for the Jeep as the entrance to the cave vanished above him.

EPILOGUE

I N T H E E N D we had something in common after all, Inspector," Gianni Lorenzo said to Ben Kamal, who sat across from him in a common room of the Vatican residence in Jerusalem. "We are both men of our word."

Diplomatic and political concerns ruled out the Vatican maintaining an official consulate in Israel, but the residence fulfilled much the same purpose by allowing church officials to perform duties similar to those of an ambassador. But the common room's dark wood paneling and burgundy leather furniture gave it a somber cast neither the soft lighting nor a crackling fire could relieve. Ben sat with his back to that fire and could feel its heat through his chair.

"You are a good Christian," Lorenzo continued. "You have done a great service to the church."

"Because the killing would have continued otherwise, wouldn't it?" Ben challenged. The aches and pains from the previous night lingered. Every motion drew a grimace from him. His right arm should have been in a sling and he would be limping for months. But he felt only anger as he faced

Lorenzo. "How many more would have died?"

"As many as necessary." Lorenzo looked at the pile of pages still in Ben's lap, reconstructed from the floppy disc Ben had left with Father Mike the night before for safekeeping. "But none now, thanks to you."

"Too late to save my nephew," Ben said bitterly.

"I was fulfilling a charge passed on to me many years ago, Inspector," Lorenzo defended. "As a soldier of the church, I had no choice. You must understand that."

"I understand that a lot of good people are dead."

"So is Mordecai Lev."

"It's not a fair trade."

Lorenzo did not look apologetic. "And what if Lev had been right? What if the scroll really had proven that Christ was no more than an ordinary man? The deaths I caused are nothing compared to the upheaval the revelation of such a truth would have wrought. People have little enough faith as it is. They do not need to be tested." Again his gaze locked on the pages in Ben's lap. "But now, with that manuscript, at long last we can offer them proof their faith is justified."

"That's what I thought you'd say," Ben said with the slightest of smiles, wincing as he twisted toward the fire and tossed the pages into the flames.

Lorenzo jumped up from his chair. *"No!"*

He lunged across the room, almost to the fireplace when Ben added Daws's original pictures and Ari Coen's disc to the flames. The pages had already been reduced to blackened embers by the time Lorenzo got there. The pictures had melted. The disc was gone.

"For my nephew, Colonel." Ben looked at Gianni Lorenzo trembling with shock and struggling for breath before him. "To honor a promise I made to my brother. As you said, I'm a man of my word."

WHEN HE ARRIVED at the church in Jericho, Ben found Father Mike still cleaning up the mess made the night before.

"Need some help?"

Father Mike peered up from picking some of the larger shards of debris off the floor and sighed. "I think you've done enough for one lifetime."

"Exactly why I thought some of the usual penance might be in order."

Father Mike pushed himself to his feet, his knees cracking. "You know, I think you are a changed man, Inspector."

"Maybe I'm just tired."

"No," Father Mike said quite surely and deposited a handful of debris into a nearby trash can. "Something happened last night, didn't it?"

Ben again thought back to the moment in the cave when Rabbi Mordecai Lev pressed the button on his detonator the first time.

The red light had flashed, the charge had been triggered. . . .

"Yes," Ben said, "something happened."

Father Mike nodded knowingly. "Don't bother telling me about it. Whatever happened belongs to you. It's your miracle, Ben. Sometimes it's better to leave things that way." He gestured toward the pulpit. "Unless you would like to make it the subject of a guest sermon here some Sunday."

"You think people would really believe the story I've got to tell them?"

"Would you?" Father Mike put his arm lightly around Ben's shoulder and led him toward the rectory. "Never mind, let's go have some lunch."

"I'm sorry about all the damage."

"The Lord's house is always in need of repair, just like the soul of man."

"Amazing what you can do with a hammer and some nails, maybe a little glue."

Father Mike stopped and smiled. "Sometimes, Ben, it truly is."

* * *

From father mike's, Ben went straight to see Danielle at Hadassah Hospital in Jerusalem. A chilly spring rain had begun to fall and the dust the hot dry wind had blown into the city over the past week ran along the streets in thin streams.

"The doctors said they can't be sure about the baby for two more weeks," she told Ben as the rain pelted the window of her private room.

"But the indications . . ."

"All favorable. Miraculous, under the circumstances."

Ben smiled to himself.

Danielle propped herself up onto her elbows with a grimace. "Listen, about how we're going to raise him—"

Ben eased the tips of two fingers lightly over her lips. "Not now."

Danielle sighed. "What about the oil?"

"The explosion came too close to the surface to puncture its reservoir casing, so the West Bank's water supply is safe from contamination. And Colonel al-Asi tells me the oil's existence will remain a secret until engineers can bring it up in a way that makes sense economically. At that point, he has been assured that the profits will be shared between our peoples."

"Not if Moshe Baruch has anything to say about it." Danielle's gaze hardened, her eyes narrowing into slits of restrained fury. "We can't touch him, can we?"

"You know the answer to that better than I."

"He'll install his own people at National Police from top to bottom. I'll be lucky to get a job as a *samal sheni,* a corporal."

"I'm sorry about Commissioner Giott, Pakad."

"And I'm sorry about your nephew." Her gaze drifted. "I wonder . . ."

"What?"

"If he hadn't been part of the team that was killed, if there was never a reason for me to call you to the Judean Desert . . ." She frowned, letting the thought go. "God works in mysterious ways, I guess."

"Yes," Ben said. "He does."

Turn the page for a sneak peek at

JON LAND's

thrilling new novel of
international intrigue

THE
SEVEN
SINS

O N E

MCCARRAN AIRPORT, LAS VEGAS

Y OU WANT THE cab or not, mister?"

The voice startled Gianfranco Ferelli, and he switched his briefcase protectively from one hand to the other.

"Yes. I'm sorry," he said in broken English and climbed into the cab's backseat, instantly grateful for the relief the cool air brought after even such a brief exposure to the scorching desert heat. The setting of the sun two hours before had clearly provided no respite, and Ferelli mopped his stringy hair back into place atop his scalp. "Seven Sins Casino and Resort," he told the driver and felt the car lurch forward into traffic.

The flight from Rome to JFK had been smooth and quiet. But the next leg out of New York to McCarran Airport in Las Vegas was packed with loud and boisterous tourists who drank and gabbed away the hours. Even in first class, Ferelli was left to sit anxiously with the briefcase held protectively in his lap out of fear one of the drunken, soon-to-be-gambling revelers might make off with it if he dared sleep.

A few times he cracked open the case and peered at the photograph of Michael Tiranno, born Michele Nunziato, resting atop the stack of manila folders and envelopes. Captured in black and white, the man's face looked to have been drained of all fat as well as emotion. Lean in shape and sparse in feeling.

But Ferelli knew enough about Michael Tiranno, things that few men did, to realize quite the opposite was true. Tiranno might not have shared his passion, or worn it on the exterior. Yet that passion had been the calling card of a rise from orphaned farmboy to fabulously wealthy casino mogul. Along the way, those who had crossed Michael Tiranno had inevitably lived to regret it, and those who had aided him inevitably prospered as a result. It was said he interviewed all of his employees personally and could greet each and every one by name, offering a hundred-dollar, on-the-spot bonus anytime he failed to do so.

Ferelli had been in the company of royalty before; he'd been in the company of fame. But something about Michael Tiranno, captured even in a photograph, transcended both. Something about his eyes, the way he held his smile. Stare at the picture long enough and the eyes seemed to rotate until they locked on to Ferelli's gaze, at which point they would not let go. And that made the task before him all the more daunting because he could not imagine what it would be like to meet Michael Tiranno in person, much less how he might react to what Ferelli had to say.

Because the information contained in his briefcase would change Michael Tiranno's life forever.

Ferelli had spent the bulk of the flight from New York rehearsing lines in his head to explain his discovery. The circumstantial evidence that defied reason. The truth discerned from a terrible lie. Tiranno had never heard of him, and Ferelli was headed to the Seven Sins without benefit of an appointment.

Just give me five minutes, five minutes, I beg you. . . .

From there, a glimpse into the briefcase would be enough to guarantee all the time Gianfranco Ferelli needed.

Ferelli felt cold sweat soaking through his shirt and asked the cab driver to turn up the air-conditioning. Thankfully, he had made it this far without incident and had full confidence

Michael Tiranno would greatly value him coming all this way to share the secrets contained in his briefcase.

Gianfranco Ferelli knew he had nothing to fear, as his cab fell in behind four virtually identical sedans on Tropicana Avenue.

TWO

TROPICANA AVENUE, THE PRESENT

THE FOUR SEDANS clung to the speed limit, McCarran Airport shrinking in the distance behind them. The cars had been left in four different long-term lots the day before, the parking stubs tucked beneath the driver's-side visors. The cars had been chosen for their innocuousness, typical rentals that cruised the Vegas Strip with frequently flashing brake lights as their occupants took in the glitz and glamour they had come to sample.

But the sedans weren't rentals. Rentals might have aroused suspicion. Instead they had been purchased from used car dealerships, where the possibility of a sale dwarfed all other concerns. Even then, added precautions had been taken. The dealers were hundreds of miles apart and none less than five hundred miles from Las Vegas itself. In each instance the buyers were trained to barter before agreeing on a price, then to return the next day with a cashier's check for the agreed-upon amount.

At that point the cars were driven to four designated load points where their trunks were packed with chemical fertilizers stockpiled over a six-month period and dynamite smuggled in through Mexico. The drivers then headed for McCarran Airport and boarded four different flights out of the city during peak travel time.

The four men currently driving the cars had flown in today, arriving within ninety minutes of each other from four separate airports chosen for the least likelihood of delays. The weather had cooperated brilliantly and each of the flights had landed on time.

The drivers were now right on schedule, the lights of Las Vegas twinkling before them in the night.

THREE

THE SEVEN SINS, THE PRESENT

MR. TRUMBULL," NAOMI Burns greeted the man seated in a hand-carved chair in the lobby of the Seven Sins Casino and Resort.

"Sorry I'm late," Lars Trumbull told her, rising to his feet. He was tall and gangly, dressed in jeans with designer tears and a loose black Dolce & Gabbana shirt that hung shapelessly over his belt. He was younger than Naomi Burns had expected.

"Actually," she said, "you were an hour early. I imagine you've seen everything the lobby has to offer."

Trumbull's expression tightened a little. His face was thin, showcasing cheekbones that looked like ridges layered into his face. "I'm impressed. Keeping track of your enemies, Ms. Burns?"

"That depends, doesn't it?" As an attorney, Naomi was well versed in answering one question with another. And, as the corporate attorney for both Michael Tiranno and King Midas World, she was equally adept at deciding who would be allowed to meet her employer and who would not. Her attractiveness— dark wavy hair always perfectly coiffed, a tall, shapely frame, and a wardrobe made up of the finest designer names—helped by giving men like Trumbull a false ease. Naomi's graceful manner could be, and often was, misconstrued as weakness, and she enjoyed nothing more than turning the tables on those who took her lightly.

Her navy blue Chanel suit, the same color as Trumbull's jeans, fit the lines of her taut frame elegantly. She wore her hair short, just grazing her collar, a style that complimented a face she had always thought too narrow, further exaggerating her deep-set eyes. A soft, powdery scent, something trusted like Bijan or Samsara, melded into the air around her, refreshing it, in stark contrast to Trumbull's drugstore cologne. Brut, she thought.

"I'm a journalist," Trumbull told her. "I'm only here because of certain information about Michael Tiranno that has recently come to my attention."

"I know what you are."

After wandering about the lobby and retail area for the past hour, Trumbull had phoned her from this chair set just beyond the hotel's entrance of glass doors inlaid between golden archways. The desired effect was one of stepping from the mundane present into a majestic and ancient past offering the spirit of adventure. A forest of golden ionic columns stretched upward from a black marble lobby floor adorned with live exotic flowers, from the radiant golden iris to rare red poppies. Remnants of ropes of amber from Baltic lands, ostrich eggs from Nubia, and a silver stag from Asia Minor covered by a delicate shower of gold rosettes posed amid golden masks, belts, discs, and shields. The lighting, adjusted automatically throughout the day to account for the sun, was soft and easy on the eye: plenty to read by but lacking the overbright glitz of the gaudy. The air, meanwhile, had a fresh rose scent to it, courtesy of carefully concealed automated fragrance releasers.

"Old news, Mr. Trumbull," Naomi told him. "The Nevada Gaming Commission investigated the same allegations and dismissed them as baseless."

"The Gaming Commission doesn't have my sources, Ms. Burns. You'd be wise to keep that in mind."

"Michael Tiranno doesn't take kindly to threats."

"And I thought that's how you must have gotten the job as his corporate counsel. Why else would he hire someone fresh off an embezzlement charge at her prestigious New York law firm?"

"So your article's about me, then."

"You're a part of it, specifically how the charges mysteriously went away after the debt was mysteriously paid. What have you to say about that, Ms. Burns?"

"It all sounds very mysterious to me," Naomi said simply, unflustered.

"Michael Tiranno swooped in and rescued you. Saved your proverbial ass and your career in the process."

"You spoke to my former partners, then."

"It wasn't necessary."

"Of course. Why bother looking for facts when rumors will suffice?"

Trumbull sniffed hard, swallowing mucous. Perhaps he was allergic to some of the exotic flora that adorned the lobby of the Seven Sins.

"Allergies, Mr. Trumbull?"

"Nothing that'll kill me."

"Not yet," Naomi said. Neither moved his or her eyes from the other until a tourist bumped into Trumbull, turning him around into the path of another guest who smacked into him and pushed him backward.

"Your guests always this rude, Ms. Burns?"

"They're always in a hurry to check in, as you can see."

True to Naomi's word, the check-in line behind the eighteen-station marble reception counter wound through an elaborate maze of stanchions strung together by velvet rope. The casino's best customers, identified by a gold medallion, used a separate, lavish VIP room where all their needs were handled. Many of them would be staying in the high-roller suites erected six floors beneath ground level, with one entire wall offering a view into the world's largest self-contained marine environment, prowled by the only great white sharks ever in captivity. Those suites not held back for returning regulars were booked two years in advance at the rate of two thousand dollars per night. One section of the lobby floor was glass as well, allowing strollers a clear view of marine life captured in a perfectly re-created ocean habitat and, if they were patient, a glimpse of a thirty-foot great white.

"Can we cut the bullshit, Ms. Burns?" Trumbull snapped suddenly. "Am I going to get to see Michael Tiranno or not?"

"He asked me to see you first, give him my opinion."

"Have I impressed you so far?"

"Yes, as a hack, a journalistic hatchet man."

"Behaving like a lawyer, in other words."

"Bad lawyers can be disbarred. Bad writers end up in rehab. So," Naomi continued, after a brief pause, "can I get you a drink?"

"What exactly am I doing here?" Trumbull asked, recovering his bravado. "Why grant me an interview with Michael Tiranno if you had all these suspicions?"

"I granted you an interview with me, not Michael Tiranno."

"You said—"

"I said Mr. Tiranno was appreciative of your interest in him and expressed a desire to make sure you had all the facts straight."

"Which means you've already made up your mind."

"That doesn't mean you can't still prove me wrong, Mr. Trumbull. Mr. Tiranno has asked that I give you a tour of the casino," Naomi told him. "Who knows, you might actually like what you see."

Four

THE SEVEN SINS, THE PRESENT

R OLLER'S OUT. NEW roller up, please."

Edward Sosa accepted the dice from the stickman and moved what was left of his chips about the pass line at the no-limit craps table. The last five disastrous rolls had nearly exhausted his two-million-dollar line of credit.

"I need another million," Sosa said to the boxman before rolling.

"Sir, your credit line—"

"Fuck my credit line. Do you know who I am?"

"Sir, I'm not authorized—"

"Then find someone who is."

The boxman rose from his chair and approached a pit boss who was already speaking softly into a wireless, handheld microphone, his eyes fixed on a security camera mounted on the ceiling.

"Eddie," Jeannie, the luscious and willowy blond showgirl who was Sosa's companion for the night, said softly, looping an arm around his thick bicep, "why don't we just go back to the room?"

"Because I'm losing my fucking shirt here," Sosa snapped, rolling the bulky shoulders his former days as a bodybuilder had gained him. He had never once expended his entire line of credit, at the Seven Sins or any other casino, and he wasn't about to tonight. With the roll having finally come round to him, this was his chance.

"Eddie," Jeannie started again.

Sosa jerked his arm from Jeannie's grasp. "Stop calling me that!"

"But—"

He wheeled and backhanded her face. Blood trickling down her nose, Jeannie lurched backward into the arms of one of Sosa's two hulking bodyguards.

"Keep her the fuck out of my sight," Sosa ordered, swinging back to the table to find one of its two dealers glaring at him. "What the fuck you looking at?"

Before the dealer could respond, the pit boss slid in between him and Sosa. "Your line's been increased, sir," he announced, "an additional one million dollars as requested."

Sosa seemed to relax a bit, enough, anyway, to accept another one million dollars in chips, half of which he began to disperse about the table. Why not? He'd never gone this long without a winning roll. Now, when it came, he'd walk away with his original stake and then some.

"New dice," he ordered the stickman, who proceeded to peel the plastic off a fresh package. Sosa accepted the assortment of dice from him and selected a pair that felt right in his grasp.

He ran a hand through his thick, gelled hair and shook the red squares in his closed hand, listening to the reassuring plastic clack, willing them to be kind to him. Then he looked up at the same hidden camera toward which the pit boss had turned.

"You just made the biggest mistake of your fucking life," he said to the man on the other end.

Sosa snapped his hand open and flung the dice. They skimmed across the felt, banged up against the bumper on the opposite side of the table, and skittered to a halt.

Sosa saw a four and, he thought, a three. Seven, a winner!

"Six," said the stickman, "the point is six."

It was a two, not a three, his eyes having deceived him. No matter. Six was an easy point to make and, once he did, the payoff would be even greater.

Sosa took the retrieved dice from the stickman and squeezed them. He could have played the table conservatively to cover himself, but felt his luck about to change, a winner coming on, and decided to press. When his next three rolls failed to produce the point, he had his entire one point two million remaining on the table, eight hundred thousand on the numbers, and another four hundred behind the line. Make the point now and he'd be even. Not a bad night's work, considering how much he'd been down.

Sosa rattled the dice about in his hand, snapped open his fingers, and launched his toss.

"Seven," the stickman announced.

Sosa gazed down in disbelief, his throat heavy, something sharp churning in his stomach, as the dealers collected all his chips and slid them away.

"Roller's out," the stickman continued. "New roller up, please."

For a long moment Sosa didn't move at all. Then he stormed away from the table toward the private elevators located in the far rear corner of the floor, trailed by his bodyguards and knocking anyone close to him from his path.

Jeannie snuggled up against Sosa in a show of comfort once they were inside the first compartment to arrive.

"Get off me," he snapped.

"Eddie—"

"I told you *not to call me that!*" Sosa flung her off him the way he had flung the dice across the green felt table. "It's *Edward.*"

Jeannie hit the wall hard and bounced off right into Sosa's hand crashing against her face. He felt her nose compress on impact, the cartilage absorbing the brunt of the blow. She slumped to the floor, teary-eyed and belching blood from both nostrils.

"Clean her up and get her away from me," Sosa ordered his bodyguards. He looked at the blood running onto Jeannie's gold silk blouse. "She's bad luck."

IT TOOK BOTH bodyguards to hold the whimpering Jeannie up while Sosa slid his key card into the door of his Daring Sea suite. Entering the most exclusive lodging in all of Las Vegas, if not the world, promised to make his losses almost palatable.

The light above the lock flashed green. Sosa started to push the door inward.

This suite, and all the others composing the hotel's underwater levels, featured a twenty-four-foot glass wall that offered a view so clear into the waters beyond that it seemed high-roller guests like Sosa shared the Daring Sea with the various sea creatures roaming it. The wall extended across the width of the suite's living room area all the way into the bathroom and exposed glass shower. When staying here, Sosa especially enjoyed lingering in the shower in hopes of spotting one of the Seven Sins' great white sharks, preferably the largest, while wet himself, to magnify the power of the experience.

Sosa felt the latch jerked from his grasp, the door rocketing inward as a figure burst out. Motion flashed, everything a blur mixed with grunts and moans. Sosa pinned against the wall, trying to register what his eyes showed him, make sense out of the impossible, as a hand locked on to his throat and began to squeeze. Then a voice in his ear, muted, disembodied, detached: "You just made the biggest mistake of your fucking life."